# S. Ó CEALLAIGH

ABHARLANN

CH

# 100k

**Beware: the future may be happening to you right now.**

ISBN 978-1-78222-493-8

Book design, layout and production management by Into Print
www.intoprint.net
+44 (0)1604 832149
Printed and bound in UK and USA by Lightning Source

Morning and I arise at the crack of dawn. And the old jokes still run around like children in a playground. But it really is first light; barely light at all, simply a light-grey beneath the dark grey. The same thoughts, like a repeated morning prayer, smothering and torturing. Cast them out, these demons. They can be thrown off like a blanket and what remains is good. It seems so long since it was good to be alive, but a monstrous phase has passed; some of the old self has been resurrected. Maybe this was inevitable, but, abandoned, one has to discover this. Many people never discover this and an appalling truth. Long have I known that I am unbelievably lucky.

John plays outside. 'John' is probably to protect the innocent. But these days I'm never quite sure who's innocent. The guilty are obvious, once one has discerned their rules. Never assume that other people live by the same rules. They only appear so. Most people present themselves adhering to the rules of which they think other people approve. They are imitating the rules they imagine are the best in the circumstances, whatever the circumstances appear to be. They are playing a game, a game of pretence in which cunning triumphs. There are no rules.

John plays outside. He always plays the same game in which he is the hero. He plays Superman and he is always Superman. He never plays the baddies. I watch him through the net curtains, as one does in this culture at this time on this planet. It wasn't always like this. Net curtains did not always exist; they gradually evolved over time. Sometime in the distant future net curtains will become extinct. No question about this: extinction will always happen, and it will happen to net curtains, as with everything else. So, for the time being, we have a simple choice: either enjoy or be miserable. But it is not really a choice. We like to think it is. This is one of the silly rules that people copy from each other and then promulgate.

I watch John play outside. He always does at this time. As I with great ease on this lucky occasion threw off the awful thoughts - there was a time when I simply couldn't, and sometimes, even now, it's impossible and I suffer the torture - I had looked forward to seeing John play outside. And there he is, after the sunrise, beginning his game. He is such a sweet boy and reminds me of my childhood. We like to think of an age of innocence. But it is not really innocence; it is simply not knowing. Indeed, often it is the very opposite of innocence. Some games are quite awful and shouldn't be allowed. But they are impossible to stop because the imitation has become serious and being followed-through in earnest. The deadly imitation and the learning of respectable and pretend rules have begun. This social learning is underway and cannot be stopped. That is myth: everything can be stopped.

The day has begun. There is something ominous about the real day. The optimism is there, the good feelings, the feeling that anything is possible, being in love with the world and everyone in it. But we know how it is going to end. The inevitable darkness, the feelings of failure and depression. The best thing is not to sleep and then the day carries on, except in darkness. There is nothing bad about darkness. Darkness is really interesting because it brings forth a whole new world. So much is happening under the blanket of darkness, the scuttling of clichés. One can buy special lenses to observe the world awake when we assume it's asleep. After a while it does not require special lenses to see through people.

Suddenly, John looked straight into my eyes, right through the net curtains, which he has done before, and offered me a brief salute. Maybe he is playing soldiers and pretending to salute his senior officer. I returned a semi-salute. I am sure I am just as predictable as him. He knows my habits and games as well as I know his. But it is still unnerving to be seen through the net curtains. It is like watching little creatures in the dark when suddenly they stop and sit to watch me and give me a little wave. That doesn't happen, at least not yet. And I know John's salute carries no respect at all. I know this because I can tell and so can he.

The sun is now bright in the sky. If it were bright somewhere else, it might not be bright at all. We would demand proof. But today has begun and the City sparkles in the usual places, on walls of windows or wet roofs. I can see this thanks to the panoramic view from our flat, some people call it an apartment. I don't mind what it's called. Some call it a dwelling. This is to do with social status, one of those silly pretend games, embedded in conditioned attitude and expressed in language. But the view stretches far, towards the estuary, and to the left are the large chunks of the sparkling city, disappearing off to the left in a haze of sun and buildings, and to the right (north), my view obscured by concrete and more thousands of rectangles of white light.

The river far below stretches out like a great widening, unhealthy-looking tongue, too far to see the water and no sparkle as yet. John gives a last brief wave, not to me, as he reaches his car in the corridor. A sparkle begins to spread the entire length of the river, and this is always beautiful, sublime, with the rising of the sun, the play of light.

This is a summary of hard-core data, which is reliable at the highest level. This may be real or imagined, and is probably happening.

## 2

No point pretending that the sun shines on all equally. It shines not on the black soul or the soul in torment. Such a soul arises from its darkness and wanders its darkened world. Bronnie woke from her dream of graves, her eyes opaque with secrets. She watched lights and shadows scatter across the ceiling, the usual reflections of the movements of the city and the dark flash of a bird interrupting the light. He snarled her awake. She probably blinked once or twice, a heavy weight already upon her after so many years, drilling, drilling, teaching her who's boss, eyes green like a wolf.

It seemed like yesterday, the secret war she had denied. She remembered the signs. Every morning she remembers the signs. Like a terminal disease, the seeping sores never heal. She wondered many times if things had actually been different. Had she misunderstood everything? Had she got it all wrong ever since? Had she got *everything* wrong? She was thinking that right now. Her worst thought. How do you know *ever* if you are right? Too much. Stop. Stop right now or she'll die. Some people die a thousand times and nobody has the decency to bury them. If anybody finds out the truth, it will be over. But it wasn't her fault. But it must have been. She should have taken action. She had seen the signs.

"Morning, hun! Oh, dear, drunk again!" he chuckled as he placed her cup of black coffee on her side-table. He was far too old to be worried about last evening's behaviour. Anyhow, his behaviour was perfectly sociable. He was more concerned about her. She was never quite 'with it', frequently distant. Oh, well, it's normal to have secrets, he told himself. He certainly had a few that he intended to take to the grave! What's the point of spilling the beans now? He had a vague hope that God's detailed files included photographs. He'd like to be reminded of what they looked like! He'd stand up, be a man - he certainly did in those days! And once a couple of months ago - and accept his millions of years in Purgatory. Not Hell! A ridiculous notion. No point dwelling on the past and... what future?

"Yesterday was a laugh! Great to see everyone," he said as he sat down on her side of the bed and stroked her available arm briefly. Every morning she looked shocked to be awake and to be alive.

She was taken aback to discover him up. She hadn't noticed that he wasn't in bed beside her. He was often up early, a lifelong habit, part of the old training and discipline. She adjusted her face. Come back from Hell and go into role. Leaning on one elbow, she reached for her coffee. He watched her sagging skin and tried to find light in her eyes. Ah, there it is! Switched on like a Christmas tree.

"Yes, great to see the family. Everybody seems fine. Did you hear from your lot? I can't remember ..."

"Yes. Remember: a couple of dictanotes late afternoon. Covered the lot of them. Nobody available at the last minute." He brushed it aside. It wasn't the first time.

"Shame, but never mind." She had used those exact words yesterday. People are like that. They develop certain verbal habits, certain verbal skills, and you can tell it's them straightaway!

He did mind, but she didn't. One has to compromise; everybody's different; be cool; don't make a fuss. He'd spent his life trying to be cool, stiff upper lip, stomach in, chest out, be a man. No matter how much it doesn't really make sense, too late to worry about it now. How would things have been different? Probably education, I guess, the habitual thought flashed through his mind. Gone! It's good it's gone. Self-torture is not his thing, in his State of d'Nile. One of his favourites, that one. That was definitely a mistake. But that thought is unbearable. Leave it! What can one do? It's all too late. Attractive woman, mature, sex, comfort - what's wrong with that? It was just great for quite a long time - quite exciting when approaching middle age and it's all happening again! Everything just coincided as if planned: wonderful, out of the blue, and loads of loot wandering about, coming our way, inevitably. Then a gradual awareness of poison, something was festering in the kingdom. Last evening, quite frankly, was a nightmare. He sighed slightly. Careful, there is no point.

"What are you thinking?" She was awake. She barely slept, apart from her chemically-induced comas, and she rarely went outside. In a flash, he was back in his bunker.

"Oh, the usual: today, things to do, places to go, people to see, a very tight schedule."

She nodded with her painted clownish smile. He knew the score. He thought he knew the score.

"Go for a stroll, buy a newspaper, have a coffee somewhere, *mug* a couple of senior citizens. Then they can mug me. Make a change for all parties concerned." He might actually feel something. It would be interesting to *rob* somebody as in those old stories. The only drawback is that the ability to run is required. Left everything a bit too late. She was musing on the word mug - he talks such nonsense. He wants to be popular and have plenty of people to talk to. Nobody really listens to him. He was telling himself that he could have achieved things. He'd still had time before this: all this comfort, the comfort of a prison. And no visitors. They didn't even write. What is it about this woman? Her family are...

"I'm going to paint today." She finished her first cup. There would be many more. Some breakfast perhaps. Yes, he headed to the kitchen. Cooking gave him some satisfaction. A hefty last meal! Maybe it is, who knows? *Something* for her, something delicate. Something cheerful.

# 3

Merkan rose from his slumber. An indisputable fact: it doesn't need to be discussed; no tutorial or seminar needed; it is not a hypothesis or an hypothesis; nothing Greek, Latin or Hebrew; nothing requiring a mathematical model; and e may well equal m c squared (but probably doesn't), but the speed of light is irrelevant. It is an indisputable fact that Merkan rose from his slumber and felt very lucky. This lucky rising has occurred 27,393 times. One day it

Professors are Men of Words, although when they take a breath, we ponder the fact that brevity is the soul of wit. Some of them are Women of the afore-mentioned, not necessarily wit but words, whilst some rare and interesting ones are both. These are particularly interesting because they are gentle and then go into a rage, from nought to sixty in one second, and then snarl and bare their teeth. One does not know whether to wrestle them to the ground or buy them a conciliatory cluster of olives. Merkan's morning micturition is well advanced. He was relieved to get through the night.

"Merky, I'm not pestering. You asked me to remind you. After work, shopping."

A brief "Yep" from the bathroom, the toilet, the lavatory, the men's room, the bog, the pissoir. Merkan easily managed not to sigh from the little boys' room because she was absolutely right - the absolute - he had asked her to remind him. Must not complain; like one's ablutions, it has to be done. Shopping. I suppose hunting and gathering used to be much worse. Patience is a virtue. The patience of Job. The patience of doctors. Doctors are teachers. Teachers must be patient. Merkan had such musings between himself and his little pal held between fingers and thumb, then shaken, squeezed and half strangled. Not too much or he might get to like it and there is no time. Time to wake up and be sensible. Face the day, do one's duty, and indeed, it is all quite enjoyable. I am just so lucky, always have been. Things could have been so different.

The prof is admired. He had retained his sense of origin and self and, after years of not bothering to pursue happiness, he had returned. Through teaching, papers, books, the wife and children (somewhere in the world), he had achieved happiness enough. The components of his world fitted together. He considered himself a very lucky man. Things had worked out.

Merkan had not retained his jet-black hair. He could have, like so many others, but it would have been unimaginable in the case of the brainiest person I have ever known. He just turned grey and dignified as good old Mother Nature had intended. But I am sure he was happy to have retained his hair. Some men do and some men don't. And a few unfortunate women don't. But mainly it is to do with genetics and testosterone and that's the end of it.

The beginning of the day for the professor some people considered 'mad', a man, ironically, immersed in madness. He was washed and dressed with monastic precision. Habitually: be on the ball, plunge in, don't *prevaricate*, he who hesitates is lost. Prevarication had been his life-long enemy. He had spent years thinking until he came to the conclusion that all that thinking had been a waste of time. It had been avoidance behaviour, a conclusion which had to be thought out. Finally, he concluded what he had known all along: avoidance behaviour is driven by fear. He was, indeed, a creature of fear and habit. This is perfectly normal if you happen to be normal. Merkan was way outside the norm, way above the 95$^{th}$ percentile. This was not the conclusion of an arrogant man, but another fact. On the contrary, his humility had produced too much thinking, which, in turn, had produced non-productivity, a production in which nothing was produced. Then he met his wife. Wives tend to stop men thinking. Wives tend to do things.

Merkan had settled down - in all senses and in every way. He had realised that all the thinking had not been a waste of time after all. It had produced a whole library of half-written books in his head. Now he could settle down to complete some of them. And he did.

"Breakfast!" he called efficiently. He had heard his wife was up and on the go for some minutes, those well-recognised sounds of decades. If it wasn't her, then it must be him. The four children had long flown the nest. They were *somewhere.* He had given up trying to keep up with their whereabouts. He had also given up trying to remember the names of their *partners.* He knew words in several languages to describe those relationships and none of them translated as 'partner', but he held his tongue. His wife was upset that the children rarely made contact; Merkan was relieved. He tried not to say so, but she knew.

"Oh, well done, darling," as she entered, acknowledging that, in a loose way, it had been her turn.

"Are you going to dust your bookshelves? Your desk must be a culture lab of diseases! I just had a peek. You haven't even made a start!"

"I keep forgetting to tackle it. I'll have a bit of a dust tomorrow."

"Merkan, I'm not doing it. I'm telling you now and I've told you before: I'm not going anywhere near your study unless I have special protective clothing, the kind of suit they use when dealing with radiation!"

"Very funny! You are a whole cellar of barrels of laughs. Tea or coffee?"

"I suppose you're off to the University. Any excuse."

Women and their dust.

Merkan and his prevarication. It is usually disguised as his favourite armchair and his one and only favourite newspaper - he has to keep up with the news! Today it's the University, where he doesn't need to go at all.

4

The Hermit had been up before dawn. He didn't have a bell because there was nobody to ring it. He had seven alarm clocks, manually wound. He had spent years thinking about the problem of the bell. Hermits mustn't think too much because that may be vanity and the waste of life and all its abundance. He was a curious and discerning man, indeed, a scientist.

"Things work out," he said, "Miracles happen every day." I am generalising from data, although these are his actual words. I must be precise and that is one of the reasons I 'empathise' with the hermit - precision.

After seven years things had worked out: he had a full collection of alarm clocks. People had given him theirs, found in attics and cellars (although both are few in number). I know that one had been their child's clock. The child had died of an incurable disease. The child had wasted away and there had been nothing to be done, nothing known to medical science.

"Some things can never be known." The hermit said many times. On many more occasions he said, "God can never be known." It would be a tedious statement, repeated so often, if he had not said it with such seriousness. It was almost a prayer, the bottom-line of his Creed. "You will eventually write your own Creed." There were tears in his eyes that day when he held the dead child's alarm clock. He hadn't always been a hermit.

So, winding-up alarm clocks, set for seven different times was not a waste of time. Like all things, this had been arranged by God, an evolved eremitic ritual, taking a few seconds at the end of each prayer session, every twenty-four hours. But each winding is different and is based on the previous amount of winding. You must never over-wind or you will break the mechanism. Wind just enough; never go too far. This is a good principle for living: never go too far. And remember: alarm clocks of a mechanical type have a twelve-hour cycle. Therefore, if you expect a specific clock to ring in twenty-four hours' time, then you must set it *after* the first twelve hours have elapsed. To aid the hermit's memory, he had a chart on the wall and he wrote a tick, or a check, to indicate that he had set a specific alarm clock. He liked charts on the wall and avoided anything involving electricity. He lived by the Rule, but, as the Rule implied *each man according to his needs*, he had modified the Rule, e.g., concerning alarm clocks and charts.

In the dark, he lit his candle. He had stopped worrying about the cost of candles and the fact that matches could only be used once and most of it was wasted. Some things must be accepted. Often he simply remained in the dark. These were the best times because it was only a physical darkness. But often he could not make contact. The thing that prevented him was himself. He was his own obstruction and he could usually work out where he had gone wrong. This morning, he had to light his candle because he was in the dark.

At this time of the morning, it's always cold, especially as he has turned the heating off permanently. His breath drifted before him. At least he's still breathing. That must be a good thing. Perhaps. But who can tell? He never dressed properly until later; there is no need; there is only one important thing. His feet were already cold when he pulled on his socks and tucked his pyjama bottoms inside them to provide a degree of insulation. Then his sandals, simply because he preferred sandals. His two dressing-gowns, permanently one garment, were already on. Immediately on leaving his bed! There are no uniforms for hermits, although it depends on the circumstances.

On very cold mornings, and this had been one, he draped his double jumpers across his shoulders, pinning the arms at his chest, just under his beard, using a safety-pin he had found under the sink. We are not sure when but you can find out by making a request to Central Computer.

Then his woolly hat. He had spent some time thinking about a hat. He had come to an ingenious conclusion. He had taken a never-used scarf, folded it exactly in half, lengthways, so it was half the length, and then folded it again to quarter its original length; then he aligned the four edges and, using a needle and thread he had found in an otherwise empty cupboard in his 'guestroom', had sewn the four edges together from the top corner to half the length of the material, this being one eighth of the original length, thus forming a perfect woolly hat. It was perfect, not only because it fitted him perfectly, but because it would fit any adult perfectly. However, it kept flying open at the front. So he pulled the four lengths together comfortably under his chin and sewed them together. Although he could not do the sewing while he was still wearing it. Therefore, he used his safety-pin, temporarily, to pin the four lengths together; removed the hat, inserted a few stitches (unknown number - ref. Central Computer), and removed the safety-pin.

By this time, as I am sure you have already guessed, his double-jumper had slipped from his shoulders and he was beginning to shiver.

When I first 'met' him, one early morning three years ago, I had been taken aback by his strange attire. When I realised he was a hermit, I realised that his appearance was perfectly normal... for a hermit.

Now, he is still, seated with his holy book. I know this is true and I know that by now he has blown out the candle. He may have taken off his woolly hat. Some things are best left unknown. Let's call the Hermit Praman, which is his name.

## 5

Halaigha Longbottom rose from her slumber. (You mustn't believe everything you read).She is another one who rises from her slumber. Her life is a permanent slumber, she is permanently aslumber. She blames William Shakespeare for much of her difficulties, but not as much as she blames her dad. A little learning is a dangerous thing. She often quotes Shakespeare for which he should not be blamed. Despising her father is like despising Adolf Hitler. If Halaigha had heard of Adolf Hitler she would despise him because he wasn't very nice. But he had the right to express himself freely and he chose to use his right. The problem was that other people listened. People listen to Halaigha. She demands her rights. We have improved on that idea, about rights. Now it is illegal to elicit racial hatred and it is also illegal to be a social parasite. Both are significant improvements. You have no idea how things have improved, but you are about to find out. Strangely, things have also got worse. It is clearly obvious that ideas evolve, albeit sometimes very slowly indeed. Some ideas have not evolved at all, ideas concerning Good, for example; still struggling with that one. Halaigha can't tell good from bad, so it doesn't affect her. She doesn't worry about right and wrong either, which is peculiar when you become aware (she ensures that you do) that she is a multiple graduate of the University. Amongst her many disorders - she collects them - she suffers from the God Delusion. This is when someone believes they are God. When you challenge her *Godhood*, the consequences can be very unpleasant, and include hearing damage, emotional trauma, smelling salts and an ambulance, the first two for the speaker and the second two for Halaigha. Sometimes all you have to do is say hello and all heaven breaks loose.

So, Halaigha rose from her Shakespearian slumber and emerged, although not quite, from her Hitlerian cloud of unknowing and surveyed Slumberland House located in her own Sleepy Hollow. She would call it Reality, but nobody else recognises the place seen from her bedroom window and synthesised in and through her brain. Her Reality is a kind of Utopia, except it keeps changing. It turns into what she wants it to be and is projected onto everybody else whether they like it or not. She is not to blame, she is a victim, a professional victim. As she speaks so beautifully, most people quite like it. I suppose most people are not very astute; unpleasant, but you have to accept the facts.

When a few brave, or foolish, people, or people who are not very astute, or indeed not totally dissimilar from Halaigha, decide to challenge Halaigha's views, the consequences can become, as previously stated, very quickly a matter of Health & Safety. They either avoid Halaigha in the future or quite enjoy punishment which is the reason they return for more. There may be other reasons, but one cannot always tell what's going on, but one certainly knows when something is downright morbid. You have to decide for yourself. Usually, this decision is so quickly acquired that you have no time to think knowingly, so to speak, and, therefore, it's not a decision. But we like to believe it is and it is ours. We really love to possess things. Central Computer possesses the data.

Halaigha loves to possess the morning, her womanliness and her view of the world which, like the sea and the clouds, is ever changing. You must try to keep up; otherwise there may be trouble. She stretches in a graceful and feminine way; not too much in one direction or the other, unless she is doing special female exercises to tone-up specific parts of her body, particular emphasis being on breasts, especially on breasts, (such a lovely and perfectly formed young word), tummy (never stomach), bottom (never buttocks), and thighs (thighs are apparently acceptable, but never quite right and always have to be worked on). Some women concentrate on these collections of muscles and tissues. Strangely, they pay little attention to hands and feet, which are horrible looking objects, although women do spend time adorning them in bright colours. My favourites are Cocktail Passion, Vrai Rosé, and Velvet. Surely, reconstructive surgeons could give more thought to hands and feet. But then they would become cosmetic surgeons, which is not as impressive. It is not only what you do, but why you do it. Intention is everything. We must hand it to them for what they do because some of their feats are truly astonishing. So, let us leave them to get on with their real work and try to ignore those four horrible extremities and the fact that Halaigha is waving them about, as she pursues her programme of self-improvement. She is unaware of the cries of abandonment of a young child. You have to get your priorities right.

Halaigha trailed like a Faerie Queene in her flowing gown past her fluffy slippers towards the bathroom. I could say she slipped on her slippers, but that might be misunderstood and, either way, is not true. She was in a hurry. Her morning had suddenly warned of the arrival of Santa Claus, the bringer of bad news, as she made her entrance to yet another final scene of yet another tragedy. Other people who'd run out of patience might well find themselves laughing, or just stay at home, claiming a tummy ache, and avoid the tragedy. Halaigha had felt the trickle of blood running down her inner thigh. As she crossed the floor, one or two small droplets fell on the soft pink carpet and formed fluffy little clouds. An Auschwitz of a day had begun. Another abysmal failure, but the show must go on, and at least there would be many curtain calls – brava! - thanks to the small, but discerning audience, the members of which had very little choice, but seemed mesmerised.

Lakota attempted to emerge from the self-imposed fog. Kicked her way out of the duvet and heaved herself to the sitting position on the edge of the bed, sagging head denoting a physical weakness not easily described, although another person might describe it as 'physiological meltdown' - an appropriate expression, which in both cases excludes a headache. This may be genetic. But an indescribable 'ache' permeates their entire body, and renders standing, walking, sitting, laying, reading, writing, and all kinds of arithmetic impossible. The only cure is patience and these tasks attempted in short bursts: a little standing followed by a little walking followed by a brief period of sitting, and so on. The one consistent activity recommended is the 'making' and drinking of many cups of tea. Whether or not people actually make tea is a matter of philosophical debate best left to experts. The 'cups' are also referred to as 'mugs', but this is not true of everybody. 38% of adults in the City use the terms interchangeably. After many mugs of tea, the victim in this investigation will usually attempt a mug of coffee ('instant' of course, but only because the term doesn't relate to 'speed', but quality).

Lakota trudges straight for coffee, being a modern person easily influenced by television, which may be out of date by the time you read this. I predict that technology will already have appended a footnote explaining 'television'. Who or what is going to define 'footnote' is another question. Perhaps these definitions, indeed all definitions, will be implanted at birth or maybe at conception. Such possibilities are under discussion by our Ethics Committee. At this moment, which we are all sharing temporarily, Lakota is not capable of any such thinking, regardless of her intelligence and beauty. Yes, tall, elegant, intelligent and beautiful, stumbling somewhat to the toilet prior to the kitchen to handle in a befuddled way the electric kettle, the water flooding, yes *flooding*, into the kettle, and deafening poor Lakota. She lands heavily on a kitchen chair, regretting immediately the speed of descent, having spotted a packet of cigarettes on the table. But, [expression deleted; C.C.: silent], no lighter! A deft twist clockwise of the cooker knob (a strange little word) and the problem will be solved within seconds. Easier to wait quietly than to stand up, although it's good that the water is approaching boiling point. It's all coming together, hardly a plan, just a routine.

"Want some coffee, darling?" Lakota calls gruffly, in no mood for niceties, to what could have been mistaken for a corpse in the other room, if it hadn't been for the ongoing physiological profile. A soft moan came from the bed followed by "Yes, please, that would be really nice" and it was so slow and soft and gentle. And then she rose from the dead and also from the bed.

You see, not even I can predict the future. Usually, of course, prediction is very straightforward. History repeats itself, baselines have been established, etc., and the future is easy. But, on this occasion, the boring routine is shattered: out of the blue, a dove fluttered, she swanned naked and silent across the carpet, scooped up a nearby dressing-gown and robed herself, a balletic grace, although evidently somewhat tired. I could describe her in detail, but some things are best left to the imagination.

"Gosh, what a great night! As far as I can remember!" She laughed, leant down and kissed Lakota on the cheek who, in turn, hugged her round the waist. For a few seconds they were one. Then the kettle boiled.

"Two coffees coming up! Do you fancy some toast, boiled egg, cereal, something like that? I don't usually bother with breakfast. Help yourself."

Oh dear, it seems that Lakota is being deliberately off-hand, cold. This is so typical. What's the problem? I know what the problem is. Make the effort! Don't be afraid.

"I'll just have some toast," she says, leaning against the sink, waiting for a response. She has visibly shrunk. Her sadness is beginning to register.

Lakota gazes into the coffee, as the steam rises and the smoke from the cigarette. "Yeah, it was a laugh. I like the club, go there a lot. Your first time?"

"Yes, it was fun. And my first time in the place. You certainly know a lot of people. Have you lived here five years? Is that what you said? It was so noisy."

"Yep, about five years. This is my second job in this neck of the woods. The first one was a bit of a bummer, didn't get on with one or two people; strange power struggles going on; got to me in the end. I really don't like being pushed around by people lower than myself. Do you see what I mean? Lower in the qualifications and skills-type areas. I'm a lawyer and I know I'm young, but I'm not going to be ordered about by somebody my age, with virtually no relevant qualifications at all, just because they've been there longer than me. That kind of thing got on my nerves. But it all worked out, relatively speaking. If it's not one thing, it's another." Something else was brewing. Something is always brewing.

"Do you remember my name?"

"Of course I do!" Slightly peeved, Lakota flicked ash into the ashtray, "Samantha. Sam. Of course I remember it." More gently this time.

"Lakota, shall I make us some breakfast?"

"Yeah, go on. I'll try and be a bit more civilised. You'll find everything in the top cupboards." The first smile of the day and it was a real smile. "But I must have some more tea - a couple of gallons should be enough! - because I've got the real jitters!"

They both had to get to work, but they had a couple of hours. Lakota, recognising the sudden onslaught of that old oppression, distracting herself by her new friend, hoping this might be something good.

# 7

Psybunes rose in his bed. Young men do. The sun tinkled through the curtains and draped itself across his bed. He rose for a tinkle. The guitars lounged against various walls and had been joined by several other musical instruments like men having chinwags in bars. It was all muffled and confidential, discussions about sex (very limited), the weather (somewhat more detailed), and football (elaborated impressively). The only discernible sounds were not discernible: the blur of traffic, the smoke on the water, the creaking of floorboards and joints as he padded barefoot, the black sabbath of his dazed and confused thoughts beginning already to reach a crescendo. More to life than sex and drugs and rock and roll, he told himself, but he couldn't think of anything. These are not his words, but things don't change.

The day lay behind him. He felt slightly, just a little iota of a modicum of a soupçon of a scintilla, depressed. But not a lot; just the usual amount which didn't last long. He was used to it. He combed it away as he briefly combed his hair, just after a pee, just after the washing of hands for no good reason, just out of habit, when he had had no choice but to glance in the mirror. He laughed out loud at himself in the mirror, his silent joke - it was a mistake! Still young enough to laugh. The fact is you just keep on laughing, sometimes because there is no reason, no matter your age. Comb the hair, comb the skin, comb the beach, if you are still be able to. You think you have choice?

"Hi." A man of few words. Too busy laughing into a telephone. Or is it a television, or a library, or a secretary, or a tape recorder? Yes.

"Okay." A buzzing sound, not to him, to me, amongst the blurring and the absence of creaking, as he is now seated.

"Yeah, see you then." Ooh! Several syllables. Let's make the most of it. Sometimes he never stops talking, in that desperate competition. Sometimes he becomes a drone, a foghorn, when he is midst that flock of *wolves*. The thought makes him tired.

Very tempted to stretch out on the bed, just for a few more minutes. No, must contact the bit of brainless fluff. Not his words today, but they have been. Not now, maybe after breakfast; but gave that up some time ago. Can't quite face it; sometimes food is such a useless chore, worse than dusting. Dust once a year or, possibly, to celebrate special occasions. But he had given up special occasions; or, they'd given him up. They just evaporated. He had reached that age, when there is nothing to look forward to except the things he created, which meant every day was special because he was creative. Anyhow, what's wrong with titbits of dried skin and hosts of living organisms which have always existed? He was contemplating - he had been advised on more than one occasion to cut out all that thinking, nobody else does it - as he scrutinised the uneven line of grey matter along the nearside of his right index finger. Now, what is going on way down there amongst the dusty multitudes? He wondered if he'd said it out loud. He rubbed his thumb several times and rapidly along the grey matter on his finger, rolled it into a ball, like snot, and flicked it away. Through the air it sailed at heart-stopping speed and plummeted, asteroid-like, towards the rain forest. The hordes are having a bad day - as they certainly will, if *she* comes on the scene with her madness - and now they're trying to disentangle themselves and to meet up with their cousins who had long ago, for them, taken up residence in the carpet. So, not such a bad day after all. You never can tell how things are going to work out. There's going to be a party!

He looked at the straight clear line of cream paint on his bookshelf. It was about six inches in length (probably only five because men tend to exaggerate) and about an inch wide. He sighed. Once you start dusting, there is no end to it.

He decided to telephone the bit of fluff amongst the dust. He was awake and much more cheerful. She always cheered him up, once he was capable of being cheered up. Make a cup of tea and make a call, almost certainly, a mating call. But, unfortunately, no reproduction; that idea is just so *passé*.

Psybunes was heading for thirty-two and his girlfriend. How had these things happened? They had just come along when he had least expected them. He was not fazed by either, but greatly cheered by the latter. His thirtieth had come and gone almost unnoticed. There was so much sadness he had simply learnt to swim through it, just keep going. He was used to it. Then she came along, a breath of fresh air and twenty and still with him three years later. She hadn't understood his thirtieth. She had been warned, but she'd thought he was joking. He wasn't. He was almost totally alone. How had it happened? "It's a long story," he'd said, "I'll tell you when you're old enough." The pretend insult had turned into a giggling and tickling wrestling match when she had retaliated. She'd never quite got to the bottom of it.

In his mind he was now heading across town in the blaze of morn. That's how he felt. He had virtually moved into her place already. It was just a matter of making the final decision. He wasn't afraid, he was just being cautious. Things could turn into a terrible mess. He had long experience for his short years. That kind of mess doesn't go away. It is like a festering disease. It just keeps gnawing away, its own kind of slow death.

# 8

"Oh, God." It was a near-whispered sound of despair, as he rolled over towards the spacious room - he imagined the expensive and tasteful ornaments and paintings he intended to buy in due course - and away from the body beside him. An inaudible "ow!" went through his mind as a small and shrivelled part of his shocked anatomy unstuck itself sharply from the bottom sheet. At least, it wasn't the duvet. That would have been worse and more inconvenient. Just another sheet to join all the other sheets in the laundry basket. He recognised the sudden discomfort - nothing to worry about. It will pass.

Oh, God - undoubtedly, his silent reference, this time, to the same hypothetical construct, in his educated opinion, referred to the fact that he could not remember the girl's name, not that, irritating though it is, he was in bed with her. Indeed, if the truth be told, and I am obliged to do so, he was annoyed that she was still there. He always referred to them as 'girls' and made the mistake of extending their stay. This needed better organising. The following morning of useless *socialising* impinged on his alone time. He had things to do, like gazing in mirrors and feeling triumphant. So far, none of them were *girls*. It might happen eventually, in which case he will spend a lot of time in prison being beaten to pulp every day by people who don't mind murder or gang rape in the shower but they really take exception to *that* kind of behaviour. Every institution has its rules. Often, the rules are quite surprising if one takes into account the full story, the big picture, the real context, as well as all the subtexts, all of which can rarely be known. But keep that to yourself, we mustn't spoil the story.

Oh, God, what's her name? He had promised himself on many occasions to make more effort to remember the names. He must find a way of surreptitiously noting them down, he was berating himself, as he fondled his best friend in order to remove the unsightly flaky bits. As it will become apparent, he rarely had anything to do with flaky bits. Just be kind to them. Kindness is like good manners - it costs nothing. He still had not learnt that in the end you pay. Ah, it's beginning to wake up. Time for a quick one before departure? Only fools miss an opportunity. She will probably be duly impressed, and so she should be. If not, then it doesn't really matter. He's more than willing to make the effort. He spent so much time writing and, yet, in these circumstances he always got carried away and forgot to note the name. Maybe a mnemonic? It would be easy with practice. It is, indeed, very easy: call them all 'darling'.

Was it Sarah or Sara? Certainly something upper class. Certainly not Sharon. God no. It would never be a Sharon. He'd never a touch of a Sharon and not even a little maul of a Tracy. The appalling thought of a Mary-Lou! An Emma would be acceptable; a Poppy or a Jemima would be a bit hopeful unless she's not very tall, although a granddaughter of somebody *really famous* was easy. So anything is possible. Keep an open mind.

"Morning, darling." What! She's not addressing me as darling? What a nerve. Just ignore it. Play it cool, but firmly put her in her place, if necessary. They usually get the message without too much fuss.

She had opened her eyes in a cute and groggy sort of way. Oh cripes, who is he? He leant over and kissed her on the cheek. She is such a cutie and so clever. She's very well liked, but she does get herself into such a mess. Now she feels awkward and embarrassed, but it's her own fault. She deserves no sympathy at all. Try to stop convincing yourself that this is normal and consenting. You know perfectly well that this is not consenting. This is learnt behaviour, conditioned by society. If you were born somewhere else in a different era, you would behave differently. And alcohol really doesn't help.

Oh, God! Our hero is praying again, this time with an exclamation mark! Her breath stinks! Oh dear, this must be bad because it has earned another exclamation mark. That is how one can tell when something is serious. This is very interesting considering our hero has significant problems with punctuation. Some people can talk about the work, some people can do the work, and a few lucky persons can do both. Suffice it to say, the funny little creature in question - some would call him an amoral, self-seeking reprobate, others would call him a hero and role model - is a wonderful talker and, it is a well-known fact that all posh talk and no brain make countless thousands mourn, or maybe dozens, certainly.

She lay there trying to collect her thoughts. She has very nice and well-mannered thoughts, which is the reason she satisfied his criteria and was so privileged. She glanced under the duvet, although she knew almost certainly that her fate had been sealed by a previous unveiling. Yes, and another chunk of her self had been chiselled away. She raised herself above his turned away back. Her clothes were scattered across the floor, a trail leading to the door, which she cannot recall, in front of which, on the floor, lay her new jacket, the jacket she really *loved*. She thought that she must have enjoyed herself, but she could not feel it or remember it. She keeps making this mistake, this abandoning of clothes, in her search for an adult male. Certificates and an elaborated linguistic code do not an adult make.

"Can I make us breakfast, or are you in a hurry to leave?" Mosimenadue asked, imagining he had thoroughly digested the Principles of Good Manners.

## 9

Radmilla rose and then fell back again and rose. Is she still asleep? She could not be still asleep, although people are never still when they are asleep; and they are certainly never fast asleep. The body is always moving. When it's not, you have nothing more to worry about. No need for aims and objectives; no need to write it all down or write it all up; no wild ambitions and no do-able ambitions; no fantasies, wild or otherwise, and no dreams. Nothing at all, possibly; some would say probably; some would say definitely. Some people are extremely foolish. Probably, according to probability, that is: one standard deviation either side of the mean, which is the norm and 68.2%, as everybody knows. Possibly. Radmilla is one of those people who are always sure, simply because she is clever and honest. She is also a statistician.

Now I know for sure she is awake. Never jump to conclusions; ensure you have enough data. Sometimes this takes decades and patience. She must be awake because she is laying on her back *and* listening to the World News on her alarm radio. She does this every day: awake at dawn and listening to the radio. This is what they do in her country: up with the lark (they are known for small birds) to do their chores and jobs before it gets too hot.

She's listening and inwardly sighing. She rarely sighs outwardly because she is so used to bad news. She is mentally noting the list of tragedies and disasters humans are prone to, most of which are self-inflicted. She stopped being dismayed long ago. Knowing her useless memory for personal dates, I am sure she has no idea when she stopped being dismayed. It was probably a gradual development, a gradual process of satiation, of being gradually overwhelmed. She might appear to be cold-blooded, but she is, indeed, the opposite, something to do with coming from a hot country perhaps. Only sociopaths and lizards are immediately, and permanently, cold-blooded.

Goodness gracious, what is she doing under her duvet? Oh, she is only scratching. Scratching and listening to the news from the world, news of more catastrophes: murders and earthquakes, uprisings and things collapsing (governments and buildings and the lives of babies); the collapse of banks, the collapse of economies, the collapse of roofs due to baby tsunamis. Ah, somebody has won a prize for doing something worthless or for something they found extremely easy. Radmilla appears unmoved, although extremely itchy. That is probably to do with the soap or detergent she uses. Maybe she is suffering an allergic reaction. It is possible that she is having an allergic reaction to bad news. This can happen to some people on occasion. I have seen this before. It can become quite serious and debilitating. Somebody has just won a prize for allergy research, but I wasn't really paying attention. This is one of the great problems: we do not pay attention, although we pretend to. Both phenomena cause serious problems. Some would claim that this includes tsunamis and earthquakes, but I do not agree with this. Certainly, wars are due to not paying attention and, also, pretence. Wars just begin quietly, at first, when people are playing golf. That is one of the reasons golf is not a good thing. I know for a fact that Radmilla has never played golf. This is not one of the reasons she is likeable. But it could be. They say 'writing clarifies thinking'. Somebody in a distant land said that long ago. I was far away once, but now I am here and so is Radmilla. Everybody was always so far away they were sad. But now they are much closer.

Computers do not like the name Radmilla, which is ironic, but Radmilla is a beautiful name. There is no point arguing about this. Go and have a game of golf and calm down; have a few drinks, close a few deals, make friends and influence people. She moaned and gasped audibly and opened her eyes, her beautiful brown eyes to match her beautiful brown name. She seems to have recovered from her allergy and the starving millions, who will never recover, but it is certainly not her fault. She has done everything she could for years.

Having had her fill of the World Noise, she suddenly leapt from her bed like a young gazelle. A slight exaggeration, especially at her age, but she certainly slid gracefully from beneath her duvet and into her dressing gown. Not a gazelle in the City. No, a gazelle in Africa I once spotted as I was passing by. It just leapt several times. That's what gazelles do. I was lucky to spot a Dalmatian, but that is another story, but quite interesting. I was told by a reliable source, who must remain anonymous, that it was a Dalmatian from Alsace.

Memory can take one back. I suppose Radmilla must be dealing with her ablutions. Ah, yes, the sound of running water, one type or another, no matter. She must keep her bowels regular. I know it sounds peculiar and obvious, but it is fundamental for R. Otherwise, she will not be sitting comfortably (only a smirk of a pun intended) for the whole day. She will be miserably uncomfortable and she will not be able to concentrate or even eat lunch. Everything will be out of synch. We all have our little daily problems, apart from the massive ones that plague us, and this is one of hers. Things sound as if they are going well. Already in the shower - a good sign. You have to be able to concentrate when you are a statistician. She was once an accountant. A different collection of lists denotes accountancy, so I am told, few of them amounting to catastrophes, except every ten or twenty years when things start collapsing, no doubt something to do with playing too much golf.

## 10

She had lain there watching the sunlight slowly smother the stars. It was another death of a day, neither alive nor dead, just a zombie of a day. Gelasia could not quite place when this had happened, the beginning of the end, the slow demise of the unsick, but it was a long time ago. It could have been childhood; it must have been. This is what everybody says, moaning about their childhood and its devastating consequences. A deep sigh would have swept over her at that point if she'd had the energy. She was sick of her own sickness which she knew was there, but could not quite put her finger on it. But she was even sicker of everybody else's, their *relationships.* Was it her mother, her failure to love? And what about everybody else's mother. And father. Oh God, let us arise and go, and go to... well, anywhere to get away from that subject, the real zombie in her life, the non-event of her upbringing, the speechless man. Just too tiring. But was that, in fact, it? The it of her zombiehood, the original knuckle dragging chimp of her childhood. You could not call him a great ape; Neanderthal would be a complement. Some men are just shadows that hang around and, on occasion, let a terrible shout to frighten little children because they are the only people such terrified chimps are capable of scaring. Did she know before that horrible day that her mother did not love her? Then her mother didn't deny it; indeed, she revelled in it: "I've always preferred boys." She had said that so many times. Way into adulthood her mother had sounded more and more like a paedophile. Gelasia rolled away from the hulk. If only she could cry. The alarm clock almost had time to go off.

She was up, not quite wide awake, facing the day, another useless dad of a day. Thinking of the men at the office almost stopped her in her tracks - the smart alecs, the tedious salacious jokes, the condescending attitudes, the patronising comments - but she carried on with her routines. Stick to the routines and you may remain sane. The greatest gift is a sense of humour. Now, where did she put hers? Ah, still in her briefcase, unpacked from the evening before. Mustn't forget it. The evening had been a fetid corpse of an evening; no doubt more to come. Things are not getting worse, they are staying the same. She could tell when they were getting worse. So, count blessings, count umpteen other things, recheck today's list of things to do, and stop thinking. I think therefore I panic. Don't think about the men at the office or I might commit suicide. She knew exactly how she'd commit suicide. Gelasia envied suicide bombers. She smiled at the thought. She had read about them at school. She was smiling at herself smiling at herself. She had no clue how to make a bomb. Indeed, at this very moment she was having difficulty making coffee.

Too many ruminations cause problems and that's the reason they're called 'morbid'. So many labels. We're just so clever. A shame we can't do a thing about the downtrodden. You'd think that would be simple enough. She was astonished that such unfortunates still existed, but she couldn't remember locations - she recalled photographs though.

Food, jobs, lazy, one thought leading to another. She ruminated morbidly and briefly on the hulk, apparent and still in bed. Sleeps like a log and resembles a hog, covered in some very colourful material. Indeed, some things should remain covered up. Could be a dead hippo. All that jogging for years. Now he's into energy conservation. What you become is what you've always been. People do not change; they just discover themselves. When they do, they appear quite alarming, unrecognisable. "What a piece of work!"

"Hey, hippo!" she whispered gently towards where his ear should be. A large head rose above the surface, two bleary eyes the first to appear followed by the large snout that, she noticed, needs trimming. Men and their nostrils. That will be the title of her next novel, although so far she had only produced a very long list of titles. She was astonishingly good at titles and summaries of all sorts, especially of people she didn't know. After her career as a suicide bomber, she thought she might found a company of Titles For All Occasions! and charge a large, albeit appropriate, fee - she wasn't claiming to be a rocket scientist! - and then do something about the labouring poor. She liked that expression - she felt sophisticated. Where to start, but something about fresh drinking water? Such a problem was hard to imagine.

"I think the water's gone off!"

"What!" His head fully emerged abruptly from his comatose sea of tranquillity. She was grinning her clownish grin, head on one side.

"I think *you've* gone off!" he said, heaving his bare and hairy arm towards the coffee. "Thanks. I feel like death warmed up."

"You look like death warmed up, my little sex machine."

"What do you mean 'little'? And don't even think about it. I feel like... "

"death warmed up. Yes, I know, you have made your position clear. And think about what? You'll be lucky! Anyhow, not in your rotting carcass condition. I hate to remind you, but today we are busy busy busy, so we must get a move on."

"Yes, I know." He was almost wide awake and threw his legs out of bed.

She chuckled to herself, as they flew through the closed window. How would she explain it to the neighbours? And what about the broken glass? The neighbours were so gossipy.

"Ah! Thanks very much. I knew they must be around somewhere. When he got home last night, he was totally legless!"

He decided to make no comment re. her chuckling: things complicated enough today.

Start a story with an eye-catching line, or don't bother. The latter is Purvanos' lifelong attitude: straightforward, common-garden-variety, and staid to the point of perfection. Steady as a rock; cautious as a cloud - and why not - never a bungee jumper be, neither a parachutist, nor a multi-coloured jumper he; more a school-grey pullover firmly on the ground; at this moment, groggy in bed, dreaming of his Great Novel. He couldn't decide whether to remain groggy or not. Let it sort itself out; no need for him to intervene. That would demand taking a risk, making an unnecessary decision, which might lead to action, and it might not work out; better to garner the facts, garner the salad, but in due course; better wait and see; no need to rush in where fools and angels have opinions and clash. Guard your tongue, your wherewithal and your possessions. Not being simply lazy, but unhurried, he rolled over and snuggled into his duvet in order to think things out, weigh up the pros and cons. Another fifteen or twenty minutes will still give him plenty of time, as planned. He listened to the clinking of cups, the shuffling of slippers and the swishing of a dressing gown. Yes, things as usual.

One eye peeking over the duvet watched the sun... doing nothing. He mused on the plurals. If there were suns, then there would be skies. Therefore, if it is possible to count the suns, then it's possible to count the skies. He came to the conclusion that this must be correct. He liked counting and calculating. Counts had to be checked. This was perfectly reasonable because it was perfectly obvious. He liked facts. That's the problem with the world: no serious acknowledgement of facts. It could be extremely annoying. Sometimes it made life almost impossible, extraordinarily frustrating. He stopped peeking and snuggled further into his pit. It was his bed, his time and he felt no guilt, guilt being a useless emotion, although he had never really thought about it. Accept the facts; acceptance is convenient. He accepted this without thinking. Now that he was thinking about how frustrating life could be, he felt depressed. But not a serious depression: he estimated a 2 out of 10 score. Nothing to worry about, just a little sample of depression, a little experience of depression, set up by his own mind for the stimulation, something to do with last night's booze no doubt. Now he felt much better. He was conscious that it was time to get up. He had this thought four seconds before his second alarm went off.

He watched the insides of his eyelids change colour, from all sorts of pinks and reds, to blotches of dashing colours, to streaks of black.

The casino was crowded and becoming increasingly excited because he was on a winning streak, he was on a roll. He loved being the centre of attention, and he was brilliant at poker (it could be roulette), a hero, a superman, so skilful, handsome and daring; a self-effacing international spy from an old story, tall, dark and handsome, although he was seated at the table and fair-haired, turning grey above the ears; obviously distinguished. And, of course, the women, one young and beautiful at each shoulder, almost wrapped around him. He could feel a breast at each shoulder. You could tell. And more were joining the group; more breasts attached to more women. Imagine the miracle: women haven't one, but two! Now things were becoming really exciting, the crowd gasping at his skill and manly prowess.

He was smiling from ear to ear, the smile being a "ah, shucks, it's nothin'" kind of smile, "I'm used to it." His attire was of the most expensive and the people around him were beautiful. Even the men were beautiful, but not as beautiful as him.

The chips stood in four piles and growing higher. The crowd emitted a sedate and well-mannered cheer when his winnings were pushed across the table to him, yet again; and again...

He had to keep reducing the piles to form more balanced piles. Soon there were ten huge piles. They would surely topple over. His piles were making him uncomfortable. But he knew everything would work out, as the chips transformed into large currency banknotes. Somebody must have slipped him a leather bag. It was just like one of those old movies. It flashed through his mind that he was certainly being watched on-camera by the surveillance team. But he was not cheating. He was just dazzlingly skilful and incredibly manly. In fact, irresistibly manly. Money and women, women and money, and, especially, being a winner, a man amongst men, makes a man incredibly manly.

Wiping another wad of loose banknotes from the table, just to make room for the next inevitable wad, with his forearm, into the large leather bag on his lap between six-pack and table, he discerned his wife's chuckle. He froze and blushed, like a teenage boy caught doing something rude and private, he glanced across a crowded room, the very one he was in, and there she was, all motherly. He tried to nudge away the beautiful women as if to suggest he had, only just now, this very moment, noticed their presence. He honestly hadn't noticed them. How long had they been there? His wife was saying something about water, chuckling something about coffee; they were having some kind of inane conversation. Not another one.

"Yes, I know," he said rolling over and sitting on the edge of the bed in one movement,   which was optimally efficient. He felt deadly, much worse than his first awakening. He had exactly 1 hr. and 59secs. to get to work. Still time; mustn't panic. Glancing down: yes, still there - behave! - just checking. Purvanos was a numbers man, solid, and forgot little - mainly because he had little to forget. Cluttering his mind with abstract concepts was wasteful and untidy.

## 12

Awakened with a start by terrible shouting. Dismayed and angry, and almost sixty years of age, and Belbiana is still having to explain to impertinent people the meaning of life. Even in her dreams, they manage to arouse her anger. She is tired and worn out by their cheek and stupidity. How dare they challenge her! She is already tired and her day has barely begun. What a way to begin the day. Her perfect husband is still asleep. She lays her hand on his shoulder to reassure him that she is still there, and feels his body rise and fall. It is mutually comforting. She begins to calm down. Such insufferable people! They people her daydreams and nightmares, but on every occasion, she puts them in their place: beneath her, where they should be and this is obvious. The fact she has not spoken to any of them for eight years. Goodness, how time flies. It is eight years since that appalling Christmas. No, I am mistaken, which does not happen very often. She smiles at her own joke. She is beginning to cheer up. That's a good thing, considering her extremely important job. Ask anyone how important it is. They will tell you. How many lives has she saved? Too many to count. But not on her own, of course. She played her part, an essential part.

"Nine damnable years!" She hissed it out loud, and her great husband, the greatest husband in the world, stirred, but was not shaken. Nine years and then only one of the obnoxious prigs turned up to our party, my husband and mine. The others were, apparently, otherwise engaged. Such feeble excuses! So down-right anti-social and ignorant. Too stupid to know how ignorant they are. And what did he do, the arrogant prig, with all his useless certificates? What good have they done him? No good at all. He is completely useless and jam-packed with highfalutin opinions on everything. What did he do? Ate like the pig he is and drank himself into a stupor. He criticised everything about Tab and me, but was quite happy to eat our food, drink our drink, and then collapse into uncon-sciousness in our guestroom. We'd worked so hard to make them comfortable.

A contributory joined the river at this point. Breakfast: a pot of tea for two, boiled eggs, toast, dripping in butter because that is how her darling likes his toast. She had a vague awareness that she could not remember much of that party, but put it out of her head. It may not have actually happened *precisely* the way she remembered it, but that was the gist. That is the way things usually went, for years, for decades. So tedious, so tiring, never ending. But everything ends and then they'll be sorry. And before that, the others? Oh, twelve, fifteen, twenty years, something like that, different for different people. Her sister is obnoxious, twenty years for her. And her rotten husband. He is probably a bitter and twisted old man by now, probably lost all his hair. He was always bitter and twisted. I do not understand why she married him. He was always a bully. My husband and I are quite sure of that. We saw the signs. I had to explain them to Tabantate, but he always agreed that my interpretation had been correct. No children is a sure sign of male immaturity and bullying. Why she agreed to that is beyond me. There is more to life than a nice apartment and holidays. That is so unreal and pathetic. That is not a life at all. And tons of credits in the bank. So what! We have all those things.

She looked around her sumptuous bedroom. Tabi had worked hard on the apartment, and all the previous dwellings - she had a recurring need to move, to sell-up, make a killing, to improve their lot, to achieve their just desserts, proper status for a respectable couple, who made an effort. Every few years, must relo-cate; up-sticks, move on, dump emotional baggage, get a life. She felt that terri-ble thing rising from her stomach. Must resist the flood, she thought somewhere deep inside where there are no words. Must escape or drown. She felt the floods coming.

The room was beginning to swim. It was surely moving, moving in on her, the walls closing in, the usual world glanced through the window was beginning to recede, reality disappearing. It looked a nice day, a nice day, a very nice day. Things would be okay, things were okay, everything was fine, fine, it was fine as usual. Nothing unusual; everything fine, fine and dandy for my husband and I.

Tea and toast, and tea, no, no, boiled eggs. Yes, that's it; must get things in the right order, things must be ordered. Law and Order, that sort of thing, for proper, mature, respectable people of mature years who have always taken proper responsibility. Five minutes to brew the tea, two and a half minutes to boil the eggs, but the toast takes longer. How long does toast take? So: kettle on, then boiled eggs - better make it two for Tabi - then two slices of bread, to begin with, into the toaster, no point putting the grill on, pointless, unnecessary. Get things started.

She slipped out of bed, not to wake Tabantate. The flood had not overwhelmed her, not this time. Her face was flushed, but things were under control, everything was normal. Sitting on the toilet, she felt much better. She imagined her throne and she waved to the adoring crowd. She chuckled and started humming an old song. Things were looking up.

In the kitchen, she majestically prepared breakfast, perfect, fit for her king. Breakfast for two, always for two.

"Two eggs for me, darling." She froze at the sound of his voice, caught out like a child.

"You're awake, hun?"

"Obviously so, darling. I've been awake for a while."

## 13

The brat of a sun had prodded him sharply and he opened his eyes to stare at the ceiling. A startled awakening, from a dream which had immediately departed; or was it a nightmare, his ex? He rolled away from the morning sounds. He imagined the neighbours knocking furiously on the wall to complain about his snoring. He grunted a laugh to himself. That had never happened, but it might one day. The daftest things are possible. That is just the way things are, whether you like it or not. Experience and age bring their own rewards... and punishments. Whenever he slept on his back he snored, and very loudly, so he'd been told.

He had heard neighbours making a racket. It certainly sounded like lovemaking, but not recently, not in this apartment; in previous abodes, as his wife called them, involving previous neighbours. The love-making sounds always caused sniggering and a shaking of heads, coupled with a few salacious comments. And then: stop listening! He wasn't the sort of person to enjoy voyeurism. So he would go into the other room or turn up the radio. He tried to recall some of the 'other rooms'. There were many.

Similarly, he disapproved of pornography, even in his rampant youth. In those days, it was almost entirely pictorial. He mused on the fact that he hadn't been to a shop for some time. Things were being delivered, although he and his wife weren't rich. They would be described as comfortable, but not as comfortable as he was at this very moment. Yes, shops had been radically weeded to allow the growth of very large and colourful markets, which had developed into supermarkets, and then hypermarkets, which had all joined together to form shopping malls, a very peculiar expression. A mall was surely some kind of alley. Oh well, he was thinking, things change. Go with the flow, but try not to drown.

It was some time since he had actually stood and looked. The last time was probably with *that woman*. Like any normal man, he hated shopping. That hadn't changed. Shopping was *not* like hunting and gathering. He tutted audibly to himself. What a stupid comparison. He had never actually hunted and gathered, but you do not have to do something to know what it is or is not. Way back in those days of wife and children, he had tended to wait outside and encourage his wife to hunt and gather. It didn't take much encouragement and he'd stay put to look after the children and stand and stare, more akin to scrutinise.

He scrutinised buildings and watched them grow taller and wider until they'd become enclosed worlds unto themselves. He imagined the front doors being locked and bolted and everybody inside living happily ever after. But what about supplies? All the shopping malls could be joined together by underground rail-ways. These giant buildings could include farms, factories, schools and hospitals, and now they do, except for farms. Everything is possible and every problem elicits a solution. You just have to be reasonable. He also scrutinised people. Peculiar looking objects, with all their silly notions, mainly about themselves. "Get a proper job!" Idle hands spoil the broth, or something like that. The prob-lem with the world: too many lazy people.

He was a builder by trade. Sometimes, he would try to calculate the number of bricks (of all sorts) that would be necessary, and were already necessary, to produce these huge structures. His children were safe enough within a few feet of his legs. He was good at looking after kids and catching the eye of women. Kids attract women. He'd always been such a flirt!

There'd been a few women. He had been frightened of his mother since the beginning. By the time he was a teenager, she had become positively dangerous. Nobody would believe the tales he told. They weren't *based* on fact; they *were* fact. But there was no point talking about these things. He and his father had 'emigrated' way across the City. That is when he'd learnt his trade. All the trades, in fact (except 'electrics', and he made that clear) and not a certificate in sight! He could build anything involving bricks and mortar entirely on his own... except for electrics. He loved his children.

He realised he distrusted his wife. He'd got her trapped at home with the children. She had to be kept in her place because women can be very violent in every respect. A few kids will keep them under control. He *sensed* this was true. And he and his father could clear off - and they did frequently - to earn a living. Father and son working together was just fine, some of the happiest days of his life, working with other men, doing a proper job. She and the kids were also fine. His father always sent money home, mainly for his other children, but could never return home himself.

Tabatante mused on these things, this sunny morning. An ill-defined sadness, but put it out of your mind. It is life. He saw his children now and then and their children. His own father was long dead when the grandchildren arrived. He'd never reached hobbling old age. Our musing hero had tried to help his present wife come to terms with certain things, her family, his family. But he really wasn't sure. Let it go, it'll be okay, we're happy. She says she's happy, apart from...Leave it. He had learnt not to rake things up. Anything for a peaceful life and a happy marriage. His first wife had become extremely threatening, as predicted, and his present wife was prone to *outbursts*. Why can't women be more like men? He loved musicals, but he didn't love shoes!

He heard clattering from the kitchen. He fancied two boiled eggs and damn the expense! Life is simple, enjoy it. He recognised the tension in his wife's voice.

## 14

Lazed, blond on her pillow, blue eyes dazed, shocked at the light. Amazed to be alive, but it just keeps happening. One day it won't. She never quite believes it, but she knows it must be true. Hence, her suicidal tendencies, all unacknowl-edged. She cannot face the facts. If you do not know the facts, then you cannot face them; something to do with her childhood, although it was not too bad, not as bad as other people's childhoods, people she knew. She had heard many tales of woe, personal testimonies, mainly relating to parents and their awful attitudes and behaviours. Strangely, she had easily understood, being clever, and it is official, how awful the awful attitudes and behaviours were, and how damaging they are, she had acquired both awful and damaging attitudes and behaviours herself. It is sad and, quite frankly, unacceptable, that clever people become awful. Not full of awe, but rotten to the core. She was too smothered in unlove and cleverness to understand herself.

She turned her head towards the light and the alarm clock. Sachikaka felt nauseous and wished she could pray for a miracle, but all that was long gone. Lessons at school do not amount to much. Something about God and *things*; all a blur now and not much better at the time. The teacher waffling on about something, the kids whispering rude things to each other and giggling quietly. They were sure the teacher wore stockings. They were quite convinced. She remembered his polished black shoes - always polished - and he wore the same suit. For years he wore the same suit. Maybe he slept in the classroom cupboard and did not have a home to go to. They could not imagine him kissing anyone or anyone kissing him. He walked into the classroom of her imagination right now and sat behind his desk. She could not hear his voice, although she could see he was saying something. Now she would love to know what he was saying. Years after being a mouthy teenager, they had all begun to understand that he was quite decent after all. He must have been, even in his stockings. She'd had worse men than him. It is funny what you learn eventually.

She wondered about the hairy arm she could feel against her naked skin. She shivered inside; she felt worn out and old. It was a waste of time promising to give up or cut down on alcohol. She had no intention of doing either. To get drunk is perfectly normal and great fun. But the consequences are a pain, literally painful in every way, almost every time. This is what her parents had taught her - the importance of networking - especially her mother. They were very well-off and still are. Her father is somewhere else and always has been. He could not quite cope. Sometimes she cannot remember her mother's husband's name. They have been a whole collection of them; she gets mixed up. For several seconds, right now, she could not remember the current one's name, although they had spoken, all three of them, on the telephone yesterday. First, she put her loss of memory down to alcohol and then remembered that this particular loss of memory was normal. She could not keep up with her mother, although she tried. Hence, the hairy arm. No husbands yet, but there will probably be a few in due course, without prejudice. They use that expression in her profession, although she did not actually enter it. She never felt quite right; lots of I.Q., but something was missing. "Money property, money property" is the old mantra, her mummy's mantra. So she decided to follow in her mother's footsteps. It was not a real decision, of course, but she thought it was. One must be sensible and provide for one's future. Money property, money property.

He seemed handsome, now she chanced a look. Blue shadow of morning beard, smartly cut natural blond hair (although she couldn't recall) and tanned muscular shoulder. They'd make a perfect couple... for a photograph. More names to remember. What was his? Which mnemonic had she used. She usually used one because they had proved so helpful in exams. Her cousin gave her the idea, hardly original, but helpful. But thanks to alcohol, she could rarely remember the mnemonic! If she were drunk, she would remember. She knew this is called state-dependent learning. As she's frequently in a state, she must be very learned. Name name name - what is it? Oh well, she'll get by. He cannot remember her name either, but no need to tell her - she knows. All is fair in love and war. All is fair in lust and pain for Sachikaka.

"Are you awake, handsome?" Try to be friendly, cod them along, no need to be unfriendly. She nudged him. She recognised the kind of grunt which meant "Yes, almost."

"I'll make some tea. And coffee," she said as an afterthought.

She rolled into the sitting-on-the-edge-of-the-bed position and immediately regretted her offer and being alive in general. The room swam around. No oxygen in her brain and she felt so nauseous that she was about to vomit. She had to concentrate. It did not work. She had to get to the bathroom. She stood up, walked a couple of paces, then collapsed on hands and knees, face on the carpet, the room spinning around.

At this unfamiliar noise, he sat up, blinked wide awake, taking in the unfamiliar scene, trying to recall last night's events. There was certainly an attractive woman. Then, being alerted by a moaning noise from the far side of this strange bed - just another strange bed, no big deal - he leant across to investigate and encountered a joyous scene. The rays of sun peeped through tiny slits in the drawn blinds and a million motes danced in the lights.

"Are you okay?"

The gorgeous, tanned backside made no reply.

## 15

Bobbing on the shipwreck of his life, Makallee reached shore. The white sand was warm under his body; the sun beat down on his eyes closed against its glare. He imagined palm trees and the chattering of exotic birds. He felt the presence of vultures. He was terrified. He wasn't dead, but he couldn't move; he was trapped, weighed down, inside the giant cigar he had considered home for so long way out in the briny sea.

He awoke to the chattering of the radio. His heart was beating ten to the dozen - he often talked nonsense - and his fear was almost smothering. Some things are so real, it's unbelievable. He kept reliving the fear his own mind had concocted, that *stuff* from way back, all jumbled up. He hadn't closed the curtains and the blue sky blazed in upon him. He threw off the covering and sprang from the bed. He was free and alive! That's what men do when they must, in an emergency, in the terror of action, when no thinking is necessary, when they just do exactly what they've been trained to do. He threw himself to the ground, sailor-like, and completed ten rapid press-ups. He felt better and went to the toilet - a sailor home from the sea, from the very depths of the ocean, home from his giant metal cigar container.

He sat on the toilet, straining for his first poop-deck of the day. He chuckled audibly at his own joke, our little nincompoop of a hero, his toes barely touching the floor. He pondered on the ancient concept of monarchy and country and the great mystery of why people have toes. His seemed to be of little use. What is it like, he pondered, to have your toes blown or burnt off in a battle?

This thought floated like driftwood in his brain, together with other flotsam and jetsam gleaned mainly from pub quizzes and wild imaginings. He had not seen action yet, but he had been there and that's close enough to tell *tales*. They had patrolled the enemy seas, out of sight, out of mind. Not exactly the enemy seas because the enemy didn't have a sea, and, in fact, there was no enemy, but nevertheless preparing and practising for 'Action Stations!' and plenty of blood and guts! He mused on body bags regularly airlifted home. He wondered what it was like to have your genitals blown off. He watched the thing, not for the first time, changing shape of its own free will. He wouldn't like to lose his best friend. He imagined himself bleeding to death, as one does. He had real friends, lots of them. He was quite sure they were real friends. How would they react if everything was blown off in the thick smoke and chaos of battle. Sinking, he wouldn't stand a chance. He wouldn't like to live even if they weren't sinking. He had made up his mind that it would be better to sink. He thought of his present girlfriend and watched it take on a life of its own. Okay, might as well, he decided, not being a person usually prone to decision making.

After a more determined bout of exercise and a shower, he still felt hot and bothered. He realised that it was too hot in the apartment for unnecessary exercise, but it was too late. He had to cool down. Some cereal and cold milk would help. He sat to breakfast, thoughts dragging themselves over the rough terrain of his brain. It is funny how many thoughts you have. Yes, it certainly is. He crunched through his bowl of sugary air and scanned absentmindedly the cereal box. Thousands of words... and he slammed it back on the table, a cereal box of a slam. Why was there so much writing on cereal boxes? It was annoying. It was like reading a novel on a box. How stupid is that? It's everywhere: road signs, shop windows, every known form of container, you can't even cook a meal without having to read tiny instructions! Why all this writing? Sometimes he felt imprisoned. Get all this rubbish out of his mind. That family of his, they're not a family at all. Having to deal with them is a nightmare, the whole lot of them! Why don't they do something useful? They treat him as though he should be in prison or killed in a war. Being in the military is a good way to keep him out of the way. They don't see how important his job is. They're all *intellect* and talk. His cousins are probably all virgins! They should be got rid of! Get rid of useless youth; they are only taking up space. Things are going to get worse - there are going to be billions of them, eating and breathing, using up oxygen, exhaling carbon dioxide, poisoning the useful people and eating their food. Something will have to be done. Wars are a great help in this respect, unlike plagues which are indiscriminative and frightening. Plagues can kill powerful, clever, and useful people - must avoid plagues. That's what he is thinking of them and he knows perfectly well that's what they think of him!

Our heroic sailor is admiring himself in the mirror. Indeed, he is admiring himself in several mirrors, two appropriately angled, as well as one handheld. Yes, he is looking good. He decided to wear his white trousers (which he had taken to calling 'pants' in recent times due to his experience as a world traveller), not because of his marine status but because he simply looked good in white. Quite irresistible, he concluded, as he did a near jig for his mirrors. He was ready for the day and the girls! The uniform would help with reconnoitring and conquering. The 'girls' were women with a mental age of fourteen. So he was about to have a good and fanciful day.

She arose in her jungle, hacking at all around her, where the sun never shines. The sun peeked through her blinds, saw her awake, and withdrew. This cannot go on forever; surely there will be an end. All things end. Into her sixties, she moaned at still being alive. Nasichisha didn't realise the cause of her moan. She considered the day ahead: so much to do. She hated the way people are: always picking on her, putting her down, never appreciating her efforts. When you hate other people, you always hate yourself, although some people are hateful, and some people are full of hate.

She couldn't leave the room, regardless of her bladder. The bed. Not much to do, but she recalled the days of sheets, blankets, eiderdowns, and pillow-cases, usually two per pillow, one going in one direction, one the other, to stop feathers escaping. Instinctively, like a robot, she scanned the bed, floor, and room for feathers. She knew there would be no feathers, but there was always the possibility for one feather nestling, hiding, having escaped. She glanced under the bed. In those far-off days beds seemed so big.

Starting at the pillow end, she smoothed down the under-sheet, puffed up the pillows and placed them perfectly aligned, perfectly smoothed down. Then she worked her way down the sheet, smoothing out every wrinkle until she reached the bottom, still under the duvet, which must not fall on the floor. Very aware of dust, dead skin, and living mites, but could not be seen, her smoothing was also a scraping of this debris towards the edges of the bed and into the air to float to the floor, the air full of the living and the dead, all around her, and the billions of tiny creatures grazing on the surface of her body, in her most private places, amongst moist oases of heat and hair, which to these creatures were enormous forests. And individual hairs like sequoias , which rose and fell, due to temperature changes, over the heads of the munching creatures, eating at her, eating at her.

Finally, she pulled the bulky duvet into its rightful and proper position, three hands, as you measure a horse, over-hanging on each side, having shaken it to distribute evenly the internal contents and to send countless debris into the air to fall silently and invisibly like snow. Circling the bed, she smoothed out its final surface. Appearance is importance; appearance is everything. Sometimes she watched the 'snow' floating in those tunnels of sunlight. She did not like that, turned away, and put it out of her mind. But nothing bad this morning. She felt just fine: everything smooth, covered up, in its rightful place. A place for everything and everything in its place. He used to say that, but not quite the same saying, but the same meaning and in a different language. That language, the one she tried to avoid, although she was fluent. A little practise and she would be very impressive indeed. No one could tell she'd been born in another country. But she would never do that. She hated the language; she tried to avoid it. She often pretended she'd not heard it on those rare occasions when it was being forced upon her by relatives or guests. She would not be forced; she would not be forced to do anything against her will ever again.

She glanced under the bed. Things under beds have to be retrieved, dusted, and put in their right places. A child stared back. The tears leapt to her eyes. No, no, no. No feathers, no bits of fluff, nothing unruly. A man who really liked her had called her a bit of fluff. It was only a joke. But he was punished; she got her revenge. She waited until he really loved her, then she took revenge. There had been others.

Before leaving the room, she glanced back just to double-check. She returned and pulled very carefully at the left hand, bottom corner of the duvet. That will do for now. Relax, she told herself, he won't be back to check. He won't be back ever. Everything appropriately plumped, no bits of fluff. But she noticed her dressing table. Is that dust? She will check later - must go to the toilet. Don't want to have an accident! She laughed to herself. This is going to be a good day. She felt it in her water.

Her breakfast was a sad scene of loneliness. Always the same, but not actually alone, she had learnt to be alone; it was safer. Healthy cereal, the highest quality muesli she could afford, low-fat milk, followed by herb tea, no milk, no sugar, slowly and sedately sipped, like a young lady. Other people were rough, avoid them, "They are not like us. You are judged by the company you keep." Drummed into them, part of them, they were taught to be *nice*. But some nice people are bad. Aren't they?

She nibbled the cereal politely, chewing each spoonful, although, of course, not a full spoon, several times to aid digestion. She had tried chewing everything twenty times, but had discovered that that was often not possible because there was nothing left to chew by number ten or twelve. She had tried it for several years, but had given it up because it was not practicable. You must be sensible and use your judgment; even a girl has a certain degree of judgment. She remembered the dust on her dressing table. She gobbled down the last vitamin supplements and her teaspoon of dry lecithin. She had given up eggs completely - eggs are bad for you. She had read that in a magazine she had grown to trust completely. Every week she looked forward to the current issue. Now, to complete her chores; then places to go and people to see. A jolly time to be had by all - the play's the thing.

## 17

The sun slavered over her face; she awoke and turned away. For a second she could not remember her husband's name. Staring at the back of his head, she closed her eyes in relief. In a flash she had scanned her list. Sixty-one soon. It just goes on and on, the routines which evolve into new routines orbiting her sun, centre of the universe. Jardena was once a sweet child, but that seems very long ago, several lifetimes. Misery begets misery. Lies radiate like the initial tiny waves caused by a pebble plopped into a pond. Lying is a bacterium which keeps dividing and subdividing indefinitely until it contaminates the world. You must understand what a person is. But people are different, you will say. Of course they are, but all human beings have that handful of traits which make them human. They must have all of them. One or two missing and they are not human. They are some kind of ape that imitates human behaviour. It is simple enough. These are the things you must come to terms with. There should be short courses on this subject, so that these essentials are clarified. Otherwise, people become increasingly confused. Appearances are frequently deceptive. More on this later, or possibly not - who knows how things will work out. But eventually you will understand, if you happen to be human and live long enough. For most, without tuition, it is all very difficult.

Now, gazing at the back of his slightly ruffled head, she remembered who he was. His freckled shoulder and white vest reminded her of a time when she would never have slept with a man who wore vests. She had almost forgotten vests. No vests needed in those hot countries where she was something special, way above the common people, the people who cleaned, served, people who did her shopping. (Hard to believe, but these places still exist! Some things never change). They were her servants and those times were good; sunny times in the sun far away where people spoke exotic languages, although she had tried to teach them to speak properly. When she and her well-designed family returned home for holidays, not real holidays, they'd already had those, the folks at home had been appropriately impressed and jealous. That was a good feeling; and so they should be. Let's be fair. Nobody knew the real reason, but she was just obnoxious in her own right. It came naturally to her, so it was said. Some people are, aren't they? Nurture? Hmm, a good question. Laters. (What a strange language!).

She stretched and felt trapped. She didn't want to touch him. As with the others, she didn't want to be touched. That feeling of 'dirty' went back a long way. First, lust and power, then depression and filth. Long ago, she used to cry on her own, but she'd passed through that phase. Now she grins and bares it. She thought of the expression. Yes, she certainly bares it, and they do not nail *her*, she nails *them*. One after another, she nailed them, and made them pay. It is amazing how men simply pay. One way or another, they simply pay because, basically, men are stupid.

Time to get up and count her worth, assess her economic standing. Not literally count, of course, that would be common, but to survey her metaphorical kingdom, ponder on the peasants toiling for their good, but especially for her good. That is the way it is and that is the way it should be. Let's just accept that her feelings of superiority are not her fault, at least, not to begin with. But there comes a time, in the life of a *compos mentis* adult, when rational decisions are possible, at which point, badness, in its multiplicative carnations, and all known bouqueic combinations, is, indeed, one's fault. Some people would disagree. "Everything is relative," they might say. And: "Keep talking 'til their eyes glaze over." Somebody claimed that as eminently sensible advice in certain circumstances. I could tell he was famous because his wife was so unhappy and his children were almost silent. It is unlikely you will ever meet him. It is unlikely that you will ever meet his wife. His children are...

Our heroine, high on the greatest drug in the world ("Self-Delusion", as it is known on the street) had never met him, according to data, but his wisdom is her wisdom, apparently, the Wisdom of the Ages. Keep talking, the more impressive the better, say anything at all, make it up, (deviscerate, for example, discombobulate), say anything to get your own way. The world is your oyster - whatever that means - so, be assertive. Assertiveness conquers all things. Except pimples, but that's another story, although not irrelevant, if you know the *connections*.

The day lay ahead. The Queen, her own creation, to walk amongst her subjects, collecting rents and explaining the meaning of life where and when appropriate, our expert on family matters and relational difficulties and dilemmas, based on her forty years of adulthood spent destroying people's lives and explaining why they should *try* to be more reasonable. The property owner, shops bought with ex-husbands' involuntary contributions, and houses acquired dittoly (just make it up, she does), as well as from her poor and downtrodden tenants, scanned her mental list. Even in our wonderfully modern world, the poor and downtrodden insist on existing. Lots of shops, lots of houses - these are the reasons she has acquired standing in the community and we are all most grateful. So are the people of Ping Pong.

No love today, my darling. She thought this to herself, but only the smirk was recorded and, therefore, available to later interpretation. Her husband, eyes still closed, turned away from her departing form. She closed the door quietly behind her. She deserved some time to herself. Keep the farce going; it is a convenient arrangement for the time being.

## 18

The Rising Sun has come to visit us and guide our feet in the way of peace. No, this is not the priest. I changed my *mind* at the last minute - it's our preroga-tive - and decided to waft through the mind of the writer where there is plenty of room. His name is Damodural and, like the others, things are complicated. Things certainly get complicated for many for no good reason. In this case they're certainly complicated and that's the whole point. Plenty of data is available, which reminds me of Kelly's Law. She is a very popular and a good friend to many, and clever. But relationships are difficult in general, and with men in particular. So I will just tell you Kelly's Law, which you may well know. If you do, you can skip the next sentence. If you don't, this may be helpful. No, the previous sentence was not intended to be the next sentence. Oh dear. I suggest you look it up in an encyclopaedia. Believe me, it is very interesting and very pertinent to everyday life. One of the criteria is to be obscure and obstructive because... everything's covered up. Or, is that two criterions?

Damodural is tossing and turning in his impressively extra-long bed. His feet aren't covered up, they are sticking out of the bed, this morning at the bottom end. It's not simply assumed, because he's a very restless sleeper. He is very sensitive; somewhat hypersensitive. Some people have used different words, but it depends who they are and what they do. Once or twice words such as 'bone-idle' have been scrawled in the margins of official notes. On other occasions, in low, discrete tones such expressions as 'directionless fool' have been uttered, but out of Damodural's hearing. But on one very embarrassing occasion, a foul man actually shouted, "You are a pompous idiot!" right in Damodural's face, turned on his heels, both of them simultaneously, and marched out of the room like a sergeant-major, although I haven't accessed data on a sergeant-major. Now, what can you expect from a *scientist*? Really, no class or self-control, no proper learning and, therefore, no sense of *culture*. Typical of a person trained in the collation and analysis of facts - social skills: zero. But a noted degree of pleas-ure when I analysed this scene, this collection of interactions. The other people in the group voiced no objection. They glanced around, quite cool, collected, looked down, looked away - there was a tense moment of silence when I really thought somebody might have been asked to leave. But, as the vile and socially inept person had already left, the awkward moment passed. Damodural tutted, shook his head, waved his hand in dismissal of the ruffian, who was no longer present, and offered to read one of his poems. The 'fidget factor' was noted. The chairs were proving uncomfortable. When the alcohol arrived, they appeared noticeably less fidgety.

Damodural lay gazing at the ceiling, aware of his chilly feet, and the day creeping up on him. No escape; brazen it out. Words formed on the ceiling: The Case of the Hand. No, corny. A Quiet Belief in Demons. Now, that sounds pretty good, but rather familiar. And then the words: She smiled enigmatically. Yes, that's excellent. So, let me see, what to write in between? What could the 80,000 words be? Suddenly, he felt so tired. Yes, Damo, have a little snooze, you have earned it. He rolled over, hugged the duvet, and brought his feet into contention with duvet and bed.

There were times when he made a living, but he was going through a lean period, another one. He thought of his guitar - could have a little practice. He could have been a rock star; he could have been an astronaut. But his height was always against him. Nobody recognised his true talent. At that thought, he rolled lithely out of bed with the grace of the ballerina he could have been. Almost immediately, he stubbed the middle toe of his right foot on the left, bottom leg of the bed, jumped aside in pain and shock, and banged his left shin on the seat of the dining chair permanently parked beside his bed on which were neatly draped his very long trousers, on top of which were folded ever so neatly his pants, a lifelong habit. Talk of pants and trousers will be confusing to some people, but it must be continuous prose and no diagrams, but Dam, as some whisper at his arrival, on the other hand, is very good at drawing. Indeed, he could have been a great artist. At this point, he uttered a series of words, which included a reference to somebody's mother as well as the immanent, words only a true rock star would know, colourful terms , but the volume was too low to elicit intervention.

When the various pains subsided, Damodural being a multiply sensitive person it took some time, he saw the funny side. It could be a scene in his next book. His *next* book? His next production of something or other, a letter to his mother, perhaps. He thought of his young child. Then he thought of breakfast. First things first. He noticed the sun was shining as he passed the full-length mirror. He caught his attention and stopped. The sun blazed on his still blond hair and made his blue eyes sparkle. Even at his age, he could still be a model. He reminded himself of a Roman gladiator. He spotted the red horizontal line across his shin. Looks sore, but it will probably heal. And the rest - still a fine looking fellow. He felt much better; always look on the bright side; onward and upward; must hold the old tummy in. At this point, he started to leak and rushed to the toilet. His backside was decidedly saggy with the sudden movement, but keep that to yourself.

## 19

We must have a detective; everybody does. This one lives a couple of clicks away. I have no idea what a click is, but it must be quite nearby, within walking distance, certainly within crawling through the underbrush distance, or through the forest, hunkered down distance. In this case, he lives down the road and round the corner from a... *load of people*, near the hypermarket. He lives in a very comfortable apartment above a superstore. It's a strange place for a policeman to live, but he has lived there for years and he is well set-up; in other words, he is very comfortable. Take it or leave it, these are the simple facts, and his name is Bill. Yes, some people will find his name humorous. His full name is William Cody. His parents had certain peculiar heroes. His sister is called Jessie.

D.C.I. Cody was up and about, already fully dressed and breakfasted. He had been in the City for twenty years and it was something to do with the in-service exchange programme, or program, and somebody had forgotten to recall him. Pogrom is something completely different. Cody was enraged by anything that *smelled* of a pogrom. There are all sorts of pogroms, he would argue, not using quite the correct definition. He had moulded the word to suit himself. It was one of his favourite words. The feeling was mutual: it had adopted him.

Bill is as straight as a die. Few are his equal: he's an MD4. He collects stamps, not real stamps, but photographs of stamps. He has acquired the usual stamps, but he would never possess a rare stamp because that would deprive everybody else of it. He feels sorry for people who do this and are that obsessed. He considers they probably need psychotherapy. Obsession is a terrible thing. He has a vast and remarkable collection of photographs. He also has a very discerning knowledge of whiskey. He likes the finer things of life, stamps, books, whiskey, in moderation.

Bill also collects criminals, but not in moderation, sometimes dozens at a time. He regards it as a kind of pogrom. To round people up and destroy their lives is a terrible thing, as most of them are already living disasters, walking train wrecks, some are beautiful houses with rotting, infested interiors, but he has no choice; so he does it: it's the Law. That word always has a capital L in his mind. He feels sorry for mad people, but more sorry for their victims, as he was reflecting this very morning as he was reflecting on his face in the mirror. He always shaves, he goes through minor phases. It doesn't bother him one way or the other. He had a beard for a long time. That didn't bother him either. Then his wife said she was fed up with him looking so ridiculous, suddenly out of the blue, and if he didn't shave off his beard she would divorce him. He couldn't take it seriously. Women can be ridiculous. She claimed irreconcilable breakdown. The items listed on the divorce petition were mad, as he once commented, mad that *that* amounted to a legal document, but the divorce went ahead. Then, finding himself (relatively) free, he decided to shave off his beard just for a change. He did look younger, although he wasn't slightly bothered. So he left with his few belongings and his collection of photographs, only quarter its present size. Then he came here for a new and foreign experience. A change is as good as a rest, he said on occasion.

Socio- and psychopaths are awful, he had reflected before breakfast, and so are narcissists and border lines. He couldn't decide which category was worst, amongst so many others, or the order of severity. He knew a lot about this subject. His ex-wife was a sociopath, and still is. These disorders are, basically, incurable. Her attitude was nothing to do with his beard. Her 'agenda' was deeply complex and it had taken him a long time to put two and two together, to join the dots. Then one day the penny dropped, the jigsaw fell into place. Years of working with criminals had helped. Many of them were deeply disturbed. He mused on this over his boiled egg, three slices of buttered bread, and mug of tea, his favourite mug, the one with the red horizontal stripe around the middle. One tea and no coffee before eleven o'clock. If work intervenes, then forgo the coffee. Charming sociopaths drink decaf. Sociopaths are always charming, praying at the temple of their body, whilst clawing at the mortar of other people's temples. (Hmm. Skip that one, he decided, for a Team briefing or a lecture at the University). It's how they get by: charming, sociable, personable, persuasive. It takes normal folk years to figure out something is wrong. They sense it, but they can't put their finger on it. But not Bill. Bill is like a speeding bullet on this subject, since he focused his mind, got the message. It is shocking how many anti-social people exist. There are millions of them. We are producing a society of sociopaths. The same old thought sat on a fence in his mind. Surely this is true and they are all undiagnosed. What sort of a society is that? No society at all; a contradiction in terms.

At this point, he was chewing his last slice of bread - he'd put marmalade on it - and wiping his lips with a piece of tissue. He cleaned his teeth, glanced at the weather, threw his raincoat over his left arm, placed his briefcase into his left hand, surveyed his apartment - all was in order - tapped the digits into the small panel on the right of the door, and locked the door behind him. No calls so far. TOA: 0859, including purchase of a newspaper.

Now he raised his eyebrows - the word is klick.

## 20

"Her soul was destroying her body: and the teeming thoughts that troubled her poured into her veins a poison yet more dangerous than that of the high-est fever." What a thought to begin such a lovely day! But all is well. Ah, the old memory is still hanging on In quiet desperation. He had read that the night before. A little concentration and it always worked. Eidetic, or something, but he couldn't remember the term. Eidetic will do; must look it up. But he forgot.

Might write a poem: The Lonely Bed and the Sea. A lonely moan of delight as he stretched his limbs. Busy as a bee, so much to do, so little time, but who cares. It always works out.

"Morning, you sexy little beast!" Jeevalani shouted down the telephone. He always shouted.

Admittedly, she was quite small. Some people would describe her as low-set. A low-set wall is one you can easily sit on. Being 73 probably helped, and being a retired nurse was even more helpful. She had dealt with many people, some of them extremely peculiar.

"Good morning, Father. Breakfast in thirty minutes?"

"Great! Just throw it on the table!"

"Yes, I'll just throw it on the table." Patience.

He leapt out of bed like a deer yearning for running streams, but more of a muscular bull, heavy-set some might say. The women he had had to fight off, not to mention a few men! It's not easy being a celibate. People don't believe it. But it's straightforward enough. It just takes the victim ten or twenty years to get used to it and then it's easy.

Do a few press-ups, for goodness' sake, then a bit of running on the spot. Skipping would be good, but not indoors. Maybe a jog before lunch. But one thing at a time. Thank God, no telephone messages. Nobody had died yet today and no child, mangled and half dead, in a hospital bed. Thank you, Lord, for small mercies. Thank you for saving me from other people's sufferings. They under-stood one another. It had been a long time and a hard slog, much of it uphill.

It was more than strange to be back in the big city. He was not happy, if the truth be known. He preferred the bush to the beach, and the jungle to the concrete jungle. He preferred real people. He couldn't cope anymore with city slickers, who were not even slightly slick. They were just lazy and devious. They were unmotivated physical and intellectual slobs, but never short of opinions. That is what you learn in the city: opinions. But that awful desperation, the desperation of the hopeless. It was thick in the air, along with all the other toxins. The air was filled with talk. That's why he had to shout.

Breakfast lay sprawled over the table where she had thrown it. Breakfast had submitted. Everybody did, believe me. To Jee, everything was a feast. He was a man of hungers: good company first and foremost, followed by food and drink. Sometimes you could skip the food. But now it is food time and a minor feast. His housekeeper was old-fashioned and great, in your face and down to earth. They were well matched. For as long as this 'today' lasts, keep encouraging one another, and they did. She did not live-in and was there as early as he liked and left when she fancied.

No Sisters this morning, thank God, no early Mass. Ten o'clock is a long way away. Lots of time to think things out, but not too much thinking. Thinking had led to depression when he had first arrived and it had been awful. He'd felt suicidal. That data was a surprise. His job is the loneliest job on the planet, when other people behave like zombies, wandering around in a stupor making inane noises. There were more committees than confetti at a wedding and nothing ever achieved. So clever they are unable to think. He sat and pondered these things, but not too much, just a quick mental scan of today's things to do. Meetings to discuss the organisation of future meetings, to decide on the creation of new committees, or to which outside committees' representatives should be sent. This is how the rich behave, the people who have very little to worry about. Sometimes they discuss the poor and decide to form a sub-group and a study group, both of which are to report back to the committee in due course. When due course arrives, a Committee Report will be presented to the Parish Council Rep., who will take the report to the Parish Council. This item on their agenda will be discussed in due course, after consulting the appropriate expert groups. Thank God it is only starvation and not something serious.

Suddenly, he felt tired. Maybe this fatigue resulted from too many physical jerks in combination with too much fried food. So he decided to have another couple of slices of bacon to give himself some energy. The jerks went through his head. He shook them off. Must not drift back into despair. A couple of years, maybe, and he will be allowed to return to the bush where the real people live. We all have secrets. I hope he has his.

He tore from his chair, grabbed his jacket and, heading to his office, let a roar:

"Thanks for the breakfast, Delilah, it was great!" The sound tore through the building like a holy wind on Mount Sinai. He should have been an opera singer. He knew she was there somewhere, in the bowels of the building, which were actually upstairs and also known as 'umpteen rooms'. He could hear the vacuum cleaner somewhere near heaven, probably in a room he had not yet discovered. Imagine, he once said in dismay, the priest living in the biggest and most valuable house in the parish. What the hell sense does that make?

## 21

Handing out tissues, the City an opulent whore in the morning sun. Temptations aplenty, but it's a long time since choice was simply a choice. It could be the *alma mater*, but a mother who is under control. A certain mentality has evolved, thanks to the Cat (called the Shoah by the professor). Sometimes nicknames conceal multiplicities of pain. Pre-Cat is now studied in curricula. It's like the expression 'the War' for generations long passed. It became "Which war?" Collective memory fades, and there were many wars. I was instructed to set the scene.

The City would be described as a megalopolis in history books. But there are six hundred such Cities, so *mega* is the norm. Two thousand years have flown away! The land was cleared, the wall was built, the rest is history. Interestingly, it is a common history, with few variations. The sea lays eight miles downriver to the west. The river flows through the centre of the City. 'Busy' describes everything. The City is an ordered colony and there is nowhere to go. Central Computer keeps watch. The management system is remarkably simple, based on sensible ideas, shared history, applied science, and the Committee of MD5's. A World Congress is scheduled for the near future.

Education provides a good start. Merkan is wandering the corridors of the University. He isn't sure why; something has disturbed him. He has reached that age. STM is going, but he isn't worried - it'll come to him. He thrust his hand into his jacket left pocket. He found his pen. Good. You can't trust anybody, a typical elder. He'd been disappointed too many times.

"Hello, prof," a young man said as he passed, in a hurry.

The professor glanced after him, adjusted his glasses. That was surely, gosh, hasn't changed a bit, still looks so young, remarkable, catch up with him later, have a couple of beers, learn his secret of eternal youth, no, mustn't, the shopping, leave the beers, maybe tomorrow, and submit the exam questions, or have I done it, oh, left my pen in the library, ah good, remembered the second one, always have at least two pens, only sensible, pens are like gold dust in this theatre of war and learning, but mainly acting. He chuckled to himself. Two young females stepped aside and watched him go by. They chuckled. Young women do a lot of laughing for no obvious reason, he mused, happy to be alive, apparently.

Degrees pour down on the place like a summer shower. It was sensible to reject the concept of failure. It took long enough. Students have to satisfy the criteria. Attend, produce assignments, complete fortnightly tests, take the three hour papers in June and, after three or four years, the overall average is calculated and stated on the certificate. After all, this is not the end, it is the beginning, the beginning of the rest of their lives. It took centuries to understand this. The question is: what do students intend to do *next*?

We also dumped old titles: bachelors, masters, and doctors. What was all that about? And that word 'honours'. What a peculiar word, straight out of the Ark, and meaningless. We reached the point where nobody had a clue what 'honours' meant. A famous and documented encounter long ago: a famous professor blurted out that it was all a load of, well, something extremely vulgar. He received an immediate vocal warning, as well as many raised eyebrows. "Let's just fire on, everybody," he demanded famously and he did, "Let's not become distracted by nonsense. It'll all work out in the end. Take my word for it; nothing to worry about. Everybody knows everything about *honours* and nothing about *honour*!" The Committee acknowledged the truth of that statement. In short, now we call them Primary, Secondary, and Tertiary Degrees, and they are of increasing difficulty, as you would expect. The rest of our education system fits together fairly well although nothing is perfect.

The place is buzzing with its millions of little bee creatures known as students, or 'butternuts'. They come and go, logging in and out, satisfying the criteria. The whole complex is dubbed 'The Quads', an ancient term (Pre-Cat) , comprised of four hyperstructures and situated to the west on the north bank. It balances our Parliament to the east. Wits have suggested the two represent *doing* and *talking*. (But which is which?). Our Parliament is comprised of four hyperstructures nicknamed 'the Gospels' due to the fundamental requirement of honesty. Hence, although (generally) we believe in democracy, we demand that minimally MD2's can be elected to Parliament. Initially, this guarantees a degree of Moral Development, but as you would expect...

Merkan returned to the office he'd retained post-retirement and entered his cosy domain. He had wandered and chatted. He had been doing it for three hours, if you include his walk to 'work' from his university apartment. Some days he didn't manage to arrive at all! Part of his job, his vocation, is to *encourage* students and anybody else who happens across his path. He may have one or two visits by uninvited students in the course of the morning: reduce anxiety and encourage! And now, down to work. He opened several books at their marked places, remembered a couple of journal articles and logged on to find them. He glanced around the room for inspiration. Those bookshelves. Oh dear, they are becoming very messy, he may have said aloud, very dusty and not very welcoming. He rummaged in the bottom drawer of his nearest filing cabinet to find the cloth he used for dusting. He recalled that he had bought a special aerosol of 'fresh air' that smelled of flowers. The cloth's quite disgusting! he thought, needs a good wash. If you want something done properly, do it yourself. But not today - one must get one's priorities right, otherwise nothing will be achieved. One step at a time: complete the task. Then the wife.

## 22

The sewage system was a major achievement. You can enter the system at several locations around the City. A colourful entrance is along the Riverside, just before the Cathedral going west from the East Council building and opposite the popular Whistling Dick pub. The four Councils have viewing galleries and the proceedings can be interesting for a time, if you have a taste for municipal management - most don't. Horses for courses might be an appropriate old expression, although long forgotten and incomprehensible for residents of the City.

Here I picked up Halaigha strolling the Riverside. She hasn't been in a Council building for seventeen years since her school project, so it's unlikely she has come from the Council. It is also unlikely that she has any substantial memory of her project. Not her cup of tea-free tea! But strolling she is, in the bright mid-morning sun, glancing to her right across her river-audience of fishes and swooping birds, giving her imaginary waves, then to the right towards the Bohemian Sector, a higgledy-piggledy area of side streets, cafes, bookshops, and bars, where people chat earnestly, with notebooks and pens at the ready. You never know when the Muse will arrive, or all three of them. Notebooks and pens can be bought in special shops. Some unfortunates have been given reduced prison sentences if they accept Community Service in the Bohemian Sector, a temporary position, for example, at the Tin Dipper Tea House.

Halaigha bounces along on high heels, long light coat open and flowing behind, her silken headscarf gypsy-like. Surprisingly, she has the strength to bounce, luckily there is no wind. She has been drifting in and out of the arms of the authorities for many years. Ironically, although she loves to talk, she won't take advice; she cannot be reached.

"Hi!" she projects a smile at a person she doesn't know. They smile back politely. Like most cities, this one breeds anonymity. Some people are very suited to anonymity. There was a time when people hid in cities, but those days are long gone. Nowadays, we can only hide emotionally. The predicted probability is correct: she is heading to the Underground.

Skipping down the steps, in her public, purposeful, and meaningful way, she enters the sewage system. We call the system The Rose. The reason goes way back. It is one of those slang expressions that caught on and became official. The entrances in the City are brightly painted with roses round the door, so to speak; elaborate designs beyond the scope of this account, and each unique. Halaigha is in Tunnel 14 and following signs to The Underground. She knows the way very well; she doesn't need the signs, although it is easy to lose your way.

At first, the air strikes as musty. She waves her hand in front of her face as if to fend off attacking and obnoxious sprites, and coughs to clear her infected lungs, affected would be more accurate. Her crisp footfall on the clean walk-ways echo through the tunnels and the beautifully painted walls. The place is well lit and the sewage flows in the wide channel between the two walkways. There are occasional bridges to connect the walkways. There are many tunnels branching off in all directions, each numbered, and fairly frequent 'You Are Here' signs. If you happen to be hopeless at reading maps and schematic diagrams of networks, and some people are, there are frequent telephones. Press the red button and you will be connected immediately to the Control Room. You will be given spoken directions and a print-out, if necessary. Halaigha has done this several times, just to talk to someone. On one occasion, she went too far in her hopelessness, an acquired condition she thoroughly enjoys. But she did not enjoy it on this occasion. A uniformed attendant arrived very quickly on his motorised vehicle to 'rescue' her, realised her 'warped attitude', as he described it later to a colleague, and issued her with her first caution. This meant that she was required to attend the Psychiatric Department of Central Hospital, Inner Circular Road (N.E.). Everybody knows where it is because it is taught at school as part of the Civics Curriculum. Halaigha easily talked her way out of the place because she is very clever. She was extremely annoyed that they should treat her with such disrespect, but she was sensible enough not to voice these opinions to the medical practitioner who interviewed her. Her friends were regaled with this story in detail and they sighed in disbelief. Apparently, like attracts like.

Halaigha spotted Ophelia and waved. Their hearts rose. Halaigha trotted across the bridge to greet her friend. Ophelia mirrored and had slowed her pace in order to coincide with the bridge crossing. They hugged each other and four kissing sounds flew past ears as both sets of cheeks met alternately. It was beau-tifully choreographed. It's what they do.

"It's so nice to see you, sweetie!"

"And you too! How are you?"

"Oh, the usual, no change there. People are so ridiculous and my boyfriend getting worse! He's becoming a total pig! Really, he's too much; has had virtually nothing for almost a year! And it's not the first time, as you know, incapable of earning a living, the complete opposite of what he claimed when we met. And I believed him!"

"Oh, dear. Any news on *your* professional front? I'm working on a script, but it is fairly hopeless, quite frankly. My director is a fool. He's done a few things, but I'm beginning to think he's a phoney."

"So many are. They are not trained professionals at all, and it is painfully obvious, eventually."

"Something interesting at the Underground, so I hear?"

"So avant-garde, it's behind the times!"

The boyfriend? Yes, we have tabs on him. He's been *ensnared*. But there have been many of them - they come and go. If they'd any sense, they come and go as soon as possible.

## 23

Half a candle, three matches, two dinners of dog food, a little milk (sour), eight tea bags. No, he couldn't put it off any longer, even with all those tea bags. Maybe he'd head for Paddy's Hen and Chickens for his provisions. The dull vibration of the train alerted him to the time and the need to go forth. It was sinful to keep putting it off. Wastefulness is a sin and prevarication was one of his major sins because it was almost continuous, except when postponed. Before his clocks, Praman had even put off praying. Imagine not finding time to communicate with God, especially as he had been given so much time for that very purpose. Even when a clock crew, he still hesitated. Another few minutes won't make any difference. But how can you tell? This is terrible pride, assuming you have some say in these fundamental matters. The only thing you have a 'say' in is doing the best you can. Maybe. It has to be discerned.

Walking along the balcony outside his apartment, he stopped to gaze over the vast range of green land to the north. He was on the 17th Floor of the North Estate, its full title being Hyperstructure Residential Estate (North), usually HRS North. The building towered above him. And he towered above the city wall. He watched two watchmen chatting. He waved, no response. All jobs were boring and part-time. He had been a watchman God knows when, probably forty years ago. He wouldn't be asked again. It was the Rota. In those days it was one day per month for twelve months. Now it was much less, but he was out of touch, being a hermit.

The farm lands stretched for thousands of acres, way off to the horizon to a stretch of green distinguishable on very clear days, but not today. It was too sunny. The atmosphere had to be just right to see the strip of green on the horizon, the beginning of the wild, wild (extremely wild) woods. To his right the mines and, if he craned over the balcony, he could just see the beginning of the jagged mountain against the blue sky. He had climbed it twice (the easier routes) on official Mountain Trips in his youth. The North Train was just passing under the Upper Road and heading for the huge city gate and off towards the farmlands.

He decided to skip the many shops in the North Estate and head straight to the Shopping Centre. This building contained everything known to man, and that includes woman, and, in fact, child. You could spend a month in the place, and many people did, because it includes several hotels and all those things people call amenities. In addition, sports stadia, swimming pools, concert halls, you name it! What about a place for raiding, rioting and arrhythmia? Yes, we have schools for those activities, thought the hermit. This place has its own perfect rhythm, everything up and running, and nothing out of synch. Some people believe anything. It also has its own platelets: an inter-floor taxi service. Thus, the two Shopping Centres (North and South) were cities within the City. Praman liked such places (when unavoidable) because he could watch people and have many an idle conversation with total strangers. Even hermits need to talk. They can't be expected to talk to themselves all the time. People would think they were crazy, if they knew which they don't because there's nobody else present.

Praman made his way to the second floor by elevator. He walked the Upper Road westwards. He was aware of the noise of the City, a constant whir. He stood for a few minutes on the bridge above the Rail South track, the road, and the Rail North track heading out of the city gate. He watched the watchmen, now above the city gate chatting briefly with the watchmen from the other direction. Then he walked the rest of the Upper Road and entered the Shopping Centre on the second floor. He enjoyed the scene from the viewing gallery or the internal balcony. The place was a massive hive of activity, the giant interior of a living organism.

The majority had lived in the City all their lives. There was nowhere else to live. Travel outside the City was *quasi*-illegal, discouraged, without official or travel permits. Yet, certain things were so far beyond human scale that one never ceased to marvel. As Praman rarely left his apartment, he was still amazed by the scale of the building. It was a wonderful, somehow thrilling, to watch so many people inside one building with its monstrous ground floor space. He reckoned there were several hundred thousand people on the ground floor. Looking upwards, there were over two hundred floors and viewing galleries. Way up, half way to heaven, or so it seemed, he couldn't make out the faces. Were they men or women? Did they notice him? Those across in the distant gallery resembled one vibrant insect. Colours blurred into one dark rippling giant millipede, layer upon layer reaching up to the sky.

"You should get out more often, old friend!"

"Mo! What a pleasant surprise." His hand shot out in the old-fashioned way and he felt like hugging his old comrade.

"Not allowed, Praman," he indicated the handshake.

"What?"

"Handshakes. Illegal a few years ago. Too many germs."

They laughed, shook hands and spontaneously hugged.

"Germs are good for you."

"Yes, Praman, I'm not surprised you believe that."

"Of course; everything is up for discussion."

"Not true. Some things are not a matter of opinion. What about oxygen? *And*, more pertinently, what about Baldy Smith's for some light refreshments and an update?"

When men had been friends for so long, real discussion is nearly impossible because they are so comfortable. They are like children, permanently on the verge of giggling. Maybe there was simply not much time left. In the end you just laugh.

With a head full of World News, today's list of things to do, a briefcase crammed with relevant information, but gone are the days of weight, Radmilla is queuing for the bus. She is prim and proper and as tidy as her kitchen cupboards. Her bedroom is the one place where she lets her hair down and every known garment. The floor is an army assault course on a tiny scale and includes a whole collection of stumbling blocks. It's like the Battle of the Crater Nite Club without the nightclub! She is fine with cupboards, but she has a problem with surfaces. Nowhere else in her life is there such mess. Her relationships have always been neat and tidy, no-nonsense affairs of which there have been few. Her marriage quietly disappeared sometime in the past, but no one of her present acquaintances knows quite when. It's nobody's business; it is in the past when all is said and done, and that marriage is definitely done and gone. She may be in love, but it's not quite clear. She is a long way from home. Tasteful photographs of family, friends and country litter her home, but no photos of her ex-husband. Her presence was requested and she agreed to come. That was years ago and people have (almost) forgotten. She rose rapidly to Administrator Grade 2 and she speaks several languages.

The RBC (Rapid Bus Corporation) arrives exactly every two minutes (usually) at the stops along Extra Billy Road bordering the vast Single Houses Estate where Radmilla lives. This estate is a throwback to an earlier stage of development and is considered somewhat 'slummy' because it has few of the modern amenities of the hyperstructures. This is an old-fashioned social class issue. Many people are astonished that such attitudes still exist, but this a social phenomenon which is difficult to eradicate. Education has failed thus far. Radmilla really doesn't mind, as the hyper-shopping centre is only a pleasant bus ride away on a day such this, under the tunnel beneath Airport Road, and then directly to the Basement bus stop. She is free to use the amenities of both the Shopping Centre (S.E.) and the Hyperstructure Residential Estate (S.E.). When she decides to walk some of the way, she enjoys the walk and it does her good!

The smell of the bus is the usual pleasant leathery smell, more to do with the cleaner used rather than the smell of leather, a material rarely used these days. As for the smell of the cleaner, I was referring to the substance used rather than the person, who probably smells of leather.

Familiar faces are rare, but one or two have already exchanged a nod and a smile. That looks like Rod who gave the nod, he looks unwell. Radmilla wonders about other people a lot. It is the way she was brought up. Now she is concerned about Rod and his wife - she was very unwell for a long time, in and out of hospital. It is so difficult to keep in contact with people. She strains to catch sight of Rod again, but she can't spot him amongst the crowd. Maybe it wasn't Rod.

The bus winds its usual route, although not much winding and as smooth as a baby's bottom: along the eastern side of the Single Houses Estate, turn right still bordering the estate, then left along the road parallel with the giant East Council building, left along the front of the building, right over Regatta Bridge. Radmilla's view of the river is the western view towards the sea, but still not in the City Centre. Her heart rises at this point. She has many thoughts of a childhood spent near the sea. She could swim before she could walk! She rarely suffers nostalgia; she is rarely negative; negative people bring her down, but only if she allows them. She feels great on this sunny morning, crossing the river alive with activity - the living waters.

Left along Embankment Road, right on the corner of the Parliament Building 1, left under Upper Road, and she arrives at her stop at Government Offices. A brisk, business-like walk, with the aid of moving pathways and elevators, she arrives in her office fifteen minutes later. She has done it in twelve minutes, but not this morning; she found herself dreaming about sailing on the river. With the clicking of fashionable heels, albeit sensible, she announced her arrival, here in the heart of the building; or, maybe the right lung or left kidney, but certainly somewhere quite essential and definitely confidential. Much in the City is confidential. This building is more confidential than the average. No information leaves this building. This is to do with our ethics, to do with privacy rather than security.

Many nods and salutations of the personally habitual kind greeted her and were returned as she traversed the huge expanse of open office space towards her private office. She entered and was given a cursory greeting by her first class secretary. She didn't comment. Josh had worked for her for five years soon acquiring his First Class Secretary status. He was an ambitious young man and had demonstrated a genuine interest in the work. He had passed the skills training programmes, but, most importantly, he had passed the Interim and Advanced Personality Assessment Tests. He was possibly Administrator material; only time would tell. Everybody knew that time and commitment were not enough. Disappointment is not *really* a problem: either you have what it takes, or you don't. This is the same at all levels of City functioning, and if you fail at one thing, there are plenty of opportunities in other fields. Radmilla and Josh were an excellent 'senior-junior' team at this level, the penultimate level for her.

"Radmilla." His tone registered.

"Do we have a problem, Josh?"

"We certainly do. Well," he said, handing her the file, "you do." He was only the Secretary (First Class).

## 25

Time doesn't fly, time crawls; but once it's gone, it has gone. It's gone and it will never be back, in its unique little units. Time dies.

A bicycle trip from the south side of Praman's building, then right, going north, brings our vitamin-swallowing heroine, who would never contaminate the temple of her body with illicit drugs, to Dunkers Station, the first and last train station inside the northern wall. Riding a bicycle in the fresh air is good for you, although the evidence for this belief is insubstantial. 'Good for you' is not easily defined. If it means that you live a long time, then longevity research has always suggested that doing absolutely nothing leads to a long life: the less you do, the longer you live. Volunteers are difficult to acquire for this research because people find doing nothing extremely difficult. It takes a lot of practice and a very special kind of personal trainer for this work, which, of course, could not be described as work. Special trainers are hard to come by for the simple reason that they are reclusive (by necessity) struggling to do nothing. Never be tempted to become a devotee of such a 'trainer' simply because they have a reputation for expertise and successfully trained followers who have 'benefited immensely'.

For reasons, which should be obvious, such a *busy* guru knows nothing about nothing. Nothing is a highly specialised area of study. And cycling the road route is better exercise than weaving the interior route of the town within the City which is the HREstate. Nasichisha cannot be persuaded of anything against her will.

She has parked her bicycle outside the station. She has no worries about her bike going missing, thanks to its numerous nanochips. She can't go missing either, for the same reason. She has studied many things at the University; nearly twenty years wandering the corridors of the Humanities building becoming increasingly inhuman. Her financial arrangements have been somewhat mysterious for some time. She sort of exists, like a leaf fluttering in the breeze. She laughs a lot. But things are becoming clearer. Her personal state of terror has never been fully acknowledged because the vast majority of relationships are superficial. The man who just nodded and smiled 'hello', as he usually does, has no idea how perilously close he is to disaster. His or hers? Eventually, you are forced to use your own judgment. The amiable professor of our acquaintance will chat with anyone... almost anyone.

The road was busy and the platform is almost packed. Her briefcase looks very impressive amongst all the other briefcases. She is an impressive figure: tall, slim, attractive (obviously), intelligent, and humble. I know these things are true because her database makes it clear: *she* has made these things clear. She ensures that everybody in her circle is duly informed. It is only fair.

People are perky on this fine sunny day, not a cloud in the sky. Some might say the birds are singing, but they are not. Firstly, birds don't sing; birds make noises relating to food, territory and reproduction; only human beings sing. Secondly, most of their 'singing' finished a couple of hours ago. Presumably, they had sorted out their food, territory and reproduction needs for the day. But the sky is certainly busier than usual. Nasichisha is a sweet singer, but it is hardly appropriate to sing in these circumstances. She feels like singing and believes the patient crowd would benefit from this, but she is not quite that brazen, not on this occasion. There are certain social norms and she likes to present herself as 'respectable', an old-fashioned word back in use. The station is being automatically and artificially cooled. The train pulls into the station exactly on time.

In the Official History of Railways (all 'Official' books are sponsored and credited by the Government. For example, the Official Guide to City Birds was published recently. Apparently, the more colourful a bird, the more depressed it is and less able to reproduce; suicidal pigeons abound (and rebound!) in certain traffic density, and so on), the train model is a 3-2, which refers to the 'three track, two aisle' model. There are other improvements, but widening the gauge was a major and necessary project due to the steady growth in our population. Now: three passengers sit abreast, times three, divided by two aisles. Easy to imagine - you don't need a picture. This morning the lead engine is called Traveller, the back engine is called Old Jube. The health and safety record of this model is almost perfect. A man broke his wrist eighteen years ago when he stepped on and stumbled over his untied shoe lace. Thus, there have been no train accidents in the modern era. It is capable of incredible speed, but not possible or necessary in the City. Out of the City, it flies along. The South-North trip, for example, takes several days. It is an amazing experience, although passengers are not allowed to disembark. The reason becomes obvious very soon after leaving the City and the reason the Wild Lands are called wild. These are beyond the Farms to the North. We have no West-East route because it is not economical, although the issue has been raised in Parliament more than once over the decades. Parliamentarians have claimed that it would be within our Safari Experience projects, considered extremely worthwhile and, therefore, a good thing. However, the proposal has always been voted out, a sensible conclusion, due to the large investment of personnel and the dangers to same to facilitate such a project. There are always certain social problems to overcome in the meantime.

A little shuffling, a few "excuse me's", and everyone seated and comfortable. No longer the Fidget Factor; seats are optimally designed and adjustable. The City slides by like a scalpel across skin: the daily sights, but always the possibility of something different in this megalopolis. Nasichisha works in the Prison.

## 26

For Bill, it is always quicker by car. Say 'hello' to the regulars, the neighbours; nod a greeting or two. Anonymity is the norm, friendliness costs nothing, and politeness is a demand. The 'unsubs' , as Bill calls them, can be spotted. He likes old-fashioned language. He has used the term with certain people he can trust. They can trust him. He knows he can be frank, although his name is Bill. He knew a Frank a long time ago, but Frank died and that was a shame, albeit inevitable. "Don't waste your life working," said Frank on his deathbed, but not to Bill. Bill has a talent for understanding what people are and remembering the oddest things about them. These are not odd things because they indicate something about the person. We all produce our assessments of other people, although frequently inaccurate. But not in Bill's case. He had made it one of his few serious 'projects': to get things right about other people. It is very useful in his line of work. Or, maybe, his job was very useful for him.

The place was itself: busy, buzzing, throbbing with people in a hurry, being efficient; nodding, smiling, a brief hand gesture, sometimes a wink, a thumbs-up; except for the unsubs or the miserable. Don't get the two mixed up. It really doesn't help in the great constellation of social life. People can die of being misunderstood, but it is not physical death. It's a long shrivelling process of drying up.

The huge underground car park (the Bloody Lane entrance) always reminded Bill of a morgue. It was perfectly designed for the job, hygienic and bleak, and not suitable for a relaxing stroll. The sound of his closing the car door behind him recalled in an instant the man he had noticed strolling on the fourth floor of the South West car park, the multi-storey near the railway. When was that? Ah, yes, that homicide, the first matricide he had investigated. Such murders were becoming increasingly frequent. He sat for a few seconds gazing at the wall. Research at the University on that very subject - not walls, matricides. He had noticed the man's hat, of all things. He looked quite splendid in that hat, although Bill had no positive interest in hats. It was either raining or it wasn't. It might be a chilly, hence a hat. But the strolling wasn't normal. It is peculiar how the mind works, still an unknown continent. But no time for daydreaming. He had already forgotten his newspaper, so must get one the other end, if he remembers. There are more important things. The engine started with the red light and the barely perceptible vibration. Reverse with care. The first human voice of the day.

In due course he turned left into the Great North Western Road. He joined the large orderly army, marching south, in their armoured cars, collisions impossible and almost silent. Four rows abreast, they could nod and wave if so inclined; certainly inter-car conversations were possible. Sometimes the day's work had already started, but people tended to avoid this - a bit of alone time to gather one's thoughts. Remember: anything is possible. Keep your eye on the road and relax, but not too much. The car could malfunction, it has been known, and it can be embarrassing. But don't dwell on the negative. It drizzled briefly.

Bill dreamed of murder and mayhem. The things that people are capable of... Sociopaths are the most dangerous types. You never know what they're up to. The vast majority are not killers, but they are so *difficult*. Maybe the person in front is a sociopath. He strained and could make out long blond hair. Probably a woman and certainly a sociopath! He laughed out loud. His ex-wife was blond. Oh dear, listen to some radio and stop laughing out loud. It doesn't give a good impression. He glanced at the driver to his right. His glazed look straight ahead appeared decidedly peculiar. Ah, some classical music! Such music is similar to the mind: as far as Bill is concerned both are dark and mysterious. He had attempted a few courses at the University in Music Appreciation, but it didn't really work. It went in one ear and out the other. He'd picked up a few facts, something about syphilis and concupiscence, the usual. Anyhow, get away from maliciousness and murder, at least for the time being. Ah, a little opera. Otello? I'm sure that'll be interesting. It will, Bill.

12.5 miles, then turn right at Salt Junk Corner and into the West Circular. We use 'miles' based on the average measurement of the adult male thumb. This needs clarification, but being helpful is often not very helpful. The Age of Devastation was comprised of many coinciding components and culminated in the Catastrophe. Two thousand years later our anatomy hasn't changed significantly. We still have two hands each, a right one and a left one. The hand is comprised of the Carpus, the Metacarpus, and the Phalanges. Bill studied his hand on the steering wheel. All seems in order. There are five collections of metacarpal bones. The thumb is one 'collection' and is shorter and wider than the others, and its palmar surface is directed towards the palm (i.e. the metacarpus). The thumb is comprised of three major bones (the other four digits (phalanges) have four bones each), the bone in question, the measurement, being the extreme and final bone, the one with the fingernail. Yes, it's called a nail. The thumb is the extreme collection of bones on the radial side. It is accompanied by four aligned digits, the fourth being the smallest on the ulna side. Therefore, it follows logically that Bill had travelled 792000 flexor longus pollicis bones of the average adult male before turning right into the West Circular road. Sometimes, Bill found the journey tiring. But still 855360 to H.Q. Then he recalled the story of Othello.

## 27

Tabantate had injured his back years ago, being physical, as opposed to *cerebral*. How this difference arises in the population is still unclear. It has moved from psychology to genetics, not for the first time. This ongoing reductionism: when things cannot be explained at the 'higher' levels, we inevitably head for the cellar. Why Tabantate, although clever, is not cerebral is much to do with his mother, if you recall. Ah, mothers... When his back injury happened he doesn't know. (I have accessed the data). Suddenly, he had an excruciating pain. One day, when plastering a wall, he stumbled from the stool and became embroiled in a grotesque dance, which would have been impressive if it had been a football. The stool entangled itself around his left shin, having cracked hard against his inner right ankle. But it wasn't the crack that injured his back, it was the prance of the dance. The following day, a slight discomfort; on the third day the beginning of years of every known medical intervention, some unknown, but when you're in agony...

Time passed and his vertebrae got used to it and so did Tabantate. Always active, he is a frequent volunteer, strongly encouraged, with the Community Programme. Retirement gives him time to think about his next *assignment*: sometimes active, sometimes contemplative, or, more precisely, sedentary, to give the old back a break. But, being seated for long periods gives him terrible backache.

Forty hours in the mines over seven days is what he has signed up for this time. As a retiree, he has a wide range of choice. He fancied the mines again, as it has been some years since his last assault on Mother Nature. He wanted some male company. Women tend to avoid the mines. He will be resident for seven days rather than return home at the end of each shift. It is a very long journey and, quite frankly, amounts to a holiday from 'Mrs Bouquet' and that routine of dusting and polishing. A couple of his old pals have arranged for the same holiday. It will be like the old days. Her Ladyship knows exactly that it will be a break from Tabantate and his slipper-shuffling about the apartment and getting in the way, even though she's out most of the time. He does tend to *disturb* things.

As he lives diagonally across the City from the direction of the mines, he knows an early start is favourite. Hyp. Res. Est. (S.W.) is breasted by Upper Road 11. One would guess UR11 as it is HRE South West. It makes sense, if you happen to know the City. You might well guess UR12 if you were a visitor. Tabantate could do the whole initial journey by the Upper Road, but that would take at least two days by bicycle, possibly three, just to reach Mines Road, which heads north-east out of the City. The Upper Road is a circular road, pedestrians and cyclists only, paths being signed 'Clock' and 'Anti-Clock'. The bicycles remind their temporary riders of directions via virtual map screens and vocalisations, both on request. They adjust immediately to the rider's voice - they 'know' who it is.

It takes Tabantate half an hour to reach the nearest UR11 Entrance/Exit. Once on the UR11 a bicycle is usually available within a few minutes at this time of morning. In no time Tabantate is flying along, wind in his hair, like being young again, the five miles to Albert Cashier Turning (he was a man of historical interest), thirty yards above the ground.

Naturally sociable, it is great to be outside; but the numbers impossible to estimate. He doesn't expect to see a familiar face, but all faces are interesting, especially women. He never misses a pretty woman, although there's no such thing as an ugly one! He must be careful of speed and has already received a vocal warning. Don't get carried away, he tells himself, or, at his age he might be carried away. He glances to his left towards the river, but no possibility of sighting it yet: at least thirty miles away and beyond huge buildings. With binoculars, the bridge can be seen from A.C. Turning.

Depositing the bike, he descends to street level by means of one of the many public elevators, the escalators being packed with patient, orderly bodies; a very good opportunity to have a chat, but not today - get the journey over with. He queues for a City Centre bus. There is always minimal talk. It's best to keep one's own counsel. It's the way it is; certainly missed opportunities, as well as difficulties avoided. Weigh up of the pros and cons; err on the side of caution; keep things simple. His timing was good luck or perfect. The second bus was a Mines bus. He imagined the thirty-five miles to the Hornet's Nest Community Centre prior to crossing the river, then right along Embankment Road, the Park on his left, the relatively steep decline into the railway tunnel, emerging to pass the Zoo, then left for the long haul of Mines Road.

He sought a seat at the back near one of the toilets. He recognised a steward, who had worked the same route for many years. Hellos were exchanged. It's comforting to greet a familiar face. He's embarking on an adventure. Tabantate's compatriots aren't due to board the bus until the other side of the river. He had driven the entire route in his adventurous youth, but even in an armoured car, it was a strange and lonely feeling leaving the City. It was like being born and dumped into a savage world. Beyond the City Wall was real danger and civilisation gone! He recalled the thrill of danger, but, when he was young, it was discouraged: public transport highly recommended. At his age, he comforted himself in the safety of the bus. Within a few miles, still south of the river, he dozed off.

28

The Greatest Husband in the World had departed and Belbiana's sense of relief was palpable. She put it down to work-related stress. It's hard work. Her work is hard and serious, but her marriage is more important; hubby doesn't complain. She sighed at the state of her crumby kitchen. Crumbs everywhere! Several dozen of them. One more cup of tea and try not to think. If she did, she would begin to dissolve, to disappear. Why did she think so often of the Canned Hell Fire Music Festival she'd never attended? Every year it reminded her of the things she hadn't done in her youth. Why that? It's not even that time of year. When had it become part of her, drifting inexplicably into her mind at odd moments? Why? What's the point? It's childish, all that teenage stuff. She's being ridiculous. Get a grip, get real!

Crumbs everywhere. There may be thousands of them and some could easily be *chips*, watching her, reporting back. She was sure he had conspired against her. You can't trust anyone. Jealousy is a terrible thing. The government is always collecting useless data. She poured more steaming tea into her steaming mug. Some people like such terms. She actually poured lukewarm tea into her china cup from her china teapot. The meaning of the adjective is long forgotten.

They looked at each other in a state of mutual contempt. The stupid gaping mouth of it! So many people like that: all dressed up, with their fancy talk and empty brains, back-stabbing. She gulped down her lukewarm tea ladylike. She wouldn't let it get the better of her. It was going to be one of those days if she allowed it. She wouldn't. It was her day off. Her special mugs ran through her mind. Anything can run through your mind. She thought of the possibility of some of the girls from work visiting. Why she refers to them as *girls* is not quite clear.

They had visited once or twice and they really liked her special mugs because they were in some way friendly, the mugs, not the girls, although the girls were quite friendly, although not that friendly because they had only visited once or twice. Indeed, thinking about it, individually, they had only visited once over several occasions, which didn't make sense. Maybe it was twice spread over several occasions in different group combinations. She suddenly felt panicky; she could become dizzy if she didn't leave it. The mugs hopped back into her cupboard above the sink. She imagined the dust collecting on her mugs. With some effort, she pushed herself to standing position, hands on the edge of the table, fingers whitening, chair scraping across the polished floor. She took a couple of deep breaths. Must deal with the crumbs.

Pottering soothed her nerves. We long since renounced the guilt associated with pottering. That guilt had produced so much unhappiness. A tertiary (TD) thesis claims that pottering associated guilt (P.A.G.) had been one of the major underlying components behind the Cat. Nobody has read the thesis, but a few have read the Bibliography and noted pertinent references - I have accessed the data - but Belbiana wasn't one of them. She has a head like a sieve, except for the clogged bits. Some people would call it selective memory. But it is more to do with fear.

She took the hand-held Sucker from the wall - she felt calmer - a biome-chanical device invented by a Helen de Roo, Sci.Ad., (a top Administrator in Science). An admired elder, she died some time ago. She was one of the young-est members of the University's Recycling Engineering Group ('Reg'). To describe that city-wide, multifaceted system would require several books. But the books have already been written. Hopefully, you'll find some remnants in the inevitable rubble when the time comes.

So Bel sucked all over her kitchen, removing crumbs and other scraps of detri-tus. She whipped around the rest of her apartment (self-flagellation and self-torture are things she can rarely avoid), tidying away all sorts of objects into their rightful places, mainly 'de-located' by her absentminded, silly husband, who doesn't appreciate her efforts *sometimes*, before activating Reg in order to remove every known germ, mite, and other tiny objects or organisms which should not be there. Everything was new and shiny and she felt much better. The day ahead was like a very long corridor in a deserted building.

She thought about the girls. They might pop in at the end of their shift. They live in the same building and are her closest colleagues in terms of having much in common. She likes to give them the benefit of the doubt. She imagined their day's work in the large Maternity Ward: the usual routines, the odd emergen-cies, rushing here and there. The thing she really enjoyed because it blocked her morbid ruminations. Morbid? She didn't know all her co-workers (the girls referred to themselves as cow-workers, just for fun). There were two hundred of them in all, fifty percent were men. Coincidentally, most of the men lived in the North-East Quarter, south of the Plank Road. No particular reason for this - one of those things. Rarely met the majority socially. The traffic would be bumper to bumper at that time of day. (Molly preferred to drive. More fool her!). The radio news reader had announced something about sexually transmitted diseases. Bel regretted that she hadn't been paying attention. Millions of people on the move at any one time. A bird would take a glance ground-ward and decide to fly on, as far as possible. She would like to be a bird... Millions on the move, unneces-sarily and not good for them. They are such fools, she thought to herself. Things could be organised much better. All these so-called experts sitting around, gazing into space, chewing their pens and producing nothing, and they think they're so clever. The room shone back at her.

The Bohemian district, so dubbed, is part of the Old City. Some of the original stone buildings still exist, the remains of the original settlement south of the river. There's a whole history encapsulated in this twenty-five square mile area, well documented at the time, and extending to Sky-Parlor Hill, these founders being the surviving community of a vast and ancient civilisation. Indeed, a whole collection of cultures. The Old City is a mini version of the present City, the original buildings tending in circles radiating from the centre; the major roads developed like spokes on a wheel. There is no sentimentality attached to the Old City. Sentimentality is a false and damaging emotion. These buildings simply stand because they have never been demolished. They are of interest to photographers and other kinds of visual artists. There is no such thing as a tourist industry, although foreign visitors view the place to satisfy their curiosity and to compare notes concerning societal development. The majority are visiting scholars. All visitors are only allowed such travel thanks to the respective governments' mutual agreement. All citizens are free to apply for a V.Doc. If you have special reasons for the visit, then you may be given priority. Otherwise, your Visitor's Record will be taken into account and you will be placed on the waiting list. You will be given a couple of months' notice of permission to travel. It is not as complicated as it sounds and there is as much negotiation or flexibility as necessary. For example, you may be surprised to learn that personal political views are irrelevant. However, Moral Development Scores will be an essential component of the assessment, together with prison and psychiatric records and outcomes where they exist. No single component precludes an applicant from travel. The Profile is already known. Morbid curiosity, like sentimentality and similar emotions, is eradicated generally, but never totally, during our education process. Total eradication would be considered a miss-use of the educational experience, which is life-long. Attempts at indoctrination inevitably arise and are monitored. Excessive emotion, on the other hand, such as sentimentality, is, by definition, morbid and sooner or later, if not treated, drifts into mental illness. There are several hundred closely defined mental disorders. Mental illness, like chlamydia, will always be with us, but is far easier to go unnoticed.

Damodural, our multidisciplinary genius, lives in the Bohemian district. He is being closely monitored. He wanders the road sharing his load (a folk singer, naturally) with anyone willing to listen. This means many people who don't know him. Some of them, within a few minutes, begin to consider themselves as victims of their own kindness and sociability. Next time they must remember to exercise more caution with a stranger. Remember the old adage: Don't talk to strange men - some men are very strange indeed - and don't forget to login your 'feelings of discomfort'. Many have, and this is but *one* reason Damodural is being monitored.

Striding the busy pavements, the pedestrian walkways, we easily spot our cosmically creative, comically-enhanced mythical character, a man among men; our true artist among fantasist artists who have little talent, as he is happy to explain with his usual subtlety. Past ancient stone buildings, long ago turned into convenience stores and apartments, and many a café for appropriate conversations, our knight in shining armour, rescuer of damsels in distress, walks with purpose to the Golden Circle Café.

Dreams of past achievements greatly enhanced - imagination is a wonderful thing, an instant video in our skulls, in which we play the starring roles - he prophesies his future glories. One must admire optimism. Positivity, that's the thing! he doesn't need to tell himself. Positivity is a good thing, albeit a component of many mental disorders. Happiness is another of one of those problematic and sought after imagined conditions. The *pursuit* of happiness: only a mild implication that it may be caught. It's not the catch, it's the chase, shouted an irrelevant noisy person. Scraps of litter mixed with leaves, swirling in tiny whirlwinds, or scuttling gossipy along empty streets, not a soul in sight. It has been known.

Not so today: busy busy busy, the City's music. I've always liked the bodies, he thinks, the damned and the melodramatic. Our hero likes the audience. He thinks of his little child. It is amazing how so many children are regarded as trophies. When all else fails, bung in another one! And carry it round on your head, literally on your head. Such strange displays! It would be much easier to acquire a very impressive wig, or, indeed, a beautiful hat (beauty is on the head of the beholder), or both. Why not! A huge, curly, ginger wig would suit Damodural, topped off by a bright sky-blue top-hat. Wonderful and eye-catching, it would suggest unquestionable depths of creativity. A couple of ear-rings, an after-thought probably best ignored. But some after-thoughts are better than some before-thoughts. The advantage of wig and hat is that when not in use can be put in the cupboard and then you can get a proper night's sleep unlike one's symbol of masculinity and failure, a thing that cannot be stored in a cupboard when not in use. Furthermore, wigs and hats can be worn out ambiguously, but you can't destroy their lives by turning them into vengeful psychopaths. Now, that seems a serious advantage in favour of wigs and hats for heads, as opposed to babies for heads. And the possibility of babies depositing certain unwanted substances on the head has probably crossed your mind and, possibly, run down Aaron's beard at some time in the distant past. Damodural has never given it a second thought in his brilliantly creative way that he will be long dead by the time his child becomes a serial killer, which appears fairly inevitable. Let's leave Damodural to his ramblings. He is being pursued by feral thoughts biting at his heels. Not a happy bunny.

## 30

The Mighty Man offers the Sweet Chick a short menu of fast breakfasts. She accepts coffee with sugar. Surely sweet enough? A very weary wary smile lights up her face, but not her eyes. There are books and papers, some in mixed piles, at the study end of the large room below. It resembles a small earthquake, its epicentre on his desk at the far window. She can see from her perch on the kitchen stool that the window offers a panoramic view over the Eastern Wall towards the sea. She pictures Sea Horse Quay by the river. She figures that the river must be to her left and, therefore, they are located north of the river. You don't have to 'major' in geography to work this out. So, the Mighty Mosimenadue has pursued one of his favourite hobbies, capturing a colourful bird ensnared in the insect colony known as the University. It will be released into freedom a.s.a.p. All things in the universe have their chameleon qualities. Slugs slither into a palace of dreams. Yes, she has sad blue eyes, but she doesn't deserve this. Her fault?

She sips at the coffee cupped in both hands like a begging child. We still have begging children, but they don't know they're beggars.

"Have you been here for long?" She slides elegantly and almost silently from her tripos and pads across the floor towards the window. She glances back, the smooth movements of a dancer or a gymnast. He finishes his coffee, rinses the cup, and places it in the dishwasher. "Yes," not ungentlemanly, but she registers the curt slam of the dishwasher door. His smile is charming, as it was last evening. Beware of charming men, her father advised. Her dad is charming.

"Seven years to the T.D. and here ever since. It's a tough old life!" Still giving little, as little as possible: it's a privilege they don't deserve.

"All jobs become tedious and tough in their own way. I'm sure the books are heavy."

Sarcasm? He sighs and considers. He starts to load his briefcase and scans his notes for nine o'clock. Always the same: they give it out, but they can't take it themselves. If you can't take the heat... Remembering a textbook, he slides the loose pages into his briefcase and heads for the bookshelf. Red spine, towards left, near top.

"It's one of those views. It's magnificent. I just want to fly away!"

She looked across towards the City Wall. Things already busy with two-way traffic, some heading to the river tunnel, some on the northern route towards the junction with the M.11 and a straight run into the City Centre. No one would be heading out. She'd never been out of the City. Some were descending by foot to Corn-Shucks Road to take that route into town. These early morning commuters disappeared in their hundreds beneath Uni Resid, which stands astride Corn-Shucks. Therefore, Upper Road 14 was directly behind her. Through University Residential would take the best part of an hour, unless she could catch a Seater. She had decided to have a day off from the grind of study and visit her mother.

Sky and land merged into a giant quilt of summer colours. The sky was blazing blue with a hint of rain. She could almost hear the hills singing and the trees clapping. She liked that one. Maybe it was her heart singing because she had risen above the mud she had allowed herself to sink into.  It was a celebration. This would be a good day. A brief silent prayer for her mother.

"It's beautiful. You've been here for years? You're lucky, certainly to get an outer apartment. Sometimes it takes years. Most people give up, although most don't care."

Oh dear: short sentences, confused, barely literate; typical *geography*. I must have been totally out of it.

"Yes, I've been lucky in some ways, but it took hard work."

"I was referring to your accommodation." She looked at him for a second. He was handsome, but edgy; he didn't smile so much as smirk, like the cat who always got the cream. It was time to leave.

"I think we should wend our merry ways!"

"Great minds." Wither goest thou, fool? To his first lecture of the day. She handed him the cup. Know your place, sir, her eyes sparkled. Way up on his pedestal, he didn't notice. She felt sorry for him.

He closed the door behind them and activated the voice recognition lock. They keep inventing the unnecessary and then have to invent something to tidy the mess caused by the previous invention. It was a pre-Cat phenomenon. We haven't learnt.

They performed their cheerful cheerios, never to meet again, one of those well-rehearsed and poorly acted rituals. A perfunctory peck delivered in the direction of left cheeks, little sounds fluttering away into the perfectly balanced ether of the busy corridor, and they away in opposite directions, she to the high-way heading to Corn-Shucks and he towards the adjoining University. He glanced at his watch and double-checked the wall clock, one of the habits that irritated him. He would be there in an hour if he made the connections. If not, he would still be on time. Her comment about her terminally ill mother in the General Hospital came to his mind. He shrugged it off. He had learnt many things, but empathy wasn't one of his strengths. He didn't feel good about this, but only because it was an area of 'paralysis', as pointed out by a friend. There was that portrait of his charming mother. She smiled. No, not now. Other members of his family paraded like spectres. It was the nightmare that kept recurring. Not now. He tried rehearsing the facts and figures of his lecture. He knew the girl didn't like him. Well, he didn't like her either. She was pathetic and stupid. He was beginning to sink. The face of his charming mother.

## 31

The shop owner, Jardena, the house owner, Jard, and the discarder of husbands, some of them her own, Jardy darling, decided on breakfast. She decided on everything. She thought of her husband. Yes, well under control and doing very well in their business, thanks to her. Well, he had to be good at something. Bed was definitely not his speciality, not that it made any difference to her. Everything was an act and she was good. She thought of her children and her grandchildren. They were drifting away, but no problem, she would haul them in as and when the mood took her; they would be brought to heel. Loosen the leash and watch them chasing their tails and running around barking mad. It was quite fun; it made her laugh. Her son-in-law? She laughed out loud.

"You're in a good mood this morning," hubby said, entering the kitchen, his dressing-gown flying open as planned. Oh, God, he disgusts me. A negative auto-matic thought was immediately repressed, to join her vast collection of those rarely disturbed memories.

"Oh, food's nearly burning!" any excuse to turn back to the cooker. He hugged her from behind. She felt her bile rising and her usual sense of disgust. She felt his bile rising too, prodding and rubbing against her backside.

"Oh, come on, big boy," she said, turning round, glancing down and smiling her whore's white teeth, "You've left it too late." She pulled away and carried the frying pan to the two plates on the table. His breath was vile and tinged with the distinct smell of tobacco. He thought she didn't notice. Well, let him kill himself.

"You know we have so much to do today. You should have been up earlier, so to speak." Still teasing, still sumptuous lips, still a salacious sixteen. "Now cover that irresistible beast, sit down for breakfast, and then straight to the shower!" What a child! He tucked in. Ooh, yummy, mummy, it's my favourite! I can see exactly what she means and I can see exactly what he means, but he'll never see what she means. None of them do. She is the puppeteer.

There are still many thousands of privately owned houses in the City. Ownership still carries some status amongst certain types of people and research has shown that this 'need' correlates positively with several types of emotional disturbance. However, as with much research of the psychosocial type there are no definitive conclusions. A property owner may be perfectly sane; they may have inherited, for example. Our biggest health problem is mental illness because it is not acknowledged as an illness, and most victims remain undiagnosed and, therefore, untreated. But that's another story. Not quite.

It is written into the Constitution that private ownership is considered unhealthy and will be abolished in time. But ours is a democracy and so owner-ship continues, albeit on the decline. People are educated to avoid the tempta-tion of useless acquisition and to *pity* the *victims*. Inevitably, some look down on property owners for being mad fools and undermining society! Suffice it to say, this attitude doesn't hold water with the majority. Owning a house or other types of property is like having a boil: it can be dealt with and eventually you will completely forget the discomfort it caused.

Thus, predictably, the delightful Jardena and her pet puppy (all the others had run away) lived in one of the private housing areas, this one located beyond the S.E. Circular Road. To be more precise (you might want to find it on the map), it is about twenty miles south-east of the Bohemian Sector, beyond Five Forks and the S.E. Circular Road, as I've said, but not as far as the Heliport, which is 'connected', so to speak, to the Police Station (S.E. Sector), which is connected to Upper Road 7. If you get lost and find yourself asking a policeman, then you've probably gone too far south.

Today is rent day, probably her favourite day of the month, not so much for credits, but for that splendid feeling of power. She breezes into somebody's home, making it plain that it is *her* house, all fluffed up like a courting peacock. Mating and threatening behaviour can be very similar. It is all part of her life, the way she was brought up. She knows some of her tenants very well. She is not so fond of their wives. She concluded long ago that women have to be kept in their places and that men obviously know their places already. Hubby is very keen on sport, as were all her husbands, and that's the way it should be.

She was as bright and cheery as the weather. A brief departure ritual and off they go, hubby's routine towards the giant Point of Rocks Shopping Centre off Forest Road, to open up for early customers, so he tells her, and she deeper into what she calls the labyrinth. It was far from being a labyrinth, this private housing area, with its little boxes made of ticky-tacky. But she liked the sound of the word and it just stuck as one of those secret, cosy expressions of married couples. This would be her day of showing how grand she is and counting credits.

Hubby glanced over his shoulder as if he expected to spot her trailing him. He was relieved. He was aware his feelings were irrational. But the rest wasn't irrational. He was quite sure they were being monitored and it could only be the Government concerning undisclosed income. He had warned her several times. She had told him to stop being such a fool. He was rarely wrong on such matters, as he'd pointed out. What about what's-his-name, an acquaintance of theirs, in the Dry Valley Quarter? He'd been spot on then. But not on this occasion, hubby darling, not on this occasion. You're not entirely wrong, but you've completely missed the point. For you, easy to do.

Psybunes the Musician - people are many different things - was thinking of venturing abroad, an impossibility, but he might go outside. No need to rush into these things. The morning was fresh and bright. The City sprawled massively in front of him, spreading far to the coastal west. He had no eastern view. It was a five mile walk to the other side of 'Writers Block'. An apostrophe? It was only ever spoken. The psychology of a people is often expressed in their language. To the younger generation everything is new until their discoveries dissolve and evaporate or fly south for the winter.

There he peered, six years after University and before *co-habitation*? The next stage - so he'd been told by people who'd had umpteen next stages. How many next stages are there? It always sounded like prison. No need to rush into *that,* he counselled himself, being a musician - a certain tradition to keep up apparently, something about drugs and groupies.

From way up in the sky, from his apartment window in City Point, from where he could feel the low vibration of the building, he never tired of the view from one of the tallest buildings on the planet. He had been to the top to watch sporting events under the dome, or to wander the many roof telescopes. Many's the summer day was spent chatting, swimming, sunbathing, or picnicking. People gathered (as people evolved to do) in parks and stadia. One of the great telescopes was housed on the roof and so was a military unit. Both were out of bounds to the general public, except 9 a.m. to midday, Wednesdays, for the telescope. 'First come, first served' for access to the Viewing Gallery, Monday to Friday. From the Viewing Gallery you could observe the scientists, but the enclosed Gallery permits no communication between the viewers and the viewed. The Gallery is partly lecture theatre and partly interactive museum. The military unit is inaccessible. The children's game, No Front Door!, and there are many versions of this game, is based on the design of military installations, as well as certain government buildings. People make up stories, myths, and legends, children's games and nursery rhymes to rationalise fear.

Today Psybunes was not above the clouds. Indeed, there were no clouds and he was clear-headed. He'd had a lot to put up with, but he had survived. So far - unlike certain 'survivors'. Sometimes the place seems to be crawling with them.

He rarely thought of the busy politicians to his rear: the huge Government Offices connected by underground tunnel to the Parliament Buildings (Restricted Personnel), as well as over-ground access, and Upper Road 4 (Rips Raps Road) running parallel and attached to both buildings. Unbothered by politicians at his rear, Psybunes contemplated the hazy distant horizon clarified by his own telescope. Very tempting though it was to invade other people's privacy, he avoided the temptation because it was never worthwhile, except on that one occasion. But he liked watching people in the streets below. That was okay; they were in the public arena and there was no salacious intention on his part. Being watched was expected.

Views north and south, to his right and left, were obscured by massive structures. But he had seen helicopters rising from the Heliport to the south, and had mused on the possibility of the Immanent when straining to his right. If he stretched out, he could see the spire of the synagogue amongst the Towers of Butler's Order. He had often wondered... but he had never been there. He's a curious young man, full of curiosity; *almost* full of curiosity. If he'd been quite full, then he would have discovered that that building couldn't be a synagogue. But never mind, he's on the right track - the synagogue is just *beyond* the spire and out of sight of Psybunes' telescope, as is the temple. These things are all a blur to P.

Situated north of the River Sticks (because of all the sticks!), the view straight ahead is the most perfect, east to west along the river. And the people in the streets below cannot be counted - rhetorically speaking. We can know exactly how many and who they are, if we need to. The river blazed steel in the morning sun. Psybunes had 'done' the river as part of a student field trip. It had been more enjoyable than studious; more incidental learning than formal learning, although there had been  nine o'clock lectures. He could remember those who'd had 'difficulties' making the 'early' start. He often thought of that week as he watched the variety of watercraft way below. It was one of the most enjoyable weeks of his life; not a care in the world, it was party time! He had been transported out of sight, out of mind, but mainly the latter. The prison of his childhood was gone! That prison, which won't go away, and its torture chamber.

He could just make out the Zoo buildings and enclosures, including the Centre for Zoological Studies. Across the river from the Zoo, he hovered upon the magnificent St. Francesco Cathedral. He loved buildings and this was one of his favourites. Religion had been beaten out of him by its contradictions and his parents' contradictions. They take turns to run the torture chamber.

Immediately beyond the Zoo, the railway and North-South Transit cut at right angles across the river, road, rail, and river, busy as a million house flies trapped in a room. His next stop, still on the north bank, is the Park and its six square miles. But he didn't tarry - he was in no mood to think about that dark subterranean world beneath the Park. He was looking forward to seeing Sylvia, his wild woodland creature, so time to clear off and enjoy the day! No flood of morbid thoughts; please, no torture today. He hadn't decided as yet to whom he was praying.

## 33

She easily rid herself of the strange young man. He seemed nice and irrelevant. She had lent him one of her toothbrushes, pretending it was unused. It makes no difference; it was quite germ-free. One must have good manners. She noticed his perfect teeth and broad smile as he reminded her of his name across the breakfast table, although neither ready for solid food.

"Oh, I'm terrible. Can never remember names," she quickly added. He knew exactly what she meant. Yes, an amenable guy. As she was heading for work, her expensive and well-packed briefcase taking on a life of its own, her elegant self, to match her briefcase, walking resolutely towards her deserved destiny. She was trying to remember his name. She's terrible!

Things to do, things to do, so many things to do. Oh, no, she had forgotten her 'To Do List'. She had left it on her desk. Too much chitchat with what's-his-name. But she could remember the important points. One thing leads to another. Associative. Her secretary. Of course. No problem. Many people have 'no problem'. Aren't they lucky. She reminded herself that, from now on, the first item on her To Do list would indeed be her To Do List. Maybe it would be a good idea to blu-tack, no, white-tack, a small note to her front door, on the inside, of course. Then, before leaving her apartment, she would be reminded not to forget her To Do List. Naturally, she had already worked out that she would, very quickly, become desensitised to the existence of the reminder. Therefore, she would have to put a note somewhere prior to her arrival at the front door to alert her to her note on the front door. On the other hand, the warning note would remind her not to forget her To Do List, which means she would not need the note on the front door. But that depends on the path she decided to take to the front door. There are several possible approaches... It would probably take a few weeks to develop an efficient system. She'll start this evening, if she remembers.

Stupidity is not her problem and neither is poor memory, but a collection of confusions developed from childhood. She spent much of her time struggling with her demons, but she wasn't quite aware of them. People say all sorts of fancy things about their 'demons', but demons have become a fashionable accessory, a bit like body rings. She had very beautiful hair, blonde and full-bodied. She was clever, but her brain didn't quite correlate with her hair. Something was missing. Her life had become disconnected. It seemed to float about beyond her reach.

Clickscraping to the U.R.11, she shook off the usual fatigue. She was beginning to wake up; her body had adapted to abuse. She was young and fit and she still had time - surely, she still had time. Of course. Get away from that person, get away from the confines of the apartment, shake off that feeling of being trapped, that old feeling, and think positive thoughts. But she still felt like an ant. She nodded at one or two as she weaved her way through the hordes. She knew she was attractive. She spotted a community bike (seemingly appropriate) to take her the couple of miles to Monongahela Road and then into town by public transport, one of the huge yellow buses marked 'City Centre'. The sky seemed so far away. She had been to the top of Brush Mountain Tower once. What a view! She thought of her fiancé and smothered the thought. Think about work.

The bus journey was uneventful, apart from the tall blonde man. He had caught her eye, much older than her, she had lingered too long. He knew. So? He had reminded her of her father, but a taller version: exactly the same sort of person, the same air of confidence, the same air of arrogance, the same hair, the same swagger without swaggering. What is it about people like him? Clever and empty, and seductive. And what's the point? The pit of her stomach fell away. She just wanted to cry. She was falling. But she wouldn't. Where is he? I wonder what he is doing at this moment. Whatever it is, he is doing it well. In his youth, he was an amateur sportsman and a professional businessman. He was one of the men, one of the swaggerers. Everybody liked him, with his blonde hair. Everybody liked him. I intercepted his message: he intends to come to her wedding. I hope he brings his new knee.

The bus swept along Monongahela, a non-stop city-bound, the driver studying her console inside the perspex cubical, permanently in contact with H.Q., inaudible to passengers. Sachikaka had often wondered about that job. It doesn't look boring. But she had never seen the same driver more than a few times. The back of this one's head wasn't familiar. Oh, she's wearing glasses. So, perfect eyesight is not a prerequisite for the job. Where do all the drivers go? She'd learnt to focus on distracting thoughts. Maybe somewhere in the City there are millions of bus drivers heavily sedated so no one finds out how boring the job is. Nothing would surprise her. She has had much stranger ideas and assumes they're all original. Sometimes, she feels a strange kind of fear when she senses bad and secret things are going on all the time. Maybe, she needs a break, a holiday. Maybe, she needs to escape. Not actually escape, of course - nobody really escapes. She believes her heart rate has increased.

A tinkling sound accompanied by an electronic written message simultaneously spoken: the City Centre Stop in sixty seconds. Time to be sensible; no silly childish stuff; time to be adult. She tightened her grip on her briefcase on her lap, as if to make sure it was still there. Sometimes she couldn't feel anything.

## 34

Jeevalani the Priest, the well-stocked priest, had returned from the Bush, as he called it, relating to some traditional idea best known to himself, several years ago, and had presently returned from the well-stocked Mass. As a person of certain sensibilities and awareness, not one to believe, simply, that everything is relative, he had entered this morning's data on his graph. His housekeeper, the Diminutive One, who bowed in front of the alter, but scraped to no one, tutted and, on occasion, sighed in front of his graph. Her tut, or sigh, was always just audible. Some people have the remarkable skill of saying nothing, but communicating a lot.

He had tapped some data into his wall console. Leaders of the Major Religions have a legal right to access a certain level of confidential information to monitor the comings and goings of their people, their flock. Parliament has decided that this facilitates the calming effects of religious beliefs, a set of otherwise irrelevant concepts.

Jeevalani then studied his graph. It was simpler to do it this way: sheets of A4 graph paper sellotaped end to end to record Sunday's and Weekday's attendances. No need to overcomplicate things; it was only for his personal information and the few people who came into his kitchen, not that many noticed. The general lack of involvement was the greatest stressor in his life. He'd forgotten how disinterested they were in this neck of the woods. Only D.I. Cody showed interest on that one visit, a visit out of the blue. Now, what was that about? The thought raced across his mind and away into the distance, leaving a small cloud of dust in its wake. He felt poetic this morning, but must be focused and serious.

A straight line on the graph was not a good thing, although one mustn't judge, or be downright jokey - a time and place for everything. A straight line could be a good thing and demonstrate optimum conditions, above which would be unreasonable expectations. On the other hand, and certainly more probable, let's face it, and our priest has a thing about honesty, facing things, and the positive avoidance of self-delusion, a straight line could demonstrate stagnation; and stagnation could indicate a whole collection of the worst possible scenarios: destructive and aberrant, misunderstandings and misconceptions, concerning emotional balance, or the lack of it, and Faith, or, indeed, the dreaded Loss of Faith! He chuckled audibly, the best way to chuckle, at this point in his reflections. Religionists do a large amount of reflecting. Fortunately, his house-keeper was nowhere to be seen, so to speak - she must be somewhere to be seen. If their religious practice had become a habit, he continued interiorly, like cleaning your teeth - he glanced down at his unpolished shoes - then, where are we? Nowhere.

He now sprawled on his settee, both feet on the coffee table, stretching his crossed legs, stretching his spine, and still digesting his breakfast, as well as a small white disc, a bit cardboardy to the taste, and a small portion of wine. To explain what these last items are would plunge us into such terrible conceptual difficulties that you may not, literally, survive. Some kind of illicit drug or an extra-terrestrial virus, perhaps? Hundreds of millions of people have already died prematurely because of these disc things and mouthfuls of wine. But we better leave It - it's a bit difficult. There he is, mug of coffee in his right hand and some horrible looking object in his left hand. Oh! Be serious! Not *that!* It's a Report of some sort.

His turn to sigh: he had skimmed it, scanned it, even read some of it - its four hundred pages! He'd certainly read the Recommendations at the end of each chapter, this report from the World Federation of Religious Practitioners; now to the City Annual Conference (C.A.C.). Some preliminary meetings had already been 'attended' via teleconferencing, but the annual meeting hard to avoid. He had made his notes, his own recommendations, which would be rejected, of course, and was at this very moment imaging his journey to the Palace, twelve miles away, simplest by car. He hadn't visited the Palace for donkey's. He liked things stated briefly - 400 pages, for goodness' sake...

As his pastoral duties included prison work, the first part of the journey was simple: head straight for the Prison, but, keeping Dowdall's Tavern to the left, take the road through the Park, i.e. over the Prison, then right, along Embankment Road. Now, he had to think. He couldn't quite place the Palace: directly across the river. Ah, got it! Left and over Hooker Bridge, and left again, along Riverside, right to the front door of the Palace. Yes, straightforward enough, just took a bit of thinking, like everything else, but not too much thinking. The truth is he was looking forward to the meeting, but mainly to meet up with the other members. The 'Ten Majors' would be represented (covering the Four Quarters), so a few hundred people - large enough to be interesting. No difficulty persuading a few religionists to reassemble later at the Old Griff Bar. No difficulty because the official meetings are guaranteed to make participants extremely thirsty and sociable.

The Palace is a marvellous place, built entirely for its aesthetic qualities, and based on the oldest of principles from pre-Cat times. Built to be inspiring and beautiful, a Work of Art of the visual and architectural type. This would be Jeevalani's first visit as a member of any kind of committee and, almost certainly, his last. These annual meetings are usually held on religious premises, where they deal with premises of a religious kind. "You'd think religion was complicated," he said out loud. "Of course it's complicated! Soon you'll be saying anybody can have religion!" He jumped - the swishing of agitated skirts and aprons along the corridor - he would have sworn she was out shopping.

## 35

An old-fashioned breakfast had soaked up last night's poison, layered his stomach in some mysterious way never quite explained, and he had departed for his newspaper and daily constitutional. Everything about the man was from any earlier era, a much earlier era: he was some kind of throwback, a cocktail of a man who never drank cocktails and was not quite *masculine.* He was soft. This is what had attracted Bronnie in the first place and then it had turned into mockery.

He was a great hulk of a man, well-dressed, well turned out, and soft. She said behind his back that he was feminine. Whatever it means, theirs was obviously not a match made in heaven. Be careful of people who mock. The foolishness of men is expected, but the mockery of woman...

She sat at the kitchen table gazing absentmindedly at the clock and sucking on a cigarette. This kind of oral behaviour is very common. The name of the implement is very old indeed. Most people are not even slightly aware of its origin, being something to do with the burning and sucking of dried vegetation in a tube of paper. Its etymology is interesting. Today's versions are completely different, but have similar effects, i.e. mildly intoxicating, especially when coupled with coffee. Bronnie had many of both in the course of a day.

She had started to parade herself as an artist since she retired. In her loose, sleeveless dress, she crossed the kitchen. Her naked feet left moist prints that immediately dried. She turned down the thermostat on her way, returned for her forgotten cigarette, and retraced her steps to her tall stool by the window. She placed her coffee on the inner windowsill, sucked once from her healthy cigarette, turned it off and placed it on the sill. Thus orally above average, she frequently talked to herself. She settled into humming an old song and tapping along with her fingernails on the sill. She was no singer, but one of her few pleasures was singing on her own. She sang many of the songs her mother used to sing. At the moment, a little humming.

Her view of the river was an uncontaminated joy. At this point the river was about two and a half miles wide. Sabine Crossing Tower provided some of the most splendid views of the river along the north bank. She was lucky - she lived on the sea side of the Tower and, with binoculars, she had an unhindered view almost all the way to the sea. She had painted aspects of this view many times. She had enlarged a photograph and had labelled many of the buildings along the south bank of the river. The long photograph was admired and studied by family and friends; it was in the adjoining room on the left-hand wall. Needless to say, there was a standing telescope. That room has the feel of a museum. Her artistic side is real. She and her husband have very few visitors.

She opened the window at the sight of a helicopter, above Libby Point, heading down river. She just wanted to hear it. Sometimes the silence is oppressive and she feels she could easily die or somehow dissolve. Sometimes she has a strong feeling that she doesn't exist.

Still a low blaze from the western sky and she notes the bulbous pink clouds, broken in places and patched with grey; the brush strokes of pink on down to the horizon. She has to imagine the masts of moored boats against the sky. She has hundreds of photographs to aid her memory and colour her imagination. There are the usual clusters of boats along the river banks. Boating has always been popular. She once belonged to a yacht club, but did little yachting. It was more to do with the prestige of membership and the amount of liquid consumed rather than the amount travelled. Alcohol is like revenge: best served cold and preferably alone. Her socialising had failed. No amount of gargling and giggling will compensate for a life bone dry. No amount of feminine sweetness or masculine charm will work. People see through it and, eventually, untie the rope and hoist the sail. Somehow it fell away like dry leaves. She watched two police motorboats leave white trails as they headed downstream. She was curious, but probably nothing. No point being curious, no point listening to the News, it had nothing to do with her.

She slithered from the stool, thanks mainly to gravity, grabbed her painting apron and stepped into her shoes. She didn't like her legs or feet. Now she didn't have to think how ugly they were. Decades of creams and skincare, toning and pampering for nothing. Her colourfully splattered apron tightened her dress to her body, her feather light gloves protected her painted nails, her hands and her veiny arms to the elbow. Elbows? Ignore what you can't see; turn a blind eye.

She studied her painting, a small canvas secured to her easel, a depiction of dancing men. She checked the tightness of the screw and that the legs were wide apart. So annoying when the whole thing topples over! Or, when the canvas slips its moorings. But this was a small canvas - only a touch of her superstitious behaviour. These days she did a lot of checking.

She studied the two dancing men. Her two husbands danced through her mind. This was nothing to do with them. And this was nothing *unconscious,* or even subconscious. It was being copied from her photograph of a photograph, in a book she'd borrowed, of two dancing men. That's all! It was nothing to do with them and certainly nothing to do with that vile... Her thoughts trailed away. Just one more cigarette and a coffee, and she'll settle to her painting. It was a lovely day, lots to observe, to ruminate upon, and she was an artist. This is all perfectly normal.

## 36

No need to check his watch. The man of facts and figures, Purvanos, the rock of common sense, decided to tear along the dotted line. His wife hadn't questioned him, although she'd noticed the briefcase. Somewhat behind schedule, a soft computer voice urged, "Manoeuvre discouraged... This manoeuvre is strongly discouraged! *Three seconds to respond!*" The voice brought him back to his pinnacle of calculability.

The expression of alarm he uttered is difficult to translate. It doesn't imply bodily orifices, the digestive system, genitalia *per se*, the legal status of offspring, extremely holy people (corporeal or incorporeal), or waste products. This list isn't exhaustive. 'Mary's vaginal' was very popular at one time and could lead to the shedding of blood; whilst 'you whopping willy!', an insult with phallic overtones, so it is claimed, came and went. Further examples: 'you rattling bucket!' was an abusive insult, especially amongst women, but disappeared in the late Ninth Century P.C. 'Mild as a bunch of daffodils' is a major insult presently and strenuously avoided. Purvanos used none of these.

What he said is impossible to transliterate. The expression *implies* the suspected collusion between a tactless strawberry bush and a profoundly sexually wayward butterfly. You can see how serious this would be *for the targeted victim.* Naturally, as an insult, it has nothing to do with reality. But in this case, Human Operator:

"Purvanos, your expletive has been recorded."

The voice made P's heart jump and then his recollection!

"I'm alone, Operator, nobody else heard me."

"We are aware of that, Purvanos." Of course, they are! He felt an even bigger fool.

"I'm terribly sorry. I do apologise." A few seconds of ominous silence passed.

"Thank you for your apology; it has been recorded. Have a *calm* day, Purvanos."

"Thank you very much, Operator."

"You're very welcome." The finality of the sing-song, two-tone.

Nothing happens. The operator is being helpful.

He had already responded and returned to the legal traffic lane. He had also remembered that he'd retired a month ago. This is what happens when you are over-tired, he told himself. He pulled off the road in the area of Cavetown and sat listening half-heartedly to the radio: popular music, idle chat, news headlines. He'd realised something else important, but...

"Just decided to go for a drive."

"A drive? Where are you?"

He really didn't like telephones *everywhere* and frequently 'forgot' his.

"Just along the S.E. [Circular Road, for the reader] -White Oak intersection - parked to have a think and listen to the news. Home soon."

"Okay." She thought of his briefcase and said nothing. Silly sausage! Probably misses work and getting a bit doolally!

"Can you pick up a few things?"

Having acquired the *millionth* list in his life, he clicked off. He slipped into the backseat. The car could self-drive, stopping at the shop, opposite the renowned Alvord School, which he'd attended. He'd give instructions after some relaxing music. Too much of a good thing last night is not necessarily a good thing at his age. He had made a fool of himself twice over. Retirement was turning into long periods of wasted time... joined together. Had he ever been ambitious? No. Is that a bad thing? It hadn't felt bad. Now, he was feeling miserable again. The flush of youth was gone. The embarrassments of old age were creeping closer.

One disappointment was his failure to become an Operator. It was hardly surprising that this came to mind. Approaching thirty, Stage 3 Moral Development had to be passed. Operator was a valued role. He'd failed MD3. Such is life. That's the way it is. When he was debriefed, he'd been advised to spend more time in the pub. This institution is the Public House, an ancient idea, pre-Cat. The Pub admits any adult to talk with strangers and drink alcohol. We have the Adolescent House for youth between 16 and 25. It is soundproofed because adolescents are unable to behave appropriately. The staff is comprised of bartenders and very strong and well trained assistants. All staff are obliged to wear ear defenders and special clothing to protect against high levels of sound and vibration. Adolescents can be dangerously noisy. When the sound reaches 150 decibels, red lights flash for sixty seconds. If the warning is ignored, then the *siren*. This includes danger-ous frequencies outside human range. If the ambient sound does not reduce *quickly* to less than 150 decibels, then adolescents begin to lose consciousness. Some of them have already lost consciousness, but that's another story. Use of the siren is automatically recorded by Central Computer and Human Operator. Most adolescents can be revived successfully. If they haven't reached adulthood by 25, then they are not allowed into the pub. The numbers of such persons are increasing. This is being monitored.

The pub is quite dissimilar: a steady wind from the sea of talk. The 'wind' can become powerful 'gusts' admittedly, but Managers *conduct* proceedings so that players become more aware of others. A few shushes and a few waves of the hand and all returns to calm. Sometimes excitement and loud voices are appropriate - the Manager is the final judge. The sociability of the place is the reason Purvanos was advised to spend more time in such establishments. This is where you can 'shape up' your Moral Development, he was informed by an expert in the 'People Immersion Method'. It is not the only approach and the pub is not the *only* place to acquire such skills. But be warned! Some jump to the conclusion that it is the only place, spend years in the pub, and this actually *reduces* their Moral Development.

The always sensible Purvanos mused on these things, on his previous successful outcomes and those others; he mused on the unpredictability of life. Suddenly, he felt fine!

"To the shop! And then home, James!"

He didn't call the car 'James'. When you are an historian, you must acknowledge the things you make up. It's only fair.

## 37

Makallee wondered about the word 'furlough'. The family deserve something interesting in their lives. Poor little Makallee In his peculiar white suit, peculiarly dazzling in the mid-morning sun. His 'shades'- how cool, irresistibly cool! A man of experience, the mind of a boy.

"Hi, I'm home." The collector of houses was silent. Seconds passed.

"Sorry... Who...?"

"It's me, Mum, I'm home."

"Oh, Makallee, of course you are. What's happening? What are your plans? No, not today, I'm really busy. End of the week? Call the others; we'll get together: dinner or something. When are you going back?"

He slipped the phone into his breast pocket. He was relieved, but didn't recognise the feeling. A week to himself? He must contact some of the crew, the boys, the wild boys. And his girlfriend - yes, today, he's feeling a bit desperate for some how's your father. She should have no problem getting a baby sitter. He doesn't relate to her children. He's thinking of his father; plenty of fathers to choose from, but probably his real father; hadn't seen him for some years and hasn't a clue how he is. Why he bothers with his mother is beyond him. But that *connection*. Why his father bothered with her is also beyond him. On the other hand, his father has a strange relationship with his own mother who is still unbelievably alive. But then his father had a very strange relationship with his daughter when she was very young, our sailor boy's sister. He was feeling metaphorically dizzy. Why did his parents divorce? As he was heading towards thirty, he found himself being subjected to that thing people call thinking. It came unexpectedly and he didn't like it. Nothing was clear, his childhood a colourful fog. When he found himself grown up, he had the strong feeling he wasn't! He often had these thoughts when he was in the fresh air. He'd never had these thoughts in the giant cigar tube under the sea fighting the enemy. At this very moment, he couldn't remember the enemy. Several had been mentioned: foreigners with mad ideas and unpronounceable names. He was part of a United Allied Force, but he hadn't met any of the others and he wasn't too bothered. Being home, he had chosen not to stay in Bowling Green Barracks. His intention to occupy a friend's apartment was a matter of course: a scrap of paperwork, no permission required.

He was strolling through Hazel Grove Wood, a popular place for, well, strolling, family picnics, lovers hand in hand, that sort of thing. He heard children playing, but he couldn't see them through the thick growth; the shouts of "You're dead!", the howls and screeches of the triumphant and the mortally wounded. A war game. He was used to those! Sometimes, he wondered what it was all about, life, that is. It's just one big game. His mother flashed into his mind.

The leaves were thick on the ground, a multitude of shades of brown. As he walked he kicked up piles of leaves and they were surprisingly heavy and wet underneath. They clung to his foot. They had no intention of remaining airborne. They knew their place. People were the disturbers of the peace, disturbers of balance, disturbers of other people's equilibrium. In his childhood, he had ploughed joyously into a great pile of dry leaves, picked up great armfuls and thrown them up in the air, some of them had stuck to the arms and chest, his woolly jumper, and he'd tried to brush them off. He'd run and thrown and kicked the leaves when, suddenly, up rose a body! When you are a young child you don't die of shock. It's amazing what children can *survive,* or appear to survive. But when a child starts to wet themselves, or become unnaturally quiet, then you know something bad has happened. He just ran! When he'd stopped to look back, it was another boy, bigger than him. What was he doing there? How long had he been lying under the leaves in that busy place? Children are irrational!

Twenty yards ahead on the wide path between the trees, favoured by strollers and other strange creatures, two children were scrambling amongst the foliage. A young deer of a boy, all skinny legs and razor-sharp elbows, cleared the path in a few strides and disappeared into the opposite bushes. The squeals of the hunter were already apparent before she appeared, and out she tore, still laughing, long brown hair flowing behind her, a woolly jumper of autumnal colours, good camouflage for woodland hunters. (Adults *love* woolly jumpers). And she stopped dead, taking account of our sailor boy. Still smiling, she waved the rapid vibration of a child's wave, bounced, and was gone! Flailing and swimming through the bushes in hot pursuit, dry leaves adhered to her, well, you guessed it!

He realised that he must look peculiar to a child, even without the sunglasses. He'd stopped too, head to foot in white against a background of browns and forty-two shades of green. He tends to exaggerate or misquote. Anyhow, he thought, it's his uniform and, at least, he is noticed. He was overwhelmed with tears. He didn't cry, but something inside flooded. Even sardined together under the sea, you can be alone. And that feeling often surfaced.

The trees were great fat standing giants, some limbs tearing out of the earth trying to escape. There was no escape. They stood at attention equidistant apart, these silent sentinels. He wondered if the wood had always been there. It hadn't.

He was a man of action and that's official. He glanced at his watch, he speeded up, he had people to see and places to go and no reply from his girlfriend and a message for his sister. Head into town, bus it, stop kicking leaves. Nearly a whole week to the inevitable showdowns; after the hugs and kisses, one confrontation after another. Powerless. Battle Stations inevitable.

Samantha had headed off; Lakota had an 11 o'clock meeting. Time enough to relax, think things out. She had exchanged tea for coffee for no good reason.

Feeling much better and vaguely aware of her next social gathering that evening, and being a gregarious creature, she liked nothing better than to herd and flock. Some people are very sociable. Her liver crossed her mind. She was worried about her mind, but her liver seemed to be holding up. Her kidneys were in fine fettle and her bladder was in excellent condition. Her skin was taut, her muscles toned, but her love life had acquired much cellulite, was a bit wobbly and seemed to be drooping. Her heart was permanently broken.

She absentmindedly drew near-invisible patterns on the smooth surface with her finger. 'Butt' means several things. She liked playing with words. Words stood still, they didn't have hidden agendas, they didn't lie to your face, and they didn't duck and dive. They certainly didn't use their power over you as their ongoing hobby. Booze can make you depressed. She didn't believe that for one minute! She'd felt the black cloud arrive silently. Her 'cigarette' was illegal. The illegality was one of the contradictions in her life. She was convinced that she could beat Central Computer - one of those silly challenges she set herself- but she knew it was only a matter of time. Then she would receive a warning and an automatic fine. Due to the nature of this first 'crime', it would be kept on-file and confidential, not even registered at Human Operator Level. A second offence was more serious, but nothing to worry about.

The legal system had taken centuries to develop, even Post-Cat. We had been lumbered, weighed down, by the old ideas. That's how it is in everyday matters. Rightful thinking for a whole nation, the whole world? If you get stuck in the wrong thinking, you can trudge the wrong path for *ever*. A whole society, which had survived an indescribable hell, can still be well and truly stuck; no progress at all. It still happens: millions convinced of a 'truth' and completely wrong! Even in the City, where we have multiple layers of safeguards, things can go wrong. Beyond the individual and group levels, it may become Inter-City, or even Trans-Global, at which point the possibilities become terrifying, a repeat of history. Lakota mused on these things and the possibility of street parties all over the world in her honour, when she saved the world! And then she knew it would rain.

She is academically clever - never failed a test - but... She's in her thirties and thinking about Stage 3 Moral Development. She can predict the result. Leave it for now. Sooner or later the glass ceiling will descend. She must adjust, accept the inevitable. She frequently reflects on the law she practices. Nothing is perfect and she often produces ideas to improve things, does some research and discovers her ideas had already been tried and rejected. "Nothing new under the sun" is one of her favourite sayings because it's hers and original.

90% of the Legal System is managed by Central Computer. Credits and fines are issued automatically and based on Individual Data Profiles. Thus, all Central Computer Legal Outputs (C-CLO's) are mathematically related to personal circumstances. People look forward to their Monthly Credits (including their pay for work). There is an appeals system for fines, which, again, is usually computer-based and only takes a few minutes. Most adults have had recourse to this and most have been wrong! If they're wrong, it doesn't count against them. Teenagers have been tempted to fool about with Central Computer, try to trick it/them. But you know what some teenagers are like! They receive a warning and a fine for timewasting.

The adult system tends to be 'monitored' by random data collection or 'scooping' - a month's behaviour is scooped up and analysed. The Children's Reward System, however, is monitored by minutes or seconds, if necessary. This depends on the child's age, intellectual development, academic progress, and social and emotional stability. Teachers and other adults are the face on the ground, the human administrator between Central Computer and the child. Such adults undergo additional training. Parents are of particular importance. Parents, especially mothers, have destroyed entire families, and it frequently becomes intergenerational, even if the original perpetrator is long dead. Immediately a woman is found to be pregnant, both parents are informed of this obligatory training. Thus, the Children's System is part of the legal system, but rarely part of the Law *per se.* These records, like all records, are kept in perpetuity. Basically, children are considered innocent until the age of majority (25). The adults in charge of them are legally responsible for children and adolescents.

For the remaining 10% of the legal system, certain 'crimes' are passed forward to Human Operators and on to other professionals, if necessary, e.g. police.(Note: Police Headquarters situated City Centre, north side of river, on M11, telephone 111. But don't panic - they will already know).

Lakota has frequent discussions at Police H.Q., but not this morning's meeting: it's at the office with colleagues and an immediate boss. She consults with several bosses. She likes the word 'consult', but she doesn't use it in their presence. She doesn't like being told what to do. The reason is not what it appears. She has underlying assumptions. Lakota is learning to control her tongue. She has already learnt how to shower in ten minutes. She crushes her final stubberoony, takes a bite out of her cold toast, gulps down her cold coffee, and regrets it. "Oh, God!" No, not an ejaculatory prayer. She stubbed her toe on the way to the shower. "Ow! That hurt!" She grasps her toe with both hands, squeezes out the pain whilst hopping on her other leg. It reminds me of the crèche I accessed. For a woman her age, she's quite athletic.

## 39

He of the blob condition had already departed for some reason. The man of precision seemed to be losing his mind, not for the first time. She still had time to collect her three thoughts and suppress those awful thoughts that plagued her. Why is life such a ditch? If you get something wrong, but keep saying it, eventually it will become fashionable. Life is a real ditch, let's face it. We just keep falling into it and then we can't get out. You will be let out, Gelasia.

She was well liked for all of ten minutes, after which she was tolerated. It is amazing how tolerant people can be. It is one of those gifts we lose very slowly. She was on her way to the office, as described in this old language. We call it by a longer expression, relating to 'civic duty'. Our expression relates to all versions of 'work'. We do have a word of identical meaning, but our 'work' is what donkeys do. So, you can see people sitting on their ass during periods of work and doing nothing at all. This is perfectly acceptable in our society. Pretending to do something useful was one of those things that produced the Cat. Books have been written about this strange attitude of pre-Cat times.

Gelasia had people in stitches at the office. Several people used to fantasise about having her in stitches. Already she was making up some colourful and jokey comments. She was so funny! She was heading to the bus stop on Farms Road on the corner of Marye's Hill Roundabout. A quick *hop* into town, past Council Offices 4, where she used to work, straight across the S.E. Circular, and on to the Health Service Head Office. It was actually 39.5 miles from door to door, and a comfortable forty minutes by public transport.

Oh, left leg! She thought to herself, but she didn't say it. She had just missed the bus. What a rotting toenail of a nuisance! Lower limb cursing is on the agenda. She'll probably work her way up. Now she had to wait exactly five minutes. She glanced at her watch, one of those silly habits we all acquire, because she had already seen  the large round analogue clock on the top of the bus stop pole. There marched a plump pigeon as if on sentry duty. And then flew off. Typical of plump pigeons to desert their posts! "Next Town bus in five minutes," announced the voice from the pole. I don't want the *next* town, she was thinking. She's funny. What a bufflehead of a morning! Ah, today she'll be unpredictable.

In fact, she did want the next town; indeed, any town at all, to get away, she and Mr Blob. He wasn't always a blob. He used to be slim and muscular and handsome. Now look at the state of him! A man of forgotten reasons to be precise and a man of hobbies - loved nothing better than holidays, but they had had their maximum permitted for this year. Their applications were in for next year. As the queue formed behind her, she imagined what it must be like to explode.

She turned around sociably and nodded 'good morning' to a few strange faces, not strange *per se*. The City didn't breed familiar faces. They were colourful this morning, the people behind her on this bright summer day, dressed in their bright flowery dresses and sparkling head decorations. The women were sparkling too! She was a card! She wondered when the sexes would simply swap clothes again. They do it about every fifty years. Things were becoming a drag. She smiled, they smiled. Everybody wanted to be friendly. It's the way we are. She turned back. She felt a bit uncomfortable with all those eyes on the back of her head. Strange place to have eyes...

She glanced off to her left. She could hear the sound of the train traversing the City. She couldn't see it, of course, but she knew it must be the southbound at that time of the morning. She imagined that some of the passengers were certainly on their way to the agricultural areas and vineyards to the south beyond the City Wall. She had been there several times over the years as part of her Community Service. She was due another week or two later in the year, this time to the east to work in the Fisheries. The duration had not been finalised yet, but she had requested two weeks because she really loved working on the coast. It was so different. Her age might stand against her, but probably not, not yet. Any work outside the City that was not Fisheries was infinitely more dangerous. Deaths inland were far less frequent these days thanks to *extremely* high technology. The original electrified fences were still up and functioning, but backed by a 'shield' and an elaborate system of lethal weaponry. Central Computer Human Operatives monitored the system continuously. This was not left to automatic monitoring.

The bus drew to a halt beside her with a great shush! sound and brought her back from her daydreaming. As she climbed aboard and spoke her destination into the microphone (this was a driverless bus), she glanced over her shoulder at the crowd behind her, across all those heads. Experiencing the same old routine, she suddenly pictured the bodies outside the electrified fence on that one occasion. The following day they were gone 'by natural means', as a fellow worker had explained. Years later she found herself explaining the same thing to somebody new to the work. As she took her seat, she experienced that familiar tingly feeling below her right ear, followed by the soft computer voice inaudible to everyone else: "Your use of 'bufflehead' has been noted." She nearly laughed out loud. It took them long enough! The fine was fine. Today was going to be a fun day.

## 40

The City drifted into its mid-morning settled routines. The dizzying pulse had returned to healthy rates. Most people logged in or out within their preordained range of times and contracts. Many jobs demand precision, for obvious reasons, but flexibility tends to be the norm. This gives an added sense of personal responsibility and autonomy, and works well. Much is mechanised and computerised, and communication is virtually instant.

It was one of those pleasant summer mornings when most people managed to reflect the weather. We had experienced one of the coldest winters on record. We weren't physically cold, of course, but dark skies produce dark moods. The winter had been quiet. The fliers had arrived a couple of weeks later than usual, but, inevitably, they arrived by the *trillion*. It was quite spectacular, more so than usual, the sky being literally black in places, as they swooped and swerved, changing directions, like great three-dimensional clouds. They are attracted by the heat and 'flesh' of the City. This is a brief, but hectic time for scientists. It is certainly a hectic time for the military who were on permanent Red Alert; a similar situation for Central Computer personnel who are, as always, a vital component of our defence.

Stories abound for times when the fliers got through. These tales are part of our folklore, passed down from generation to generation and *embellished*. When they breach our defences, it results in chaos! It lasts for a couple of weeks. There can be several hundred deaths, caused by malfunctioning systems, and the mess these creatures cause takes months to clear up. The City is covered in their dead bodies. They are allergic to a chemical in building materials, but they keep coming, indeed, every year. But, when all is functioning normally, nothing can get through the shields. Naturally, this year several thousand community service workers cleared the bodies from outside the city walls. This stuff is perfect for fertiliser and is taken by train to the farms north and south of the City. So, we had our annual aerial spectacle and things were quiet again, just the *rumbling* of humanity, loud in the mornings and again in the evenings. Born to the *hum* of the system, people give it little thought. We have an enviable reputation for quietude. Other City Reps arrive occasionally, and are welcomed, to study our levels of calm. This is quite a complex issue.

This week will be busy for the Prison, situated, if you remember, under Mudsills Park in the City Centre north of the river. You would never know the prison, which doesn't have a name, is actually there. No society is perfect. We do our best to be humane, but some humans are simply not human. At a certain point, there is nothing more to be done. Some of us know exactly where the 'certain point' is - it is part of the prison organisation, referred to as Level 6, meaning the lowest storey, underground. Of prison workers only a select few have ever been there. This is not really public knowledge. It is one of the few things which is rarely discussed. People just *know,* or they don't. For a time, years ago, we had a version of 'Level Six' which was a swear word. This was eradicated. Few people remember it.

This is one of those weeks when the Pea Ridge Pet Food Company will get a delivery of fresh meat. It is one of the oldest processing factories still in the centre of the City. 'Processing' relates to any kind of factory. Most of these companies have been moved out of the city centre. We've tried to develop the City Centre as an attractive leisure area. However, this company will remain there for the foreseeable future. It is of historical value, so the claim goes: it is a protected building, protected by the Government. The building is certainly of rare architectural charm and beauty, and centuries ago was the parliament building.

We have an Official Language which is also the Global Language. This is used in public arenas - Parliament, Law, Administration, and so on. We also have four Major Languages, all five spoken by the vast majority. There are thousands of other languages, but these are minority pursuits, in one way or another, traditional or academic, for example, or both.

We have our one Official Religion which is also the Global Religion. Religions are very like languages - there are thousands of them! Like language, they evolve. The Official Religion was evolving before the Cat, although barely recognised, and became more consolidated after the Cat. This took about five hundred years, according to certain scholars, although its actual emergence and chronology are ongoing debates. It is considered the best of all (religious) worlds: a collection of rules and regulations, study, prayer, practice, penance, fasting, more prayer, more study and so on. There is belief in the Deity, made in our own image, of course. Apologies to my reader if I sound facetious, but religion is a collection of useful rituals for a variety of aims and objectives, and no more. There are ten Major (Secondary) Religions. One particular religion is about a hundred times more 'difficult' than the Official Religion! They believe in all sorts of strange ideas, including a Deity, but part of their religious beliefs is the belief that it is 'normal' not to understand any of it, and they don't! It seems sensible to have no religion at all. There are many - probably the majority - of the people who have no religious beliefs. They don't seem to be any more content than the rest. Maybe we should take a little time to hum one of our Official Calming Songs.

Watching activities on the river produces one of those universal calming effects. The river is the busiest thoroughfare at this time of day. It is ablaze in its own kind of glory. We are cruising towards our midday breaks.

## 41

Three hours into his day and Bill was receiving reports thick and fast from his team. There had been two briefings already - normal. He had a strong tendency to print out the electronic reports or scribble down his own notes and pin them on the board. His office was very large, mainly because of the walls. With his rank and moral development level, he had simply ordered (politely requested) the redesign of his office. A wall was knocked down, his office extended because Bill needed space - he needed walls! He sat with his back to the large window overlooking the City, across to Embankment Road and the river. He had kept the window. When he fancied a stroll to stretch his legs, he tended to turn right outside his office and head for the end-of-corridor window about a mile away. The corridor was fairly tranquil. Bill treated the corridor as an ambulatory (a new word from his recently acquired friend), a place to walk and do some thinking or no thinking at all, sometimes the best kind of thinking. The window at the end looked out over Mudsills Park, a place to reflect, not so much on the calm beauty of the park, but, if you happen to be a leading detective, on the prison below the park. He could just discern one of the entrances; none of them can be seen from the ground. He had helped send several to Level 6. No, he reminded himself, nobody goes directly to Level 6. Maintain a healthy perspective. Hence, the walls.

On the right from his desk stretched his cork notice-boards. Almost nobody used this old-fashioned approach. These were for his use and were nobody else's business! His younger colleagues thought him somewhat eccentric, but his record spoke for itself. *Colleagues*? Hmm. He glanced along the boards. Things are becoming cluttered: eight serious cases, several building up. Sometimes he felt like an orchestra conductor.

On the far wall, the white boards which contained scrawled and labelled web diagrams. Every day something was added; occasionally, something was erased. A press of a button on the wall console and down rolled the flexi-computer screens, in front of the white boards, from their long housings, like neon lights, attached to the ceiling.

On Bill's left-hand was the huge, necessarily huge, satellite view of the City. This display had the usual 'zooming' facility, and many others. Key in a person's P.I.N. or name-tag and up popped a red light and as many details as required. Therefore, D.I. Cody, having Priority Access (not *Military* Access) to Central Computer could locate anybody in the City: man, woman, child or neonate. Not to mention pets. Rats lived in a world of their own. Bill had a lifelong interest in rats.

He had re-read a minor case. His eyes wandered from one wall to the other as his mind juggled with the facts. He felt the warm sun on the back of his head. It was pleasant. He knew the rain wouldn't last, just a shower. He jabbed at the light-temperature button on his desk - down a few notches, mustn't get too cosy! The glass altered, the sun's heat was reduced and the ambient light increased accordingly. He just needed one report. He tapped in her P.I.N. and up popped the red light on the City map. She is still interviewing, must be patient - but he was quite sure he already knew the outcome. More important cases, certainly, but this particular kind boiled his blood. All totally unnecessary, not a crime at all, and yet it is! Some people are in for a terrible shock, but he didn't feel a bit sorry for them. There are no excuses. He felt downright vengeful, but being an MD4, he was more than aware of his own feelings - the facts first, always the facts first. There may be mitigating circumstances, but unlikely at this point.

A knock on the door and a face and name appeared on his desk screen.

"Come in, Tom," his voice transmitted quietly in front of Tom's face.

"Morning, Chief," Tom's anachronistic salutation, the first of the day, as he lumbered straight for the Chief's desk. It was curtains for Tom, rather than a suit. The mystery was: How, for a great mountain of a man, did he always look so elegant?

"Just passing, thought I'd drop in," which was literally true, except for the *drop*. Tom believed in face to face communication. He said it was so because his parents loved him. You never knew what to expect from Tom. His sense of humour was either appallingly childish or razor sharp.

"It's animal!" he said, handing over the slip of paper to D.C.I. Cody.

By the time the slip of paper had made contact with his fingertips, Bill Cody had decoded the message. He looked at Tom and rose from his seat.

"How is that possible? It's not."

He knew it was, it must be, as they headed for the white boards. He added a straight black line to the second web diagram and labelled it 'Animal DNA' and added the two digits indicating the day and month. He dated almost everything, sometimes shopping lists.

He looked at the slip of computer paper and the scribbled initial, as if to draw from it some kind of solution.

"It's animal. The whole thing is impossible. Any ideas?"

"Not a clue, and no fingerprints."

"So I see, and not even a suggestion of fingerprints."

They were repeating themselves and stating the obvious.

"Right, back to the drawing-board," he said, pinning the lab report on his cork board, staring, hands on hips.

"Team meeting, 30 minutes, this office." A few off the premises, but the majority were in the building. Tom was already leaving.

He wandered his cork boards like a rich man at an art auction. He enjoyed the challenge. Now, which of these miscreants is going to win the Stupidity Prize? Animal, indeed.

## 42

Thinking of nothing, suddenly a glass staggered through Bronnie's mind. Too early! The two dancing men were taking shape. Their time, culture? Her curiosity gone, if it ever existed. Life was surreal, cobbled together. She had tottered from crisis to crisis, having entered a fog from which she'd never emerged. Her denial fell like a soft boulder, crushing, suffocating. When she was a girl love was so exciting. Then it changed. The two men were taking shape, exactly like the photograph. She *must be precise*. She had a sense of scale, but no sense of proportion.

He was around somewhere, her Jolly Jack Tar. Every day was Sunday. It was so long since she hated Mondays and had Friday on her mind. She looked forward to Monday: start anew, another chance. She felt her heart sinking. Time for something tasty. Surely. She glanced at her watch. How can you tell it's too early? A blob of paint landed on her right slipper. She needed a break.

"Hello, dear, back from my ramble."

"I didn't know you'd gone out."

For a second he was still. She hadn't even turned around. They had an understanding, a combination of tolerance and ignoring. They drifted like two dinghies on a calm sea. The calm had arrived like an angel. At first it was welcome.

"Did you go outside?" She sounded curious. She remembered the outside and could see it from her windows.

"No, no need. Walked three, four miles, just for the exercise, met George, dropped into the Bean-Hole, fairly busy, people having a break, teas, coffees, a bit of a chinwag, that sort of thing. Pleasantly sociable."

No response, then she swung round, stared and was pale. She couldn't bear his telegraphese; she felt like screaming.

"His wife's not well, been in hospital, three days, high blood pressure, the usual. Coffee?" He'd slipped off his brisk, clip-clop shoes and shuffled in his slippers towards the kitchen. The usual. Transformation. Her undercurrent of irritation he ignored. No point.

She remembered the couple from *sometime*. They must have changed. The usual.

"I've forgotten her name. Did you give them my best?"

"Of course I did," he lied, "Germana."

George and Germana. Sometimes suicide seems a healthy option. If she could just survive and float about invisibly, then she could laugh again. If she could just watch the show without playing a role; if she could just stab the odd person, like Germana, whom she remembered well, with a very sharp pin. That would be just perfect!

The jet of water, that sound of drowning, the chink of china, and out came his head and shoulder, then an arm, a magic show of the grotesque, "The painting's looking good!" No response and he was gone. "Coffee coming up."

She, like a white statue, or a captive parrot chained to her perch, knees clenched. Too late now. In her next life she'd be a bookshelf. She nearly laughed. She glanced at her watch. Too early for laughter.

"Making progress," she managed.

She slid from the stool and padded to the settee. A break for coffee and some light conversation would be purrrfect. Her bones hurt.

He lounged in his favourite, off-hand chair, his long legs stretched and crossed at the ankle, his belly a dome of discontent, his large soft hands clasped north of the dome. Her body Z-shaped, a violin over-wound. She sipped her coffee daintily, focused like a cobra.

"They'll never change. This has been going on *forever*. It's like a bag of cats." He sighed and glimpsed his feet beyond the dome. He wiggled his toes - must watch the old circulation. He uncrossed his feet and reached for the coffee. She was in no mood to talk about her children and grandchildren. Yesterday's frantic 'phone calls - indeed, every messaging system *over*-activated - had been typically disastrous, stressful. She had trouble recalling what they *claimed* had initiated that particular flood of dismayed chatter. He couldn't be bothered. He picked up his newspaper. Now her grandchildren are adults, things are worse! He'd made such an effort for so long. To all intents and purposes, he's their grandfather, and yet he shouldn't have to put up with *this*. No respect.

"I don't know what's going on. Nothing's improving." As she spoke, she thought of *his* adult children. They're perfectly civilised, so it couldn't be anything to do with the breakup of marriages. And they weren't as well educated as hers. For years she'd been really proud of them, but it had turned into an ongoing nightmare. They easily avoided detection by Central Computer. A thought had crossed her mind many times. They spoke beautifully, calmly and venomously. It built up every time. A normal get-together was impossible. On those occasions, her thought was to scream abuse just so that Central Computer would intervene, put a stop to their tearing each other apart. She'd never be reduced to *that* behaviour. It would be just too embarrassing and she'd be the guilty party! That just isn't fair.

"I've suggested therapy umpteen times." He nodded and turned a page.

"Sometimes, I think they're going to explode. Literally!" He chuckled. "I've imagined them saying something terrible to a complete stranger and getting themselves killed!" He was sorry he'd said that.

"They blame each other," he continued his oft delivered monologue, "Every time I've tried talking to one of them I get a *version* of the latest event, the whole story. It just comes pouring out *in detail*. It's never *their* fault, it's always some-body else's. They are too clever by far. Sometimes I think they need a good slap! - to introduce them to what the rest of us call reality."

There was a moment of synchronised sighing. He turned another page. His feet disappeared below the horizon and rose again. He felt old and tired. It was nothing to do with him. Maybe a holiday would help, preferably on a distant planet! She felt depressed and increasingly thirsty.

## 43

A day off was a day of ghosts. Hubby had only popped out for a stroll, more of a hobble in his case. She had de-crumbed, polished, re-wardrobed, re-cupboarded, re-shelved; she had aired and made the bed (a peculiar expression); she had puffed-up cushions, relocated dust to its proper place; she had tidied up, tidied around, tidied about, and tidied away. At least, there were no bodies to keep tidy, tidy up or tidy away. Ghosts kept popping out of cupboards and she kept pushing them back and slamming them in. But some trailed behind her, clung to her back, sat on her shoulder, weighed her down and whispered in her ear. She was furious because they weren't her ghosts. They had cluttered up her life, made things difficult, rendered her dysfunctional, slightly so, of course, and less able to achieve her potential, that calm which was her natural right, her natural disposition.

He had padded in unnoticed, the Padding Man. He could have been a super-hero in a comic; he could have been a comic superhero. He was *her* superhero which sounds comical, because it made her Mrs Superhero in the way that without him she didn't exist. Every time she thought of herself she was the Invisible Woman. *She* had noticed. But keep going and remember: Appearance = Respectability.

Perhaps, the Huntress of Microbes had sensed the disturbance of dust.

"Is that you, hun?" One of *those* questions. She momentarily despised herself. If it hadn't been 'hun', there would have been an alarm from Central Computer.

"Yes, darling. Bought the 'paper; had a quick scan, nothing to report: no wars, earthquakes, uncontrollable forest fires, or tsunamis to put them out. Just the normal range of misery in faraway places; nothing to trouble us. The starving millions are still starving. Shame on them! Why don't they just get a proper job. Some people will do anything to get attention. According to scientific research we're the most boring people who have ever lived and we'll live to five hundred, once another lot of scientists have figured out how to remove our heads and connect them to an electrical source and preserve them in an upturned goldfish bowl."

That story sounded familiar. Hadn't she seen it at the Archive Cinematograph? That's such a sociable night out. They'll have to try it again sometime. She likes being sociable so that people can have a chance to talk to her.

"Yes, Tabatante the Astonishing. I told you before to avoid fresh air because it's not good for you. It gets you thinking and you know that's definitely not good for you."

He gave her a hug from behind and kissed her on the back of the neck. She shivered.

"I haven't walked in that stuff for years. You get to a certain age and you just can't be bothered. And as for thinking..." Index finger to lower lip, he stood there like a five year old trying to remember the previous lie and why this one wasn't being accepted.

"Oh, for goodness' sake, stop annoying me," she chided, "and do something useful."

"Yes, I will, honeypot. I think I'll sit down and read the newspaper or, in my case, look at the pictures."

He landed on the couch like a backward flop into a swimming pool. Where does he get the energy and co-ordination to perform such a piece of gymnastics at his age? She wondered. He landed like a large bag of something unpleasant, an elongated bag of fat comes to mind, with a childish grin from behind a precisely trimmed grey beard at one end and a pair of brown leather shoes at the other end. The shoes need polishing.

"Belbiana, I know what you're thinking," he teased.

No, you don't. If you had any idea, you'd...

"I'll polish the shoes today. Or... maybe tomorrow. I do have a lot on."

She felt herself becoming hot. Humorous people think they're so clever. I can crack jokes, but you can't do it all the time when things are serious. She headed for the kitchen.

"You seem serious. Anything the matter?"

"No," she called over her shoulder, "Just thinking about lunch." Lunch? She thought of the fly in the kitchen and the attempted suicide, when the woman slashed her wrists. It is strange how the mind works. It was nothing to do with her or any of her patients. Somebody mentioned in a book, some kind of case study, a newspaper article, she couldn't quite place it. She heard the barely audible ticking sound below her left ear. High blood pressure. She should know better. Calm down. Sit and try the thought-blocking exercise. First she put the kettle on. Not a good idea, she turned it off. Get the B.P. under control without distraction. Control is important.

After a few minutes, the ticking started to slow down. The more self-possessed she felt, the slower it became. Mind over matter. Good, it's gone. Perfect self-control with a little help, some training in bio-feedback. That is what people need: self-control and a little training. She kept telling people, but they wouldn't listen. Now she put the kettle on.

In her mind's eye, he sprawled on the couch in his self-contained and self-confident way. He had skated through life acquiring his skills in his steady and manly style, thanks to his father, learning the hard way to be a man. That's why he could cope so well. That's the reason he could overcome or even sidestep difficulties. Nothing was that important, everything would work out. She could never be that strong; sometimes he appeared shallow. He was her manly hero, her father wasn't. Daddy was a gentleman, but her mother... Nobody had any understanding of the blackness in her heart, the sadness. She had always put on a good show, but it had never really worked. Nobody had ever reached her. She was alone and her anger festered. Belbiana was off the wall! So they said.

## 44

Breakfast was either an improvisation, a drifting from the bits to the bobs of the moment, or it was his favourite quartet of cereal, fruit and tea. This is only a metaphor. Don't start counting or you'll be lost in the woods. There are stories within stories and metaphors within metaphors. Probably the thought of Sylvia elicited a sigh of happiness in the soul of Psybunes. It also elicited a sigh of concern. Was she going to be rid of him because he wasn't good enough? When you think you're not good enough, you're not good enough. If you think you're a genius, then you're definitely mad, unless you're a genius. Thinking is a good thing, but never have too much of a good thing.

Psybunes had learnt many things, mainly based on his favourite cereal. His latest unfinished book had been called 'The Zen of the Art of Breakfast Cereal Eating'. He had spent months on his brilliant opening paragraph which explained that the book was nothing to do with Zen, nothing to do with cereal, and nothing to do with breakfast. At the end of this process he had concluded that he really didn't need to write anymore. The rest was obvious. He is now working on 'String Theory and String Quartets'. The whole book is completed in his brain, but he is having serious difficulty with the first paragraph. Being a musician, his thinking is only part-time and his writing a hobby. You must understand the differences. He does. He thinks on Wednesdays. Today isn't Wednesday; today is for sighing.

Through the cobwebs of unknowing, the youth, who is heading to forty, is enjoying the sunniness of the City, the sunniness of the million bobbing heads on the river of souls beside the river of sticks down from the Keetsville Woodlands way beyond the Eastern Wall. In the sunniness he halted and leant over the embankment wall to watch the river traffic on the sunniest of rivers. He squinted through half-closed eyelids and watched the countless diamonds sparkling on the river, the diamonds turning to tiny birds and then to crucifixes. He marvelled at the millions of unknown lives going about their business amongst the diamonds. To his right beckoned the shaded Baxtersprings Tunnel beneath the north-south roads and railway akin to the bridge of the same name.  The tunnel would take him further along the embankment and into the Park. It would be cool in the tunnel. His forehead was being microwaved by the sun. You can have too much of a good thing.

He'd walked a hundred yards into the park, towards the Great Oak, when a horse and rider galloped past. He'd been dreaming - or was it a nightmare? - and hadn't been aware of the approaching hoof sounds. It's one of those things, he mused, that he'd recalled the hoof sounds *after* they'd passed. The power of the horse was majestic and shocking and, enclosed in muscle and mass, far greater than a man. And the lucky young girl as she bounced with the horse, her pigtail whipped back and forth like something trying to ward off an attack. He envied both, joined together in power, grace and freedom. He didn't see her face, but imagined she was sixteen and beautiful. She would probably envy that he was a musician! He would learn to ride a horse one day, before he's too old, and maybe she's already on her way to becoming a musician, which is a lot harder that learning to ride a horse, he told himself. He'd been thinking about his great unwritten paragraph. He was also thinking about Sylvia. Maybe they'd learn horse-riding together one day. For some reason, he doubted that this would ever happen. Things don't last.

Twenty minutes later, as he mounted the crest of the gently rising hill, he caught sight of the Great Oak and there was the girl resting in its shade, her horse grazing nearby. He still couldn't see her face clearly, but she certainly had the shape of young beauty. He imagined her flawless because that's what he wanted to imagine. He didn't want to imagine the reality of being sixteen. He didn't need to imagine that. A further hundred yards, she rose, pocketed her phone, re-buttoned her jacket, mounted her horse and was gone.

When he reached the Great Oak he was early and alone. He sat on the bench. His journey had been long enough, mainly by bus, but he had walked three or four miles, a distance which disappears in a city. He had often walked twenty miles and barely noticed, but he'd certainly noticed his hot and throbbing feet! Today was a ramble.

He watched the couples and the carefree, the elderly and the young with no need to go to work. No teaching today, he could relax until this evening's gig. He'd formed a new band. They were still at the young and struggling stage, both conditions coinciding just as bad as they sound and not slightly sprightly and full of the joys of spring. At his age... His previous band had disintegrated after eight years - that inability to cooperate makes young men feel old. He was the natural leader and he'd finally given up. They'd had plenty of need for glory, but where was the discipline?

These negative thoughts and the fact she was late led to more negative thoughts, the old ones, those thoughts that couldn't be shaken. They were always waiting to ambush his quiet moments. They were a poison in his system and, so far, there was no known antidote. Nothing had ever worked. He thought of his father. They'd talked often, they'd kept in touch, but the poison was always there. Now there was a huge chasm of silence between them.

As he watched a group of young children play and their mothers animated in a semi-circle on the ground a distant bell chimed. She was over an hour late.

## 45

Sachikaka could have been a lawyer amid many possibilities. People outside the Law don't realise this. Criminals are 'outside the law' and know more about the law than the majority of citizens determined to live within the law. Determination has little to do with it - it has more to do with fear, but this is not quite true. It is not fear that keeps people on the straight and narrow. It is a certain *understanding,* a collection of attitudes, like everything else, acquired in childhood. Some refer to the 3C's of Sapiens: congregate, communicate, co-operate. Simultaneously. Persons who can't do this...

However, our young blonde and beautiful man-manager hadn't acquired these attitudes, these human attributes which produce emotional stability. Emotional stability doesn't mean 'still'; or capacity for minimal response; or 'boring' and 'lifeless'. Emotional stability means the ability to generalise a honed and developed intelligence in circumstances, which, to a greater or larger extent, you have arranged for yourself. Nobody is completely in charge of their own destiny. That belief is immature and egocentric. People depend on other people, but there is always a 'negotiation', an *honest* negotiation. Then, in very specific and acknowledged circumstances, and after a certain period of time, emotional stability becomes apparent. Its absence becomes apparent much quicker, in which case other people have to decide how much patience they are capable of and willing to expend. In terms of other people's patience, Sachikaka was trying, very trying. She was already past her 'sell by' date: twenty-five is adulthood. She's heading in the fast lane to thirty. She is a clever girl, albeit a slow learner; a girl who demands to be treated like a woman; an egocentric five year old looking for Daddy so she can be his Princess. Where is her Daddy?

Her potentially high-flying job with the Ministry for Security was something she boasted about for a short time. Her pride in achievement had dwindled rapidly. She boasted, but the reality brought hammer blows to her brain. She made no mention of her rapid decline into alienation from the organisation because she wasn't aware of it. It was her first job after *uni* and a shock to the system. It wasn't what she'd imagined. Nine to five? *Every* day!? Two weeks off in the summer. Two!? Two *weeks*!? In fact, she'd given it no thought - she'd simply assumed another impressive item on her Curriculum Vitae, part of her inevitable rise to the top. Everything had been so easy to that point and things were going to continue to be easy. She had learnt a way with men from very early on. She was confident-to-smug on her expertise in this field: men were easy! Men had learnt that she, too, was easy.

Her five years at the MfS had proved somewhat 'difficult', although she thought none of her family and her many friends had noticed. But people *say* things. Apparently, they're not aware they're saying things. She couldn't quite adjust to the routine and seriousness of the job and that these two things went on *forever* - they aren't temporary, as and when she felt like it. The '*Firm*' wasn't divided into terms or semesters and work given an 80% mark deemed 'Excellent.' It was, after all, the Ministry for Security and an 80% was deemed poor to catastrophic. Within a few months, however, this breakdown in communication had righted itself, a few words in her ear and she had come up to standard, not so much her punctuation as her punctuality, and her attitudes, her *leisure activities* were, well, *questionable*. At the end of the first year she was warned. It was suggested that she 'improve' things. She said she would. On a global level, security is a multicultural stalemate, multifaceted, multi-networked, and multi-desperate to maintain harmony. 'Never again' is everybody's attitude. Nobody can ignore a sexually promiscuous drunk near the inner *doings* of H.Q.

After five years, and five Annual Reviews during which the advice became increasingly stern, she decided to 'recollect in tranquillity' something to do with incompatibility and glass ceilings. Neither of these factors were communicated 'officially' and, of course, she continued to impress. This was friendly advice offered by her on-line manager in the most friendly of ways, indeed more akin to father-to-daughter nurturing. It was implied that she was beginning to embarrass the family. And one doesn't embarrass that particular family. So, she informed kith and kin that, after due consideration and without prejudice, she had decided that the Ministry was somewhat limiting and she had decided to take her massive personal skills into the marketplace. (No, not *that* occupation, but she would have been pretty good at it - no problem getting dozens of excellent, and anonymous, references). Apparently, this made perfect sense, her move from the Min, and everyone wished her the very best of luck in her future career.

In her future career, which is her present career, she is a *Consultant*. There she sits at her desk in the spacious, open-plan office on the fourth floor of the great fist of an edifice called the Stones Building. She intends to work her way to the top. Intention is everything. And the top in this case is way up in the sky. The hierarchy is literally designated floor by floor. There are many companies housed in the Stones Building and her company of *consultants* is amongst the best. Consulting demands total discretion and confidentiality. Obviously, her fellow consultants must know what she does. At this very moment she is poring over pages of facts, figures and graphs. Some very colourful diagrams appear on her computer in a flash, so this must be important work. She glanced at the digital clock on her computer screen and she's not happy - not nearly lunch time. She has a meeting at eleven o'clock at which she has to provide certain data. She is not looking forward to this meeting because her rank will be painfully obvious.

## 46

Bright as a bird, charming, personable, always smiling, Nasichisha, flutters from pillar to post, has a little tweet here, has a razor peck there. Her job is as ironic as the rest of her life - she works in the Prison. She is a dissembler and some kind of psychologist. On probation. Nothing is quite what it appears. Today is an easy day. She ensures that all days are easy days. She has a way about her, not quite straightforward, not quite cunning, as far as anyone can tell, which is not very far. She flits, she floats, she drifts. Today she has to administer Personality Inventories to two male prisoners on Level 2. They are already seated desks apart. A guard sits on an aisle desk four rows behind them, feet on the chair in front. That's okay. He's a decent man who likes his job. She floats in, introduces herself, places a copy of the booklet in front of each prisoner, ensures they understand the task, and silently departs. This assessment is untimed, taking less than two hours. The guard will 'buzz' to inform her when the task is completed. She will appear, collect the booklet and the prisoner will return to his cell. Ditto the second prisoner; unlikely that they will finish simultaneously. A very easy morning. She will spend the afternoon analysing the prisoners' responses. She will ensure that this takes several days, including her written reports.

For some reason she's not happy at work. She has avoided work assiduously. She has used all kinds of excuses to explain she has better things to do, things of a higher order. Escaping into formal study has been one of her favourite ploys. She has dragged out certain study courses by *negotiating* extended deadlines. She spent years 'hanging around' the university and nobody took any notice. The 'story' was never put together because academics can be extremely easy-going and do their best to be helpful and supportive. They are concerned about 'standards' and they are always met, as far as anybody is concerned to ascertain. When individuals study this phenomenon, as all such studies, there are so many variables that their research findings are frequently open to a plethora (one of N's favourite words) of criticisms and interpretations. It has been pointed out that one hypothesis produces ten more, and the conclusions often propose the inevitable: further research is needed. A pleasant maze for the flutterings and chatterings of Nasichisha.

University turned out to be her perfect escape. Now, she is caged in her first proper job, although, again, neither of her two seniors are able to contact her. She is busy doing something somewhere. Not for the first time she has slipped out of sight of the monitoring system. This is hardly serious enough to contact Central Computer. That would be embarrassing and suggest that they are not on top of their management role. They are annoyed - this is *not* University. She has a certain attitude: argumentative, uncooperative, divisive, obstructive. They know she's not in danger, no emergency has arisen.

"Any ideas?"

"None."

"We'll discuss this later." The brief ping of the terminated telephone conversation. A calm anger in both parties. Why does she behave like this? Jo recalled her time in the military. This behaviour would be called dumb insubordination. Success in naming it was quite calming. It wasn't AWOL. She wasn't absent, she simply wasn't around. Yes, certainly some kind of disobeying of orders. She chuckled to herself. Who cares! That's not the point, she counselled herself, if you can name it, you can change it. That was her philosophy of life and her approach to her work as a senior prison psychologist. In this case, the 'absent' psychologist seemed 'madder' than some of the prisoners! Hardly professional...

Nasichisha is seated on an upturned bucket in a walk-in cupboard on the third floor. How she got to the third floor and not be seen by the prison security monitoring team is a mystery. She must have been disguised, she must have looked like one of the maintenance staff. She needed some quiet time. The reason for this is unclear. Much of her time is quiet. The only noise in her life is the noise she makes or the noise she elicits, or the noise produced by other people who expect her to do things she has agreed to do and avoids doing. It's something to do with *power*. She enjoys the status and title of her job, but she positively dislikes her boss, indeed any boss. Her intelligence has gone to her head.

Long ago 'intelligence' had been a problem. It had never quite been defined. Certificates, tests frequently did not correlate with behaviour. Experience and education, either separate or in combination, were supposed to increase, hone, refine intelligence to produce honest, decent, civilised, skilful people who were supposed to be dependable citizens playing their part in an integrated society. This was the 'plan'. We have produced our fair share of sociopaths, psychopaths, narcissists, borderlines, etc. Borderlines are not borderline, they are not *slightly* abnormal. These groups are the sociably anti-social because we don't quite know how to deal with them. We don't know what we are dealing with. Like chameleons, these people keep adjusting themselves to suit the circumstances. Such aberrant behaviour can be so low-level that it is never picked up by Central Computer, and the rest of us have difficulty naming the 'problem' without it reflecting back on us: Is it me? Am I being difficult? Is this a personality clash? Is Nasichisha sitting on an upturned bucket clasping a mop, like a queen on her throne leaning on her symbol of authority, her sceptre, in a cleaning cupboard on the third floor because everybody else is emotionally disturbed and is envious of her skills and hates her? She would claim she is misunderstood. Pity the poor fly trapped in the cupboard. It's trying to irritate her because it hates her.

After an easy start, Jeevalani received his first shock. At the Palace they wouldn't let him in!

"No C.A.C. here today, Father. Next month?"

A strange expression hissed from the priest's mouth, an ancient language not picked up by Central Computer. A curse, perhaps. The doorman seemed used to expressions of exasperation by clerics in unknown languages.

"I think you'll find it's the World Congress you're looking for."

"Of course - mixed up the dates." He looked at his shoes for inspiration, as one does. As he clicked his thumb and middle finger and index finger vibrated upwards, he uttered, "Taxi."

"Seems a good idea, Father." This fellow has a clear grasp of the human condition. There were no flies on him. Unfortunately, no taxi for twenty minutes. Another audible hiss? No point, no time saved, he concluded, as he leapt into his car, although his days for leaping had long passed.

So much for being back in so-called civilisation, he thought, everything time-tabled, scheduled, enough to drive a man to drink, unless he could get a taxi which he couldn't.

"The University," he instructed, "and like a bat out of hell!" A few seconds passed while the computer translated and away they shot! The meaning of life for Jeevalani was fun with decent people. However, he forgot to close the windows.

"The windows!" he shouted. Now, look at that: hair all betossed! Vanity, it's definitely his favourite sin.

Tearing along Riverside (West) seaward, he would have kept going, but he didn't have an Exit Pass and it was too much trouble and he must be sensible and attend the Congress. A priest could get an Exit Pass, but his lie would get another black mark from Central Computer. Right, the World Congress it is, albeit a bit late, no harm done. Probably enjoyable. Pass a couple of bridges, cross back to the north bank at Dover Swamp Bridge and straight to the University.

*Fifteen hundred* delegates, for the love of God! Yes, precisely, Father. He was already registered and was handed his folder. He scanned the programme and it appeared familiar, not because he'd heard it all before, but because he'd had a copy for the last month. He was relieved to miss the talk on Spirituality. He wasn't really into spirituality. There would be several talks simultaneously. He thought it best to have a quiet cup of tea and allow the Spirit to guide his choice, or maybe just have a chat with somebody, which *is* the Spirit.

He'd read many's the book; or, to be more precise, he'd read many books. Or, to be even more precise, he'd read the same book many times. Or, to be even *more* precise, he'd read the first half of the same book many times. He was determined to read the entire book, maybe next year, which would mean restarting the book. He had started many books, but this was his favourite. He thought it was although he'd never read it. It had been his one constant compan-ion. He'd packed it many's the time. More times he'd never unpacked it. Then, when packing, he had discovered his favourite book and had cursed himself for having wasted so much time when he could have read it. In the next country, he'd definitely unpack it. His favourite book is what's-it-called by yer man. Oh, yes, he reflected: Merton. That's the fellah. Merton was a great writer... because he'd had nothing better to do, concluded Jeevalani, who was always busy. He was busy now looking for someone to talk to. The best thing about Conferences and Congresses was the number of people to talk to, once they had emerged from the tedious talks. Plenty of talk and beer!

His eye roamed the mighty, near empty students' canteen. How many canteens are there? Dozens, he conjectured. Apart from the counter-kitchen end, he was surrounded by massive amounts of glass, two walls of windows about a football pitch away. The canteen was on the corner of the building and the views were tremendous, but he was disinclined to walk that far - he'd had a hectic morning. And, anyhow, he'd seen it all before: the wonderful view over the river, and the panoramic view towards the Western City Wall from the windows way over to his left. He was content to sit, sip his tea, and imagine the views on this glorious sun-washed morning, another proof of the existence of God. The fact that Jeevalani was still alive was the only proof he needed - he'd had so many near misses. If it wasn't one thing, it was another. Being bored to death by intellectuals was, inevitably, part of today's penance. Father rarely completed his penance. He'd discovered *technical* reasons for truncating the experience. God is good.

Out poured the beards! To his right, at *that* wall of glass, he had positioned himself for an optimal view of the eye-squintingly long corridor. To use binoculars might be considered bad manners. Right on schedule, the chattering hordes emerged from several lecture theatres. For an unholy split second he imagined a line of bare backsides doing their business. It reminded him of his army days, and that early day when their naked knees had actually touched! Like most things in the army, the first time was a shock, but you get used to it. Quite embarrassed, they'd started chatting.

"Have you ever read Thomas Merton?" the other young recruit had asked. "Neither have I," added the boy soldier. It was one of those conversations. God certainly works in mysterious ways.

God will hardly get a word in today. The beards will have the floor, most other parts of the infrastructure, much of the oxygen, and large amounts of alcohol, being sociable. The thing Jeevalani marvelled at in such a huge clerical gathering was how wonderfully colourful their garb - every colour under the sun and one or two invented by chemists. Today would be nothing if not gay.

## 48

Time to depart from the sewer, an exit , or exeunt, depending on how things go, was her aside. Enough socialising, me thinks. The Underground is rare, one of the few theatres in sewers. Such cultural centres, tastefully located, suggest a certain degree of lateral, indeed, subterranean thinking. Its café is one of the most popular centres in the City, where our creative non-thinkers gather to have non-discussions about non-events, which they call discourses. The Hot Air is another such cultural centre. Admittedly, the quality of alcohol is always the highest, and quickly turns their existential angst to a babbling brook of pleasure, which is very appropriate considering the locale. The babbling and bubbling has wearied Halaigha, the Minimalist. Today. Tomorrow she may be an Aesthete. Last week she was a Contemplative. The smell of fresh flowers is pleasant, the quality continually monitored for reasons, which should be self-explanatory.

Halaigha arose amongst the bouquets down in the Rose to bid her farewells.

Flinging one end of her colourful scarf over her left shoulder she nearly took out Oedipus's eye! Her audience was appreciative and did they laugh! They didn't applaud or shout "Brava!", and Oedipus shrugged with open hands to heaven in his Italianate way and twinkled with mirth through his good eye. He felt quite privileged to be her anointed victim. She was sure he did. Her apologies were effusive. She really deserved a standing ovation. Wobbling uncertainly on her high-heeled leather boots, the heaviest part of her, which kept her from floating away, she floated away, her cape giving the impression of a departing priestess from the alter of a sacrificial pagan mass, the acolytes to bathe themselves in the virgin's blood.

However, they decided to stick to drinks of a more legal variety and to enjoy just one more glass before luncheon, although it was heading for early afternoon for these denizens beyond the universe of common sense.  Most of us know when to pull on the reins, slow down, before we reach the end of the road to oblivion and drive our troika off the cliff.

The light was at the end of the tunnel. She headed to the light. She was being called - yet another of her many vocations.

"Hey, Halaigha! Here I am, darling, over here!"

There are times when murder is such an enjoyable fantasy. It is not as mad as it sounds. Indeed, it can be positively therapeutic. After an imagined mass murder, or a machete of serial killing, some people feel much better! It helps them sleep more soundly. Apparently, to imagine strangling the life out of some-one makes you feel more positive, increases your feelings of well-being. So, don't feel guilty. If you're normal, fantasies aren't real.

"Here, darling!"

Oh my, he's waving and definitely not drowning. But it could be arranged, especially in this place. They are about as suited as a pelican and a giraffe. The only thing they have in common is their fantasies, a Venn diagram of day dreams. Where is the law when you need it? The law is close at hand.

They kissed briefly, linked arms and away they flounced. Other people must envy their special relationship. They are the perfect couple, the perfect partner-ship, the Adam and Eve of the Arts. Unfortunately, they have avoided the Tree of Knowledge and the Tree of Good and Evil. Other people keep upsetting Halaigha because of the bites *they* have taken. Those horrible munching and slurping sounds! But these chewings are the chewings of the disgruntled, the bitter and twisted, the old and battered failures who envy the idealism and optimism of youth. Ignore the rantings of the malcontent, hobble forward at your own speed, Halaigha, and be not afraid! Thus, buoyed up with these logical conclusions and fine thoughts, she, half of the happy couple, having finally found her rightful place, headed towards the light.

The sun shines on the equal and the unequal *equally*. Light is the most caring of parents and treats all its children with the same degree of kindness and compassion. Its failure is the failure of those who have acquired a darkness permanently within them, a darkness that is impenetrable.

Halaigha and her boyfriend were enjoying the brightness of the rest of the day ahead, as they strolled the Riverside (East) on the southern bank. She glanced across his bulging stomach as the cathedral went by. Certain rowdy thoughts yelled at her, but she bludgeoned them into silence. They keep ambushing her when she least expects it, usually last thing at night when she feels so alone in their coffinbed, where she lays wide eyed and straining to see the ceiling, and imagines that somebody has already nailed down the lid. Sometimes they are raucous, ill-mannered toddlers who are demanding things she is incapable of providing. People will despise her.

"It's a lovely day for a stroll."

"It's just great, honey, perfect weather," he says smiling down on her. He is happy that she is so relaxed, although she has so much to put up with, but today not a care In the world.

They have planned a spot of lunch, something cheap, at the Cracker Line, a vegetarian restaurant on the banks of the Hard Times contributory. It will be very pleasant today sitting outside and watching people go by. There they can gather data, in an informal, polite and surreptitious way, for their great works, not yet completed, indeed not yet started. A couple of crackers lightly buttered (not *animal* butter) should suffice at this appropriately named eatery for Halaigha, already fairly full to the brim with her one pure orange juice and small bottle of even purer spring water. No need to panic! She always carries a spare - one must never become repredehydrated! Her boyfriend is secretly salivating at the thought of tearing into a giant cheeseburger dripping in animal fat, but he won't. In a relationship one has to compromise.

Where is their child?

## 49

Town was home. Makallee enjoyed the sights and sounds of the City Centre. He'd picked up the 10.45 from Pilot Knob and he'd been barely aware of the 38.75 mile journey to Bummer's Roost on the north bank. The journey was a fly-by and he had done it so often back along. His language still had tinges of his childhood dialect. His white uniform had attracted glances and he had tried to be 'sociable' in those situations in which you don't actually say or do anything. He represented the Services. He regretted wearing the uniform - he was in no mood to be an upstanding and responsible *anything*. He wanted to lounge unnoticed.

He'd watched the grey buildings poorly camouflaged beyond the trees as the train approached the Barracks to his left, but, from the front, the trees were so dense there was no suggestion of its presence. All this was cosmetic. The locations of barracks were common knowledge. Nobody in the City was a danger to security. Those days were long gone. But he mused on these things as the train passed the Barracks at a sedate 60. As he had just returned from an *official* war zone, he thought that maybe he should have elected to spend his furlough in the Barracks for the company, if nothing else. And then it was gone and the 'town' loomed and he felt better. Still nobody returned his calls.

He crossed the footbridge to the Zoo side and headed for one of their favourite pubs. Most holidays were a real drag, one decision after another.

"Hi. What's happening?"

"The usual: parents, brothers, explanations , why am I wasting my life? That sort of thing. Where are you? Oh, great! Must be time for a few beers or twenty. You're not in uniform!? Come on, get a grip, get rid of it! I don't care what you do with it! Throw it in the river! I'll muster the guys and we'll be there toot sweet, sweetie!" The black cloud lifted. He found himself smiling out loud. Who cares about mothers and sisters and girlfriends!

Within the hour, a small avalanche of youthful male voices burst through the main door of the Sunken Road Bar. The regular locals knew immediately who the newcomers were - they recognised a certain degree of discipline amid the raucous excitement. The manager glanced at his bar personnel. Yes, all was well, no problems with this group. It can happen, then *data collected* and warnings issued, but it usually doesn't.

There were multiple huggings of the manly type as if these folks had not seen each other for twenty years, as opposed to barely three days.

"Darling, what is that horrible growth on your back? On the other hand, it is so colourful, I think you're my type!" he said, grabbing a handful of Makallee's right buttock and kneading it.

"Cut it out!" He pushed the hand away and was then assaulted by half a dozen young men in their sexual prime.

He wrestled away. "That's sexual assault!"

"You should be so lucky!" They were all laughing. The people behind the bar were enjoying the light entertainment in a discrete fashion.

"But, what is it? Oh, it's the uniform!" he answered his own question.

"Why, for the love of all that's not holy, did you buy *that*?"

"I wanted a small one."

"You've already got a small one!" from somebody. More laughter.

"Any possibility of a drink?" Makallee said, pretending to be irritated, and being blocked from access to the bar.

"It was the only one in the shop and a backpack leaves my hands free for more important activities." He mimed something which seemed to suggest alcohol and sex.

"Well, your uniform will be safe unless you happen to run into a dishonest ten year old girl who fancies a new school bag." More laughter.

"Oh, you're a man of quips, no doubt about that," said Makallee.

"Oh, I'm a quipist *par excellence*."

The beer started to arrive. Let's take it easy, lads, it's still early.

They drifted rapidly down the winding river of carefree young men with time on their hands and the right to enjoy the fact that they are still alive, on down the river of laughter and alcohol towards the inevitable white water which they would probably survive. They had always survived up to now. They were home from no discernible action at all, but also home from the permanent threat of death at any second, possibly.

Makallee rode the wild current of whoops and yelps, the backslapping, bear hugging, arm wrestling and generalised horseplay; a gathering of gleaming white teeth and well-toned muscular laughter. The old mules, gathered at their usual watering hole, enjoyed the scene and recalled vaguely their youth. A few tales were swapped across the room and all was well with the world for this short intermission. A bunch of the boys were whooping it up.

He thought he was avoiding the rocks. Then his father jumped up before him, arms outstretched. Where was his Dad? Where was he living these days? What actually happened and what is still going on? Something. At his age, Makallee should understand more, he told himself, why doesn't he? Surely something is wrong with his brain - it doesn't work properly! Avoid that rock, swerve! And it was gone. But up sprang his mother. She knows. What? Someone had given him a bottle of strong beer, highly recommended, they'd said. He didn't drink bottled beer, well, not very often. Now he was curious. He dragged himself back from the river, which was becoming too much. What does it say? On the label, what does it say?

"It's only strong cider, matey. It'll put hair on your chest! And, let's face it, you could do with a bit!" The quipist wrapped a hairy arm round his shoulder and pulled him back into the group. He sensed that Makallee was beginning to go under again.

## 50

Tempted to stay, chat and watch the hordes in their giant termite column, Praman dragged himself away. He had catered for his needs, but the temptation of idle talk... Hazardous. Naturally, being a social creature was a gift, but one must apply a sensible discipline. One must discern not to go too far. He had talked with his friend and several strangers, as he had wandered this busy oasis, and now time to return to his hut. These things were about discipline and a muscular mental disposition.

He was aware of the weight of shopping in the bag he'd made, and he was sure its contents were essential. He was wearing his outdoor clothing in this city of covered walkways and tunnels joining hyperstructures. It was several months since he had been outside, or was it years? He had to think. His outdoor clothes did not draw unwanted attention, as his indoor clothes would, if they'd been worn outside his 'hut', in the public domain where he was now wandering. His beard was noticeable enough in this time of the fashionably shaven. But most people assumed that he was an old-fashioned old man. Sometimes, children stood and stared, and the very young were speechless. He would give them a little smile and a wave. Some parents don't like this. Adults can be so foolish, he often thought. Indeed, he thought this most of the time. Sometimes he realised that this was pride, but most of the time it was fair judgment. He often despaired that common sense was not very common.

Paddling the refreshing streams of humanity, he was heading home. Things are a lot calmer and pleasant at this time of day. People are vulnerable, with all their strengths and weaknesses, but fascinating. You must take the good with the bad, he counselled himself, the fascinating with the frustrating. Almost lost under the contradictory demands and drives and urges, a person is trying to survive and do the right thing. You can see it in their faces. He stopped again and looked. He wasn't really convinced that his assertions were true. This did not apply to the mentally unbalanced. By definition, it did not apply to criminals. How many mad people are not diagnosed? How many criminals had not been caught? Some crimes were not acknowledged as crimes; some madness was considered wholesome and merely eccentric, sometimes not even eccentric, but admired. Why did people allow themselves to be subjected to contradictory demands and drives and urges? How could crimes not be recognised for what they are? How could criminals be admired? Move on, head home, things to do, or preferably not to do.

At earlier and later times of the day there are the frantic tides, the rushing to and fro. Praman remembered those days, which he thought would never end, when he was young and his children were young. He remembered his young wife. Sometimes he thought he saw her in the crowd and froze. He studied oncoming faces just in case. There was no need to venture abroad, so to speak, at those times of day, but on occasion, he did in order to recall the experience - a foolish vanity and torture of the soul - to refresh his memory of his young days when he thought he knew what was going on. You can't know if things are kept secret.

He must be home for the Prayer During the Day. He would be combining all three 'sessions' today because of the shopping, the few chats and the twelve-thirty lesson. That was perfectly acceptable: one had to be flexible and adapt-able; dealing kindly with people *is* prayer. He stepped on and off moving pave-ments when available. The 'mile-long' was out of order - an electrical fault - but a speedy walk was good exercise at his age. He had already calculated this because it was out of order on his outward journey - and no carts at this time of day. These few hours each day were set aside for certain kinds of maintenance, night-time for serious maintenance. On the average day, there were no shocks or surprises for Praman. Those days were over. Some *means* of death was inevitable.

Too much morbid musing, he was definitely behind schedule. His life had been knocked out of kilter decades ago. The poison had entered the system and there was no remedy, no developed immunity. It gnawed at his innards. He started to recite the set of prayers silently as he walked. He had learnt them off by heart, like monks of thousands of years ago, when few could read. He thought of the vanity of the written word.

By the time he entered his apartment, he had easily completed the prayers, but it didn't feel right. He logged on, then he lit a candle and opened his book. He read the afternoon prayer out loud and 'slotted in' the three Readings for the day. It was all a bit of a jumble. This is what happens when you get carried away chatting and too much thinking. You rationalise so intently that indeed nothing makes sense at all! You have rationalised yourself out of rationality! He sat still in silence, except for the ticking of clocks. He waited for the silence to penetrate. He waited.

Then the trilling computer sound.

"Hello, old chap!" The irony, the joke, the humour - children are good with humour, if they are clever.

"Hello, *young* chap!" The ten year old boy smiled across the miles. Will it never end?  How can kids end up illiterate after years at school? It may be a jumble out there, but not in here. This is where Praman reigns as Master and the apprentice has arrived. It is just a matter of time and the boy will be Master of his own domain. No more rationalisations, no more shocks, no more devastations - a matter of discipline, a matter of empathy, a matter of posterity.

## 51

Litigious is how Merkan would describe some students. The younger they are the more litigious they can be. That last young man - something to do with lack of heat in his student room and how he was going to sue *everybody* in sight. He shows huge potential. Sense of humour correlates with intelligence. He not only spoke beautifully, but he said interesting things and it all related to decreasing bodily temperature. He was some kind of litterateur in the making and certainly a multi-disciplinarian, which was impressive at his age. He was making connec-tions. Must keep an eye on him and I wonder what his sister is like, Merkan mused, maybe it runs in the family. It is not off the wind you take it! He had long since decided on the nature/nurture debate. There was no debate! And he had long since ceased to pay attention to 'posh talk': it's not what you say, it's what you do. But, of course, saying can be a preliminary to doing. But not always: writing clarifies thinking. Nurture is everything and lack of it a disaster.

Thinking of children, he thought of his own. His body was almost a straight line, as he stretched back on his chair and his legs stretched under the desk. It can be tiring being a professor (emeritus). His shelves looked satisfyingly shiny and he was aware of the smell of roses. Maybe it was the smell of chrysanthemums. He only liked chrysanthemums because of the spelling. He glanced at his screen and a quick count told him fourteen. Not too bad for this morning. He would probably complete the sentence this afternoon. It needed some thinking. He was curious about what the next sentence would be. It was exciting and something to look forward to - it could be anything!

Where are they? He checked the time on the large, white framed, round, wall clock. He fidgeted when he noticed how grey the top surface of the white frame was. Wives can improve one's sensitivity to environmental factors, he mused, but he would have preferred to attend a lecture on the subject and skip the practical experience of a lifetime. It would have been more efficient. A bit like that next sentence, his children could be anything and anywhere. Were they still talking to him? He couldn't remember the state of play. Things can change rapidly. One minute it's sunshine, the next minute it's lashing down and thunder on the way. Sometimes it's just thunder, not even a flash of lightning. He tried to think back. He could ring his wife, but no real point. She would only mock his poor memory. There were certainly four of them - or is it five? - and so many combinations possible. Was there a row the last time, or was that the time before? Something to do with 'lifestyle choices' was it? Some such nonsense. And boyfriends and girlfriends - there is such a rapid turnover of these creatures. It is like being in charge of a class of children with half the class absent and you still haven't learnt their names. And then when they attend school they've changed their names! His children had ruined his Address Book: crossings out, names, addresses, telephone numbers, he couldn't keep up. Ah good, it's nobody's birthday this month.

How had things become so difficult? It was like conducting a collection of divas of both sexes. Ahm, well, something like that. He mustn't say that sentence out loud... Oh, he couldn't be bothered thinking about his children. They made him feel tired. He wasn't a lion tamer and that's all that's to it! And he and his wife deserved some peace and quiet at their age. All this hassle, it's ridiculous! Although his wife seemed to deal with it better than him. They just seemed to remain so young for so long these days. He couldn't remember this applying to himself when he was their ages. Was he like that? He couldn't remember his parents or his wife's parents complaining about either of them in these terms. Has youth changed? Have they got everything too soft, everything handed to them on a plate?

The fact he couldn't stop worrying about them probably goes back to when they were children, when 'worrying' was natural. He could see them now running around playing together, and when they stood still they were like doorsteps, as his mother used to say. He had never thought of himself as a proud parent. That was one of those foolish things that other people say. It was a sort of given, just assumed, about other people concerning their children. Those parents were always *so* proud. It hadn't made sense at all. If you apply your common sense, everything will work out just fine. What is there to be proud about? The word had always annoyed him and he had tried to ignore its use in that context.

He could feel himself drifting towards a collision with nostalgia. If it happens it will be quick, but somewhat painful. Change the subject. Where could they be at this time of day? Their jobs were all so different and not entirely *regular* jobs. And they were all so different. They weren't regular people, but then that's the way it is: everybody's different. You're supposed to help your children realise their potential, which means they are all going to be different. This is obvious. Indeed, a job well done. He and his wife could be proud of themselves! And let the children sort themselves out. So, when is this going to happen?

In a flash, he saw them when they were children, probably inspired by that photograph of them with the one bicycle. Now, whose bicycle was it? When they were young, they were perfect: they behaved perfectly, they talked perfectly, and they had bicycles! In his next life Merkan would have a bicycle and then his childhood would be perfect.

## 52

The lifelong office and party girl, Gelasia (only sixty), loves holidays and her chubby husband. You become the person you marry if you're not careful. Apparently, this is called 'compromise', i.e. the happy couple became one in order to survive. And this being joined together in holy matrimony only takes forty years. Tweedledum and Tweedledee will be happy until death, never quite deciding which is which or whom is who or who is whom.

It has been a morning of pomp and circumstance, sometimes known as work, and keeping things in alphabetical order. If we didn't use alphabets, we'd use numbers, sometimes both. But we'll never run out of applied alphabets and so Gelasia will never run out of work (she imagines), just like she'll never run out of places to go. Next year our intrepid explorers have applied for Harambee City. 'No place is too far' is their motto and their relatives' motto: 'any place is not far enough'. So everyone agrees, which is the main thing! Democracy depends on the consensus of the majority and Gelasia is nothing if not a democrat. Although, in terms of democracy and the majority, there are certain criteria which must be satisfied. Gelasia has no truck with such finer points, things to do with sanity and morality, for example; and a slight touch of criminality is always good for a laugh. If you disagreed with her, there would be a torrent of good humour.

She has been everywhere in the City, a few days here, a few days there, staying with friends, staying in B&B's and hotels, anywhere to get away from the *nothing* of home life, her comfortable home, her comfortable life. Every weekend, away. She and her husband, the forever happy couple, have been on all the safaris, which, as noted, can be dangerous-to-extremely dangerous. Any trip outside the City carries significant risk, but if you adhere to the rules and the advice of expert leaders, you will be safe. There are so few accidents that, statistically, safaris are no more dangerous than crossing the road. (Although it has been pointed out that whilst crossing the road you can't be carried away by some hideous beast and fed to its young).

If you have little on your mind, then you'll be bored. If you have minimal responsibilities and little on your mind, then you'll go on holiday. If you are your own vocation, then you will vacation frequently. But, naturally, Gelasia has paid.

Decades of going from one organisation to another, bored with the previous job, trying to find variety, trying to avoid the same boring people, she has travelled, across the City, across its institutions, a slow and steady rise up the hierarchies, which are, really, all the same hierarchy, of the same people, she arrived almost where she started. Three steps forward, two steps back, wandering in circles, she has arrived at the beginning: unemployable. She appears unaware of her predicament, but has a vague feeling her time is running out. For once, she's right! Her husband has played the same game. Sometimes he leads, but mostly he follows, so long as it's not inconvenient, depending on the context. It's not always about work. They've convinced themselves that there is more to life than work. Yes, there is - there are holidays. There are also *campaigns*.

Lifelong members of the P.P.P. (the Proles Political Party), thanks to both sets of parents and grandparents, as it tends to be, they have campaigned for the *usual* and nothing changes. A tweak here, a tweak there brings a modicum of improvement, but hardly noticeable. The Laws already exist and simply have to be applied. There are serious consequences for ignoring the Law. But it is fair enough that one remains vigilant and being positively involved facilitates vigilance. No one would object to this attitude. On the other hand... well, these two *blobby* creatures have a certain *history*, a certain reputation, a certain set of attitudes which are not quite P.P.P. Of course few people have much to do with the minority Select P.P., but it helps to have an opposition. S.P.P. people exist, so one puts up with them. Sometimes they say something interesting, but this is rare. Members of the S.P.P. are the kind of persons *picked up* for anti-social behaviour and inciting something unpleasant. A few weeks' therapy is usually enough to help them see the errors of their ways. But they do tend to  recidivism. They talk a lot about law and order, falling standards, the need for good manners and correct grammar. Many of their pronouncements start with the word 'clearly'.

Clearly, Gelasia (a P.P.P., as noted) is presently, she and her husband take turns, the Chairperson of the local branch of the Campaign for Real Alcohol-Filled Potatoes. Presently, the product in question is not real on either count, but is very popular amongst consenting adults. Gelasia has been campaigning for forty years to rid the world of the phoney, gassy product being mass-produced in factories. Such campaigners consider it a conspiracy against the poor perpetrated by members of the S.P.P.

Thus, Gelasia is a mature and experienced organiser, as well as a seasoned campaigner on behalf of the poor and downtrodden at home and abroad. But mainly she campaigns on behalf of herself and makes people laugh whether they like it or not. Her husband supports her in every way. They mirror each other.

Gelasia is looking forward to lunch at the pub, and she'll probably have one or two A-Spuds (the brand name). She can't remember exactly why her husband took early retirement; something to do with ill-health? She'll catch up with him this evening. In the meantime, people to see and to impress with her ready wit. Her family? They are around somewhere. They are *difficult* people, especially her older brother. Her sister is a nuisance too, now she thinks of it. The whole lot of them more to be pitied than laughed at!

"Tabby, where are you?" Straight to the point as usual, like living with a sergeant-major or someone planning to invade a country.

"On the bus, darling?" Better add 'darling' to keep her calm. He really didn't like having private conversations in a public place. You have to be some kind of megalomaniac to enjoy the inevitable attention.

"Oh, you're such a silly! It's the 16$^{th}$, not the 6$^{th}$. I'm reading the letter on the notice-board right now *beside the calendar.*"

His heart sank, twice. He glanced out the window and watched his freedom disappearing in reverse. Have to return. Indeed, he'd be stopped at the East Gate. Central Computer would question his reason for leaving the City. His ageing memory? He'd laugh it off. Another ten days to his Community Service. He chuckled to himself: if they find out he's becoming senile...

"Okay. I understand." He was trying to be authoritative and tactful in a public bus. Several extremely taboo expressions came to mind, but he controlled his tongue. He was naturally calm, regardless of rules and regulations, codes of conduct, that sort of thing, expected of a responsible citizen. Of course Tabatante was responsible at his age. He had learnt from his mistakes; he was still paying the penalties. Apart from his building skills, he was also above average for the intensity and longevity of his misspent youth. That's what he'd like to think.

"Okay, darling, in the circumstances," suggesting that the circumstances must be really quite interesting. "I'll just have a bit of a wander and enjoy some fresh air, then home." He was sure that that sounded just fine, casual. She understood, although he was sure she'd tutted. Why would that bother her? Women...

He requested a 'stop' and alighted opposite 'Writers Block' two or three miles city-side of Parliament buildings. He had no intention of crossing the road and having some light refreshments in *those* cafés. Those places were designed to drive a sane person mad. All that theorising by the terminally ridiculous was enough to raise his blood pressure even higher. He fancied a drink, one of those feelings which tried to convince him that he was still young. But he was far too old and too sensible to be tempted back to the joys of alcohol and the joys of pretend youth. His wife had ensured that he had learnt to be sensible. It was a compromise, his. She'd nagged, eh, counselled him on every occasion until he had learnt to behave properly. Thus, the joys of marrying a younger woman. He had weighed up the pros and cons and here he was, miles from home and decades from his previous wife and his former self. Indeed, his former self was younger than his children, a sobering thought. He checked his watch and emitted possibly a sigh. But probably home by lunch. No point worrying about a waste of time at his age. Might as well waste the rest of it!

He crossed the road at a steady shuffle, his belly leading the way and impressing oncoming motorists. Yes, enjoy the view - it has taken years to achieve that - and envy the muscle control. Naturally, his wife hadn't ironed his shirt properly. He enjoyed the attention. He imagined what he would say to explain his present impressive condition, something he'd said many times. The truth is he ironed his own shirts. You can't expect a woman to iron a shirt. They're not capable of the necessary commitment, they haven't bought into the project, they haven't taken *ownership*. Thinking is frequently self-entertainment, to be enjoyed rather than endured, and never to be taken seriously. Several stages of development are necessary before a thought can be taken seriously. Thus, in a state of reflective good humour, having ignored the sigh, an irrelevant physiological response, he crossed the six lanes safely. He'd been some entertainment! Then he lurched in the forward direction.

Four minutes and twenty-three seconds until the next 'Speedo'. See! Everything works out. He was the only person at the bus stop - the time of day. Then he noticed a young man across the road. He almost called, but there was something about his walk. He slipped on his glasses and yes, he was right, it wasn't him. He thought it was his youngest son through the blur of old age and traffic because of the briefcase and the air of confidence, but his head isn't quite right. His son's head faces the other way. Inwards. He is obnoxiously self-obsessed. One thought was leading to another when the Speedo arrived.

Feeling light-hearted, these buses, appropriately nicknamed, remind him of the funfair. Tabantate wanted to be the driver! But these buses don't have drivers; so he'd have to settle for sitting at the front, but no empty seats. Oh well. And then whoosh! If he'd understood G-forces, then he'd have known that he'd just experienced a few.

His son, and the other kids, who are no longer kids - where exactly are they? They are probably doing well. They usually are, but they're beginning to disappear; or, more likely, he's beginning to disappear. This has been going on for some time. When did they last get together? When they do, it's appalling! And his grandchildren - they must all be a lot bigger and unrecognisable. Why does this happen? Is it the coming of his second wife? Hmm, rephrase, he smirked. Is it the *advent* of his second wife? Her arrival caused chaos. He didn't like to think about that. He couldn't do anything right back then. It wasn't his fault. But his wife, who became his ex-wife, was just awful! She was terrible all along. Surely she must take most of the blame. These thoughts cut through him like a knife as he flew through the streets towards the City Centre.

Must make a few 'phone calls when I get home, he thought. He hated making 'phone calls. Telephones are totally unnatural.

## 54

His lecture was impressive and his students suitably mesmerised. He'd learnt to keep it down to their level. He was handed three essays and had looked appropriately cheerful. He'd suggested, very subtly, that other areas of the curriculum, taught by his colleagues, needed more work. Thus, most of his students presented no essays. You have to use your brain if you work at a university. Essays: the same boring stuff from tedious little people. They're so *ignorant*. He would prefer end of course three-hour papers. This meant a week of marking short, scribbled and badly expressed essays. These were easy to assess and, quite frankly, who cares about the results? Nobody. These people were dross. Give them their degrees and get rid of them, prior to his long summer of relaxed musing, socialising and self-promoting. He had his book to think about. He'd been 'teaching' for ten years and no candidates for higher degrees. He'd had keen students, but it's easy to spot them - making the usual noises from early on - and, therefore, easy to *redirect*, preferably out of the University all together! They were a waste of space and wasting his time. Let some other misguided masochist supervise their puny efforts.

Lunch loomed. Deal with a few of these silly e-mails and then quietly slip away. Have a walk, get some air and then head home. No lectures for the rest of the week and the two tutorials over and done with. The Faculty Meeting had been the usual monthly entertainment, if you like farce, but everybody knew the score, except for the usual pushy people with their hobby horses and bees in their bonnets. They were so predictable. Just take a deep breath, bite the bullet, nod sagely, smile knowingly - like visiting the dentist, it must be done, the discomfort doesn't last long. Talk about loquacious! Something about improving our approach, developing the curriculum and being more student-centred. What's all that about! Nonsense. The knowledge exists, let the dummies get it into their thick skulls, which is *their* responsibility, and move on, preferably *out,* and as soon as possible. Demand more independent learning and shorten the terms! What about more computer-marked assignments? An excellent idea! But never accepted. Mustn't push it - his seniors might get the wrong idea. The Government also had a say, of course, certain Acts of Parliament, Minister for Education, and that kind of malarkey, perpetrated by the dimwits in charge.

Therefore, the working week is over by day two lunchtime - not bad for a full-time job. Mosimenadue stretched and yawned. Being kind and patient could be exhausting, but he was used to it. Give it another half hour, then march towards his next battle: a high class restaurant for a spot of lunch. There was a waitress he had his eye on. But just some light entertainment. Don't get involved with waitresses. They might get ideas above their station. Stick to mouthy, self-obsessed post-grads. Easy pickings for the odd periods of drought. But not a drought, of course, more a period of self-imposed exercises at the gym - good for your cardiovascular system - or a series of easy victories in the regular skirmishes in the Battle of the Sexes. Not for the first time in history, the battle was turning into a full-scale war. There would be casualties. Such is life.

Thus he mused, Mosimanadue the Conqueror. When he was feeling good, he was feeling very good. One of the great problems, perpetrated by the good, is the 'delivery' of too much positive reinforcement. Mosi the Magnificent had barely experienced an adverse criticism his entire life. When they came, criticisms, they were obviously caused by personal jealousy and such darts had to be borne. One must ignore and persevere. Women easily become distraught and over-emotional - best to soft-talk them and quietly depart. They'll get over it. He was well used to hours of screaming and shouting the house down, not his behaviour, hers. He was well trained in the art of war. He had spent so much time helpless and cowering. He'd learnt to smile, cajole, to duck and dive these emotional onslaughts. They were to be expected.

At times he was being attacked from all sides. It was never-ending, even in his dreams. And those letters! What can one say? Suddenly, out of the blue, from his siblings, his parents, just when the blitzkrieg had stopped, the campaign had calmed, when negotiations had progressed, when peace had reigned, an unintended (?) cross word, a Freudian slip (?), and the bombs rained down! The campaign was not even co-ordinated, although it seemed to be. It seemed as if all the bombs were timed to explode according to a pre-planned schedule, some simultaneously, others in rapid succession. Sometimes it was horribly mystical and for a split second he believed in the existence of the Devil.

"Hi, Mum," he was suddenly very hungry, "didn't expect a call, nice to hear from you." He scanned his office instinctively, checking and rechecking: all in place.

"Ahm, I'm not sure I can make it. I'll just check my diary, a bit inundated this week. We've already had one meeting." He tapped his closed diary. Must get it over with.

"What about next week? Wednesday would be good for me. This Friday evening? Is he? Oh, of course, slipped my mind - a lot of marking recently. Yes, fine, about eight then? Okay, looking forward to seeing everybody. Yeah, me too. Love you."

Suddenly his office seemed smaller; had to get out, fresh air and food. He scraped with his finger nail at the tiny line of grime which had accumulated in the groove below the 3-6-9-hash buttons on his telephone. He hadn't noticed that disgusting muck before. Indeed, there were lines of disgusting filth all over his telephone. And countless flecks of dust on his laptop. And his desk... fluff on his jacket... a thread on his trousers... dust on his shoes...

## 55

"I know everything."

Radmilla could have said that, but she didn't. She absorbs facts like a sponge absorbs water; she grasps a situation quickly, sometimes as fast as lightning. She has a very peculiar sense of humour, which is the only peculiar thing about her. Except for her 'funny voices' - they're not very funny. She has absorbed the contents of the updated file in the last few intense office hours, with the help of cups of decaf. It's all a bit shocking.

"I've got it clear in my mind," is what she actually says. "I presume you want me to cover the legal angles. Okay, I'll make the recheck calls, but I'm confident it's all been covered. I'll get back to you as soon as possible, hopefully within the hour. I presume the others have been alerted - they know this has been initiated. Right, talk to you later. "

She looked through the glass wall that fronted her office. She could see across the heads of the open-plan department in her charge. Sometimes she felt like a judge surveying her court, but she didn't have that attitude - she was a senior administrator. Her job was to co-ordinate the collection and analysis of all kinds of data important to the Government and the Legal System. The case in question was solely of a legal nature. Thankfully, there is no hint of a Government scandal, a very rare event for obvious reasons.

She made the telephone calls, systematically ticking off the list she'd compiled. She knew some of the numbers by heart. She had to leave a few messages and then received 'acknowledgements of receipt'. She flicked through the file once more, looking at photographs and re-reading some statements. She'd been alive for too long to be shocked. Her probationary first assistant had described it as *just awful*. He was clever, but melodramatic, overly dramatic - he enjoyed the drama. She had noted this as a 'personality fault'. She imagined his histrionics if he read *that* file. He would be informed in due course anyhow. At that moment he passed her window, raised a questioning eyebrow and she smiled a "No, you're not required, pass on!"

She was disgusted that some people loved other people's misery. The people in this file were real people and real freaks! Be still, oh beating heart, remain professional, she counselled herself.

She thought about her family, the children, her siblings, her late parents, even her ex-husband. He wondered what people were really like. How can you ever know what a person is really like? She pondered on her latest lover, not that there had been many of them, you could count them all on one hand, and she felt so sorry for him. He'd tried so hard and things had gone so badly. How does that happen? She flicked through the file again and stayed on one smiling photograph. *That's* how things go badly wrong. How could anybody see behind that smile? The evidence seemed airtight, but she was not part of the legal process, so she was welcome to her opinion in silence. She checked her watch. Almost lunchtime.

Project 14/32256L is on schedule and looking pretty good. Radmilla is experienced enough to be able judge these things accurately, this case being Parliament-based and may eventually become law or effect international law; to do with courtship behaviour in specifically named ancient and modern cultures. This sounds anthropological and something of an historical or sociological matter, but, in fact, is highly relevant and at this time highly confidential. It will eventually enter the public domain, as one would expect, but not yet. On the other hand, 13/22524D had encountered certain difficulties and has been dragging on. Ask the right questions and you will get the right answers. This dictum has always been true. Radmilla is excellent at producing the right questions when everybody else is well and truly stuck! The research involves infant mortality around the world and has ground to a halt again - there are so many variables as yesterday's review uncovered. When people are very good at working with other people, there is always something of the therapist about them. Radmilla had managed to get the researcher *disentangled* and focused again. Radmilla was watching her at this very moment. You can tell when someone is happy in their work. But be careful of the word 'happy', she reminded herself. Things *look* good. She glanced down at the file, not realising that her hand had been flat on the file throughout these few musings. Yes, things can look very good, but things are rarely what they appear.

There were the hungry and coffee gurgling sounds from her stomach and she thought of her family. Maybe it was something to do with those meals together. Throughout her childhood they had always gathered (just about!) for a hurried breakfast, although her father had usually already left for work, but always the family gathered for their civilised evening meal. The children had grown up and drifted away, but this tradition had continued. For some years Radmilla had not recognised it as a tradition - it was just normal - until she began to notice how other people behaved. It was all so uncouth! she had concluded. She was quite certain after all these years that it was definitely not a good thing.

She imagined her family and they appeared like a living portrait gallery: the children, her siblings and other members of the family scattered all over the City, two of them in two different distant Cities on temporary research visas, the 'news' of their lives being a regular 'admin job' outside working hours. This evening at least an hour of 'catch up' conversations. It was unplanned and inevitable: *somebody* was bound to call. For a few moments she despaired at the state of other people's lives, the cruelty and isolation caused deliberately. She placed the file in her top drawer and locked it.

We haven't had a serial killer for decades, indeed, centuries. We are top of the league for peace. This standing amounts to a whole collection of statistics of violent deaths and includes accidental deaths of the physically intrusive type, like being sawn in half by accident or falling headlong into a cauldron of boiling oil: human error and loss of concentration can have fatal consequences. Serial killers? Yes, the child, innocent though he be, it really is a matter of nurture versus no nurture, that old chestnut. You don't have to kill in order to destroy. You can do it very quietly, one scrap of personality at a time screwed up and discretely discarded. By the time the kid is twelve, he is ready for anything.

Damodural the Delightful had managed to gobble down a giant cheeseburger when Miss Delicious had disappeared into the Ladies. He knew she'd be a long time. On her return and departure - she was always busy - she was sure she could smell something animal in his kiss goodbye for now. She put it down to his personal manliness. Then she had this horrible feeling of imminent death and gave him an especially enthusiastic hug, her short-term investment. At least his stomach had stopped gurgling. She'd told him that a light salad would do him good. She would eat later. She couldn't quite see his face because his head was a blaze of sun, just like a halo. And off she went, muttering something about the kid and loads to do. They would catch up later and have a lovely evening of arty talk and one's struggle, smelly nappies, slow development being a sure sign of creativity, food as passé indulgence, and their involvement in the Campaign for Special Needs for Children. What do we want? Special Needs! When do we want them? Now! That sort of thing. Damodural was the Chair of the local Branch, obviously on his way to national level. He was just *so* clever and, therefore, so was she. The child would watch them, the giant planets, orbiting. There was always that droning sound. They seemed to be taking turns. He'd been wondering about the drone from way back In the warm darkness. He felt a keen aloneness, a phantom limb.

The afternoon lay comfortably ahead, a time to relax in the sun and just enough money for another coffee. These outdoor cafes were perfect, mused our literary genius.

Then he remembered the letter. He didn't really know why he'd taken it with him. He might re-read it on his own undisturbed. He took another sip and felt the well-packed envelope inside his jacket to convince himself that it was still there. The sheets were stapled, neatly folded and carefully squeezed into the envelope. He'd had difficulty replacing it himself.

Was this the place to read it? He looked around. People were engrossed in their lunchtime snacks and conversations. One man seemed to be enjoying his soup, rolls and newspaper. He was a neat and dapper individual in middle age, younger than Damodural. He was wearing a gold wedding ring. A feeling of envy washed over Dam, something to do with marriage and stability. Things could have been different. Nothing had quite worked out and now things were much worse. No point dwelling on what might have been. This place was spacious and nobody was paying attention to him. For once it suited him.

He scanned through the many pages to remind himself of its contents. He guessed it was several thousand words and the strangest letter he'd ever read. He really didn't know how to deal with it. It was very verbal and to the point, but there were many points. The vocabulary was impressive and the text flowed like a somewhat polluted river. It was alive! It was alive with anger. The writer was enraged and for some time. "For forty years I was wearied of these people." It's weird what comes to mind. Damodural tried to pick out the salient points and mark them with a pencil. He really shouldn't deface the letter. If even half of it were true, then it was bad. Either it was a group assassination or a group assessment. Both. For the first time he was worried - maybe he didn't know what he was dealing with after all. It wouldn't be the first he had been tricked. He gazed into the distance. When he returned from his reverie, he was staring at the man with the wedding ring.

The place was filling up with the second wave of lunchtime customers. He was being nudged inadvertently by passers-by because he was big. There was no point staying here. Things had taken a nasty turn in his thinking. He was no longer relaxed. He was worried about his blood pressure. He had enough problems already - certain emotional involvements suddenly out of the blue. Things had looked brilliantly good and had then taken a terrifying nosedive. Still trying to recover from those events, the letter had arrived. Sometimes life starts to spiral out of control. But there is always more to it than that: people are deliberately *doing* things. He had no belief whatsoever in the concept of luck. Indeed, the letter in its very essence, in its strange format, confirmed his own view of the world. Almost shockingly, he found himself on the same wavelength as the writer, which, in places, was brutal. The whole thing was unnerving. There was some kind of battle going on. The combatants were obvious enough, but the cause was vague and unstated, or never admitted, and the aims and objectives could not be discerned by him. Certainly, this must not be avoided because it is all too upsetting, although in a cowardly way it would have been easier to turn down the invitation to read the letter again and give his opinion. This was all too close to the bone. He had unavoidably been drawn in.

## 57

A morning of alpha-chat, dominance-smiling and pathosociobility added colour to Jardena's cheeks already sensitively coloured to coordinate with her subtly colourful existence. A pocketful of hard credits and a small wad of cheques produced a comfortable drive home via her local bank where her gleaming teeth were well known. No bank transfers, it was simply this way, and gave her huge satisfaction. She wanted to see the whites of their eyes, she wanted to handle and count the stuff herself - the best way to keep track of things. Lodge the cheques and deal with the credits in the usual way, under the mattress. Anyhow, you needed credits to live your everyday life, nothing questionable about that. She didn't mind queuing in the bank and allowing people to admire her finery. Even at her age men of all ages looked, although she still found the grey baldies disturbing. And there were no 'difficulties' this morning: they just paid up. Excellent. Their personal problems were none of her business. She had her own problems. Would she get sympathy from any of those lowlifes? No. And that's the way it is and one has to accept the facts. The real facts of life can be far more downright devastating than all that biological stuff which is neither here nor there once you get used to it. She'd tried to pass this message on to her children and she'd been very successful. Her husbands had made no effort. They'd been completely useless on this or any other front. Men were only good for one thing: mindless productivity.

She had every intention of calling into the shop and then changed her mind. Leave it - let her spondulicks machine, Mr Gormless, get on with it. All staff at work today, and all was well with the world on this sunny afternoon. She checked her watch. Yes, just gone noon, so home sweet home.

A tiny red light flashed on her dashboard. Now, what are these funny little creatures up to? she thought to herself, always checking something, these nano nuisances. She tended to personify Central Computer. It had been a very long time since she even received a caution, and only once by a Human Operator, and that was back in her drunken youth! She was far too careful. But she was never quite comfortable knowing that she was being monitored, even if it were by an inanimate object or, indeed, several million inanimate objects. What are they up to? Why the sudden interest? She reflected on a few possibilities. Most people did, there was nothing abnormal about curiosity. It was obviously a random data collecting exercise. A typical waste of time, this constant collecting of data. What was the point? When they'd been needed, they were nowhere to be seen. No flashing lights in those days. The whole City would have turned red if the facts had got out! She suppressed those thoughts in an instant. The red light had stopped her happy rent collecting happy thoughts. She was returned to her own strange reality.

Her reality? It was no one else's, not even her sister's. She had to make those calls when she got home. Don't put it off. Her silly sister had never grown up, her arrogant children all over the place and she still a giggly, nonsensical school girl. She had to telephone her and then she could do *her* share of phoning to help arrange one of those wonderful family get-togethers - the weekend had been mentioned. She hardened at the very thought: if she crashed the car now, then she couldn't attend because she'd be in hospital! It'll just be the usual nightmare. All that clever-clever wordplay and smart alec competitiveness and alcohol flowing... What a total waste of time and energy, not to mention the cost. It was like distributing alms to the poor. It was the same every time. All that fancy talk, all that intellectualising, all that empty chatter, all that hot air - it was like a gathering of angry, hysterical tits hopping from one posturing branch to another and these people didn't have two credits to rub together and barely a job! They drove her crazy; quite frankly, they made her skin crawl. How they hadn't been prosecuted for something or other was beyond her. Surely they were breaking the law. Her sister living on Welfare all her life!

She parked outside her large house. She inhaled the pleasure of her fine property. Rare in the City, a private garden. It was considered *historical* and eccentric. It should be a tourist attraction. This area of houses and gardens was certainly regularly visited by groups of children on their educational day trips, and so it should be. One had to keep one's garden up to standard and in all aspects of her life Jardena was above standard.

"Yes, I got a message this morning. The weekend would be convenient for all concerned and he is short of time. Sometime next week would be pushing it. Let's make it Friday and get it over with. No, yes, okay, well, you know what I mean. I have to make a few other calls. Can you get on to your lot? Probably. Yes, I'm sure there are messages flying all over the place, but can you sort out your kids? Yes, I *know*. I know they're far from kids, but try not to be difficult... How are you? You *will* deal with it? Good. So: how are you? Everything okay? Oh dear, that's a shame, but I'm sure it will work out. Be patient. He's always been difficult..."

At the end of the call Jardena felt drained, she felt she'd run a marathon. She'd been pacing about and now she just had to sit down. She felt that the life had been sucked out of her, and that was only fifteen minutes. That sister of hers! She never changes. How do people put up with her?

## 58

Sleeping three times in one morning had produced a cerebral disaster. Purvanos was more confused and exhausted now than he'd been at 3 a.m. Indeed, if he hadn't gone to bed at all, he'd probably feel much better now. He'd had such a busy morning although none of it necessary. In fact, he needn't have got out of bed at all. In the meantime, he had been all over the place and much of it whilst asleep!

He walked into the apartment greatly relieved to be home and carrying a bottle of milk only to remember he'd forgotten the eggs. The car had taken him to the shop, but somehow had misunderstood his next instruction. Purvanos woke up perfectly parked and facing a huge wall. For a split second he thought he'd been abducted by aliens. It was one of those mornings. The car informed him politely that they were now situated north of the East River City Gate. The wall towered above him and Purvanos wondered about the number or bricks... To his right, a mile away, the Gate and, to his rear, Parliament Buildings. He had poked at his itchy right ear and scratched his right eyelid. When agitated, he started to itch and the itch travelled. It all seemed in the misty past. He put the milk in the refrigerator and noted the one egg. He also noted that his wife was out. Good. Maybe she could buy some eggs. One must remain calm in difficult circumstances.

Dictanotes flew back and forth, something about gatherings here and there, something about meetings, things about bits and bobs and eggs. Notes and conversations seem to reproduce themselves by some kind of exponential principle, something mathematical on a graph never drawn, busier now than when he worked full-time. What does this mean? Thought he might contact Central Computer and request one of their Summaries, but shelved that idea, applying his old adage "What they won't know won't trouble them" together with "Never give bureaucrats too much information because they may become confused". He should know. Avoid anything causing inconvenience. Purvanos refused to undertake anything that was likely to inconvenience him, a lifelong principle.

A social evening this weekend? What was that again? A console message. He went back to the console and flicked through the messages in its memory. Ah. He stood like a heavy statue, slightly hunched, podgy hands on hips, somewhat mesmerised by the message displayed on the wall console. He liked the green light and that's all he liked about the message. He seemed to hope it would some-how change, another message would superimpose itself, a friendlier message, a message cancelling the invitation. Waking up at the City Wall miles from home was quite pleasant after all. You never know what's round the corner. Best not to turn the corner. For a few seconds he missed the predictable routine of work. No avoiding this. It won't be that bad: a few drinks and lots of idle chat. Everybody will be there. He scanned through the 'everybody' in his mind. He wondered where his wife was. Had she already seen this and was in the process of stowing away on an aeroplane bound for a distant country? But she positively liked this sort of thing. Weird or what? Women.

He turned towards the kitchen. You could easily imagine a grizzly bear covered from head to foot in brown hair after an excellent meal of salmon: heavy-laden. Then he turned back. Should he send a message to his wife? So many media to choose from: via the console? But what for? Something to do with *comfort*? For goodness' sake! Go to the kitchen and eat. The bear was starving.

What is it with these people? He mused to himself whilst constructing and then deconstructing a generous cheese sandwich. His own family was bad enough, luckily most of them were dead, but this shower left him speechless, mainly because he couldn't get a word in! Everybody present would be overwhelmed by *their* education, especially them. It was always one massive, unrelenting free-for-all to find out who's the cleverest. Who cares? They do. And they don't know a thing that's important, important issues, world politics, economics... He decided to console himself with another cheese sandwich. This time throw in some lettuce and tomato to counterbalance cholesterol. Everything was a chore since he retired, even eating. His wife said he'd finally become a glutton, although no such advice from Central Computer. She'd always been self-opinionated, that woman, always the same.

"We can discuss it when you get home," he was addressing his wife on videocall. "How are the children, same as ever, I suppose?"

"Right on the button - no news is extremely good news in this case. She has the usual fuse already lit. I don't think it ever goes out. There is always something tearing away at her insides. It is so tiring." And you fan the flames, he was thinking.

"It'll be on Friday. Is it Friday?" She nodded in confirmation. He had received a text message.

"I think your memory is going!" she laughed heartily. He thought she was putting on weight, or is it a faulty transmission, or are his eyes still out of focus?

"I hope it's completely gone by Saturday!"

"Oh, don't exaggerate!"

"Yeah, okay, but it's different for you. You kinda enjoy the chaos. I get quite stressed trying to dodge the verbal bullets. And there's always an *explosion*! Considering the sort of people they think they are, they're extremely uncivilised."

"I know. It's all so predictable! And we've discussed it a hundred times. Nothing to be done. But it's a laugh!"

"That's because you have a perverse sense of humour." He wasn't joking.

"Okay. Gotta go. See you later. We'll have a chat to calm your nerves."

"Right, we'll have a chinwag. Oh, and don't forget the eggs!"

"I won't! You and your eggs!"

"They're not *my* eggs!" She's definitely putting on weight.

59

In her grey business attire and white open necked shirt, Lakota lounged at her desk, the silver chain peeped discretely at her throat; the heavy, gold watch and loose bracelet her trinity of accessories. The meeting had chipped away at her consciousness, but barely penetrating, the reason she took notes; looking wise, nobody would bother her. She got through the hour without saying a word, although alert enough. It is sensible to keep tabs on them: know the enemy. Her childhood had been trillions of words thrown in her face. She was used to it, better qualified than the average. It was handy to tell when people are lying. She was highly experienced, so trust nobody. She was wrong on both counts.

She fancied a cigarette, but it's too much trouble. She would have to go to that disgusting smoking room, and so many angles to cover, so many recriminations to expect. Such behaviour would come under the generic term 'liberties' because she wasn't senior enough to absent herself. Then, of course, the smoking room was a dead giveaway of her 'antisocial behaviour'. Addiction was frowned upon in the legal profession. If all the illegal legals were rounded up... She chuckled and swung round to look out the large window. No, they weren't that bad. They just had a few questionable hobbies like everybody else. Everybody?

The City stretched into the distance, the same scene for the last two years, a collection of huge boxes containing millions of windows. Sometimes she fantasised that she were a window cleaner and then she wouldn't have these *snide* comments to put up with and this stigma. She would definitely be *outside* the system and getting plenty of fresh air! Way below her, people were experiencing the City's very own atmosphere. She wondered about their weather; hers, enclosed, was a fine summer's day. Her watch flashed in the sun. Stop pretending to read notes, she chided herself, and do some work! Nearly lunch.

Footfall! She swung round casually and closed the file she hadn't been reading. Her ear had attuned itself to that floor material. Being aware is plain sensible. She had learnt that long ago. Oh, it's that creepy little... person. He stopped abruptly, the creepy little person, indicated that he had absentmindedly taken the wrong, turning just as she looked up from her work and gave him a welcoming smile. He reciprocated and turned on his heal.

She was lucky to be placed out of sight and almost out of mind. Her intelligence and rank had led to this little niche in the open office. She was a shirker of a worker at times, but always got the work done. So what was the creepy little person up to? He was definitely up to something. Men can be such irritants! They are always working on some scheme and plotting some ridiculous move. Why don't they just get on with the job and earn promotions the honest way? Men are a bit like gnats on a summer's evening. On the other hand, let's face it, some women are just as bad, but different. Talking of evenings, some kind of evening 'do' coming up. Not this evening's shindig. That one has been well engraved on her brain. She recalled the other text message. If it's not one nightmare, it's another. Now she knew why she had repressed the memory. Don't even think about it, enjoy this evening.

Who was that girl this morning? Samantha. She said she would come this evening. No pun intended. She is certainly beautiful, one of those classic beauties, although Lakota didn't really understand the expression, but she certainly knew what she liked. Something to look forward to then, and, if not, then there might be something else to look forward to, she told herself.

Then her siblings came to mind. Did they all receive that letter? She could hardly forget it, but she hadn't had time to read it properly. They all wanted to talk, as usual, but she wanted to reread it first. It was just so weird and abusive.

What was he on about? Get over it!

Thoughts flew through her mind, the long-running saga, scene after endless scene, a web diagram of unhappiness and emotional brutality. There was no one to talk to. How could that be true in this day and age? In order to talk about something, you have to be able to describe it. Where does one begin? This was monstrous and baffling, everybody furious at everybody else. The others are no clearer on this subject than she is and, therefore, this is nothing to do with intelligence. There had been *10,000* clever discussions, emotional outbursts, rivers of tears, and blazing rows and... no progress at all. This had gone on for years, her whole life! How long had it been going on? It is some kind of unkillable virus: when you think things are under control, it springs up from nowhere and explodes in your face! It's back again.

"You seem deep in thought." She managed to control her shock and physiologically-based urge to spring up and explode in his face.

"Oh, yes, miles away. What can I do for you?" O creepy little know-it-all, squidgy slug, creeping up on me.

"I was right all along, you know, a few minutes ago. These documents are for you, part of the industrial accident case." He did his best to smile, but he found her unfriendly, unapproachable.

"Oh, right, okey-dokey, thanks very much," she called to his retreating back. "Nearly lunch."

"Yeah, must admit I'm famished!" She was trying to be friendly and informal. He's not too bad, really. Quite nice. It crossed her mind that she might have been moving her lips whilst having one of those awful interior arguments. Well, if she had, so what! It's only what children do and everybody else, in fact! Probably. No, he's not too bad. There are much worse around than him and a lot closer.

## 60

I suppose John has had his usual morning, although I couldn't say. One advantage of being elderly or having young children is that you can apply for an apartment anywhere that's convenient to you, and you always get it. I haven't a clue who John is. I know his name because I've heard his wife calling him and I've seen the children get into the car, so I've suggested the obvious conclusions. I've had no reason to investigate further. My 'curiosity' might be considered downright intrusive and certainly illegal.

Passing the Pierian Spring, I thought I'd sit down for a spell. I started by trying to spell Cerebral Autosomal-Dominant Arteriopathy with Subcortical Infarcts and Leukoencephalopathy, but that was too difficult. I found pnemonoultramicroscopicsilicovolcanoconiosis much easier, but relaxing can be so exhausting! So I've heard. I found that pneumono word in this old language in a course for teaching children to read long ago - and it never failed! In those days, illiteracy was the norm at school and daily sex was the excuse (you have to think about it...), but no longer. In our City, as in all Cities, illiteracy amongst children is a form of child neglect for which there are serious legal consequences. It is ensconced in most City Acts of Parliament relating to children. The bit about Pierian Spring is a metaphor.

When I started to take notes for this account, not real notes, you understand, I had the notion that I would write a description of everyday life for future generations, the obvious aspects of the City: its educational system, political and economic system, social mores and sociological structures, its place in the world, and so on. I know that hundreds of such documents have been produced, but everyone has a story to tell and every story is interesting and different. I had no idea how different this one would be, once I was *orientated* for the task.

When you reach a certain age things take on a significant hue. Your values become more firmly established, whilst your confidence has been gained through hard labour, experience. It might still appear to mimic the brash idealism of youth, but there is a calm, a knowing condition. You are no longer *attached* to your ideas and feelings, in the thrall of some kind of personal investment which you must protect. You are in charge, they are yours to use as you will and not as somebody else might elicit for their own purpose or amusement. You can see them coming, you've heard it all before, you are well practiced, you can foresee their weaknesses and ploys. That life is a struggle is obvious. But the real struggle is to decide: why? And you know for certain that nothing is perfect and also compromise is frequently expected, and not always a good thing. There *are* facts, there *is* truth, there *are* such things as right and wrong.

"I thought it was you. I thought I'd come over and say hello."

Yes, I know you did. Her friendly wave like a shot from a starting gun.

"Having a relaxing spell in the shade? It's a wonderful day for a stroll."

"Yes to both." You are wise to listen very carefully. "How are things, that old song called Life?" Ah, poetic, a poetic wood nymph, one of the ageing variety - an old nymph. She'll play along if it suits her.

"Oh, life just trundles along, you know," Yes, I know. I wonder if she does. "One has to be patient and stay on top."

"On top?"

"Of things, the usual: family, daily chores, the necessary routines." She seemed to dance in the sun, or was she squirming? Settle for a squirm of a dance, some kind of cover-up, somebody's working her strings.

"How's the family?"

The 'the', as if she cares. She doesn't like me. She has never liked me. Why she talks to me is part of her game. Why I respond is simply good manners, but I am far too long in the tooth to partake in her bouts of ping-pong. I wonder why she's thinking this, if she is. The probability that she is is high.

"Oh, everybody's fine, plodding along, generally enjoying their lives, which is a good thing. That's the way it should be. I know a lot of people in all sorts of difficulties. I feel sorry for them, but, really, I am often bereft of advice. What can one do? One simply isn't in a position to do anything but offer a sympathetic ear." Whoops! I sense that someone has taken the wrong turning... even at her age.

"I know exactly what you mean." Oh, dear.

"How's your, eh, sorry I've forgotten his name." What word do they use these days when it's all about appearance, status and sex? And what is his name? I have difficulty keeping up. Which letter of the alphabet are we on? Surely, they must have a system.

"Boyfriend? My boyfriend's fine. Joe. Seph. Joseph." If she's unsure, I'm not surprised. The name sounds familiar. Yes, it is the same name. She could be working her way through the Josephs of the City. Maybe that's the latest fashion.

"That's good news. And your children. Are they settled or, em, still in the same areas? That sort of thing. Same jobs?" Oh, just when I was feeling on top of things, like a wise elder of the tribe, this happens and I can hardly communicate. I'm just not that cool. Indeed, few people make me as hot and bothered as this woman, who can't decide whether to retire gracefully and act her age, or start a new career as a lap dancer. I have a horrible feeling she is going to tell me all about her wonderful children and how they take after her. One must be patient, well-mannered and avoid bad language. These facilitate harmony, which doesn't always help.

As for me, I'm not eavesdropping, I'm collecting data.

## 61

He had wandered off early afternoon as he always did, being a person of habit. Bronnie had already had her first drink. She'd waited, it seemed, politely until he had gone for a snooze. She had painted whilst he chatted to his probably terminal son. Lunch together had been *pleasant*. His telephone conversation irritated her - she couldn't concentrate - because it was so predictable: the usual thing about nausea, pain, insomnia, treatment, the possibility of remission, the probability of continued treatment. The inevitable never mentioned. Why hadn't he taken himself to another room? It was indulgent and selfish. He knew she was trying to finish her painting. Then he had taken himself to another room where he snored loudly fully dressed under a single sheet and in the foetal position. Now she could relax. She could relax because she'd done a good morning's work. And she could dream, with a little help, with a little something to stimulate her imagination.

She had draped herself with something loose and flowery, one of those modern, silky fibres, a kind of light-flowing smock drawn in at the waist, covering her less than youthful backside adorned in elegant navy blue slacks. She used that word. On this occasion, her white shoes worked very well. You could tell that she had artistic tendencies - her sense of colour without being ostentatious and showy. She had long given up being affected, almost as if affection had, like life itself, worn her down. She would never be a great artist. That dream had been murdered long ago. That monster. The bracelets, earrings, makeup and brunette dyed hair - just fine. She always dressed for the afternoon. She had smiled at herself in the mirror. She was smiling at somebody from sixty years ago.

She began to sink under the weight of the rest of the day. Although she couldn't have many left, this day, again on her own, would be too long unless she could rouse herself from the weight of her memories, memories more like the stuff that hardens arteries. Another drink would sustain her, energise her. She poured another generous 'shot' into the crystal glass. Its many panels reflected the sun's white light as she twisted it one way, then another. She appreciated the play of light as she wandered through the years of browns and greys. Every time she thought of those early years she could see no colours, not even her children were real. When she thought she could remember them, she knew they were only moving colour photographs forced into her black and white video. She couldn't see them as they were. Those times weren't real. Not just gone, they didn't happen at all. It was all some kind of dream. Maybe she would wake up and find herself eighteen again and it had all been a dream, a nightmare. She swallowed most of her drink and it burnt its way into her body and she felt alive because the pain, minor though it was, was real and familiar. This was the beginning of a daydream and, after her work, she'd earned the right to relax. Now she was floating. Her spirit rose. Her anger returned. She was no longer a victim. Everything made sense. She could explain everything because she was in charge. Anger is good, anger is righteous. It wasn't her fault, she was powerless, she had no experience to deal with those things. Not like now. Now she was in control.

She listened for the snoring. Yes, she was still free and the wide window seemed to give her a sense of flight. She could fly! She could fly away, away to the sea, sweeping under bridges, soaring to the sky, following the river to the sea and away, away across the sea. She wondered about birds that travelled thousands of miles without landing. Maybe she would never land.

The phone calls had started, together with all the other messaging systems, as predicted, messages flying back and forth, increasing to a crescendo in a few days no doubt. Those so-called happy gatherings. She needed a secretary, she needed a boss like the old days, when she could ring in and say she was sick even when she wasn't! She needed an excuse to act: coughing and sneezing into the phone, wheezing and gasping, actually holding her nose, but not over-doing it, "Sorry, I can't bake it today, I have a heavy cold. Hopefully, I'll be fit tomorrow. If not, I'll give you call." Those were the days! No, on second thoughts, they were definitely not the days. If those days were supposed to be halcyon, they weren't. She pondered the word 'halcyon', one of those words that didn't make sense. Then she remembered that when she had tried to send a text, the system was temporarily out of order. "No access at present. A temporary fault," said the recorded message. It was always the same woman's voice. She couldn't remember the name of the woman who had become famous for those recorded messages. She had retired a long time ago and was front page news at the time! One of those light-hearted pieces of news. So, a temporary fault, she'd remembered. Good! Some peace then.

She wondered about the boy, probably wearing his white uniform at this very moment. He saw himself as irresistible and he was! She looked over her shoulder towards his portrait on the far wall. He was quite perfect. She couldn't quite make out the painting without her glasses. She should offer to paint an up to date portrait. That idea was rejected immediately.

She jumped when the doorbell rang. Her reaction was not unusual. He often chuckled and reassured her, but he was sound asleep, the huge plump baby. No one expected, who could it possibly be? Oh, not one of the family to waffle on and on about nothing, the nothing in question being the coming weekend. No peace for the wicked.

## 62

Fumbling through her day off was like struggling uphill carrying a heavy suit-case. Belbiana's attempts to relax made her tense. Her calling made her very aware of her own physical condition - if *she* weren't aware, then who would be! Hence, her request for physical monitoring (e.g. heart rate, blood pressure, oxygen uptake, bloods) was happily accepted by Human Operator at Central Computer. It was *professional* for an objective person to do this rather than herself. This was the fourteenth request in the last twenty days off, including today. They were happy to oblige.

In her young life her own deterioration had become an awareness; death all around, her vocation, had rendered her extra... *alert*. But there were other reasons. The database existed, but had never satisfied the criteria to elicit human intervention. Some people can go *very* quietly amidst the noise and haste, suffer terribly and their suffering remains unnoticed. Not anymore.

Thus far she blundered through the early afternoon sedately: dignity above all. Her heroic little boy had to be looked after, her six year old with a grey beard playing with his toys, frequently immersed in a hobby, which kept him out of trouble. He was so different and difficult in company. He drank too much, which is very bad for his health (she frequently took his pulse, informed him that he must slow down, and he did), he laughed and joked (which was bad enough!), and then he would start singing. Everybody would join in: they would drink too much, laugh constantly, and then start singing. They were only trying to be sociable. It was so embarrassing! Belbiana had no choice but to join in, get horribly drunk, and sing songs. She could sing beautifully. Everybody agreed that she really could have been a professional singer. The next day, hardly in the *morning*, her bad feelings about the behaviour of the previous evening were powerful and awful: those terrible people (most of them had stayed overnight, as per invitation - don't say 'invite', it's common), those old sentimental songs, her husband... It won't happen again, she determined each time.

That *hadn't* happened for some time. In public. And it wouldn't happen this weekend. A sudden invitation. She'd almost forgotten about that shower! Though she couldn't quite get them out of her mind. There were periods of peace, during a 'crash call', for example. She really enjoyed the excitement of a crash call. Her husband didn't understand. He'd never had power - he was too efficient, he didn't need power. He didn't have emergencies. But, usually those *creatures* were a ghostly presence destroying her peace, not the dying patients, the weekend ahead crowd. The dying patients were interesting and under control. The weekend ahead people were... What's the word? It would come to her in a minute. But she's not going and neither is her husband. Their cheek is unbelievable!

She looked over her magazine at him in his silent sprawl on the settee, her dozing lion seal. She knew that a bit of fresh air, even if it wasn't actually fresh, would send him to sleep within five minutes of attempting to read his newspaper. Why he bought his 'daily' was beyond her. At his reading rate, he was about five years behind the news! Silly old thing, but clever.

She really should do something useful and not just sit around having morbid thoughts. Her dead parents had already popped up exactly as they were when she was ten. They were instantly suppressed. Ten was the last time she positively loved both of them. As she began to know them properly, she was increasingly appalled. Nobody had parents like hers, certainly none of the other children at school. She had to keep her parents secret as well as her parents' secrets. Her parents disgusted her. All that rowing was terrible. That's when she started to reconstruct herself, bury all the family secrets. This required some small degree of dishonesty for the greater good. She was good at this and, after all, at the end of the day, in the final analysis, life was but a game, or was it but a dream? Same thing, she doesn't split hairs. Her darling, naturally brainy husband would agree. They were a perfect couple and many people said so. Look at him now: a perfect specimen of manhood. Of course he's a bit old, but that aside, there was a lot of jealousy surrounding them as a couple and one just had to put up with it. You can't even trust the girls at work who became close friends, well, *quite* close friends. Some of the neighbours were just awful! She hadn't been unaware of their lasciviousness. It was *so* obvious and at their age! And their ridiculous impertinence. One of them actually suggested recently that both she and her husband needed therapy. Imagine that! Oh, it wasn't a neighbour, it was that awful... Oh, the weekend - that woman would be there, hogging the centre of attention. Unbearable. Tabby is so clever and tactful: he pretends to like her! He's right to claim that it's only sensible, as there is no point adding to bad feelings. He's absolutely right to remain calm. Yes, they'll go, but only to best *that woman*.

"Oh!" she said out loud. She was really taken aback, being a highly strung and sensitive person. Hubby stretched and smacked his lips. She felt very tense. She always did in these circumstances. Somebody at the door. Nobody expected. Who *could* it be? Oh, he looks such a mess, sprawled out like a pile of washing.

"Tabby, darling. Tabby!" she hissed. "Somebody's at the door. Tidy yourself up."

She rose from her chair majestically: best foot forward, best face, best voice, best self for the public. Could be anybody. Oh, no! She whipped up the inside of her dress, wiped the photograph and then the surface of their exquisite antique pedestal table, on her way to the door.

## 63

Unexpectedly, Sachikaka had the floor and rose to the occasion. Several men in the large, polished conference room behaved like lizards during her presentation, sunning themselves on their rocky prominence, still as a stone, flashing tongues. She was good at this. The woman, Head of Accounts, was also somewhat *aroused*, hanging on Sachi's every word. Other senior executives took unnecessary notes, fidgeted, met each other's eyes and looked away. Sachikaka had a way with people and was very confident in this area of social skills. She was a People Person. Ask her and she'll tell you, even if you don't ask her. Her C.V. is powerful: highly developed communication skills, brings out the best in people, creative, innovative, and developed analytical thinking; acquired legal expertise, a proponent of embedding regulatory functions, systems cleansing, lean techniques applications, enterprise advancement, market navigation, utility spacing, Z.E. co-ordination, prefabricated modular delivery [as opposed to FMD, which is quite old fashioned], complex intelligent solution building, integrated target driving, D-automated systems analysis, adaptive content enabling, aquaflow analysis, hotair dissemination techniques, procurement processes, buy-side and sell-side processes, DBO, SLA, LCC, and so on. She was brilliant at procurement, especially in her own time. Education is a wonderful thing and, doubtless, her interviewers had learnt a lot. The lady in charge of accounts had become noticeably glazed on more than one occasion accompanied by certain gasping sounds. That was two years ago and Sachikaka had grown to simply *hate* her job: not stretching her enough, not using her potential. It's just not right, is it?

She enjoyed her own office. Those communal offices were too *democratic,* all that forced sociability was unnatural. After lunch she always felt groggy. She made a strong cup of coffee and prevaricated concerning the rest of that report - she still had a few days and plenty of other less demanding tasks on the go.

Her family took up much of her thinking. To have to listen to other people's problems concerning their family was just too much to bear. Why don't they just get themselves sorted out? Therapy of every hue is available: family, couple, child, adolescent, work, school, you name it. So why not? Most of them need *sex* therapy, in her opinion. Talk about *inhibited*! How do people end up in such a sexual mess? she often asked herself. Now, must have a peek at the Appointments page, but which medium is the most sensible? She didn't want people to find out at work. Best to be discrete. Ah, 'discretion'- must remember that for the C.V., in a discrete way. Being brazen suggests overconfidence, not a good character tray. Ah, that word - sometimes things just don't make sense. A quick gander via her computer.

"What!" she said aloud. How peculiar, she can't get outside the company network. There must be a fault. She walked over to the large window overlooking the office and couldn't see anybody else looking perturbed. She was good at non-verbal behaviour. Maybe they already know, better leave it for now.

She flicked open the large report at her marked page. Scanning a few paragraphs made her feel even groggier. It wasn't confidential as such, she might feel better tackling a chunk of it this evening, a couple of hours when the kid is in bed. Her husband won't mind. She tried the console on her desk. Okay, a bit weird, but that's happened before. They really should ensure that other systems aren't down before starting maintenance work. Very inefficient. About time they were more organised, better co-ordinated across systems. It crossed her mind that it is the sort of work she could do, but it might be somewhat limiting. She tried to imagine the job itself. Somebody must be doing it and not very well.

She looked for her handbag. It was on the back of the office chair, the one being used as a kind of in-tray, just out of reach. She felt so tired and fed up. She really wanted another job, one more demanding of her real ability. She felt her motivation had taken a serious hammering. She looked at the pile of files and sheets of A4 on the chair. Things were piling up and it doesn't give a good impression. She glanced at her watch: tidy up first thing, get her office back in order. No, do some of it on her way out in two and a half hours. Get that pile out of sight for a start!

The third option was the mobile phone in her handbag. The thought of its contents, the list of names depressed her. That was it, for goodness' sake! That was the thing breaking her will again. It was there all the time eating her alive. She dreaded the promised call 'for a chat' from her loving mother. She was relieved that so far no call. She'd probably forgotten, which is typical of her - selfish what-sit! She'll ring when she feels like it. Obviously, she doesn't feel like it. As for her father, they talked a few months ago. He hadn't even seen his grandchild and the kid is nearly three! What is it with men? But, on the other hand... For goodness' sake, what had Sachikaka done in a previous life to deserve those two? A professional torturer? She laughed at the idea. She chuckled at the thought that she might be one in her *next* life and then she could deal with her parents and the rest of that obnoxious family! She probably wouldn't have to torture them - they'd come back as slugs and she'd just stamp on them! That would be far more convenient and no explaining to do!

Do you see what happens when you procrastinate? she asked herself - you start fantasising about murdering slugs who used to be your parents! She felt more awake and reached for that tedious report. Leave the career thing until tomorrow. Then she noticed two official-looking men approaching her office.

The fly zigzagged and swooped a downward arc towards the open door. With its ski jumping and ski flying, it flew to freedom. Nasichisha followed at a gentler pace, her peaked cap placed low on her forehead and matching her maintenance overalls. Then she stopped abruptly - too abruptly? No - and turned serenely to return the mop. She had a *penchant* for mops, vacuum cleaners, indeed all things related to cleaning. She had a lifelong interest in stain-removers and assorted cleaning aids, from hand-driven right through to electricity-driven in their many forms; the complete continuum from liquid to powder to stone to metal; and, as for water... temperature... the consequences could be dire. Whiter than white? On *proper* inspection, only white. And the smell...?

At this moment she resisted the urge to mop the corridor (two and a half miles): the cleaners had been despicably negligent. There was dust everywhere. She wouldn't report this; she was having trouble enough with her superiors. Her superiors - so they imagine! She'd probably report anonymously. Mustn't be impulsive - one must have self-discipline and control. She quickly and neatly folded her acquired uniform and secreted it in the usual place.

Heading to collect the tests, she thought of her children and that nuisance, that interference in her life. Why couldn't he just disappear? Why couldn't he get the message, sent clearly and loudly so long ago. How many Court Judgments? He's just making a fool of himself and upsetting the entire family. Things are going well and he pops up again like a case of incurable syphilis. Did she have the right disease? Well, *something* nasty. But the children know what he's like. She's told them often enough. He was seriously ill recently, why didn't he just die?

And the children. Why aren't they shacked-up and moved away? Marriage! Huh! Even *further* away. Oh, another glorious and loving family celebration coming up. They'll all be there and she'll just have to keep them in their place. It's like herding cattle. They'll bring all their boyfriends and girlfriends, probably more new names to learn and be polite with people insufferably arrogant. They always choose the same types. I wished they'd tell the newcomers who their mother is, so that she doesn't have to. Hasn't she enough to put up with: ongoing income problems, a demanding job, having to get up every morning for work - for the last *months*. Is this it, the meaning of life? What, another ten or fifteen years of this and then what?

"Hi, she's turned up."

"Who? Oh, her."

"Third floor."

He tapped the code. "Yes, got her. What's she doing there? Where has she been? It's like dealing with some creepy little animal, some ferule creature." He chuckled. "Sorry, that's a bit extreme and unprofessional..." He was lost for words. She was acting like a teenager.

"I've decided. The thing we discussed at lunchtime. Can I depend on your support?"

"Yes," without hesitation, "I don't think we have any choice, *you* have any choice." He'd forgotten her promotion. "You've been through full procedure? Three warnings? Of course you have my support, as second in charge. Quite frankly, well, I'm repeating myself, but many of the prisoners are more reliable than her. I don't know what the problem is, although, I suppose, we, of all people, should know." They were silent.

"Okay, I'll tell her in the morning. Will 10 o'clock be convenient?"

She glanced through the window. One prisoner had completed the test and departed. She'd forgotten to turn on her bleeper, but it didn't matter. She entered the room authoritatively, nodded to the warder and picked up the test from the desk beside him.

"Everything okay?" she asked gently, as she leant towards the prisoner. She was very caring and maternal.

"Yes, ma'am," he answered in the formal protocol of the institute. "Straight forward  enough."

"Good. I told you it was not *that* sort of test, not like school."

Both men watched her as she returned to the front of the room. The prisoner was annoyed at himself for watching her at all and for being so diligent with the test. There was no point doing it badly, but he'd certainly been 'schooled', conditioned some would say, to do this kind of classroom task, having spent years at the University. He was only 'inside' because of those 'outbursts' at political meetings. The authorities had expressed concern about his emotional stability. Surely she knew his background and that he had been given four months on Level 1 for DC (Directed Counselling). It was apparent she didn't. So much for her sweetness and light. He finished the test quickly and departed in silence, accompanied by the warder. She was glad they were both gone. Now, back to her office. Two and a half hours and then out of this *mistake*! Maybe she could get back to the University somehow, but there had been one or two difficult people... One being that vile old man.

A tiny ping alerted her to the hour. She stretched. Going through these tests was always tedious: she had to read the lot, allocate scores, check the Manual, fill in boxes on charts, complete graphs, write a Report, etc., all of it computer-aided. Most of it was not even slightly interesting. She had no interest in statistics. She could easily get by without all that male thinking. Where's the female intuition?

Bored, she 'twiddled' with the monitors just to see if anything interesting was happening. Highly unlikely. But, lo and behold, there was a uniformed policeman coming along the corridor, together with a female (probably plain clothes) - that's a smart suit, she thought - and between them that awful, bossy woman. It crossed Nasichisha's mind that her boss might be under arrest and serve her right! She was mildly curious: you rarely see a policeman *inside* the Prison. Oh, well, she'd be informed in due course, probably one of those terribly clever *initiatives*.

## 65

Something moved in his trousers. Jeevalani awoke from his dream (Goodness, even at my age! he probably thought) and instinctively sneaked a peek at the man beside him - he was sure it was a man, sometimes difficult to tell - who responded with knowing raised eyebrows: "Would you please kill me before I die of boredom?" No, it would be a sin and thinking that way is probably a worse sin. Jeev roamed the backheads of several hundred delegates. Some nodded sagely, some nodded off. A distress signal from Row 13: hair hair hair bald bald bald hair

hair hair. The brain is amazing: just one glance.

It was his sensible habit to choose an aisle seat near an Exit, which in this case is also an Entrance. There may be an emergency and a priest needed in a hurry. Even in these circumstances, you really don't know what the future holds - earthquakes, fires, mass incapacitations? The Bar is just beyond the exit and people may need water in a hurry. Jeevalani is always prepared.

He'd managed to fill with his tiny 'conference writing' the first quarter of his folded sheet of A4. When he'd turned it over, the tiny blank page had dazzled him, creating a kind of snow blindness, and he'd lost concentration. This response recalled his childhood: the blank page, thousands of them, the three-hour exams he'd passed, but barely. He was a dreamer. And a doer. During this talk (Interfaith-something or other), he'd thumped cartoon-like from head to head, as light as a feather, and out the window and away into the clouds! He'd been gone for *ages,* probably, he estimated, ten million words, when there was a rumbling in the cellar which brought him back to earth with a bit of a thump, albeit as light as a feather. He noted his folded paper and his still as a leaning tower pen, and placed both nonchalantly into his breast pocket, where he kept his supply of folded sheets for talks. He hated being laden down. His manly bulk travelled light, like the old song. One had to negotiate crowded bars and enjoy the pleasure of other people without being a mobile obstruction, laden with briefcases, umbrellas, hats, newspapers. Imagine squeezing towards a crowded bar carrying a rucksack, tent, manly hat with dangling corks, walking boots, kettles and pans banging against the backsides or seated heads of chatting customers, clattering amidst the chatter. He'd learnt from his mistakes.

When he read the name on his telephone, he was somewhat surprised. Although he should have expected a further contact. It could be something serious. He rose silently like a small hot-air balloon from his seat (small?) and drifted towards the Exit. In his youth, he could have been a gymnast, but he'd had more important things to do at the time, like socialise and chase girls. As he opened the door, it creaked loudly and made a watery sound across the carpet, like surf on sand. He looked over his shoulder as if to apologise and slipped out. He hated people who interrupted the speaker by unnecessary noise or by asking sensible questions. No point prolonging the talk.

The corridor was long, empty and still. His baritone voice would usually echo like a thunder bolt, but a little positive discretion may be needed.

"Hello, just received your message," he almost whispered to the wall as he headed away from the conference room, "What can I do for you?"

He had already examined his conscience in the last few seconds. Now he was doing it again. Immediate feelings of guilt. Had he done anything? What a horrible feeling. This reminded him of *other* aspects of his youth. Does that stuff never go away, always lurking just out of sight, ready to surface like a shark? Certain things did rattle his youth, apart from academic examinations. And, of course, he dealt with so many people on a daily basis. Had he been implicated in something? Or, even worse, accused of something? He racked his brain. Things are not always black and white. Had he 'stumbled' into something awful? Even in our society, scandals can spring up anywhere. Just when things have calmed down, up springs something else equally monstrous. You didn't need the Devil when people were well able to organise their own villainy!

He stopped still, puzzled, but somewhat relieved. "Yes, I know..." he glanced around - still nobody in sight, need for confidentiality -"that person."

He leant against the wall for support. He wasn't shocked, but he imagined that some kind of boulder was heading his way.

"Yes, I see

"No, I don't quite follow

"As you say, for many years, probably twenty

"Yes, I know that person too, for obvious reasons, the usual connections

"I can't speak freely at present. I'm at a

"Of course, you know

"About five... maybe six

"No, I've never met... Okay. May be called?

"Right, I'll wait. I understand. Bye for now."

The recorded message immediately followed. This has happened a few times over the years. It's not a problem. In his position it's bound to happen. Being *incommunicado* for a while is no big deal. He's hardly on a deserted island. There are fifteen hundred delegates at this conference, indeed, *congress*, in a City of 80 million! No, sociable though he is, loneliness has rarely been a problem. Not being able to use any kind of telephone is a relief, almost a holiday. But, joking aside, what is going on? He noticed the public phone on the wall and he knew that if he even picked up the receiver, he would immediately receive the recorded message because it was him. He has lived in places not as 'covered' as this, but they are few and far between these days. And there is always satellite-tracking. Musing on these things didn't calm his nerves. Surely he is not implicated. But somebody may have said something. Don't panic - born guilty!

## 66

They would be home soon, Halaigha and her mincing man. Their flowing scarves signalled an impressive couple. Her family had acknowledged this, except for the bitter and twisted ones. They could make more effort to control their nasty tongues, their personal frustrations. A few certificates and they think they're God! What about her certificates? And what about her boyfriend's lifelong achievements? Even his wife had become a serious nuisance, an interfering, vicious, dried up old hag, with her nasty comments delivered via their eldest son. Halaigha was quite sure that the young man had no idea that he was firing barbed and poisonous darts. He was like his father, kind and considerate. What *is* her problem? It's probably her upbringing and adult *addictions*. The authorities can be very remiss.

Out of the sun and crowds and into the relative calm of the hyperstructure where they live, Halaigha is now focused on their young child. The child minder is not *special* - they are entitled to one. Bureaucracies really get on your nerves! You'd think they'd put the child first, as the kid was born dangerously premature. Look how bureaucracies behave! They all make people's lives even worse. It's appalling! They should be ashamed. And the involvement of the police? It was shocking. But best to put these horrible thoughts out of her mind. She must be positive. She knew that long before her therapist told her. Her mother always said it. The therapist had taught her several mental exercises to block destructive thoughts. These exercises were taught as each one proved ineffective. She ended up with an arsenal of interesting possibilities. (She might become a therapist!). She thought about these exercises a lot and this helped block her morbid ruminations. Sometimes she and her boyfriend talked about this for hours and even invented new exercises. Not only were they totally blocked, but they slept soundly.

The woman from the Welfare looked after the child six hours a day so that the parents could get their lives organised. Things were difficult although it was nobody's fault; one of those things, mishaps, bad luck, social and medical problems, the breakup of his marriage, etc. They were advised to attend certain classes: psychotherapy, counselling for various purposes (parenting, preparation for return to employment, applying for jobs, and so on). Things were so hectic you wouldn't believe it! How people found time to earn a living was beyond Halaigha. She said it often: "I can't imagine how people find time to go to work!" Certainly, who could argue?

Halaigha didn't take to the 'lady' from Welfare. They referred to them as 'ladies'. This lady was *matronising* and fat. Halaigha found that disturbing, quite disgusting. She wrote a letter of complaint, claiming that Mrs Jolly was too fat (she didn't use that word) and uneducated, an inappropriate role model. Firstly, the woman's accent... How she had studied childcare at the University must be to do with positive discrimination. Not surprisingly, she hadn't received a reply yet. Typical. Everything's so frustrating, and now she has to take charge of her child for the rest of the day. And that woman can't wait to go home.

"Everything okay, Mrs Jolly?"

"Yes, everything's fine. We played some games, she had a nap, I did some tidying, then we played more games. She's very clever, you know. I read some stories and we did some drama. She's extremely good at language, advanced for her age. She's beginning to read and finds it very easy. She reminds me of my children when they were that age. They were all excellent readers, thank goodness. That's a great boon for a child and a great relief for teachers, I imagine!"

Yes, typical. She's read a few books, did a course, has a few adult children and thinks she's a world expert on child development. Halaigha could see that Mrs Jolly was *anti*. She probably had a lousy childhood and has a lousy marriage. Her children probably don't talk to her.

"Yes, I know she has a natural interest in literature - it runs in the family. Thanks for tidying up."

"Any luck on the job's front?"

"No, it's hopeless, you know how it is."

"Oh, yes, I do. My eldest had a terrible time finding work. It took him a solid year to get a teaching job, even with his qualifications. It was just as bad for the others, although all very different careers. But all five of them sorted themselves out. You must be patient." Her eyes had obviously betrayed her thoughts - Hallie could tell that. That woman should leave before things get out of hand.

"Okay then, same time tomorrow?" She didn't wait for a reply and put on her coat.

"That tub of lard gives me the creeps."

"Ignore her, darling." He wasn't quite sure what she meant, but he understood her frustration. People are difficult when you're creative. He was bouncing his perfect child on his lap - he would be so old when she reached twenty. It was quite likely...

"I better 'phone Mum about Friday. I suppose it's still on." He said nothing. His little one gave him a big hug.

"Strange. Let me borrow your phone." She just took it. "Typical! I'll do it later." His phone made a soft landing on the pile of arts magazines.

A tingling below her left ear. "An aural," she announced. His raised eyebrows questioned, "Something interesting?"

"Hello.

I see.

What, right now?" She glanced at her watch.

"Okay. Fifteen or twenty minutes then?

Fine. See you then."

He knew it wasn't positive.

"What a nuisance," she said. "They want to see me at the Office. You don't think that ridiculous woman has made some kind of complaint?"

"Of course not! What kind of complaint? They just want more info for their files. Where would the poor little clerks be without their files? Just tell them what they want. Not too much!  You'll be back within the hour."

## 67

He had blood on his hands. He is being manhandled, the room is hot and filled with smoke. The room is spinning, he cries for help, he can't hear his voice, nobody comes. Why can't they hear him? Someone's right there and they don't care. Nobody cares. No hope, he is lost and falling into blackness.

The ocean heaves, like a thousand invisible hands, he is raised and rolled and plummets. He's drowning, then sees her and calls. She turns her cold, unseeing eyes, round and white. Two strong light beams scan the surface, blind him, sear right through him, wait and move on. She's seen him. She hasn't. She must have. Why doesn't she reach out and save her child, her little boy? And *he* is there as always, immobile in the distance across the marsh in the dark mist. He waves, his mouth moves, that's Makallee's name in the silence. And the mist turns to blackness and he's engulfed; he becomes part of the fog and vaporises. Makallee gives up, he stopped crying long ago.

In the tube no one can move, pale with despair and stiff with terror, they wait. The bleeping sound like a heartbeat amid the silence of the dead, and the real hearts, deafening. In the tube no one can hear hands trembling. Wrapped tight as a new-born babe, unable to breath, unable to scream, and no possibility of succour, they begin to hope for luck, they dump their disbelief in God. They would give up anything to get out of here, the death chamber they voluntarily entered.

Music means life. They begin to dance. It is so crowded, the music so loud, in this space nobody can hear you scream. These places where crowds gather to be cosily hemmed in, to laugh, to sweat, to move to the rhythm, flail their arms, but not drowning, in an ocean of bodies, some so tempting, irresistible, right here right now, right here right now. The laughing faces, the perfect beauties designed by experts in seduction, swimming like vertical fish out of water to be hooked and hauled in, but gently, so gently, no need to rush, be cool, no hurry, this is a game for the unhurried, the prey and the preyed upon in mutual embrace. This is a game, a matter of time, anything can happen in the next half hour! Anything you've heard, anything you've read, anything you've seen, anything you've imagined. Power power power - now you can have your say, now you are in charge, now you don't have to follow orders, now you are the boss and what you say goes. And what you say may be weird, but hardly original, and she'll do it because she's here.

It is crushing, deafening, he can't breathe. They are laughing, they are screaming, but there is no sound - it must the music, but he can't hear it because he's deaf - their fangs, their wild eyes, their claws, they are tearing at him, digging their claws into his flesh, tearing lumps from his flesh, but he can't feel the pain. They are going to slaughter him, tear him to pieces, disembowel him, his intestines wrapped around her waist, butcher him, dance his flesh and bones and blood into the floor, skip with his guts, play netball with his skull, tear off his testicles and flick them funlovingly into the air with whoops and cheers. He lashes out, tries to fight them off - it hurts - but it makes no difference. He is going to be raped, but these are women, but they are going to do it with their knives and their truncheons and their screwdrivers.

His mother's had a stroke and can't speak, her beauty is gone, her smile deformed. She doesn't seem bothered. He's surprised - her vanity? -nothing touches her. She's the same, unrecognisable, he knows it's her. You never forget your mother. You can never forget your mother. His father is old and bald and shrivelled, as he remembers him from that wedding. Where is he now? Here he is! Daddy? He knows it's him, although he is limping and hunched. It's the operation. He'll be okay in a few weeks, right as rain, young again, athletic and sporty, member of the local gentlemen's club, where Makallee had never been with his Daddy, and then Daddy was gone. Where did he go? Why did he leave? Mum said loads of things about Daddy, but they weren't true! Makallee knew, children can tell. And now he's back, but he can't speak and he can't reach Makallee because of the crowd and the noiseless noise , and Daddy's disappearing again, far off on the ocean of bobbing heads in this stormy sea. His aunty appears with her cancerous face and she's trying to kiss him! She's horrible! Don't, please don't. He feels guilty for being a bad boy, for being naughty and rude and unkind. "You mustn't be unkind to girls. You must look after your sisters because they are not as big and strong as you. You mustn't be too rough with your little sister." What little sister? They're everywhere! "How come they're not kind to me? It's just not fair." "Don't be silly, you're imagining it. They love you." He's falling falling. He's suffocating, choking, disappearing. He's going to be stamped into the ground, turned to sticky dust.

"Oh, what a mess!" Makallee is being pulled into the upright position. He gets a very strong sense of vomit. There is dry blood on his left hand and flakes down his front. People in uniform. Who are they?

"Your brain is about to re-enter orbit, son, prepare for a crash landing. A shot of A.E., Sarge."

Anti-Ethanol painlessly entered Makallee's bloodstream followed by a few seconds which feel like being hit by a hard ball *inside* your skull. The room stopped *undulating*.

"You'll be okay, matey. You need to come with us, when we've cleaned you up."

His wife interrupted his thinking and it was a relief, it stopped him going round in circles. He'd learnt long ago that you could get stuck in the same vicious circle for years; indeed, the same box from birth. Merkan was humming an ancient song about boxes.

"For goodness' sake, Merky, are or aren't we?"

"Are we what?"

"Are we nearly out of decaf? I forgot to check."

"No. Well, yes. Or, at least, by next week's big shop we'll be probably be out."

"So, we should buy a jar?"

"Well, I would. Definitely."

"*You* would? Well, why don't you?"

He'd been happily interrupted, he'd always disliked shopping. Shopping made him anxious, something from childhood, maybe he was suffering from post-traumatic stress disorder related to his mother and shopping. Men were genetically programmed to be hunters and gatherers, not *shoppers*. Where were the men, the honed skills of co-operation; the forest and the danger, the chase, the blood, the death, and the triumph? Shopping was unnatural, against human nature.

"Now where are you, darling?"

"In a forest, dear, but no need to worry, I brought my spear."

"Ah, I'm glad: I feel much safer. Now, if you could possibly return to the present era and, preferably, this planet, could we do our best to finish the shopping, bearing in mind the coming weekend?"

You could see his mind flicking through the index cards towards the double-*ewes*. "Ah. A flocking of those strange creatures is expected, if I'm not mistaken."

"Yes, Merkan, those exotic little creatures of the forest, also known as our children."

"Will there be many of them?"

"Probably a small herd, *flock*. You should recognise several of them from previous sightings."

Good, something to look forward to, like falling overboard during a gale.

The shopping was indeed a triumph, apart from queuing and paying. He couldn't understand why feeding wasn't *automated* like so many other aspects of life: just press a button and his stomach is filled. They're probably working on it.

He was tall and looked across the bobbing heads. There were thousands of them. He had enjoyed watching the heads exploding. It was like the Grim Reaper having his usual reap. As he stood in the queue behind his wife, he looked down on her, but only in the physical sense, on her neatly brushed and dyed hair. It is strange how women do that. Not much has changed over the millennia. Women have always covered themselves in colours and smells. None of it necessary. They probably do it because they belong to a different tribe, a different species. For centuries, men had assumed that women did it for *them,* for men. Then it became apparent that women do it for each other! How peculiar! It makes no sense. He concluded, not for the first time, that he should leave that to anthropologists, and their ilk.

Looking over his shoulder, he scanned the miles of aisles. Satisfyingly, the floor and freezers were covered with dead bodies. A deep squelchy carpet of human remains. One of them came into focus and nodded 'hello'. Merkan nodded back. It must be one of his old students. People change. Did she always have a beard?

His wife was gazing up at him. She had that knowing look in her eyes. Only one customer in front of them.

"Have you enjoyed yourself?" she asked in a low voice.

"Well, the same as ever. You know. One of my ex-students, I think," he said, raising his eyebrows and nodding over his left shoulder discretely. He was hoping she might recognise the person. She ignored the comment.

"Was it the machete or the machine-gun today?" she whispered.

"A machete? What gave you that crazy idea? That's horrible! But I must admit that I did take a few pot-shots, now you mention it, just to keep in practice."

"If anybody found out, you'd be carted away!"

"I would be carted away if it weren't for the fact that the people who should be carting me away are too busy slaughtering the entire population, apparently, according to you, with machetes. You don't seriously believe that *this* is normal," a slight wave of his hand to indicate the hypermarket and probably the entire City.

"It's what we are and it's pretty good." She's right, of course, but one is entitled to one's fantasies. But everything on such a giant scale, thousands of people in any one place at any one time. Sometimes, it's just too much.

He heard the tinkling of her telephone. He avoided telephones and the 'aural' behind his ear was frequently turned off, neutralised. Age and status had earned him this perk.

"If that's my mother, tell her I'm out shopping. It won't be a lie."

"But it would be a miracle! Hello…"

Ah, miracles. Where would we be without them? What would life be without its miracles? What are you if you don't believe in miracles? Miracles happen every

"It's for you."

"Me?" He was always surprised to receive a phone call. He considered it somewhat abnormal. Maybe he had been traumatised in his

"Hello." A moment or two of silence, as he absentmindedly placed the last items from the trolley onto the conveyor belt.

"Yes, I understand. Thank you. Goodbye for now." He had no idea why he said 'thank you', but he'd be contacted again.

He handed back her phone. She looked quizzical, slightly concerned.

"Nothing to do with us," he said close to her ear, "I'll tell you on the way home." Only give his wife the barest details, just to put her mind at ease. She had already discerned that it was something serious. He doesn't know the details. It couldn't be something he has done, could it? Or a member of the family? Explain that it is something confidential to do with work. A few quips about machetes? No, she's a lot sharper than a machete. That's put a damper on the day somewhat. What's going on?

## 69

It is neither good nor bad: in, out. Prepare for the worst. It's best to occupy yourself in a meaningful habit which you accept has no meaning. Thus, Praman had convinced himself that he had to go out to purchase certain essential objects. He had also convinced himself that it was essential to interact with others to maintain psychological equilibrium. It was good for all parties to experience pleasure and avoid pain. These things are normal, healthy, and positively recommended. At this very moment, Praman regrets his actions: although enjoyable they increased his pain. Essential purchases? Who can tell?

He is sensing that paralysis coming on, creeping through his clothes, into his bones, heading for his soul, and he has no protection.

He feels someone has shot him with a dart of curare and is watching him turn into a lump of sculpted wood, a statue, just breathing. Someone? He knows who it is, injecting him with *their* diseases for *their* entertainment.

He sat down in time for his alarm clock, in time to light his new candle. The candle kept falling over, dripping wax, threatening to burn the wooden table, and extinguishing. What was wrong with the candlestick? Was the candle too tall in the saddle? And the matches kept breaking or refusing to light. Was it the matchbox? Was the world not bad enough without this conspiracy by inanimate objects, these supposed bringers of light? Why didn't people make candles properly and matches that worked? How many thousands more years will it take to produce effective matches and decent human beings? Where is all that 'sapiens' that people claim to own?

Then the candle remained upright, the match lit and the alarm clock went off. The world will go on without Praman. No one will notice he was here.

He scraped his chair into place, sat down heavily and 'jumped' the dead weight into position, his legs in their usual place and his arms clasped on the table. He reached for his book and felt he was lifting a dead body. *Something* had died. He slammed down the book. The vibration made the candle jump and flicker, but it stayed alight! It was an insult.

He lay his head, right cheek, on the cool the table, arms stretched like a plummeting diver. Can he please be released? He lifted his head in his hands. He was still. He could hear the ticking, each tick gone forever. That millionth of a millisecond has had its time and it was for nothing. Nobody noticed.

Life crawled across his skin like scorpions. Why did it keep him alive? Why did he have to keep reliving those appalling events, the disempowerment, the loss, the bereavement, the smirking faces that nobody else noticed, in that virtual video that was real and keeps increasing? How bigger would it become? Helpless, incapacitated, enraged, the battle had passed into his being where it was re-enacted over and over, whilst the protagonists had wandered away for a chat and a laugh and some light refreshments, to flirt and to tease their lovers, to negotiate their careers, to enjoy their triumphs, to be hugged for their upsets, to plan their holidays, to boast of their children, and to laugh off their treachery.

The noonday demons comingled with the post-lunch dip orchestrated by Nocnista and Krisky and Plaksy, having volunteered for the day shift. The weight on his back could not be shaken off. "The sorrow of the world that worketh death." The sorrow of the scourged man.

This came from *outside* the man, by people who enjoyed their work, the torturers. The thought of night, followed by another day, was dreadful. The sadness was a straitjacket. Night-time would be worse. He had tried everything. His relationships with others, some of them the closest to him, had been contaminated forever. He had attempted escape, but not possible.

"You'll never escape from yourself. You must come to terms with things and move on."

"But it is not me. I am not the problem."

"You're in a state of denial."

"No, I'm not!"

"Oh, come on, try to be reasonable. They can't all be wrong."

"But they *are* all wrong. Ask me anything! I'll tell you the truth. Anything: difficult, personal, embarrassing, sexual. Don't feel awkward, be brave, spit it out, say what's on your mind, some minor curiosity, some major question, something important you've been told. Ask me anything and I'll tell you the truth."

"You need to talk to someone. You know what I mean. It might take a few sessions, but I'm sure you'll feel much better. You just need to get things into a proper perspective."

"I don't need to do any of that. I've covered all the angles a hundred times and it has turned into decades. I need the Law to actually exist!"

"That's ridiculous and you know it is. This isn't about the *Law*. This is about messed up relationships, things you can't get over. You're sounding increasingly paranoid and it's obviously gone on for far too long. You are destroying your life. You must talk to someone."

How many times these conversations, which weren't conversations at all? What has happened that people cannot understand these simple things? What has happened? We seem to have produced a society of lunatics, or people who have very limited experience, or both. Where are the normal people, *adults*?

Praman had stopped talking. He didn't know anyone who understood human emotions. They talked in labels and clichés. Praman stuck to politics, religion, sex, the weather, football. The real man was no longer recognised. Had he ever been? He no longer existed. His innards had been gouged out. He was a walking talking smiling handshaking shoulder tapping waving hello nodding chin rubbing earlobe pulling nose stroking chuckling waving goodbye machine.

The hermit's baseline is normal. Apart from many taboo words in anger, he has remained unnoticed by Central Computer. Decades ago his distress was normal. Now he's just fine.

## 70

Gelasia was jolly and tipsy. The girls had returned, all giggles and flowery dresses, a vertical rugby scrum of clutches and unsteady intimacy, with their whispers and secrets and waves to encompass the world; or was it the unattainable men with suggestions of bad intent? She was in their midst, the belle of a ball that nobody attended. The men looked up, shuffling paper, tapping keyboards: the usual scene, nothing special, the returners from lunch precisely on time. Gelasia had been doing this for forty years. If she couldn't make it to the top, she'd learnt to spread her influence sideways. This is what she'd settled for, her acquired smugness based on experience. She played the age card - the Head Girl with no competition. She was making the most of it; soon she'd be left behind again. She was a stone in a stream, meeting all the youngsters on their way to the river. Why not have a giggle!

She placed her jacket it neatly on her chair, and took her place in this human battery henhouse so beautifully organised. In the City everything worked perfectly, except when it didn't. She cleared her throat, beamed around, put on her glasses, pulled into her desk, a slight creak of a wheel, to form an efficient unit of production. She neatened papers, tapped in instructions and printed out a table of figures. For a second her desk seemed to float, she seemed to rise weightless from her seat, and the pit of her stomach fell away. She sighed, but nobody heard.

She's used to it. She gripped her desk. It will pass. The call of nature is a good, but inconvenient sign that she's still alive. Sometimes death would be easier than facing the trail of white paper and useless data from her long past and disappearing into her shortening future. More get-togethers, more festivals, more holidays, but one day it will end abruptly.

Sitting on the loo was a relief. It was the privacy and relative silence and nobody else present, just the echoey emptiness and the smell of disinfectant and perfume. A world of extremes, a life of extremes, ups and downs, back and forth like a fiddler's elbow... Keep calm, enjoy the silence: no constant tapping, creaking of chairs, turning of heads, mumbled and earnest chatter about nothing important, exaggerated laughter at a joke too far away to hear, make the most of the white door and the two white walls, a meditation chamber, a meditation chamber pot! She thought she might have giggled out loud. Too much booze spoils the broth. Many hands make clit work. A hand in the bird is worth two in the bush. Does anything make sense?

More liquid within the hour and idle chatter when she'd crack her jokes whether they liked it or not. People wandered around her brain distracting her from her 'information management' tasks. Those dimwits who thought they were so clever. But she could multitask - decades of switching attention, but she didn't know that expression. Her parents stumbled in and out, knocking over furniture, spilling drinks, talking too loudly in public, making fools of themselves, interfering with her life, a couple joined together forever and from beyond the grave in holy embarrassment. Messing up their children's lives, what a shambles they were. Men die younger than women and it was a relief to get rid of him, but that obnoxious woman carried on *forever.* Unbelievable! Then the great relief. How will it be for her and her husband? She didn't want to think about that. Make the most of things! But he wants to be cremated - simple enough. At least he's always been objective and sensible. They were well suited. She had been lucky. She could have married a fool who *didn't* die young. Her mother was lucky in that respect.

Her siblings were obnoxious and still alive. Luckily, they stayed well away in every sense: no contact at all. One lived in the Leafy Lanes of her mind. How such a ridiculous person imagined she'd actually risen in the social hierarchy! With her concocted 'posh' accent gleaned from television.

And the other one was even worse, but different. Talk about all mouth! - a screeching little wimp, ranting and raving about imagined insults. A few University certificates and this is how you end up: totally dysfunctional, stuck in the past, unable to move on, a raving paranoid. She and her husband had simply been sensible, accepting the *real* facts of life: knuckle-down, skip all that education nonsense and the fancy talk, and sort out your life. It's obvious. She couldn't understand why she was plagued by these thoughts, by these people. It must be to do with her upbringing. Her husband was *so* rational. No children was agreed before they married. Fine! What's the problem? What business was it of her parents? And, she was quite sure her siblings had opinions, although it was none of their business. His nervous breakdown? Work-related stress, not his fault. And she always overlooked for promotion. All those graduates: a few weeks with her and then straight to another department, something to do with *Fast Track*. Nonsense. How was that fair? She knew more than them and she'd been a Company Person, a team player all her life. Same for her husband - both married to the firm, all their firms. But things were okay really, just hunky-dory.

The beverage break was another fun time with the girls. The afternoon was flying by, as usual, apart from the black thoughts, flashbacks and those awful sinking feelings, feelings of being trapped. No personal phone calls during office hours, please - one of the rules of work, and Gelasia had no reason to sneak any or receive any. Her husband was known to make a quick call to remind her of something. Not today because her telephone is temporarily out of order - in a very pleasant voice. Good! It happens.

## 71

Sensuality has its time and place and its many modes. He missed the primal type and decided that he might try it again sometime. The fact that his back was giving him jip was neither here nor there. It was sometime in that week thirty years ago when he stumbled off that silly stool. Was it twenty years? Whatever! But still young enough for lots of shenanigans of the sensual type and to venture onto an old stool to plaster a wall. He should have set up the two ladders joined by the plank. It would have taken a few seconds. The problem with injuring your back is that very often you don't realise you've done it. He just landed on his rump and he leapt up and kicked the stool! He was still very strong in those days and the stool went flying through the open French doors, newly installed that very morning! He looked round in dismay and was relieved that nobody had observed his multiple foolishness; a sigh of relief that the doors were intact, and the windows. He could tackle all aspects of building work except the 'electrics', as he often said. He had started work early that morning and was on his way home by the time the children of the house arrived home from school and were bereft at the discovery of their dead tortoise. Apparently, it had sustained a fatal injury, somehow involving a stool. Children love a mystery...

Tabatante the Sensualist sat at his work table, his back much improved after trying every known treatment thanks to *her*, having found his way home after his mishap concerning the calendar and his attempt to escape early to his Community Service. He liked being with men doing something useful, physical and skilful like the old days. There were wood chippings and sawdust everywhere, and he foresaw his wife tearing in from her outing like a whirlwind of indignation concerning the 'mess'. He would easily fob her off with a few growly, well-chosen flirty words of assurance and reconciliation. She was a sucker for a manly hormones, his! Of course he would tidy up as usual when he had finished his session with the magnificent wooden model he'd been working on for months. Of course he would, darling. They were proud that one of his models had been on display in the City Museum for some years. This one hadn't been commissioned either.

His father had introduced him to this hobby because he wanted his son to stop being so wayward and such a wastrel, and settle down to acquiring some real skills. It was one of those peculiar moments. Tabatante had always loved his Dad and gradually grew to despise his mother. She was dangerous and venomous. Her husband had no insight into her personality and when the son had grown up a bit, they'd departed together, driven out. Tabatante already hated his mother and became an amateur womaniser. His youthful vigour and natural lust encouraged his hopeful fantasies. His father had commented that woodcraft was the work of real men, as they examined a piece of irrelevant carpentry. That was it: the moment.

It was not only sensual, it was also contemplative. While working with wood, Tabatante had travelled far and wide in his mind. He had passed beyond fancy words and difficult concepts without ever stopping and had arrived had the station of silent understanding. In his mind everything was simple. Life itself was a dream, a pleasant dream. Other people brought aggravation in a rucksack that weighed them down. He tried not to be unkind, but was often short of patience. Why did they arrange their own crises? Bored with one crisis they worked on the next and jabbed at people to ensure it happened. The weekend loomed.

He stopped chiselling, sighed and gazed at the blank wall. He had painted it a shade of yellow. He couldn't recall its name. It would come to him when he stopped thinking about it. He had some vague intention to decorate the wall further, with a few tasteful paintings perhaps, bought from their favourite Arts shop. Then it became a giant television set. There they were! Not floating or swimming in space, but a near-perfect projection of those people. They were all there with their drinks and their chatter and their *crises*. The music was too loud to hear what they were saying! He chuckled to himself - you've got to see the funny side! But he could tell by the agitation of their bodies, the usual posturing, and waving of arms. His wife sat to one side, her face smoother than a well-plastered wall, the ice in her eyes focused on the ice in her glass, as she patted her brow with a white handkerchief. He had seen these white squares of cotton or silk (decidedly unhygienic!) used in period plays or old films. He imagined his wife had emerged from a time machine which had dragged her kicking and screaming centuries into the future and had deposited her unladylike in this uncouth City.

And where was he? Ah, there he is looking very suave and sophisticated, a maestro dissipating the heat, keeping the peace, and bringing the whole orchestra to a satisfying conclusion. Mmm. He sighed again: nothing like a pleasant fantasy to help the afternoon pass away quietly. The reality: there would be no passing away quietly this weekend unless his time had come.

"Righty-oh, I'll put the kettle on. Course the place is tidy, darling. My room's a mess, but a quick sweep and... Pardon. Repeat. Ah, righty-oh, it's on then, all systems are go. Just have to check the machine guns, have the SWAT team standing by and a rescue heli... Sorry? Oh." She's gone. Tight as an over-wound violin string. It begins. The weekend is confirmed. Boy, oh boy, patience is a virtue.

'Optimism'! He knew it would come to him.

Or was it called 'Cowardice'? Nah.

### 72

Tick. Tick. Ehh? Two vertical parallel red lines shot into the margin. Generalisation! Mosimenadue fidgeted, sighed, and stretched briefly at his desk. Life can be tedious if you're expected to do so much stretching. Another couple of thousand words, ten/fifteen minutes of the usual guff, with the odd feeble attempt at humour by people who really see themselves as stand-up comedians, and have as much insight as a trained parrot. He'd already decided his short para of brilliant advice to be appended in his eccentric scribble to denote genius and vast experience. It is interesting that a frustrated stand-up comedian mocks people who want to be stand-up comedians. Lest we forget! Indeed, forgetting is one of his greatest achievements, apart from holding the World Record for Typographical Errors. Embarrassment is not one of Mosimenadue's problems. Problems?

Ah, yes, the family. First things first. Deal with this immature dross and tick off a few items on the To Do list. Don't forget the Departmental Record. He checked his computer screen, which sounds superstitious, but once the lot was deleted! Some technical foul up; what a mess. He was being overwhelmed with sighs. Quick scan, a couple of words here and there. Dit dit dit. Yes, why not, couldn't have put it better myself (joke!), great, wonderful, astonishingly original - only read that five hundred times before! -tick, tick, scribble, scribble, scribble, tick, tick ,tick, scribble, scribble, and, after some high-speed, educated 'chunking', the final huge tick. And now for something erudite beyond compare from his personal collection of Things Erudite Beyond Compare. That took about three minutes, could be a new Personal Record. Don't forget the record on-screen. No! - couldn't possibly face another one. The students can wait.

The afternoon lazed ahead, sprawled on his chaise longue or maybe his traditional rocking chair - had to get one, his mentor/surrogate dad has one. He had no intention of becoming a mentor himself, but he could certainly acquire the rocking chair, fine wine, avant-garde works of art, and a much better, i.e. more expensive, residence in due course. It is perfectly normal to have a role model, but when you have a role model, you must know the 'bits' that apply to you, Mosi. Rocking chairs, traditional or otherwise, don't usually have much to do with role models. Mosi didn't quite understand. For a start, M's role model had worked his socks off! M. avoided work like the plague, this being a terrible disease from pre-Cat times. Mosi was not simply bone idle. There is always more to it.

The afternoon wandered about aimlessly, with Mosi a reluctant companion, listening to music, making coffee, replying to some useless e-mails, yawning, scratching, picking his nose. Roll on the evening! Then he could demonstrate his brilliance and roll on some impressionable and easily impressed young thing. Life was good. But - there were always buts... The afternoon is not a good time to be aimless - disturbing buts make their entrance.

The buts started to poke him painfully between the shoulder blades. He tried to ignore them but he couldn't.

The steam from his coffee clouded his thinking, blinded his eyes, and drew him into the black shiny liquid which reflected and magnified the light.

The weekend lay ahead. His overpowering mother, always there, hovering, casting her spells, smiling, the obsessive cleaner and cleaner of common sense, the expert crisis provider, impossible to live with, impossible to deal with. His father passed by, long passé, smiled a nod, cracked an inane joke, and was gone. The clown would definitely not be there, no possibility of that, not invited and would never attend. He had said so many times and in writing recently. If he was ever present (by accident), then blood would be spilt. No, it would be civilised, if you call *that*, that ship of fools, civilised. His maternal grandmother and her crude, arrogant and simple-minded husband, good only for inheritance, sooner rather than later, and the sooner the better. All this hanging about, going from one medical treatment to another. For goodness' sake, how much does all this longevity cost? Just get rid of them, shed a histrionic tear, pick up the inheritance and get on with your life. The kitchen became crowded!

The siblings, together with their gormless boyfriends and girlfriends, had just dropped by, popped in, came a-calling, to emphasise the 'hell' in hello. Oh, Mother of God! (What a stupid idea!) - now, look what he has to put up with, all that ridiculous, empty brained chatter! All those rationalisations of their minor catastrophes, as well as nonsense about their fantastical lives. The same rubbish as the last time and the time before that... never-ending. But why the torture now? Why is his brain rehearsing the coming weekend? Things are not (*never!*) resolved. Most of his consciousness was drowning in this swirl of aggravation because... he enjoyed it! These walking, talking failures cheered him up no end! They should really listen to his advice, which he was rehearsing right now, but not too much or they might improve their lot. The Eldest Child Syndrome (something he'd never heard of) suited him just fine, being the Golden Boy, and he always would be.

Naturally, that aunt creature and her mouthy children, his cousins, would be there, and a collection of *things*, their quasi-spouses. Mosi really needed secretarial assistance to keep track of this ever-changing list of paramours associated with his family: names, addresses, telephone numbers... And, shockingly, they'd started to reproduce - there were a few children toddling about. Really, it should be illegal. But, again, he did experience a degree of satisfaction.

When he emerged from his floating and diving in the shallow end, he discovered that his coffee was cold. Ah well, a quick blast of the microwave and all will be well. Might call one or two friends and have a little pretend rock at the same time. Mosimenadue: a man comfortable in his own skin.

## 73

Lunchtime had drifted by uneventfully, as expected. Radmilla frequently remained at her desk because it was convenient. No more rushing about at lunchtime, being sociable and socialising, those days were gone. Anybody was *usually* welcome to come in for a chat, those for whom there was a natural rapport after years of working together, or she might wander along the corridor to the staffroom for the same reason, or to converse with some of the less known colleagues, but neither happened today and she was quite pleased. Over many years, friendships had rarely developed at work and beyond the work context. For Radmilla, friendships, as such, had begun to develop decades before in her childhood or youth, two friends from schooldays and two from her first year, of many years, at the University, for example. It had occurred to her some years ago that the four people in question had never met each other! She had arranged a social evening for all five of them and the other four really didn't get on. There were so many 'personality clashes', she couldn't keep track of this four dimensional chess match! Or, was it five? The evening was a disaster and became one of her many funny stories of her particular sample of life's rich tapestry. These were her best friends - separately. She had learnt long ago that people relate to different aspects of different people and that's the way it is! It's not a mystery. It is simply that people are simple and complex simultaneously and, quite naturally, play different roles in different circumstances. You have to be experienced, decently tolerant, and very *cool*, as opposed to *cold*. A sense of humour is essential and also one of those many natural attributes. A person with no sense of humour is a peculiar object! Radmilla was all things to all people. Her 'primary' family and all the younger relatives were still the most important and loved people in her life. She considered this perfectly normal and didn't question it. Thus, in the many busy lives involved, weeks would pass and not a 'friend' in sight - perfectly normal.

Today, Radmilla was more interested to ensure that that file had been received and acted upon and, therefore, didn't mind at all chewing her tuna and mayonnaise bread roll in silence. It was not her direct responsibility (the file rather than the roll), but she knew perfectly well that time was of the essence in this case. It could be postponed, if necessary, but if it could be facilitated today, then ensure that it is done! Thus, everything was on schedule.

It had taken many months to get this far and several interim reports. There was a direct line of directives, an awkward, but accurate descriptor. It means that there are a minimal number of persons involved, in rank order, and the process demands total confidentiality. Indeed, it is impossible to access the files on such a case. The *few* know the facts - the *raison d'être*, the big picture - and the many assistants do their specified jobs and have no idea what is actually going on. Years of experience will produce very good guesses, but, then, nobody discusses their work or speculates on its context. Integrity is everything and is expected without question or encouragement or order from above. Radmilla, her seniors, and her juniors only work in Central Computer because they have already proved their moral development. There is a *silence* amongst such people. Josh, one of Radmilla's many Secretaries (Probationary), was beginning to concern her. He seemed too personally involved. This is not a good sign, but only time will tell. She had known many people to suddenly get into line, so to speak. Josh probably would. In terms of satisfying natural, but silent, curiosity, all would be debriefed in due course. It is a rare case which must remain secret in perpetuity. Confidentiality is not the same as secrecy and discretion is not the same as underhandedness.

She pondered the case idly as she picked a crumb from her front and placed it between her lips, then stroked between lower lip and chin. It's very annoying to discover a crumb on your chin or a speck of anything at all in the very fine hairs of your upper lip hours after you thought you'd eaten it all. There is a small mirror in one of her lower desk drawers and also one in her handbag, now she thinks of it. Vanity is a bitter and twisted view of self and the world and should be long gone by about twenty. Her attitudes to crumbs and mirrors is not about vanity, it is about efficiency and other people's comfort. She mused on the 'vanities' in this case. How can people be so shallow and vicious in order to achieve nothing that is valued or can even be named? Radmilla wasn't even sure if 'vanity' was the right word, but it covered a multitude and would do for the moment, this moment of tuna and mayonnaise. It was in these moments that she was grateful that her fairly complicated life was so simple. The horror facing these people because they refused to understand. No, she didn't really believe that. They would experience horror, but it would be part of the saga, part of the role they have been playing and their awful determination to keep it going. She thought she might start a rumour: tuna and mayonnaise help you think clearly. Young people would believe anything, they really would, and she had a peculiar sense of humour. Sometimes it was just so nice to go home, kick off your shoes, watch the television news and know that you are not on the edge of the biggest shock of your life.

Gosh, crumbs everywhere. Crunchy bread rolls are never a good idea for the office, but a combination of hunger and temptation can prove lethal. Now, that little pan and brush?

He had strolled and scratched and pondered. He had an itchy spot on his buttock. It happens, too much sitting around. Maybe his buttocks had a mind of their own and were telling him something. He was hoping they'd put their heads together and take him hostage. Nothing is quite real. It was great, then it was terrible, then it was great - and now? One must persevere, be patient, always look on the bright side. Thus thought Damodural, thinker and litterateur, as the afternoon formed into a black cloud.

He'd strolled and now he strode. He headed for his private shelter through the teaming streets, awash with the toings and froings of the busy afternoon, the involved and connected. He should have stayed put, with his sedate coffee for another hour or two, and watch the rush flow by.

The eyes everywhere, watching him but not seeing him, not recognising him. One day they would because he was still a contender. He was still young! He nipped sharply into a darkened cafe, like a rabbit chased by a dog. He almost cowered at the wall, not easy for a person of his mass.

"A table for one?" He was startled by the unexpected formality.

"Yes, and just a coffee."

"We have a minimum charge." The young man said discretely and indicated the menu.

A minimum charge. Typical. He felt hunted.

Damodural spotted a table in a quiet corner, stood up, caught the eye of the waiter and indicated his preference. The waiter waved a friendly "please do."

With his back to the wall, in privacy he scanned the letter. It was monstrous! But clever. Surely, it couldn't be *accurate*. Surely, it was exaggerated and pretty vilely inappropriate, written by an enraged old fool. Why can't he just get over it and move on? Some people are hopelessly stuck in the past. But... there were certain things in *his* past that just wouldn't go away. The past is not a foreign country, but it can be a boulder you drag around, which is who you are. He thought of their child, a vulnerable kid, cute, innocent, and full of the joys of spring. Sometimes clichés are okay. If this letter were even nearly accurate... some kind of inherited disease. But this *thing* isn't physical, it's psychological, or maybe psychosocial, or something like that. He wasn't sure, not his subject, all this psychobabble. Nevertheless, he found it unnerving, like the appalling events in recent years. The letter didn't mention any of that, but the implications were there. The letter described the past and predicted the future without being specific. It was appallingly and deliberately obtuse, *slippery*. It skirted the issues in an expert and violent manner, but not threatening. It was sad and prophetic, it bode ill. He'd gobbled his *doughnuts*, but had forgotten his coffee.

"Hi." No, he was fairly certain he hadn't said that, but he probably should have because he'd recognised the man passing in the opposite direction, although the man had looked away immediately. Maybe Damodural had said something on a previous occasion. He looked very like Dam's brother, although he didn't have one. But if he'd had a brother, that man would be his spitting image. You are attracted to people similar to yourself. Or, is it the opposite?

"Hi." This time he had said it and too fast before the recorded message that his telephone was temporarily out of order. What a nuisance. He really wanted to talk to his girlfriend, just to hear a human voice, hers. He felt alone. There was no point looking for a public telephone, hardly an emergency. Life can be overwhelming in its contradictions and ambiguities. Is anything real?

He was enjoying the cosy bus. The light was too bright - he wasn't in the mood for all that vitamin D! You can get too much of a good thing. He tapped in his request and the light was reduced by a few *international candles*. So precise. Nobody nearby objected and, feeling full and safe, he dozed.

It was a magnificent party! He didn't recognise the place or any of the crowd. It was a great bar. He could hear clearly so many conversations and a band was about to strike up. He spotted three women buskers who had just made their way to the counter. One was a 'one man band' (large drum on her back, harmonica still attached, acoustic guitar, cymbals between her knees, brightly coloured clothes and a beautiful white smile); the second similarly attired, with guitar; whilst the third pea in the pod carried a string instrument he didn't recognise. The one man band smiled at him. He was young, tall and good-looking, a combination of cute and rugged. He was as free as a bird and knew a drink would facilitate making her acquaintance. Their eyes met again and the ship's bell was clanged behind the bar: last orders! She smiled, he mustn't hesitate, as he frequently did, not this time. The bell clanged twice and he was too late! How could that be? He felt a rush of despair and inadequacy. Ting ting ting - a tiny sound below his ear.

He stepped from the bus, feeling groggy and a blast of cold air was unexpected, but not unpleasant (as planned). Heading home, his long shadow, cast by the solar streetlights by this time lit, slid along silently before him, reaching its optimal length, shrinking rapidly and, as he imagined, skulking behind him, before appearing suddenly by his side and leaping ahead. This was morbid and obsessional, he thought, and he could feel himself sinking. The fact that his shadow was interrupted by hundreds of others helped to distract him, but it wasn't healthy. Snap out of it!

If that angry old fool was right, then that woman shouldn't be allowed anywhere near his child. He had to go there to collect his kid. She was their occasional child minder, his girlfriend's mother.

## 75

Back in her multi-roomed family home, replete with manicured garden, deplete of family, thank goodness, Jardena checked herself in her very impressive - indeed, envious - living room mirror. With her middle finger she moved a gathering of rebellious hair carefully back into its rightful place over her right eye. She studied her face, first moving to her right and then slowly to her left. She smiled. It would have been alarming if it hadn't been for the purpose of scrutinising her teeth, all well and delft-sparklingly in place. Her tongue shot out almost to her chin and resembled an off-yellow doormat on which many a boot had been wiped. She put it away, remembering the boozy party of the coming weekend. These modern fillings are brilliantly realistic! She was never unpleasant to her dentist, her hairdresser, her beautician, or her coach at the Ladies Gym, although, believe me, these people could be extremely irritating. One has to be pleasant. And we mustn't forget her dress designer and fashion consultant.

It brought another smile to her face to think how *anybody* can call themselves 'consultant'; but go with the flow, let them dream. Jardena had been a Consultant in many of her previous incarnations, although she rarely furnishes details. Her friends are an ever-changing circle, the members of which cannot quite put their fingers on Jardena's many former professions. She admires her lips, still opulent.

In no need of a mirror, she smooths her blouse and skirt, fingers her taut tummy, palms her pert buttocks, and inspects her shoes. All in excellent order. You wouldn't believe that forty years have passed since University, except for the clothing, of course, which is the latest for a woman of her age and class, although one is young at heart. Scanning her mental list, she concluded that all necessary tasks had been completed - rents, lunch taken, business calls, husband under control, children pleasantly distant, maids elsewhere for the afternoon. Thus satisfied, she decided to check her finances.

Jardena repaired to her office, her inner sanctum. In this role, she is extremely efficient, far better than her husband who was barred from her office. He had to be taught that there are limits. He stays out of her room and her affairs. Jardena has a large mouth to accommodate her large and perfect teeth as well as her sharp tongue. Unlike her sister, she doesn't shout, rant, screech or sob; she simply focuses like a sniper. Hence, she has never been 'picked up' by Central Computer: no inappropriate 'noise' or physiological 'blips'. Other persons in her company have produced such graphical jumps and their inappropriate behaviour has been noted. Her husband was warned several times and now keeps quiet. Her children were brought up to keep quiet. Her ex-husbands didn't learn this in time. Jardena collects property and husbands. Some of these husbands were actually hers. She likes husbands, but she doesn't like fathers. She understands control, patience, using her brain, waiting for the right moment, keeping things under the radar, as people say. That's how she was brought up. Little is known of her childhood; she tells little stories, some of which are almost true. But if you ask the right questions, you'll get the right answers from Central Computer if you have top level clearance.

She uttered something - we could access C.C. - and her computer sprang to life. She pulled some files from her cabinet and started to enter figures in both file and computer. She double-checks. It is her wont. She treble-checks herself, double-checks her credits, and skates gracefully across all aspects of her life. There were so many *objects* to deal with. It was irritating. If it wasn't one thing, it was another, so many ornaments to coordinate, organise, order and polish to shiny perfection. Who invented families! All these parasitic creatures flitting in and out, biting and stinging like gnats, leaving itchy lumps in their wake. They were enough to drive anyone to distraction. Why were so many well educated people of her acquaintance, indeed, her family, so dysfunctional? It was one of the great mysteries and they kept calling on her to actually do something. What exactly, pray tell? They never could. It always started with little chirps, some hopping and perching and twittering, but rapidly, aided by large amounts of alcohol, they transformed into menopausal vultures that had given up the carcass of increasingly competitive discussion and had started tearing lumps out of each other. It was all so predictable and - talk about green-eyed monsters! - why couldn't they just get themselves organised and get on with it, life? Why is everything such a hassle? Oh, a mistake? She checked her figures. Typical. They interfere with her life even when they're nowhere around! She almost chuckled.

She sighed at the very thought of the weekend. And those telephone calls, those ambushes, those predictable skirmishes, but they'd reduced in frequency. She'd ensured that. Some people just won't die off. Several ridiculous creatures, mainly men, still causing problems after a monstrous number of years! Still they emit poison these retards inhale voluntarily; their own worst enemy. What about that appalling wedding speech? Men.

She threw down her pen, exasperated. She'd decided on a large drink before tackling those calls. Get it over with. A quick, agitated gulp, a few deep breaths, thinking herself into her calm and mature voice, she had a pleasant surprise. She knew she wasn't putting it off; it wasn't her fault. Dismayed, she was still reduced to such childish reasoning. But, nothing she could do: her phone was temporarily out of order. It correlated with all those awful people permanently out of order. Those children of hers and their cousins - which pod did they arrive in? In her next life she'd be a C.E.O. with lovers and respected for her charity work and donations to orphanages. Enough time-wasting and back to some satisfying arithmetic! Her tongue momentarily flickered into sight.

## 76

Samplers and sequencers cluttered the playroom of his brain. Sometimes the music wouldn't stop. Being relaxed and edgy at the same time, one of those days; he kept stumbling into a deep hole. Dad had said be careful of women, they acquire too much power; then complain about being disempowered. They should try being a man! Some do. Why hadn't she rung? Surely they understood each other by now. Two hours lounging in the park watching the day go by - it's really not on.

Pacing the apartment, looking out windows, watching the boats, the millions, looking for a place to moor his ocean tossed mind, he had slopped coffee down his leg, when a bird crashed into the window and plummeted out of sight. He swore very quietly, at everything, more of a hiss than a curse. The day was becoming a void. He waited: nothing. Calm down. Don't phone. That was the deal, the agreement. She'd ring. Nothing bad had happened. Obviously. She'd decided not to ring? Just work! Do the serious stuff first, *then* relax, but know *when* to relax. His father's advice from long ago, or was it repeated? Those things were always blurry, but it certainly wasn't his mother. Don't go there, not into that murky cave where the shape-shifters live, the creatures with their umpteen versions, changing the rules, moving the goalposts. Goalposts in a cave? Ah, so what! He picked up his favourite guitar. "I got the goalpost blues hangin' round my brain..."

He worked on the same series of songs at times like these. He found it his natural escape, these songs that stretched back several years. They had gradually collected themselves around him like old friends. They were his, but never quite right. This didn't tire him, it enervated him. They were his babies and he the nurturing father. They would grow up to be fine songs. He suspected that they might turn into something big, maybe an opera. But let's not get carried away; one step at a time; lots of other things to do. But it could happen. He drifted into this world of words and sounds and he was himself, at home. He didn't have to prove anything, he wasn't in competition, there was no undefined battle raging. The coming weekend flashed through his mind and was gone.

Then the phone rang and he left the settee like a sprinter off the blocks! He knew it was her. Be cool. Men should be cool. If men show their emotion, it is somehow humiliating and anger is even worse. What's the *real* problem? Let's face it, there isn't one. It's only a walk in the Park. This will be a walk in the park.

"Oh, Psy, I'm so sorry. The Park, it went clean out of my mind! I got talking with Mum and time flew away. Then my aunt turned up - her sister, that is, and her little kid - and I lost track. Something was telling me "this evening's gig and nothing else". Are you okay? Do you forgive me?"

Of course he did. What was there to forgive? Yes, this evening. It' should be a good one.

He knew that the boulder he'd been carrying was suddenly a feather. Why was he so weak? On his own again, he was almost tearful. Why is it always there? That thing, that threat that everything is going to be taken away. It's not rational. He turned up the volume. A bit of practice for the gig would be sensible. The band's in its early days. The rehearsal was okay, but... They were all good enough to cover up mistakes if need be and it probably would be! 'Artists Block', as it is called by the locals (with or without an apostrophe), was as solid as a rock, luckily for the neighbours.

A few hours passed, a few breaks, those tunes so familiar and easy. He hoped the others were as confident. He had wondered often why some people come into the business. Even some of his fellow students had appeared bored much of the time, dragging themselves through courses for no good reason, except for some notions of inevitable fame. He'd been criticised for being judgmental and self-righteous. These days he tried to keep quiet and just wait for people to drop out, disappear quietly. He'd seen it in his own family, that kind of *pretence*, self-delusion, playacting. He couldn't put his finger on it. It was both obstructive and destructive, and damaging to others. He couldn't stand his siblings. He felt he was under permanent attack. It was awful. And his parents had torn each other apart and were still doing it. That letter? Amazing and ridiculous. What was the point? His father becoming increasingly mad!

His childhood had been one long shouting match. But when he'd visited his father at the age of twelve and his dad had lost his temper with the kids' constant arguing, Psybanes realised that he'd never heard his father shout before. On that occasion, one bellow to 'shut up!' and then back to normality. So what was all the shouting about in his early childhood? It was all a blur now, a half remembered nightmare. It was frightening then, especially when giant policemen appeared framed in the bedroom door. "Everybody in here okay? Don't worry, everyone's a bit upset downstairs. It's all quiet now. Try to get to sleep. School in the morning." That happened several times. It was always mum's voice for hours. She would start shouting and she wouldn't stop.

Such thoughts weren't new. They were like a regular beating. He thought he would ring round the guys, have a few chats and finalise things for this evening. He was almost relieved to discover that his telephone was temporarily out of order. Ah, well, who cares! The calls weren't necessary anyhow, just being sociable, a bit lonely. But he was used to it. Watch some television and relax.

The cheese sandwiches lay on the settee producing mini-volcano noises - the milk helped - while Purvanos absentmindedly surfed television channels. Surfing could be exhausting as there were thousands of miles of channel. He muted in dismay, slumped back on the cushion and surveyed the Himalayas of his body towards his feet which still worked as directed, sometimes to the right and left in unison, sometimes in synchronised opposition. He could have been a ballerina! When you are bored you make yourself laugh. In retirement he'd become a lay-down comedian.

His organ came to mind. He decided that time on that might finish him off in his present spiritual state and decided to leave it until later, but before his wife returned because she really didn't like it. She complained of headaches.

Gazing at the white ceiling, he dreamt of deserts, frozen wastes, sandy beaches. His hobbies hadn't changed in fifty years: sport (mainly involving balls), beaches (all kinds, bikinis essential), beer (a bevy of brews), and music (anything that nudged his pleasure centre). Once established, about the age of three, people don't change. Simply access Central Computer (with the appropriate authority), and trillions of records will confirm this.

Self-centredness is peculiar. No mathematico-philosophical perspective can rationalise a truly self-centred life. The condition is multiply destructive. The 'sterility' of Purvanos is, apparently, his chosen lifestyle. Regardless of recorded intelligence, such persons appear *mentally retarded!* and people say this, quietly. Purvi, *et al.,* have a deficiency of human attributes, their life untouched. They collect jokes and quips and social skills; they collect knowledge for chit-chat and quizzes and political chinwags; they collect chuckles and guffaws; hand-claps, thigh slaps and finger clicks; touches, nudges, pats and hugs. But it's like being hugged by a cardboard box with arms and pre-recorded statements for all occasions.

Purvanos hopes his wife will remember the eggs. Otherwise, things may become inconvenient, but he'll pretend otherwise. It's in his eyes. The ceiling turned into thousands of battery hens, but no eggs. There's no point having a battery hen farm if you can't collect the eggs. He started to count the hens and calculate the number, completed some of the process, worked out the best way to do it and stopped because it was only imagined. You must use the correct word: hen. It's not chicken. We don't eat chicken, we eat hen. And their children.

Although warned for bad language, he'll never be 'picked up' by Central Computer. His blood pressure barely changes! He never raises his voice. He doesn't talk to himself. He pads almost soundlessly. He doesn't read or write. He doesn't paint. On occasion, he tinkles with his organ. And he drifts. He drifts unnoticeably from one entertainment to another. This confirms that nothing is perfect. Surely, this *non-behaviour* should be investigated. He is a man without opinion, without passion (apart from the usual, now averaging once every three months), a man *without* - outside the warmth of humanity, a man of hobbies and collections.

Drifting in the doldrums, sustained by the blubber of his habitual thoughts, nobody has ever landed accidentally and built a fire on his back or warmed the cockles of his heart or scraped the barnacles off his bottom. Dragged away from his egg calculations, he was startled that the phone hadn't rung. Some people have a sixth sense. He sensed that something was wrong, but probably not. It may have been the touch of cramp in his right gastrocnemius muscle.

He is now undertaking a series of prostrate semi-genuflections, which is not like him, prayerful he isn't, unless you include the odd nod of adoration to his own reflection. Ah, these exercises of the once honed and toned, a good investment, although there is nothing more annoying than a painful cramp brought on by doing absolutely nothing. It is most inconvenient, but a few more genubendings to facilitate oppositional toe-group-flections and the cramp will go away. Everything is connected. The toebone connected to the headbone, the headbone connected to the elbone. Now, hear the word of the ... He considered whistling, but changed his mind.

Not aroused by the prospect of the forthcoming weekend. Although somewhat inconvenient, he would certainly attend - not only entertaining, but free beer - just to please his wife. It was no skin off his nose. He had his own family to think about, rarely. What's the point? They were just fine. No need to complicate things by contacting them. They were busy living their own lives, which is as it should be. A pity her side of the family didn't have such good sense. Things had gone drastically wrong, but it was nothing to do with him, but his wife enjoyed it. Talking of whom , where is she and the phone call?

He felt a complete silence, except for the sudden dry creak of his knee. Needs a bit of oiling! He checked his telephone and sure enough he'd been cut off in his prime! How did he know that? Had his wife said something earlier? Was he expecting a call from her? He couldn't remember. Well, it didn't matter, nothing to worry about. Oh, look at that! All systems are down. That doesn't happen very often. But it does happen. No big deal. He considered that, apart from several hundred thousand people in his building, he was all alone. He liked it and started to exercise his other leg just for the sake of balance. He thought of the days of his youth when he had jogged daily, thousands of miles in all. He glanced down and wondered about the whereabouts of his cast-off suits and concluded that if he'd calculated the miles he'd run, then he could calculate the pounds he'd gained since he'd given up jogging, as well as... it was complicated. Where'd he put his calculator? Probably on his organ. Within a few minutes a plaintive sound came from his caveroom, which wasn't the sound of a calculator.

## 78

She sat becalmed on the long yawn of the post-lunch-dip sea. Everything in order, no need to *liaise* - let them wait - she drifted towards the shoreline landing of five o'clock. The sun warmed her head and shoulders and she dreamed of being far away. She dreamed of running her own pub in one of the leafy nooks of the City. She was leafing at this moment through one of her favourite scholarly books pressed snugly against the inner spine of an official file held up to public view, the possibility that a creepy little person might come by, not somebody important because they'd phone, but one of the wandering minions, singing and dancing to somebody else's tune.

Some of Lakota's happiest days had been spent in the 'Peculiar Phenomena Studies Department', as dubbed by generations of students. Only a few years ago, but it seemed a lifetime, one of those distant climes she dreamed of. She thought she might return sometime, but always put it off. It was too difficult to organise, it would destabilise what little stability she had managed to achieve, and study was so demanding. "You go to university to discover how stupid you are. If you don't discover this, you were too stupid to go there in the first place." Her Dad, typical of him, the resentful old fool.

She scanned the contents page of the book she'd brought to work, from her time of peculiar studies, and hovered over the expression 'Dumbing-Down'. What was it like in those days when they were so dumb they spelt it 'dumming-down'? It must have been mad! - not an academic certificate worth a jot. How could they allow that?

The Propagation of Bastards and Demise of the Family. She glanced over the file. That is, over the *top* of the file. The corridor is clear - no point inviting trouble - and she ruminated on the chapter, which she recalled almost by rote. She pulled from her mental archive the ever increasing figures of that era and the graphs flashed before her mind's eye. Amazing! The production of illegitimate children had grown proportionately faster than the population until bastards and their unemployable mothers had become the norm. The psychological damage should have been obvious and *spread like a plague*. She'd written that in her essay and got a B++.

The Re-emergence of Fascism: The Attitude to Immigration. Now, that chapter was frightening and shocking. Imagine that happening now. Impossible. She sighed. The disaster was inevitable. Why didn't everybody realise this? Everything is joined together, one thing affects another, cause and effect, the house of cards was bound to collapse. And that ridiculous thing called Capitalism: a myth, it didn't exist, and it ruled the planet! Unimaginable. She felt even more deflated. The wrong book for a sneaky read.

She pictured the rogues' gallery of her family and felt light-headed. Was history repeating itself? What was going on? She thought of her father and blocked out the thought. They were the whole thing again, on a micro scale. Maybe that's how it starts.

She slipped the book onto her lap, laid the file down and leant to her right to squeeze the paperback into her jacket on the back of her chair. She couldn't believe how morally bankrupt people were. They deserved what they got! But nobody deserves that. Even today, she was aware that some people are fundamentally dishonest. She glanced at her watch. She had better be seen, if seen at all, to be doing something vaguely useful.

She reached for her mobile phone and remembered 'Mass Communication in Which Nothing was Communicated'. Every chapter describes (and predicts) catastrophe, indeed, *the* Catastrophe. Constant 'talk' is still going on. The weekend will be constant white noise, ranting, raving, tantrums... She must be cool: either don't drink or drink a lot. She'd already decided. They are so childish. 'Adultescence: The Disaster of Delayed Development'. Yes, it's them! Is it her? She mustn't drink too much. She is so like most of the family. She doesn't want to end up a slob in twenty years. She's already a slob! Is she? She thought that this morning in front of the bathroom mirror. 'Delusional Dysmorphia: The Evil Goddess of Self-Obsession'. Her entire family has that! Has she? Leave that book, or she might go mad. Like her mother! Have some chocolate and calm down. 'To Eat or Not to Eat: That is the Question', one of the final chapters describing the decline of civilisation as they knew it. It's happening again!

She scrabbled in her other jacket pockets for her telephone. She had to ring one of the lunatics to get an update. She was curious about that crazed letter, and the rest - after all, they are her family. At one time they loved each other.

She snarled something that was not picked up by C.C. *What's* out of order? Why can't they give proper information? She sucked a single square of her chocolate bar as she tried her other brother's number. Same response. Then her phone rang. Strange.

"Hi. Oh, yes, it's finished. I could pop it along now. Oh, sorry, forgot the 12.30 update, went clean out of my mind. I suppose you'll be in first thing. Righto..." I thought the phones were out of order.

Might as well have a wander. Ah, look at that, right on schedule, one of the creepy little people. That'll save energy.

She wiggled her index finger in a sweet and sociable way, a come-on that definitely wasn't. He knew and popped his head around the door.

"You called, madam?" Is that good-nature or sarcasm?

"Could you drop this down to *Sir's* secretary?"

"Yep, no prob, it's on my way."

I thought it might be. She tapped into the corridor monitors. Yes, there he goes, into the Gents for a quick read. They are so predictable, the creepy little people who should be kept in a cupboard under the stairs.

## 79

Notably, Lakota had no thoughts on 'Sexual Promiscuity and the Death of Civilisation' or 'The Growth of Insanity: Individual Madness & the Madness of Individualism'. It's shocking that these phenomena increase to the point at which they become 'normal' prior to collapse. The great irony of sexual activity is that it produces so much death. C'*est la vie,* to quote from another old language, or it should be *c'est la mort*. But I must not over-complicate things already over-complicated.

Arguably, all empires have declined and fallen due to individual decadence and their whispered conspiracies. This spreads like a disease until it becomes societal and then, at times, global. Hence the demise of the Western Empire, followed by the demise of the Middle Eastern Empire, and so on. We do not even know exactly when this happened because of the huge gap in written records. The Catastrophe was so total that their existences at all have become part of an oral tradition, many different oral traditions. The Catastrophe itself was barely understood. Remarkable as it appears, the Cat was described for a long time as prehistoric.

Concerning written records, as stated I was instructed to produce this account and its accuracy is implicit. I am aware that Radmilla is producing her written account. At the time of writing, I know she has chosen a novelistic approach. I have accessed the first five thousand words and note she has changed names and locations. This is how creative people work. She couldn't possibly be to protecting the innocent, but we'll see. Maybe she's developing a significant psychological depth, which may be greater than the facts. Novels must not be ignored - they tell us many 'hidden' things about the time, events and the writer. It is not unknown for writers to attempt to write sensible texts even in *our* day and age!

One of my instructions is to include a brief description of the origin of the City.

At this very moment the City relaxes in its summery stupor of mid-afternoon, the calm before the storm of the rush hour when people are heading home after their day's work. Then the place will be chock-a-block, like a colony of purposeful ants high on illicit drugs - more haste, less speed is advised. But the City is also very high up the league, thanks to its very low accident rate. Few people will be killed or injured outside their own home. The kitchen is still the most dangerous place to go unaccompanied and it is also the most dangerous place to go accompanied unless you are intent on reproduction... We have every statistic you could think of, including that one. We live in the Age of Data. We can access a googolplex (or even more!) of bits of datum on any known subject or aspect of a subject even if the 'subject' happens to be a human being within the context or nowhere near the context of a research experiment. You name it, and we've got it ragged, tagged and bobtailed. So where did it all come from? J & the One Hundred.

They emerged from the Mountain. This atop a vast labyrinth deep in the earth, some of it natural, the rest dug out and modelled over several hundred years where it is estimated several thousand people lived. Accurate records are not available. It was dictated that survival was more important than diary-keeping. It is speculated that written records were banned. As the decades went by in these desperate circumstances, a belief that the written word was intrinsically evil became established. Both reading and writing are fundamentally vain, self-indulgent and, therefore, damaging to self and society. Human beings are gregarious creatures - we congregate, co-operate and communicate. When the 3C's begin to breakdown, they are replaced by the other C's: centeredness, chaos and catastrophe. This has happened time and time again and it finally did globally and almost permanently. The book was banned and the sword was deemed mightier than the pen. People very quickly forgot how to read and write.

In order to flourish, the underground community became monastic in character. A Rule was developed and strictly adhered to. Nobody knows the originator of this, but, according to the stories passed down from generation to generation, a caste of warrior-monks developed comprised of the most enlightened and the most ferocious of the Rule's adherents. These men were trained in high moral principles and physical prowess. In mature adulthood, those appropriately 'formed' took vows of chastity, poverty and obedience, established on ancient principles. When the time was right, when the earth had recovered, the One Hundred emerged into the light. They were already ruthless in applying their principles, their Rule. The Order still exists, but is entirely peaceful, sometimes referred to as the J's.

The City was carved out of the forest which hugged the river. At first it was simply a walled city for its inhabitants' safety against wild animals unknown and unrecognisable at the time. It also protected them from the inevitable breakaway groups. The latter were hunted down and eliminated - there could be no opposition. The entire planet had nearly been destroyed by factions of every type everywhere. All societies, countries, and cultures had been torn apart. Only threads of decency and memory remained, whilst the planet itself had virtually started to implode: like a line of standing domino pieces, biological systems had fallen, destroying themselves and each other until... the calm. People learnt the calm.

J & the One Hundred mirrored the calm; their calm ordering, their fierce enlightenment. Then, when order was restored, they unearthed their Secret. Deep in the mountain they had protected their Archive. Mother Nature and human civilisation were re-established. Finally and inevitably, the Cities of the world discovered each other. This had been a spontaneous resurrection because this is what human beings are and this is what they do. Education was no longer oral: reading and writing were re-established. Literacy began to rule...

1p.m.

D.C. I. Cody glanced at his watch and then at the large clock on the wall, still several seconds fast. Nothing is perfect. Thirteen hundred hours, he breathed to himself. He was a stickler for punctuality. And then the brief knocks and in they came. Hardly a fashion parade, but certainly a parade: the long and the short and the tall, the muscular, the slightly chubby and all as sharp as pins, but not necessarily in sartorial terms. But, as one would expect, the detectives of Psychological Crimes could blend in unnoticed, and didn't miss a twitched eyebrow, a dilated pupil, a dry mouth, a licked lip, a rubbed nose, a fidget, or a sigh. The rest - simultaneous physiological data provided by ICN's (Integrated Cellchip Networks) - when requested from C.C. These police were experts in common sense, applied science, and perseverance.

They shuffled their chairs, nodded or grunted greetings to each other, and manoeuvred into two semi-circles in front of the large screen and at right angles to Cody behind his desk to their left and only thirty-eight seconds behind schedule.

"Ladies and Gentlemen: last briefing." They nodded, shuffled files, glanced at an array of electronic recording devices suited to their personal way of working, used to his formality. They might call him Wild Bill behind his back, but this characterised his calm application to the job. But try not to 'mess up' with Wild Bill.

"Sir, D.E.P.?"

"Indeed."

He fingered keys on his desk console and eleven red dots appeared on the screen and their personal electronic devices.

"As you can see they are scattered about the City. Most of us are creatures of fear and habit and they certainly are. The best way to deal with these people is to isolate them from each other. This will make our job easier today, as it will for other professionals from here on in. They've had forty years for inane chatter and now it stops. At sixteen hundred hours all telephonic communication will become impossible for the eleven. They'll be informed that the system is temporarily down. They won't give it a second thought."

He keyed an instruction and 16T appeared on each red dot.

"Local police have already received instructions to carry out arrests soon after 16:00. They'll be cautioned and informed that they are being taken into custody under the Merkan Act. They probably won't know what it means, but ignorance is no excuse - crimes have been committed.

They'll be brought here for interview. They will be brought in by different entrances and interviewed well apart from each other."

He tapped his console and individual instructions appeared for each detective on their personal console.

"Received instructions? Please check that you are clear exactly whom you are to interview and that you've received the Individualised Interview Questionnaire." There was some audible sighing. Cody smiled. He knew technology was considered by some to be miraculously infallible... except when it goes wrong.

"Yes, folks, but just call out, starting back row, nearest the door, the name of your interviewee and confirm you've received the 2IQ. We don't want you double-booked or to give the wrong questionnaire, do we?" he said, acting the caring father.

One or two red dots flickered. This indicated that they were still breathing and some of them moving around. He always enjoyed the sense of malicious satisfaction when he knew that their degree of freedom was about to be significantly curtailed: they wouldn't be going anywhere for some time. He didn't feel guilty, he felt sympathy for their victim, who still had no idea what was going on. In these cases, the victim could not be told, although there was always the danger that the victim could do harm to themselves. The probability of this was greatly reduced by data provided by Central Computer. 'Know the enemy' and, in this case, know the friend or the victim. Cody knew the victim would survive the afternoon and probably for many years to come, because the victim had survived so long. In such cases, a victim could be lost - they just couldn't carry on any longer - but none during Cody's watch. He had an impeccable record. So far. Pride may or may not come before a fall, but smugness certainly does. Never become smug, Cody told himself. "Complacency Costs Lives" was one of his mantras.

"Judges lined up, Gov?" The briefing continued.

"Yes. They've got everything in hand," Cody answered.

"I presume Habeas Corpus dumped?"

Cody sought the voice and smiled a "Yep" in an equally casual tone.

"As you would expect, detective, all these criminals have already been tried. The evidence is irrefutable. But you're right to get all the facts straight in your minds," he addressed the group. "Tie up the loose ends - that's our job. Other questions?"

He noted the resignation, pallid faces, and degree of wear and tear scattered across the group. It takes a certain type to do this job. Months of labouring over data, noses to computer screens, poring over conversations (written or spoken), asking for data analyses whilst following a 'hunch'- ask the right question and you'll get the right answer, and frequently not asking the right questions: millions of facts, thousands of hours do not produce tanned, toned and healthy-looking individuals. Cody not only thought of his ex-wife and why she left him (things could have been so much worse, but she would have had to be a certain type of person, and, of course, there were no children), but he thought that his team deserved a holiday. But one thing at a time, Cody cautioned himself, let's get through today.

Pale but primed, when all angles had been covered and chairs replaced in their original precise assemblage, the team made their departure and toward the final stage of these proceedings, a mighty shock for the captives, a sense of a job well done for the captors: the bad guys were going to jail.

## 81

The room was sparse and white, but comfortable enough. The bed appeared comfortable. Bronnie sat on it and bounced up and down briefly, still young at heart. She was sure it would be comfortable, although she wasn't really thinking. She considered trying the two chairs, the desk chair and the armchair, but concluded it wasn't worth the effort. She had already noted the privacy afforded for washing and toileting. She was relieved, but already felt 'blocked' at the very thought. It would become inevitable, but put it off as long as possible. She'd always had such difficulties, coupled with obsessive and morbid ruminations, concerning evacuating her bowels outside her apartment. No, not in the corridors or the woods or on a bus! It was very serious for her: she called it agoraphobia because it sounded nicer. This went back to childhood, as she rationalised for herself to explain her peculiar self-imprisonment. There were other reasons. Her husband had accepted her explanations and had attempted to adjust accordingly. He'd had forty years to adjust. He would audibly sigh and self-counsel: be gentle, compromise, nobody is perfect, give her space, we all have our faults. The truth is it was one of the perks of his marriage.

She'd lost track of the time. She glanced at the clock on the wall: seven past seven. Like everything else in the room, the clock could not be 'accessed', i.e. tampered with. The television was similarly part of the wall. There was a console, again indented, flush with the wall, with labelled buttons. Even the toilet flushed automatically. A vocal request for any of these facilities could produce an automated response and no button-pressing necessary.

"Flush toilet, please," she experimented.

"Unnecessary request. Automatic flush."

She should have known. She hadn't used the toilet and now *they* know. She sat still. At least she had privacy and was not under visual surveillance. She should have known about that too. She tried to imagine people with disabilities. Those unfortunate people must have different facilities and differently designed temporary accommodation. She tried to convince herself that this was temporary and some kind of accommodation, a bit like a hotel perhaps. Yes, she told herself, treat this like a short break, a little holiday, a *sojourn*, an interesting treat, a brief vacation, certainly, a misunderstanding. She was good at pretending.

The pillow could not be separated from the mattress. The pillow could be reduced or expanded by pressing the buttons. The bed could be adjusted to suit any body, but the bed was attached to the floor, and the bed coverings were attached to the bed on the wall-side. They could not be removed. How were they washed? This troubled her. The bedclothes smelt gently of lavender. The material was soft to the touch and extraordinarily tough. Suddenly, she felt hemmed in like a trapped animal. She mustn't panic.

She had panicked. When they'd barged past her, ordered her to put on outer clothing, she'd become numb, unable to respond or think. She couldn't focus on their identity cards. She was too old for all this and she felt very old and alone right now. She had been told that she could have assistance or company, someone to talk to. All she had to do was make a vocal request. She was not alone. She certainly wasn't, every movement was being monitored and recorded.

She'd been told all sorts of things, but couldn't take them in. A medical doctor had already ministered certain pills to make her feel more relaxed. She sensed that things were going to get worse. What had that silly girl been saying and doing? What were they talking about? What crime? She felt very alone.

Where was her husband? They wouldn't answer that question, but one of them mentioned he was a witness. A witness to what? He must be at home and the situation would have been explained to him, but no contact with her was allowed. He was very sensible and would be okay. But he wasn't well and under permanent medical care. This wouldn't be good for his health. This was a vague, factual thought that didn't mean much to her. She really didn't feel much. He would be looked after. But why wasn't she allowed to contact him or any of her family? She felt like a prisoner.

She looked around the small room. The predominant colour was white and the few pieces of furniture were subtle hues of autumnal colours. It was very soothing and the music was also soothing. She felt calmer. She noticed that the chairs could not be moved, but could be adjusted. The overhead light dimmed slightly. She padded over to the wall console and noticed she wasn't wearing shoes. Where were her shoes, her sensible lace-ups? The floor was a kind of carpet and slightly warm. She pressed the 'light' button and off went the light. It was a soft dusk, the kind of evening to go for a walk. She used to do that when her children were young. That was so long ago that she'd almost forgotten. She could smell the blossoms along their street when the children were little. It wasn't her fault, the allegations. She had nothing to do with that, if it were true. She felt that old despair rising. She pressed on other lights around the room. The desk light might be useful. The room was quite cosy. She pressed off all the small lights except the desk light and returned to the bed. She pressed the bedside light button on the bedside console. She pressed it off. She lay down and half closed her eyes. She felt much calmer. Maybe those pills were working. She watched the desk light beginning to weaken, its rays expanding above her feet like a silent exploding star. She was beginning to drift away into the dark, into her memories. Tomorrow all would be revealed. Nothing to worry about. Just drifting, drifting away.

## 82

The white ceiling was soothing. The paint sparkled in the setting sun from the virtual window. It was like a field of ripening corn, so he imagined from television. He wondered vaguely about the type of paint. When he flicked on the bedside light the sparkles disappeared, so it must be something to do with the direction of the light source. Now, what was the point of that? When he remembered his feet, he jabbed at the button on the bedside console and the bed extended. Hands clasped behind his head and feet crossed, his eyes wandered the top half of the room. He was very relaxed, head on pillow, mind wandering, it was the most he'd been relaxed for some time. He'd been assured that it was a matter of routine.

The window must face west. He was curious about the height of the room, but not that curious. If he jumped he could touch the ceiling. If he stood on the desk chair... his weight might break it! That sort of thing had happened before and it could be more than embarrassing! One or two memories flashed through his mind of times past and his teenage years of clumsiness. No, leave it. Or, even worse, supposing the swing chair swung, he lost his balance and went sprawling? He could break bones and have to be rescued! Oh, for goodness' sake, put it out of your mind, Damodural, and relax. He chuckled. Ah, the thought had made him laugh - he *is* relaxing. You can't always tell what a person is thinking unless you have the stats.

Although accosted on the street, he'd been reassured and informed that his presence was required and essential. The two men had made that very clear. He didn't trust people in uniform, although he wore the uniform of the free-thinking *artiste* who didn't trust uniforms. He hadn't been allowed to collect his child. The kid would be upset and that woman had begun to unnerve him. The letter hadn't helped. But he knew he was being irrational: the kid wouldn't notice a delay and she'd do no physical harm. Indeed, she was overly intent on being nice. She made huge efforts to be the most compassionate person on the planet, all heart and soul. He'd felt uneasy from the first, but couldn't put his finger on it. He'd convinced himself that it was his problem, as people do, some kind of personality clash. One must compromise. Then a few months ago that appalling letter arrived out of the blue. It was a letter of festering rage. Would it boil over? Unlikely - it was all too *disciplined*. *Boil over*, something *festering*? - but, in what respect? Anger was a dangerous emotion.

In the course of that questioning he thought it helpful to show the letter. He'd opened it, flattened its several pages and pushed it across the table. They'd both glanced at the top page without picking it up, then at each other, and informed him politely that they already had a copy of that document. They'd used the word 'document' meaning *evidence*. Ah, had it, in some sense, already boiled over? That raging old fool - well, not that old - had gone too far. So, that nasty piece of work would be dealt with. There must be things he was not aware of. A serious chat with his girlfriend was on the cards. Talking of whom...

He was informed that she was part of the investigation, part of the case, and he would be debriefed sometime this evening. He pondered the word 'debriefed'. Things certainly needed explanation, but he trusted the authorities. He liked the look of that man - what's his name? It would come to him. He is very well-read, and Dam felt he could be trusted. He was obviously in charge, DCI-something. He had wandered in, politely interrupted, asked a question or two, and had then excused himself equally politely. He probably had a dossier on Damodural and knew exactly what sort of person he was. That explains his gentlemanly demeanour. The interviewers hovered between forced politeness and a degree of gruffness, probably not deliberate, more to do with background and upbringing, and obviously not literary people.

Oh, what about his little child, his pride and joy? If both parents were helping the, eh, case, then... The thought of Social services entered his brain. Stop! Negative thinking and ridiculous. They'd all be together for tea, or dinner, or whatever. Damodural was relieved that the kid wouldn't be with you-know-who for too long. He calmed down again. In fact, he was finding this all quite pleasant, this attention. People actually wanted to hear his insights. Whatever the case is, he was essential to it, or, at least, important enough to be interviewed. It's not sensible for people to get carried away with their own importance, he told himself, a minor player in this drama. Although he had no clue what was going on, he had plenty of interesting ideas to share later this evening. Maybe they could write something together on this subject, once things became clearer. The old *King Lear* story came to mind. Not many people have even heard of it, he mused. He'd read a modern translation decades ago, the ancient language being impossible, even older that the Old Language! Not his thing at all, the language, that is. The play was interesting, about a senile old fool. You can see why *King Lear* came to mind. Pretty obvious! Damodural chuckled.

He wriggled his toes, wagged his feet, tapped his thumbs together, his hands now clasped across his chest, as he dreamed way beyond the white ceiling. Things were looking up. He hadn't been so relaxed for years, especially the last few years. Things had been so difficult. It's nice for other people to take charge, even if it's just a few hours. He dreamed of a snowy mountain peak and himself standing on the summit.

She paced the room. She estimated ten angry paces. Then she paced it consciously - five each way. It certainly looked square, but who cares! Who do they think they're dealing with? She scrutinised the nearest wall - she had no doubt - and slapped it, gently, like she'd slap a nagging baby. She knew all about babies, brats and obnoxious teenagers. And ridiculous men. That knowledge goes back a long way. And now more *despicable* men to deal with. She studied her hand and along her fingers under different angles of light from the ceiling and then from the bedside lamp. She could discern tiny sparkles. She rubbed her hands together vigorously and clapped hard.

"Now, analyse *that!*" she said out loud. She knew immediately that that wasn't helpful. She expected... But no, silence.

She rubbed her hands together, to dust rather than to destroy. She couldn't damage microchips, or whatever they're called these days. But they knew she knew and that was the main point. They couldn't fool her. Why would they bother, Jardena? She considered everything a challenge to her position, her status, her *authority*. Some people get above themselves!

She noted the silence. She'd been agitated in her movements, had 'slapped' the wall, and had emitted at least one angry verbalisation, and no intervention. Obviously, she was being monitored, but not by Central Computer. She pretended anger (hardly a pretence, this righteous anger) and produced loudly and clearly a taboo expression. She waited. Yes, she knew what was going on: in this building she was being monitored *internally* by human operators. Every movement, every physiological change, every utterance was being monitored and recorded. They are collecting evidence, she concluded. What had that ridiculous woman being doing to implicate her, Jardena, in some madcap *psychological* crime? What had that old fool been saying? She hadn't seen him for years, but he must be at the back of it. So, they're monitoring. Well, two can play at that.

It is perfectly normal to talk to yourself. If you are stressed, lonely, if you have to think something out, or simply feel frustrated, then why not! Jardena did it herself and sometimes recommended it in her professional capacity, or, indeed, capacities. Only uneducated fools believed that it was abnormal. Trying to explain anything at all to the ludicrous members of her family was one of those things to be avoided. Now, she was in some kind of peculiar mess caused by this collection of dysfunctional dimwits. She, implicated? Impossible! But she shouldn't be surprised. However, this had already gone too far. So, what we have here is a game of chess, me thinks, Jardena was thinking, you'll have to engage your brains to beat me, gentlemen; or should I say, overgrown schoolboys? She didn't say that out loud. One day they'll be able to read your thoughts, but not yet. She opened her eyes. No, not yet.

She had seated herself upright in the armchair, demurely. She already felt demeaned. She closed her eyes again, still and silent. They are watching and she is just relaxing. She was well known for her self-improvement exercises. She is very sensibly trying to calm down. Anybody can become irritated in unpredictable and stressful circumstances. Her responses so far: perfectly normal. She started some measured inhaling and exhaling. Some rhythmic sounds would probably soon follow.

Some minutes later - Jardena knew exactly how many - she opened her eyes. She was as calm as a relaxing ant after a hard day's work dragging foliage and dead creatures, some of them not quite dead, back to the colony. She'd imagined herself an active ant, using the Active Ant Dissociation Technique. How a person with such developed self-awareness and natural cognitive abilities had destroyed so many marriages, some of them her own, must remain a mystery... for the time being.

She surveyed the room slowly and carefully. She was obviously a person of discernment. She was sure they were impressed, not only by her charm and beauty, but by her poise. Let's face it she had a kind of majestic air. This would explain her success in life, the difficulties she had with the rest of her family, and yet her great success with other people, the ease with which she managed them.

"I really must co-operate to the full with the authorities, with that clever man in charge," she breathed huskily to herself and certainly loud enough.

"Why I am here makes no sense at all. What am I accused of? Something to do with my silly, foolish younger sister? Her difficulties go back to childhood. She has always had exaggerated notions about herself and no common sense. Her views? Wildly immature! I had those *liberal* views when I was a teenager, but I grew up! I did well at University, I am a successful business person, and I am proud of my two wonderful children. All those useless men... well, I don't like to be too harsh. I think the facts speak for themselves.

"I can't imagination what that stupid old man has been saying. I know it's something to do with him. It's typical. Men have no sense at all. They only have one thing on their minds. Themselves! They are emotionally stunted and dim-witted. Not the clever ones of course! I've always admired clever men. And looked up to them.

"Where are my children? They were mentioned. They couldn't have anything to do with this. They are innocent of any wrongdoing, whatever it is. We're all innocent. Is my husband here? He hasn't even met that old fool. I'm a great believer in rights and equality and the freedoms, freedom of speech, for example. I'm sure that will be clear from my record of study, teaching, business, community involvement, family, and so on. I've been an upstanding citizen and have taken adult responsibility, as one is naturally obliged to do."

Yes, Jardena, keep talking. They're listening, not that they need to.

## 84

Priests lead a singular life. They are not quite connected to the rest of humanity. They imagine their 'vocation' in youth and, if they are determined enough, it is powerfully reinforced. For years it all makes sense and is, in a very real sense, beautiful. Then it starts to fall apart! At that point they have experienced, whether they like it or not, something really unpleasant. They have been dragged kicking and screaming into what the rest of us call a combination of adulthood and reality. For some of them it's the last straw that breaks the camel's back, a desert creature not being irrelevant. Jeevalani had never seen a camel outside a zoo. He grunted in accompaniment with the wide smile showing his strong and even teeth at the thought of meeting a camel outside a zoo. He was not a man of literature, but he was certainly a man of imagination. He pictured the City amok with camels, frustrated and spitting at passers-by! He thought it might be *psychological*: maybe that's what *he* wanted to do. He was a bit of a rebel, a lazy rebel. He felt guilty, but shook it off. Guilt is a useless emotion. He wasn't quite sure that that was true, but somebody important probably said it. He sipped his whiskey.

He had drifted amongst many of those who had been dragged kicking and screaming, etc., but had been distracted along the way and hadn't quite achieved that state when the brain gets control of the genitals - the brain is still running riot! These were the academics. Jeevalani was never sure what they believed. It was all so complicated: brief showers, downpours, torrents, floods, words, words, words - it was all so *wet.* But one thing was sure: they believed in themselves. Fancy putting that lot in charge of Church Tribunals. That was like putting kids in charge of the military! Their passion was apparent and boyish. They existed somewhere between God and Golf, never knowing which way to jump and collecting facts in large amounts and equal measure. Their lives were balanced. They laughed a lot. They did a lot of *touching.* They were so... sensitive, the sensitivity of five year olds.

His chair rocked, thanks to instructions to the armrest console. It was soothing, as was the dimmed light in the room, much of the room drifting away into shadow. On such a day he preferred to sit in the dark, curtains drawn. The room was a cosy and familiar womb. The Congress had been lively and ultimately dissatisfying, but he'd made an effort. He'd shown his face and was predictably disappointed. He'd met up with one or two old friends, as arranged, for lunch. They'd updated each other about their lives, but nothing had changed. Maybe you get to the point where nothing changes, there is nothing to update.

Another couple of days of this minor nightmare... but it seemed likely that he had a reason to dip out. Things had suddenly taken an unexpected turn. He had received the follow-up phone call, as promised.

He swung his legs off the elongated leg-rest. He'd already had dinner and another one or two would do no harm. But take it easy - becoming tipsy might be tempting, but unnecessary. He needed to be relaxed, alert and cool. He strolled to the beverage wall dispenser, jabbed on a sidelight, and pressed the Spirits Button. He placed his glass into the recess and under the multiple dispenser and spoke, "Whiskey", and watched the golden liquid pour gently into his glass. He was tempted, but no, a single would suffice. He'd probably have a coffee later. He might have a whiskey in it. He scraped the glass along the lip of the nozzle. Waste not, want not. He had not measured out his life in coffee cups or whiskey glasses. He had measured out his life in people. There'd been countless thousands of them, although they had indeed been counted, but he'd lost track, didn't think about, neither a thinker, nor a counter. Jeevalani was one of the most travelled persons in the City and he didn't think about that either. He went where he was sent and now he was back to where he started, neither happy nor sad, just *there* for the time being. Who knows about the future! He'd learnt not to think about it. All people were basically the same, either in a mess, or temporarily not in a mess. He hoped the latter knew how lucky they were and that it wouldn't last. The great gift of celibacy - being unmarried - was that much of the personal misery was watered down. The great disadvantage was loneliness and other people not understanding either. The difference between celibacy and chastity is that celibacy is a unilateral condition easily explained - although people don't understand - and chastity has its own *hierarchy*. Jeevalani was a chaste man. Mostly.

And now - he shook his whiskey and watched it circle the glass in the clockwise direction before returning to his armchair - a mess was brewing. He'd seen the symptoms for years, but didn't know what they meant. He should have sensed *something* was up! But how are you supposed to read other people's minds and lives? Especially if they don't understand the cause of their own difficulties and assume that they are within the norm and should struggle on without making a fuss. Get a grip, stand up and be a man! That attitude is questionable. He took a gulp. But it always comes out in the end, one way or another. It may take a thousand years, but the truth will out. He dealt in thousands of years. Indeed, Jeevalani dealt in eternity.

The phone call had been a shock. He glanced at his luminescent watch. He glanced over his shoulder towards the drawn curtains - no, not now! Depart ye cursed! Anyhow, he'd be visited within the hour.

## 85

Our professor is confused. He's standing in the small room where he was placed and has barely moved for several minutes, his head the top of his light-house. He is almost as pale as the walls, somewhat wide-eyed and hands in pockets, consolidating himself, gathering his thoughts, his body solid as a statue. He doesn't know which way to turn, not because of the small room but because of the big picture. He's not confused because he's not a professor. He has no doubt it's just a matter of time. Mosimenadue has *notions.* This word suggests that he has grown bigger than his boots. This expression suggests that he has ideas above his station. This awful expression means that he values himself more than his actual value. To suggest that a person can be valued, like a piece of furniture, is dehumanising. So we'd better leave it there. Suffice it to say he is confused. He is also dismayed and must acknowledge his fear, which arrived unexpectedly, out of the blue, and has crept into his bones. He must defend himself.

He walks to the desk mirror. The mirror cannot be manually adjusted. It is an upright oval on a stand, a single unit with the desk. He leans down to the console and adjusts the mirror's angle until he can see himself without sitting down. He doesn't want to sit down, he wants to give a talk, a lecture. He adjusts the mirror-screen until he can see his head and torso; he focuses it to suit his eyesight from that distance. Now he can see clearly. He looks good. He will have to face a real audience in the morning. He imagines this discerning audience, something he's used to, and, in these circumstances, there will be no difficult questions he can't answer. He waits for them to settle down, their silence, their rapt attention. He is used to imagining this.

In private he does practice talks for serious occasions, but he is past that for ordinary lectures. This is more difficult: he has no notes; he has no idea of the questions; he's not even sure of the context, something to do with his parents, his upbringing, their upbringing; what exactly is going on? He'd already been *interrogated.* A crime? He'd never committed a crime. Had he? In these circumstances, it is strange how people begin to remember bad things they have done and feel guilty. Because they *are* guilty! Aren't they?

Mosimenadue started to mouth his talk. He knew he daren't speak it out loud because he knew perfectly well that everything was being recorded. He wasn't stupid! Far from it. Forearmed is forewarned. What they won't know won't trouble them. But he'd forgotten about 'Subliminal Recording', as it tends to be called. This level records *everything* from the tiniest physiological response to entire conversations *from birth to death*. The information exists, but can only be accessed by certain persons of high rank and their reasons must satisfy the criteria. Otherwise, their behaviour is illegal and may lead to serious consequences. This is due to an individual's inalienable right to privacy.

Thus, at this very moment, in these unfortunate circumstances, every unuttered word formed on the lips of Mosimenadue is being decoded and a written script is being printed out. His non-verbal behaviour, as he acts his speech, is being analysed and matched to his trillions of spoken words already on record and a vocal record is also being produced. If these records are deemed not necessary, then they will be destroyed in due course - deleted and/or shredded. The evidence will still exist, of course, in the computer Evidence File. We do not read thoughts. This means that when his lips do not move there will be gaps in the synthesised vocal and written recordings. Thus far, thought reading is illegal. It is also impossible, so we are led to believe. However, there has been talk of certain 'borderline' research.

Mosi is friendly, personable and impressive. He's an academic and researcher and, on the surface, has done very well. But he lives in a strange little world of mutual admiration. This experience has reinforced the very worst aspects of his upbringing. When he publishes something, for example, he is praised and congratulated. He earns points for his Department, but in the real world nobody has heard of it because almost nobody has read it. It is difficult to explain to academics of this sort that they have a responsibility to reach out to the larger community. The University wasn't invented, so to speak, for their personal convenience. Drink, drugs, sex, fame and fortune, all within the confines of this peculiar institution, their society of mutual admiration and mutual abuse. It is abuse. Mosimenadue is the kind of academic who is a user and abuser in a multitude of small ways. Even in the City it is an appalling fact that people like him still exist, but eventually they are caught. His present predicament has nothing to do with his academic involvement. Indeed, arguably the opposite: if he had applied his brain he wouldn't be where he is today. He was given many warnings, but was incapable of listening, literally incapable. His fault? Yes, according to the law.

He's enjoying his performance; his speech is impressive and misinformed; his destiny is to be taken out of circulation for some time. He is exhibiting his usual level of awareness.

He should have listened to advice, listened to your parents; but, as there are two of them, he should have been more aware of their agendas; tried not to get carried away with his own increasing feelings of self- worth; acquired more humility and respect for other people. Mosimenadue will have plenty of time to muse on these suggestions, the essence of which he has steadfastly rejected hitherto. Rather than raise him up, his real record condemns him. Maybe this is so for most of us. He adjusted his hair.

**86**

Goodness, it's dusty! He was annoyed that he'd forgotten his glasses. He'd been taken aback, put on his outdoor shoes and jacket, and very politely accompanied them to help with their enquiries. His wife had just slipped out - unlikely to have *fallen off* her pedestal, but kept that to himself - but no need to worry about her, he'd been assured, she would be taken care of in due course. So what is that colour, certainly a shade of white? he thought, as he scrutinised the wall and brushed his right hand absentmindedly on his jumper. He'd already lobbed his jacket onto the bed. The plaster was not as smooth as it could be. You can't get the staff these days, he smiled. Or the women. Everything can be so slapdash. When you're 75, you tend to be pompous and judgmental. The fact that you are accurate is neither here nor there. So much for being one of the elders of the tribe! Tabatante would have thought if he'd been the sort of person who did much thinking. Another fine mess you've got me into. He didn't quite know to whom that statement applied.

It's all so precisely constructed. He took a few strides in one direction and then the other, and surveyed his tiny and temporary kingdom. Naturally, he studied the finer details. We are all scholars in our own way. He might suggest a few improvements, but leave that for another time. No point in engaging them in conversation. Don't come across as a smart alec. Just carry on being polite, helpful - they are doing their job - and depart in a friendly and dignified manner. Be polished and smooth, as usual. No point antagonising people. Be friendly, good humoured and go! He would be taken home. Excellent! Now, what exactly is going on?

He sat on the bed, wiggled a bit - it seems comfortable, but he won't be here long - and decided to try the armchair, which couldn't be moved. The whole room seemed to be one unit, as if factory-produced, which is quite possibly the case. He wondered which factory it might be and probably involved the Official Secrets Act. He'd had to sign that himself at times. That building contract with the Ministry of Security came to mind. Much ado about nothing in his opinion. Who are they securing themselves against? But then you never know. Best not to ask too many questions. They know what they are doing. He jabbed at a couple of buttons and adjusted his chair. Ah, that's better - the old back is beginning to play up.

All those questions. He couldn't answer most of them: no idea, hadn't a clue, wasn't even there, had never heard of *that*. They seemed satisfied. There'd been meaningful glances when he'd said something interesting, but he didn't know why, and they had no intention of telling him. He certainly didn't ask, seemed inappropriate, none of his business. Hopefully, none of it was his business, or his wife's. He knew she was somewhere in the building. That was a bit worrying because she could be very antagonistic, but she knows how to behave. Anyhow, he was assured that he had nothing to worry about. He couldn't remember many questions. Old age...

He cosied into the armchair, pressed the 'R' button, and then the downward arrow. Perfect! Press 'V' - too loud. He'd no real knowledge of the subject, but you didn't have to *know* something in order to enjoy it. Too much education can go to your head! Too much knowledge and self-opinion, and no experience - that's the problem of the world: too much fancy talk. He'd grown to love and enjoy classical music on the radio whilst at work. As he relaxed, cradled into his own dreamworld, he started to recall the interview.

It was obviously to do with that family. Why did he get dragged into the twisted world of her mad mother? Why are there so many mad mothers in the world? It must mean something, something must *cause* them. The questioning - what does that mean? It's about the other lot. His heart sank: the weekend. No escaping that. The talkers would gather and attempt to talk each other to death. Several other people would be collateral damage. The only way to survive emotionally was to drink heavily and interrupt the flood by wisecracks. Then you would be thought a fool who couldn't concentrate on the deadly clever and informed discussions, which were actually tedious diatribes. Rather be thought a fool than drown a slow death. Maybe they'd all be sent to prison for six months! Six months of peace. But, no, that wouldn't happen: they'd talk so much that the investigators would let them go, just to get rid of them.

A thought of party and drink, and his eyes opened and, in an instant, focused on the drinks dispenser. His eyesight, rather dimmed, had noted the drink symbol on the wall. He'd had a difficult and stressful afternoon of, eh, *inquisition.* Yes, that's the word. You can be traumatised and not realise it. He held up his hand horizontal in front of his eyes. He was sure it was trembling, but he'd forgotten his glasses. He needed something to settle his nerves. But *never* before eight o'clock: a glass of red wine at dinner, poured by her, and a drop of the hard stuff topped up by a gallon of tonic water, she in charge of the drinks, of course. If he turned up about six half-cut, he'd never hear the end of it. She'd be taking his pulse every five minutes for the rest of the evening and nagging about his irregular heart rate. Oh, so what! Women! What can you do with them! He could think of several things... But first just a little snifter to settle his nerves after being traumatised. He rose from his armchair like a young Odysseus.

## 87

Gelasia plonked her fat backside into the office chair where it fitted snugly and swung around to face the mirror which also fitted snugly, a seamless join. It crossed her mind that it might be two-way, but probably not. She glanced over her shoulder towards the toileting facilities, minimalist and private. She watched herself in the mirror, slightly flushed, but otherwise fine. The experience had been unnerving, but she had purported herself well. But, for some reason, she felt that things were not looking good. That story her brother had so admired flashed through her mind. It's strange what comes to mind, although she couldn't remember the title. It was that book about the man who had been found guilty of an unspecified crime, and eventually executed. It was an ancient text. Her brother would like that sort of thing because he was a know-it-all, considered himself an intellectual. However, on this occasion, it made some sense. If you talk rubbish for years, you're bound to say something sensible! But her detention was real and, of course, temporary.

Quite frankly, she couldn't stand her brother, but she kept that well disguised. Her education and her arrogance were not well matched. Her education was very similar to the present toilet facilities: minimalist. And what she'd learnt was easily flushed away. She is one of those people who simply avoid the challenges of life. She was a person of *light entertainment.* She drifted giggling from entertainment to entertainment, from decades of T.V. 'soaps' to beer festivals to holidays to pub quizzes, one long cycle of superficiality facilitated by rivers of alcohol. To finance this she had worked and paid her way. No question about it! But much of it for a laugh, just a giggle, you mustn't be miserable at work, that would upset and annoy people, you have to be sociable and decent. She was both, she concluded, as she watched herself, although not quite seeing. She'd been overlooked for promotion so many times. Suddenly, she felt terribly alone.

Why did she avoid the difficult stuff? Low self-esteem? No way! She despised both parents, avoided her brother and hadn't spoken to her sister for twenty years. She blamed her parents for the mess of her childhood and these messed up family relationships. Her entire family was an emotional train wreck. Why she was wandering this old labyrinth was beyond her, but there must be a reason, she mused. Her present predicament was nothing to do with her family, except for her brother. Now, what had he dragged her into?

She fluffed up her hair. She studied her face from both sides, checked her makeup, with the back of her hand patted and rearranged her double chin, and thought yet again that she might get *that* removed at some time, although a bit cowardly on the surgery front. All in all, not ageing too badly, probably inherited her mother's skin (she laughed out loud; then scowled: the only thing her mother gave her) and decided to leave the double chin for another few years. See how it, *they*, develop. She swung around to consider the screen. How about a couple of soaps to kill the time? What are they doing anyhow, a load of useless paperwork probably? Typical of bureaucrats! And she should know. What are they investigating? Why all the secrecy? Although, to be fair, in her position, she certainly understood confidentiality, an everyday requirement for her, so leave them to it. It'll all be fine.

She switched on and then switched off her favourite soap. No, not in the mood for the usual lies and secrets of those stories that can really *not* pull on the heartstrings, but on your credibility, or rather, their credibility. Nobody behaves like those characters, going from crisis to crisis. But this is like a soap: a collection of appallingly dysfunctional characters.' This case - it's obviously a legal case - is something to do with that difficult *human being*. She's always been difficult, but they'd got on well, except for... well, there were times... He'd always described her as a child abuser. He has accused me of positively supporting a child abuser! He is just so malicious! What is he talking about? He has never said it to my face, but it got back to me. They're all malicious. They're more trouble than they're worth.

Gelasia was becoming more uncomfortable, a bit lightheaded and hot. She didn't need to look in the mirror. She felt almost panicky. She stood up, took a few deep breaths and walked up and down the room, taking deep breaths, yoga-like. She'd seen it on television. She was trying to calm down. It wasn't like her to become hot and bothered. She was Mrs Cool-and-Collected, especially after she'd collected a round of drinks!

This couldn't be about child abuse. That's impossible. That woman wouldn't do what had been done to her and hope to get away with it. The kids would have said something years ago. She froze. They haven't dragged her into something horrible? She hasn't done anything, she hasn't witnessed anything awful, nobody has said anything to her, she knows nothing at all. Those interviewers gave her the creeps! They seemed to be collecting evidence of something against *her*! That's what it was, that's what made her feel so uncomfortable. She'd been around for too long to miss their unspoken attitudes, that thing her brother was so keen on years ago. What was that? Non-verbal communication. That's it, that's what she had picked up, that's why she was so uncomfortable. They are investigating *her*, Gelasia! And it's something to do with that half-crazed loony and her mouthy, nutcase children! The small room seemed to becoming smaller.

"Gelasia, a drink is being delivered at the drinks dispenser," a human voice said. "Drink it and you'll feel much better. It's a mild sedative. Lay down and relax. We'll get back to you shortly."

It must be her blood pressure.

## 88

Radmilla lay full-length reading a novel. Publications are free; authors receive credits and... glory! or not. She had many favourite writers. Some friends said too many! She would retort that she was fluent in several languages simply because she read so much, not to mention her vocabulary, which she didn't. They'd be well advised to spend less time *glued* to mindless screens. These were 'art forms' she didn't appreciate. Those friendly battles might last into the early hours. But not tonight: a workday tomorrow, no late night carousing, talking about the meaning of life and other such nonsense. Nothing like a good crime thriller! And this was nothing like one. The book flopped spread-eagled face down across her belly. She wasn't in the mood, couldn't concentrate.

"Coffee," she called as she stood and stretched. She was aching. It must be old age! But not quite. She removed her mug from the dispenser, noticed the brown stains of several days and pressed the Wash button. The room was a terrible mess too, clothes everywhere, the litter bin overflowing, piles of books like stalagmites, and everything dusty and in need of a vacuum. The people at work wouldn't believe this! She had no intention of going into the kitchen. Yet.

She manoeuvred through her obstacle course, sipping her coffee held like a chalice, the aroma of home. She gazed far into the distance and could smell the pomegranates of childhood. She needed a holiday. Her thoughts were becoming morbid. That case had dug a hole in her: she felt shovelled out and thrown in a heap! Might use that image, she thought. It was one of those evenings to be tolerated, a kind of penance, a cold night in the desert where evil spirits played their games with the lost. Hmm, impressive, might slip that in too. Now snap out of it! Too many spooky crime novels and concocted psychos hiding in the woods with white eyes and chainsaws.

She placed her coffee mug on the low mahogany table in an old coffee ring. Her favourite table could do with a damp wipe, once she'd cleared the books, notes, pad of doodles, tray of gathered random objects (to be tidy), breakfast mug, pepper and salt condiments, tub of face cream, knitting needles, packet (cylinder-shaped) of biscuits (twisted-sealed to keep fresh), bag of makeup, two empty plastic bottles, booklet of common birds, packet of dried fruit sealed with a clothes peg, small doll, fist-sized bottle of glue, last evening's coffee mug, packet of headache pills, dinner plates (muckily balanced like a small spaceship landed on rocky ground near a precipice), and a pair of binoculars. No point making things worse, concerning the coffee ring.

No point making things worse? That behaviour had gone on for forty years. It's shocking *torture*. What was the point? But she could answer that question by now; hadn't worked on something like that before; live and learn.

Radmilla had thoughts of *her* family and the possibility of a chat to distract her, but no, and hoped they wouldn't contact her. This evening was not a good time. She needed to think. Maybe in a few hours, maybe after dinner, she'd have a clearer mind. At present, it was full of other people's garbage.

She removed a pile of books, three coats, four handbags, six weeks' worth of Sunday newspapers, scooped up in her arms, a deodorant spray she'd been looking for, and sat down on several flattened woolly hats (of beautiful colours) in her armchair, cradled her coffee and crossed her legs. The mess of some people's lives, she mused, was a crime. She was admired for her compassion and good sense, but in the face of injustice her eyes blazed, her tongue sliced like a scimitar. Now, she felt vengeful.

The 'battle of the sexes' floated into her mind. Sometimes one word could recall an entire book from decades ago and then she could locate the one word within seconds. She considered such *abilities* of no interest. She could make connections. The 'difficulties' in this case went back to the beginning, the beginning of the human race, to the time when these creatures stood up on their hind legs (She wasn't convinced of that claim!), when they started to think of themselves as *Homo sapiens*. That's when the 'battle' began. Down the millennia there had been a to-ing and fro-ing: the stronger sex in charge, then the second sex in charge, intermingled with brief periods of equality, then back to square one, like a Mexican wave around the planet. Every culture had been through the same experiences, probably imitating and influencing each another. Why couldn't we just acknowledge our differences? Women were obviously superior! She scanned her bookshelves. The thinkers she greatly admired - no doubt about *their* gender. The creatures who created, destroyed, then recreated the thing we call Civilisation. They may be called Naked Apes, but they can grow beards! Radmilla liked beards. Perfectly natural! Why can't we just accept our differences?

The Great Germ, for example, predated the Cat. She'd spent decades trying to convince women of the realities of life. Finally, she gave up and concentrated on forests. Radmilla chuckled: the fact is trees don't talk nonstop, rationalising their appalling attitudes! Thus, way back then, ordered society started to break down. Individuals moved into a state of personal chaos, with political and economic phenomena causing, or coinciding with, pending ecological disaster. The helpless sensible people became distraught. The rest is history; although that history was almost lost. Just when we think we've survived, it's back!

Radmilla felt a creeping dismay. This case went back sixty years, but only because of the time limit put on it. How could it have gone on for so long? People's lives have been destroyed. Why wasn't it stopped? Humans are such cowards! Radmilla decided the best thing to do was to tidy up. She'd start with her clothes. If somewhat overwhelmed and in doubt, do something useful.

89

Well, so much for watching television and relaxing! Psybunes, the musician, was thinking. That relaxation didn't last very long and now he was going to miss the gig. He'd never get there on time, but they'd be informed. Brilliant! Thanks very much. The room didn't bother him. In a very real sense he'd felt imprisoned all his life, wandering from one strange setup to another. If he weren't sleeping on one friend's settee, it was another friend's settee. He'd had his own places, but things had never worked out. School was a terrible struggle, university was even worse. When he was a 'poor student', he'd been very poor. He couldn't understand why he'd been 'poor' in the first place. No inverted commas, actual poverty of the type allowed. Suddenly, they'd been plunged downward. He couldn't remember much of that, but the umpteen conflicting accounts didn't help. In the end he'd simply blocked it out. Life is a drag, life is a struggle, just accept it, and get on with it.

The blackness of adolescence remained undiluted. It just kept hanging around and keeping a sanguine eye on his (lack of) progress, and whispering dark thoughts in his ear. Sometimes they were strange dreams or half understood thoughts. Were they memories of real events? There was no point in asking the others. Either they couldn't remember any such thing, or the events weren't as he remembered them. How come he had *everything* wrong? How is it that his memory or interpretation of events was so out of kilter with theirs? Always the same responses, the same recriminations, the same patronising attitudes. He was the youngest, the cleverest (not his opinion) and 32! Surely, he had *something* right and accurate and true! (Hey, a lyric?). No, not once. The usual stuff: dump that emotional baggage, move on, get a life; otherwise, you'll lose the plot. Why did they always use those meaningless clichés? What are they talking about? Do they know themselves what they mean? Because he doesn't! And he's the cleverest! He grinned at the thought. Yeah, well, you've got to have a sense of humour. What is intelligence anyway? What you learn is important, but what you do with it is what counts. And what have they done with all that *brilliance*? Dad had blown his top so often, telling them they're all ridiculous fools, both families entirely comprised of idiots! He laughed out loud at the thought. Dad has raged like a mad bull, but is it true? Are they all raving mad? No, of course not. But, quite frankly, lunacy would explain everything. What's going on now? This is frightening. He is going to miss the gig because the loonies have done something, or is it somebody else? It couldn't be. All those questions were about the family, weren't they? They were double-checking something. He's not stupid, he could tell. Whole truckloads of information are being collected on everybody. It's normal and nothing to worry about. Unless you're a criminal. A few gigs not reported to the Revenue over so many years. That couldn't be it. And he'd spent the money on necessary purchases; he'd kept the receipts. It was all business. He may well have *forgotten* one or two items, but he wasn't defrauding the Government. Sometimes it's more trouble to report earnings than not to. It makes no difference, just less record-keeping. It's terrible how you remember all your 'sins' when you're made to feel guilty.

He leant against the wall at the bed-head, one foot on the bed. He'd kicked off that shoe: no point dirtying the top cover. In such a crispyclean environment, he was surprised they hadn't forced him to strip, shower, and redress in the usual garb he'd seen on television; and then taken his clothes to forensics! Mum would have! She'd been cleaning mad. Their lives had been a misery until they'd all rebelled, left, the escape being University. That was easy, but any excuse would have done: to grow up, become independent, fly the nest, become an adult, but the one criterion was *as far away as possible*. Unfortunately, they didn't manage psychological distance. She was in their heads, had taken up permanent residence. Many mothers are like that. *The Myth of the Nurturing Mother* is extremely unpleasant, if you happen to believe your mother is the greatest thing since sliced bread! Psybunes didn't. Suddenly, his stomach... a bit like stage fright: his present predicament might be something to do with her.

The others? Had he spotted his sister way down the corridor? Had his view been deliberately blocked? He hadn't thought about it at the time, but now... His family wander like ghosts around the haunted house of his mind. Sometimes he imagines seeing one of them and it turns out to be a complete stranger. They're like phantom limbs.

This must be something to do with the Revenue and illegal parking. Maybe he'd parked illegally outside the Revenue. Yeah, right! Crack a few jokes, as he was going round in circles and had nothing better to do. Be patient. All will be revealed in an hour or two and then he can head for the gig. Maybe it was something to do with the Unlikely Criminals. Of course that stupid suggestion for the band's name had been rejected. He'd never actually met a criminal.

In these circumstances Dad would be patient. Although in recent years he was far from patient and said on many occasions that he was out of patience with vicious fools. Fools? He was the fool. These days you could hardly get a civil word out of him. That was the reason Psybunes avoided his father. Talk about grumpy old men! Boy, if they dragged *him* in for questioning, he'd get life for lousy speeches about *the system* and verbal abuse of police! They wouldn't get a word in. Psybunes was glad his father wasn't involved, which was peculiar. Where did that idea come from?

## 90

"I need a stiff one," uttered Sachikaka. Ooh, I'm sure you do, dear! Now I'm a matronising, effeminate homosexual! Maybe I'm imitating some old movie character. Must check databases. In the meantime, she wanders over to the drinks dispenser: ah, the full range. Great! Well, she might as well, in the circumstances... Most people would. This attractive and clever young woman doesn't know how lucky she is. But luck is relative. It was a close call. She presses the button a second time and removes the glass.

She studies herself in the full-length mirror, a little dance, a little catwalk, protrudes her bottom and breasts simultaneously, forms a curvy zed, a little wiggle, smiles broadly - her perfect teeth - pouts and winks salaciously at herself. Don't forget the eyelashes! Then she catches her reflected reflection in the mirror on the desk, and there she is, her replicates disappearing into eternity. No stopping *her*. Let them watch! Let them enjoy themselves! She didn't envy their boring jobs. Then one thought led to another and she felt very sexually aroused. No, not here. Don't! It would give them a thrill and she'd love it! Why not? It would be fun! But it might make things worse, she counselled herself. But who would complain? You don't know what's going on. She stood still, gazed at the white wall and took a sedate mouthful. That's true, she doesn't know. She's a witness of something or other. Well, they're lucky to have her as a witness! On the other hand, it could be one of those ridiculous psychology experiments: a four-way analysis of variance (whatever that is!) to investigate how people relate to stress when taken into custody. Men versus women, the intelligent versus the stupid, the beautiful versus the ugly, the long-legged versus the short-legged (she knows why she was chosen), something to do with alcohol consumption and stress. She took another sip and placed her glass on the desk-dressing table thing. They won't catch her out in some silly study. She was caught out a couple of years ago in that embarrassment study. Citizens are obliged to take part in research, be a subject, as they call it, and not complain whether or not they are informed beforehand. They must be available, of course, in the sense that it doesn't interfere with their serious duties, family, work, that sort of thing. She had made a complete fool of herself and had come over all Giggly Girl. Once bitten, twice shy, not that she could be described as shy! Anova - sounds like something astronomical. It's all rubbish anyhow. But she wouldn't mind being debriefed. She could do with a bit of debriefing right now: the weekend cometh.

She tried listening to music, but the negative thoughts were taking hold. She was beginning to feel trapped and nauseas, being sucked into the maelstrom of her own life. But it wasn't her life. It had been created by other people. Her parents were a walking disaster. Why don't they just *extinguish*? She felt like crying, but she couldn't. There was no release, there was no escape. She looked at the near-empty glass and saw that day. Oh, not that. She felt she was collapsing inward. That was so long ago. Why won't it go away? Why does it never become dull or diffused? She was twelve and almost innocent, years ago. Why did it feel like *now*? Why doesn't it go away? She was on her feet, pulling her hair with both hands. The pain felt good.

"Sachikaka, shall we send someone, or can you calm down? We are happy to help."

The human voice stopped her. She knew all along she was being watched. She felt calmer immediately. As she removed her hands, she straightened her hair, as if she hadn't been pulling it in the first place.

"No, thank you. I just feel... I just felt rather tense. Is this an experiment?"

A few seconds of silence.

"Oh, an experiment.  No, this isn't an experiment. This is real, as such. As you've been told, we are confirming certain facts, tying up a few loose ends. Some of it will be kept confidential for the present, but you will be released and seen home shortly. I see you enjoy whiskey. Well, help yourself, it's on the house! But... [the tinkly bell prelude for one of our slogans] *Drink Sensibly*," in a jokey, sing-song voice. "We'll talk later. Okay?"

He sounds  kindly and good-humoured, seems to enjoy his job. He has no idea what's going on in her head. Nobody does.

She felt sad - they do exist, men like him - as she took another measure and this time plopped in a cube of ice. She plopped herself into the comfy, white armchair, snuggled further into it and crossed her legs. She had the distinct flying thought that not keeping her legs crossed had caused most difficulties in her life; too much too young. She wondered about the man behind the kindly voice. He's probably married, but so what! He's probably not kindly and hates his job. Why couldn't she have just been allowed to grow up at her own pace, whatever that was? Sometimes she wondered who she might have become - anybody, so long as it was somebody else. What was all that open-minded liberalism about, all that frankness, all that *honesty*? She, spoilt and running wild. She felt she'd been robbed. Her parents were the most emotionally dishonest people she'd ever met. Her mother was also literally dishonest; her father was an emotional cardboard box.

This self-absorption will pass, she told herself; this feeling sorry for yourself will not do. Snap out of it! She wasn't the sort of person to be self-obsessed. Stop worrying about the weekend, that fool in white, and all the nattering nitwits.

Get a grip! She knew her worth; remember who and what you are. By the fourth drink, Sachikaka was feeling much better.

**91**

Halaigha mopped her brow and sipped water. She'd removed her scarf, undid buttons, loosened clothing. She'd become increasingly hot. The panic had started when two men, first espied lounging at the wall, had stopped her. She's on her way to the Office (they knew it was Welfare), she'd informed them. She was required to accompany them. Nobody's had an accident, she was assured.

She understood why such interviews were referred to as a *grilling*. Why the personal questions? They went back and forth, as if to catch her out. Doing what? It was all public information, meaning obvious and known; a normal, happy and respectable family. Ask anyone! Nothing is perfect, of course, she explained, we have our ups and downs. But her interviewers weren't satisfied. "Ask me anything!" she'd said, somewhat exasperated. "We shall," one replied, "We appreciate your co-operation." That woman was definitely sarcastic. No need for sarcasm. Manners cost nothing. She didn't say that because it would have been bad manners.

Stressed and pacing the tiny room, the room becoming smaller; caught in a net, being dragged along the bottom of the sea, suffocating, drowning. Why can't people leave her alone? The walls were moving in. She tried to hold them back and sank to the floor.

"Halaigha, a drink is being delivered," a voice said kindly, "Drink it. You'll feel better."

The voice was a shock. She didn't expect such an intrusion into her privacy. She stood up and gathered herself together. She was a trained actor, a profes-sional, composed. She heard the sounds from the dispenser she hadn't noticed.

"I don't need a drink, thank you very much."

"You'll feel much better."

They're trying to drug me, trying to make me say things to suit their case, whatever it is, to weaken my resolve. I'm trained. She swallowed the drink.

"That's very nice. I feel a little better already. Thank you." They knew she hadn't swallowed it. They knew she'd swallowed only water all day. Twenty years' data of body weight had been accessed. 'Weight' as a keyword had unearthed a small mountain of verbal information: many conversations involv-ing her distraught father, including eight telephone conversations (four of which had elicited computer warnings for his bad language), three letters to other members of the family pleading with them to do something where he'd failed. The symptoms were obvious. He'd been ignored. They were *encouraging* her, he'd raged. All of these interactions had remained at the normal level and, there-fore, private. There had never been alerts to Human Operators. Now her child was being monitored continuously.

She sat at the desk/dressing table, adjusted her hair and checked her appear-ance. They can't trick her. She's behaving normally; a perfectly normal young woman and *mother*. Let them remember that: she's a mother and has responsi-bilities, and a mature man who loves her and recognises her natural ability. They noted she hadn't adjusted the mirror to suit her eyesight.

"You graduated three times and entered two professions immediately. Is that correct?" They'd been deliberately difficult, stating the obvious, trying to catch her out. "Is this true?"

"Perhaps you would tell us why you haven't had a proper job in the last fifteen years."

What a stupid lie. She had explained that she was an actor - "and a teacher, Halaigha"- and a teacher, and fully registered with the appropriate official bodies.

"Yes, certainly," one of her interrogators replied, "and so why have you never had a proper job? Would you like me to define the word 'proper'?"

"No, not necessary in my case." And the sarcasm isn't necessary either. "I've had many jobs."

"Yes, you have, according records, but they were few and far between. The point is: you did very well; you are clever and capable. Your academic and vocational records are impressive. Obviously, something went wrong. We're trying to get your view of what you think this was and why it's going on so long. You haven't actually paid your way, as one would expect of a person like you, for the last *fifteen* years. Either the City or a *lover* - would you prefer the word 'partner'? - has kept you."

They had no right to delve into her personal life.

"We have every right, Halaigha, because of the nature of our work. We are trying to get to the bottom of your Curriculum Vitae, which, quite frankly, appears to be *exaggerated*. Did somebody else write it? We have your *real* C.V. Why have you never taken adult responsibility?"

"I'm a mother!" She thought that should be self-explanatory. They were invading her privacy and they had no right; this was against the law and they should know better.

"You are, indeed, a mother," - *she* was jealous and vicious, and it was obvious, a barren woman! - "and this confounds the situation. Why have you done this? You had no income, no job, no permanent abode... Can you explain why you became pregnant so often, lost the babies, and remained in such a state of insecurity? It is remarkable behaviour for an educated woman of your age."

It was none of her business, or his, and she told them so.

There must have been another hundred questions. Why all those questions about her family? Why so many questions about her mother? The less said about her the better! Although Halaigha was always sympathetic - she knew her mother had had a lot to put up with. And, as for her father, very little about him. But *he's* the nasty piece of work, the inadequate, the raging creep who should be investigated, and the sooner the better! She'd pointed this out.

She knew she had to calm down now. She'd be going home soon. Do some Buddhism, some meditation, recite a mantra. All will be well. Oh, what about her boyfriend and baby? She looked at her watch. He'll be worried sick. No, be calm: they'd told her he'd been informed. Nothing to worry about. Not really.

## 92

Merkan was a worrier. He worried that things weren't being done properly. He claimed that *normal* people set out to do things properly. He joked about the shopping, but only because his wife took responsibility for it. When he was in charge it was done properly, and he fantasised much less. Fantasising about mass murder was perfectly normal. Sometimes he machine-gunned the entire

Faculty during those long and fatuous meetings. He suspected that they might have said something interesting, but he could never remember what it was. He was there to facilitate the education of youth and to do his research. Where did it say that he was there to be roasted alive by other people's hot air? Or, to drown in an incoming tide of verbal diarrhoea? He had huge amounts of patience.

"Nonsense!"

"Excuse me."

"Oh, just thinking aloud. You do that at my age. Nothing to worry about."

She smiled. What a beautiful smile! Oh, dear me, he thought, watching over his glasses, like the well trained scientist he was. What a fine rump, well packed in its summer wrappings! But rain clouds were gathering over the trenches on his ancient forehead.

The phone call was longish. He lounged on the desk chair, dreamed his way around the room, trudged across the off-white expanse of the ceiling, noted that the spider was making steady progress, and promised himself to do something about the dust, which could well be a health hazard. But there were worse things than dust. There were diseases. And war. Now, think of that (he did on occasion): war. Like all citizens he had studied War at various times in his youth. The Great War, for example, was still a contentious issue. How had it started? Was it one war and a whole collection of wars, a boiling cauldron of wars? No, a 'boiling cauldron' isn't much good. He'd never put that in one of his books! Things boiling are governed by Laws. That war was 'ungovernable' and that's why it is still contentious. And look what came next! The whole thing is unimaginable. But people survived. That's what's unimaginable!

Why is he thinking about war? There are worse things. Yes, that's what he was trying to get to: there are worse things than war. It felt familiar. Had he said that before?

"Yes, you have, dear."

"What?"

"You've said it several times: no sugar in coffee. You gave it up months ago for some peculiar reason." His wife handed him his afternoon coffee. It was one of their rituals. She pulled up a chair.

"You still haven't started. Look at the mess. Look at that pile of newspapers. What would people think?"

He didn't say that nobody comes in here except her and maybe the children when they visit.

"That case is troubling you, isn't it?" She stroked and gripped his arm. "That was the phone call."

"You'd think I'd get used to it. I don't know the person, but I know what he is going through. How can they still not know it's a crime? People keep doing it. Then, when they're caught, they exhibit all the symptoms of shock-horror: they're innocent, it's unjust, how can they be guilty? They have no awareness, for decades sometimes. *They* are the perpetrators! How can they not know?"

"You're the expert. Brainwashing?"

"I can't talk about this case. It wouldn't be quite ethical, but the details are terrible. For a start, it has been going on for forty years. God, I hope Hell exists!" They both laughed.

"Well. A few millennia in Hell would teach them a lesson."

"Yes, but you'll have to settle for a decade in prison and lots of therapy," she patted his arm re-assuredly and sipped her coffee.

"But what about the victim? What about the *millions* of victims?"

"One victim at a time. Things will improve. What about your Act?"

"It's not *my* Act. There were a load of people involved."

"I know." She could feel his mounting agitation. "But it has been dubbed the Merkan Act and I'm proud of that. All those years of research and you were *almost* ignored and then, suddenly, it was an Act of Parliament! Well, it seemed like suddenly. Something to be proud of."

"People still don't understand the long-term consequences of child abuse and the variety, the range, of its destruction. It's monstrous! And victims still call themselves survivors. In what way are they survivors, for goodness' sake? Survivors who have had no therapy?" Merkan was becoming hot under the collar, as he always did at the lack of intuition by people who should know better. "And it mutates. It's passed on and becomes intergenerational. There's no end to it!"

He thought of his children, his grandchildren, and how things could have been totally different. He thought of his parents, how he used to mock them when he was a teenager. By the age of thirty, perhaps, he had regained the respect he'd felt for them when he was a child. Yes, he had been given that thing everybody wants. He had taken it for granted, especially in the shallowness of youth. But he had eventually understood and, naturally, passed it on to his children: unconditional love. He took it rather personally. He wasn't unaware of his wife's *contribution*. No, that word is peculiarly inappropriate, he thought. What's the right word? Have to think about that...

"And the victim? I've advised Cody to be careful. There have been umpteen suicides. We have no idea how many. How can you tell if the victim himself doesn't know? It's not really suicide; it's murder and patricide. Cody has to be careful how he handles it, but he's experienced. But I'd love to be a fly on the wall in those interviews. And the victim - something about compensation and punishment, I suppose - but it's never enough because it's a whole lifetime destroyed. You can't compensate for that, you can't buy it all back."

## 93

Well, blow me, thought Purvanos, not in the new-fangled sense, you understand, but in the old-fashioned sense, very similarly akin to 'well, that's a mystery!' He found himself almost thinking (he attempted it on occasion), this could be serious. Not for him, of course. So, why was he dragged into this? And: what is it? He's a rational person and why isn't everybody else rational? They refused to answer *his* questions, but they expected him to answer theirs. Not unreasonable in some ways, but unhelpful. They were obviously gathering evidence, but if they'd made things more clear he could have been more helpful. As it stood, he knew nothing.

It must relate to his wife. She hadn't returned home and, when he was *invited* for questioning, he'd been assured that she was safe and *helping with enquiries*. At least, she wasn't in hospital again. She'd a habit of breaking bones (hers) whilst under the influence of alcohol - she was always celebrating something. Had she fallen over last night and injured someone? Oh, God, not a Personal Injury claim. Again. When was the last one? He couldn't think. She probably insulted a few people, but he couldn't recall an *incident* involving anything physical. She was like a cow in a China shop: loud-mouthed, denigrating, flailing and stumbling.

No, just a moment, there were many questions about her family. It was beginning to come back to him. But not that despicable mother of hers. It was her brother's family. What was all that about? The brother-in-law's okay, but the rest of them, that shower of *intellectuals* would do your head in! You can't get a word in. You would think they had done something interesting, but they haven't! Just the usual university stuff. He's glad that he hadn't bothered with all that education malarkey. He was right to leave school and go straight to work, just like his Dad. What's wrong with that? He'd applied for the usual tiny flat when he was twenty-one and was lucky to get one almost immediately. The three rooms were not as tiny as this one, mind you. Hope he's not here too long - there's a match on telly this evening. Then, thanks to his permanent (and boring) job, he'd got married and his first mortgage was born. A real and roomy apartment. He and his wife felt great and still do! Apart from one or two difficulties. So, what's wrong with that? Only one of the geniuses have achieved their own place and they're heading for forty. He wondered why he was thinking along these lines. Something was troubling him, but he hadn't managed to put his finger on it. There was something just outside his thinking brain. You can tell that sometimes - you know it's there, but you don't know what it is, and yet it's in your brain! Boy, things can be really complicated.

He wandered around, examined the several consoles in turn, hands in pockets, looked at himself in the mirrors - seems to be putting on a bit of weight, must be imagining it, doesn't need a haircut, indeed, looks pretty good for his age - and sat/lay on the bed in one relatively smooth movement, hands still in pockets. 60 is the new 40? Yes, people would believe anything.

No babies. You see, realistic. They had agreed on that before they got married. Obviously sensible. Unlike her brother with his four or five children. Four! Why did he think five? Oh, there had been that time of ructions, their normal condition, not that he knew much about it. It was none of his business. But she had finally got her own way. She had spread so many stories about him, his brother-in-law. He didn't pay much attention, although she was always the 'goodie' and he was always the 'baddie'. There are two sides to every story. Best not to get involved. But his present condition was something to do with that lot, that woman and her, eh, progeny. The questions he'd been asked were coming back to him. Best to stay out of it. But, on the other hand, he was somehow in it. Why was he here?

Why can't people be normal, accept their lot? There's not much to life. Sex, work, marriage, sort out the purchase of an apartment, football, beer, pub quizzes, having a laugh, and more sex! But seriously, that's about it: Life. All that nonsense about religion really doesn't help. It's about time religion was banned; it should be made illegal. He would do it if he had the political clout, but he couldn't be bothered. Stick to what you know. Education is good, but it can go to your head! Look at that lot of intellectual fools. What good has it done them? They are almost completely dysfunctional. Look at the state of them, now he thinks of it: one has a mortgage, two have a proper job (just about - they're always threatening to give it up. What kind of attitude is that for an adult?), and the others spend their lives ducking and diving, scheming and conniving. When you think of it, it's unbelievable! Why does he bother with them at all? One of those horrible get-togethers planned for the weekend. It'll be terrible! It's his wife. What's her agenda? He had never thought of it before. God, she despises her brother! That's what it is. It's obvious. Why hadn't he realised that before? That's the connection. Somehow she has dragged him into something concerning that family and it's serious.

He clasped his hands across his stomach and found them clammy. He rubbed them together. He sat up, swung his legs, and sat on the edge of the bed. He felt fat and sixty and trapped. Those questions started to come back more clearly. This was something serious. Should he ask for a solicitor? But he wasn't a criminal, never in his life, always as straight as a die.

## 94

They had set it all up, lured her away from her sleeping husband - she'd left a note - and, within the hour, they had pounced! Well, it felt like being pounced on. Her expert knowledge was requested at H.Q., although they didn't use the word 'expert', but that's what she'd assumed. At first, it had seemed like some kind of survey - they could have sent it through the post or by electronic mail, she remembers thinking, except that people tend not to respond. People can be so lazy - but then the questioning became focused and somewhat personal. She'd convinced herself that she didn't feel threatened. In an interview she'd always done well. Although interviews were not her best experiences. Almost certainly the best candidate for the job (otherwise she wouldn't have applied), she never knew quite what they were getting at. They were trying to catch her out, trying to demean her. They wanted someone prettier and cleverer. They were legally obliged to offer the job to the best candidate, not the sexiest one, not an airhead who could be easily seduced on some future occasion. Men are such fools! They weren't going to get the better of her and, anyhow, they needed her more than she needed them.

She'd become increasingly red in the face and flustered, although her accent was cut-glass and educated. Two women on this occasion. They were young and she wondered if they had children. They must find her interesting: refined and experienced.

Now they expected her to stay in this, this whatever they call it, waiting room. What a cheek! It was obviously a holding cell. The door had locked automatically. But everything was clean and tidy: a clean sheet and pillowcase, and a duvet in a similar crisp and white condition, and not a speck of dust anywhere - she'd checked the shelves and surfaces - and the lavatory facilities were basic, but spotless. She wondered vaguely who did the cleaning. She imagined herself with cleaners - she'd call them maids - and there would be no inappropriate informality. She'd had a daily years ago, two hours a day, three days a week, but she'd had to let her go because she was inefficient and you can't trust people from *that* part of the City. We must check background thoroughly next time, she had agreed with her husband. He'd appeared typically detached. There were many things men were hopeless at! Dealing with other people, taking on a management role, completely hopeless, even when they were actually managers!

She could feel how tense she was. Her blood pressure was probably way up. She shouldn't take her pulse because, if it was high, which it definitely was, then it would probably get higher. But no pinging as yet. Must calm down: a few calming down exercises, some slow and deep breathing. But she felt too tense to concentrate. She must calm down before she can calm down... She might wash her face with cold water. She thought of the last time she was so flushed. She could see it as if an observer of the scene, everything crystal clear. "No, we have no children, my husband and I, it just didn't happen, one of those things." Once that 'video' started, it played over and over again. No, we have no... one of those things... no we have no... Block it! Count backwards from 100. 99 98 97 96. She was even hotter now.

She scooped cold water onto her face rapidly, but gently. The makeup would probably hold, but no point getting into a total mess, must be seen to be in control, although whatever this is about, it has nothing to do with her. Makeup and hair just fine, and no handbag. They'd taken her handbag into custody, together with her sense of empowerment. It's just not right, but these things have to be borne with dignity. Anyhow, only a minor inconvenience, one mustn't fuss. Helping with enquiries: which one of them said that? Was that the little blondie girl? She seemed quite nice. So did the other one, a bit older, just as polite. Helping them with enquiries?

She froze standing in front of the tall mirror. It's amazing what you miss or forget when you are being asked dozens of questions. It was an *interrogation*. Surely it was, albeit polite. Politeness is everything and it shows breeding, although those two had been trained. Obviously, they didn't have breeding *per se*. She watched herself: a fine figure of a mature and professional woman. She could have been a barrister. She could imagine herself in her robes addressing the Court. Those courts didn't happen often because of all that monitoring, but she'd seen it on television. It still happened in some countries, some Cities, to be precise, and she was very precise. She could have been someone big. Her husband was very intelligent and appreciated her real qualities, although people assumed she'd married beneath her. Fools. He was a good man and that's all that counts. His ex-wife would never appreciate that and neither would his awful children. They'd had more than enough time to get over the breakup. Imagine they still blame her, although the breakup was inevitable. It's about time they grew up, considering their ages.

She sat down heavily in the armchair because she had suddenly realised that the questioning was something to do with her brother. That malicious woman had nearly destroyed his life and look at the state of their children. The shambolic lives of these supposed adults! It was something to do with *her*. Oh, no - she was panicking, some kind *nervous* attack, she recognised the symptoms. She felt her heart racing. Pinging. That woman, that mad woman had *killed* her brother! That's why they wouldn't tell her. She started to become hysterical, she was screaming, crying, and thumping and kicking on the door.

"Tabi, help me! Somebody help me! I want my husband!"

## 95

The irony of Lakota the Lawyer; the irony of her present circumstances; the irony of her life; the irony of having no common sense. Some things don't make sense. This was one of those things, the fact that she had been 'collected' at the office by the two *plain clothes*. They could have been a bit more colourful! Although one was wearing a pink tie, which didn't suit him. Typical man! They can't even get their tie right and they invented it! The tie: the most peculiar of garments, or is it an accessory? No point asking a man. And it's always an arrow pointing to you know where, their dangly bits, as if we don't know they have them. Well, most of them do, but she suspects her brothers don't. And there they are: men, with their tattoos, body rings, fake suntan, pumped up muscles, coiffured hair, makeup, and covered from head to foot in perfume! They look like peculiar smelling clowns and that's exactly how they behave. Or maybe the prancing horses at a Horse Show. (What's that called, she couldn't think, the prancing horse event?). She couldn't think of anything more ridiculous than men, with their deep and booming voices, a bit like foghorns, and their incompetently performing, bulging trousers, most of which is as phony as their brains (you can buy the 'bulgers' in shops, for goodness' sake!). She knows about their multifaceted incompetence from personal experience. All that fancy talk and no brain. And, as for women... She knew that this situation was bringing out the worst in her. She was pacing about. Incompetent men: must be cool.

She took off her jacket and placed it neatly on the back of the desk chair, not on a hanger in the cupboard because she wasn't staying. The place looked like a nice hotel on a small scale, but it certainly wasn't. She looked at herself in the full-length mirror. She loosened her shirt collar because she was feeling hot (and bothered!). She looked fine: shirt snow-white, silvery grey silk cravat fronted by an intricately woven silver brooch dotted with a dispersal of semi-precious stones; trousers pin striped and neatly creased ; sensible shoes (slightly raised heel), black and polished. Hmm, yes, she could be 'plain clothes', she thought, now she was calming down, except for the mad tie! It's only what he'd wear for work. Must be an interesting job, meeting lots of people, maybe in her next life... Put it down to a learning experience. Being on the receiving end of an interrogation - it definitely was an interrogation. She wasn't sure what she was learning. Sometimes it takes quite a while to get the story straight. And she had heard some stories in her time. You can bet on that. She could write a book about it. Several books.

She'd figured out the gist of the interview. She'd noticed the 'lie detectors' amongst the questions, the double checking, but as she never lies - why would she? -those questions were irrelevant. Why hadn't they simply come out with it? You can hardly lie these days and hope to get away with it. But that despicable family of hers would say anything, and she knew it was about them. That long-running saga would never end! Unless it was about to? She would only be slightly surprised to find out one of them had committed a crime, but what is it? And why all the beating about the bush? She didn't know anything about a crime and yet the questioning had gone on for nearly two hours. It seemed to be all about dates and places, some of them going back in her childhood, and relationships within the family. She'd often thought that it was a very small family, even in its extended form. There were plenty of ex's. They were scattered all over the place, a serious 'body count'. There were dozens of them. It hadn't occurred to her that this didn't look good. But it's not illegal, consenting adults, and all that. Where's the crime? But there had been some despicable behaviour: all trust between members of her family had been battered to pulp. They'd committed every kind of treachery over the years , done everything except incest! Apart from... but that was nothing to do with her. And her Dad: mad as a hatter! He'd become increasingly nuts, more and more manic and spiteful and downright vile. He was now blaming them for their ridiculous mother. Lakota had nothing to do him *ever*. Enough is enough. He needs to talk to a psychiatrist and she'd told him so more than once. He'd gone berserk every time: You're not listening, he'd shout at the top of his voice... Every time they visited he attacked. He'd been warned by Central Computer to moderate his tone, but they didn't take any action. Well, enough is enough, and he dared to talk about abuse of *him*! Just plain stupid and mad, should be locked up. And, as for Mum... Lakota had run out of ideas years ago. They'd talked all that highfalutin nonsense, especially T.D. Dimwit, who thinks he knows it all, but they'd given up. Mum was always right and they couldn't get through to Dad because he was too stuck in the past. Aunty Gelasia always said that he was just like Granny: an egomaniac who'd ideas above his station; spiteful because he'd achieved nothing; jealous and unforgiving. The slightest tone of voice he turned into a major insult! You can't deal with somebody like that. And Mum should be locked up too, but not in the same cell as Dad. They should all be locked up! Lakota really did deserve a ten year holiday from her entire family. Oh, no, the coming weekend. She sank deep into the armchair. If only the armchair were a time machine, then she could fast forward a hundred years and they'd all be gone. Lakota didn't often cry.

## 96

He vomited finally. He knew it was inevitable. Gasping for air, he nearly choked on the lumps and now one was lodged in the back of his nose. He swallowed hard repeatedly, turned his nose into a tiny vacuum cleaner, emitted the necessary grunting noises and back of throat suction noises to dislodge it back down into his throat, nearly vomited again, and then coughed it like a bullet into the toilet bowl. The aim was perfect, the relief that he was still alive was wonderful and the taste was vile. Why did they give him all that *stuff*? To sober him up so he could answer those questions.

So, no kissing today, not with a mouth like a sewer, but worse. But then, no contact at all from her. You can't trust women. That's what everyone says and he knows it's true. If you can't trust your own mother, who can you trust? And, as for his sister, it's always been a shadow of a relationship. Even when they were children. Worse since his dad left years ago. Dad told him the whole story in adulthood, and it was completely different to mum's version. His family are a family of ghosts dragging chains behind them. They're going to celebrate his return at the weekend. Yes, of course they are. Stop thinking, he told himself.

He had a brief memory of hovering over the sink. The result was a sink full of brown vegetable soup with no means of escape via the blocked plughole. He would have had to *poke* it clear, arm up to the wrist... Now he vomited again, this time producing a thick pea-green liquid, which tore out his innards and destroyed all of his interior organs on the way! Being vaporised by the enemy would have been preferable and painless. He vowed never to drink again. He wouldn't stick to his vow - they never do.

A pain suddenly opened fire on his brain and pounded through his skull like the battleship guns of his training days. His head reeled, the room reeled, the sailor reeled his reel to the foot of the bed, stumble-scrambled on to it, elbowed and kneed his way, the wounded combatant, under the enemy's barbed wire, towards the pillow and sank into his mummy's , or somebody's, welcoming breasts. They couldn't be his mother's.

Why is he being kept here? Is he under arrest? He hasn't done anything. It couldn't be military arrest, could it? He scanned the room with a bleary eye and was not surprised at its military-style precision. Why all *those* questions? Maybe he was being vetted for some special op. That would give him a boost in his mates' eyes. But, of course, he couldn't talk about it. Top Secret. He'd said that before and it was true, but the geniuses hadn't believed him. They just smirked and changed the subject. They're always putting him down. No matter what you do, you can't win with them. Vetting? They know everything about him already. Anyhow, this is police. Maybe the mouthy prigs have committed a gang crime and they are all going to jail! That would give him some pleasure - he'd be laughing for the next month. It would serve them right, take the wind out of their arrogant sails. But they don't have the guts or the...

And he was gone, into the land of nod where all the children have fun all day and are loved by their parents.

And thus poor Makallee slept like a baby.

They knew he'd met up with the lads and had got himself well and truly hammered, but they'd had no choice but to pick him up and bring him in for questioning. Indeed, it had made their job easier if anything, apart from a bit of organising at the beginning, a bit of discretion required with a member of the military, especially a young guy drunk and miserable. No need to make his life worse.

They already knew he was unconscious, in a post-alcohol coma sprawled on the settee, before entering the apartment. They managed to wake him. He was dazed and confused and thought he was under the sea, but didn't recognise the uniform of the woman - and what was she doing here? And why were the two men in civvies? But he came to fairly quickly and was rather wobbly on his feet and somewhat incoherent, as they helped him into the interior taxi they'd arranged just outside the front door. They cruised almost noiselessly the couple of miles of corridor to the nearest vehicle and people elevator that took them to the ground floor; then into the police car.

He was the easiest interviewee because he simply answered the questions. He had no idea what was going on and was in no fit state to be curious. He seemed to assume that it was personal and concerned his job - something to do with national security maybe or, even worse, a spot check to do with his ability to do his job. He was concerned that he had been caught in such a condition, although he was off duty. He didn't mention his concerns; they didn't bother to assuage his obvious tension. Let the kid squirm for now; he'll be okay in the long run. In short, he had tried to be as helpful and as *sober* as possible. He had succeeded in the former. Some of his thinking was slightly irrational, as you would expect. To put it in more sympathetic (and accurate) terms his permanent condition was due to childhood neglect, and, therefore, poor education, and a lifetime of mixed messages. They knew this. Alcohol was another of his family's fine traditions. When confused or unhappy, get sloshed! As they are confused and unhappy most of the time... Quite frankly, Makallee didn't know if he was coming or going. The others, with all their astonishing brilliance, didn't know that they didn't know.

"You didn't actually answer the question."

"I did answer it, but you fail to understand how complex these matters are. Obviously, you've been told things about me, which are not true. I've always been honest and hardworking."

"You still haven't answered the question."

"Now you're badgering me. I'm trying to explain that the answer isn't black and white, and I must be allowed proper time to explain. I have rights and I believe you are deliberately trying to deprive me of them. I don't play mind games"

"Let's change tack for a moment. You are a trained psychologist to a certain standard."

"A very high standard," she interrupted.

"And, as such, you have carried out a number of experiments involving human beings."

"Yes. But it's not quite..."

"You read precise, written instructions to subjects in closely controlled laboratory circumstances."

She fidgeted on her chair, pushed away gently a cup of coffee she'd requested, but had never touched, sat back and folded her arms.

"That's not quite the kind of work I specialise in. My approach is more..."

"We don't understand how someone trained in the scientific method finds it impossible to answer simple questions."

The detective sat forward, clenched her hands on the table shared with Nasichisha and looked straight at her.

"Do I need to remind you that this is a police investigation? Are you aware of your ex-husband's present occupation?"

"I have no contact with him because..."

"Are you aware of his occupation?"

"No."

"Did you tell DCI Cody approximately two months ago that your ex-husband is a part-time teacher at the University?"

"I haven't had contact with him for years."

"Did you tell DCI Cody..."

"I can't remember."

"You can't remember talking to a Detective Chief Inspector?"

"Of course I can remember talking to..."

"But you can't remember what you talked about? Do you remember telling your son that his father has always been an angry man, jealous, and impossible to live with?"

"Which son?"

"Does it matter which son? You've said this many times. The last time was" - she consulted her note - "the 16th of August at one minute past two in the afternoon."

"How do you know?"

"How do you think we know?"

"Have you told your children their father is a violent man?" The male detective took over.

"He *is* a violent man."

"What kind of violence?"

"He used to push me around and beat me."

"He slapped you once twenty-eight years ago."

"He did it many times."

"*Once*," the detective said firmly. "Do you remember that occasion?"

"Vaguely."

"The one physical assault you only remember *vaguely*? Do you remember *vaguely* why he did it?"

"No."

"Do you remember being questioned by Social Services?"

"No."

"Their Child Protection Team?"

"No. I mean yes, I do remember. It was a misunderstanding."

"A misunderstanding?" The detective looked through his file and extracted three pages clipped together. "This is their report."

"Nasichisha," asked the woman detective, "what did your father do for a living?"

She reached for the coffee cup. Her hand shook. She took a sip. She placed it on the table. Then she cradled it in both hands and swirled the coffee. Why are they asking about him?

"He was, eh, I can't remember, I was too young."

"You were fifteen when he died."

"But he hadn't worked for a long time."

"Because he'd injured his back" - the detective paused - "whilst loading a lorry. Your Marriage Certificate states that your father's occupation is... Executive. Do you know it's a crime to lie to a Government Registrar?

"Would you describe your father as a jealous man?"

"I wouldn't know."

"But your mother complained of this many times well into your adulthood. Indeed, only a few months ago..."

"Well, yes, I suppose he was. On occasion."

The male detective intervened. "Would you describe your father as violent?"

Nasichisha froze. She was unable to speak. She must control herself. She mustn't lose her cool. The silence was deafening. It buzzed in her ears.

"We know the answer. We've seen the filmic records."

She caught sight of herself in the two-way mirror. She looked like a cornered animal. They must be watching. She must buck up.

"What did your mother do for a living?" asked the woman detective.

"She taught art."

"What did your mother do for a living from the beginning of her married life at the age of nineteen for the next thirty years?"

"Well, if you already know, why are you asking?"

"I want you to tell us what your mother did for a living."

Bill Cody sat in the darkened room watching the videoed interview. He listened to every word. It was like pulling teeth. You'd have more luck getting blood out of a stone. She's a classic, at *least* a sociopath.

"Have you noticed her contradictions?"

The other detective nodded and yawned. The stool creaked under his weight.

He removed himself to a chair. It was getting late. "She's fascinating, if you like that sort of thing, some kind of creepy animal," he commented.

"Concerning your Tertiary Degree, Nasichisha, you studied parenting in victims of child sexual abuse. Is that correct?"

"Yes," she replied.

"And you developed a questionnaire to give to the targeted subjects, proclaimed victims of child sexual abuse, in your study. Is that true?"

"Yes, it is," she replied.

"And you concluded *basically* that there are no adverse consequences of CSA, people grow out of it. Is that true?"

"Well, it's not as simple as that, but, basically, yes I did."

"Amongst this cohort of victims of CSA, these anonymous subjects in your study, did you include yourself and your sister?"

Cody sighed. "She's enough to exhaust the patience of Job," he muttered.

"Who?" Cody ignored the question.

"There would have been sympathy years ago, but not now. She's gone too far. Listen to that! What an outright lie! And she thinks we don't know. It's been a long day. I'm off. Lock up the shop, detective."

## 98

God, misery must not poison my life.
They think you punish me in your anger.
 Help, O Lord, my spirit dies of hunger,
My bodily life wastes to skin and bone;
My life's a burden I barely carry.
For how long will you observe from afar?
Return, be enthroned again in these lives.
Repeatedly I have learnt my lesson:
My insults of you have been heaped on me.
Earthly amends too late when in the grave,
Too late for them to learn when I am gone,
Too late to learn who I am, who you are.
In your great mercy, justice and great love
Stretch out your hand and quell the serpent tongue,
For in their vile breath I am disappeared.
My despair has worn me out.
These things are beyond my tears.
A rotting thing is my soul.
My eyes a wasteland in drought.
Those closest my enemies.
My life ended long ago.
Depart ye cursed! Cease fruitless torture!
 The Lord has heard my case, in patience waits.
The Lord has strengthened my understanding
And accepts my just claim, the Lord's own claim.
My enemies will be shamed and dismayed,
My bereavement and despair shall be theirs.

He had read that Psalm hundreds of times. He knew it had been translated thousands of times, into every known language over several millennia. He didn't need to read the original: if something makes sense, it makes sense. Do you realise how difficult translation is between unrelated languages which no longer exist?

Praman mused on these things. It saved him actually praying. He'd rarely managed the state of *contemplative*. He spent twenty-five years going through the motions, hoping for a breakthrough, hoping for something magical, maybe supernatural to happen. His brain was too cluttered. "You can't be a contemplative when you are being tortured," he spoke these words out loud and was then silent. You can't be a contemplative when all you can think about is murder. "Thou shalt not..." Don't bother me with that nonsense! "Vengeance is mine, sayeth the Lord." Yes, I'm sure it is. Well, bully for you. When is this vengeance going to happen? When I'm dead and gone? I must empty myself of sin, pride, self. Empty myself? I don't exist at all! I'm walking around breathing, making noises - some people call it talking - and they are still kicking the stuffing out of the corpse. Nobody has the decency to bury me. What kind of society is this? What is a human being? Homo sapiens. Where's the sapiens?

He had felt everything gradually die. His hopes and dreams, humble as they were, gradually shrank to nothing. His causes became hot air, empty words, meaningless, until he stopped speaking them. He had given up wondering about other people because they'd given up wondering about him. He was just plain tired. He was tired of their arguments, which didn't make sense. He was tired of their arrogance, their snobbery, their smugness, their failure to accept unquestionable facts. Unquestionable, for God's sake! He slammed his hand down on the wooden table. The glass leapt, the candle flickered, the prayer book closed itself with a dull flop! "Oh, for crying out loud, which page am I on?" he growled. One set of the prayers were printed on a yellow card, which he used as a bookmark. It was on the table. The other yellow card was still in its place. He clasped his hands to his face under his nose. He could hear his heavy breathing. "Which Psalm Week is it?" There were only four to choose from, but he couldn't think. He pushed his chair back and stood up.

He walked around the room, sighed, stretched, listened to the flip-flop of his noisy sandals. Not quite flip-flop, there's a dragged note of each heel. He wondered if that happened forty years ago, if it was age, or if they were simply too loose. They were certainly too noisy. His sandals annoyed him. He kicked them off. The silence was wonderful. The soft, barely heard sound of the killer. He could stalk, pad after the target and kill instantly in silence and move away into the dark. He was probably kidding himself, not as lithe as he used to be.

He glanced along the shelves of books. What was the point? What was he trying to do? What was he trying to prove, and to whom? Why did he keep them? Why did he treasure them? *Vanity of vanities, all is vanity*. He probably wouldn't even get a chance to smell. He'd read that the smell is terrible. No, as soon as his heart stopped he'd be found. He wouldn't get a chance to smell, to decompose, to putrefy. He'd be bagged, taken way and put in a fridge, all neat and tidy, and not even a bit of smell left behind. Just a load of books and scraps of paper. The books would be *redistributed* by the Council, the paper would be turned into compost. All those years of work. He made himself a cup of tea. Psalm Week 1! Office of Readings. He returned to his bare wooden table.

Praman unconsciously reached out and stroked the smooth, shiny, paper cover of his dictionary: over two thousand pages and never big enough. Then withdrew his hand as if from a flame. These emotional train wrecks, these pieces of human garbage. It's unbelievable! They don't know who he is, what he is. How is this possible? He could understand it from *her* - that freak! - but his own children? It was exhausting, it was killing him. He could always feel himself dying. He tried to concentrate on the prayer book, but couldn't. He was reading the words, but nothing was penetrating his brain.

In the stillness the candle flickered. Praman doesn't believe in angels or demons. He certainly doesn't believe in omens. He believes in cause and effect, as far as it goes. So, then, the doorbell rang.

## 99

"Bill?"

"How are you, Praman?" They shook hands. They stood staring at each in silence.

"Oh, sorry, eh, please take a seat," he said indicating a kitchen chair. "Or, maybe you'd be more comfortable..."

"No, no, this would be just fine, fit for purpose," said Bill. He looked at the dusty bookshelves on the three walls of the main room leading off the kitchen. There must be three other rooms. He looked over at the crowded double table with its piles of books, papers and what looked like charts. "So this is your abode, your hermitage."

Praman chuckled self-consciously. "You can't be a real hermit unless you're a member of a monastery and under spiritual guidance."

"Sounds a contradiction?"

"No, it's not. You have to have reached a certain stage of spiritual develop-ment before you're allowed to be a hermit."

"Hmm. I see," said Bill, although he didn't. He wondered about this peculiar business of religion: it's not as simple as it looks. But he knew that nothing is.

"Is this an official call?" asked Praman.

"This is an unofficial official call. I thought I'd let you know personally." Praman was worried and intrigued at the same time.

"Stop looking so guilty! I think I'm the bringer of good news. Well, not entirely good news. Remember, we ran into each other in the pub a few years ago?"

"Yes, of course. Oh, can I offer you a drink? Are you off-duty?"

"Yes, you can and yes, I am. Thanks." Praman poured two whiskeys.

"What's this about? Cheers."

"Well," said the DCI, "this is a long story, but the fact is you know it already. You were quite distraught the night we first met, but you tried to cover it up. Every time I asked you a question, you kept changing the subject. I knew some-thing was up. I can sense it. Our subsequent meetings were not a coincidence. I wanted to find out more.

"You talked about your children and then suddenly stopped. As if you'd said too much. Over the months, *when we bumped into each other*, you made refer-ences to what could only be Post-Traumatic Stress Disorder - nightmares, use of alcohol, you can't bear the sound of a vacuum cleaner, and you can't play certain board games. These were passing comments over several of our get-togeth-ers, but I did note them. Also, you were very enthusiastic about your interests, especially your work with emotionally disturbed children and adolescents and the reason you gave up this work did not hold water. The work, the publications, the conferences, and suddenly you retired! That struck me as peculiar. So I started to check out exactly who you are."

"You're not suggesting something untoward."

"No, certainly not, Praman. You were a main mover in the City, ahead of your time, and suddenly you stopped. You became increasingly alcoholic and reclusive. It looked like depression.

But your sense of humour remained razor-sharp, and probably kept you alive." He finished his whiskey.

"I'm trying to get to the point. Your letter. The one you sent to your children."

"My letter? But how do you ..."

"Don't!" Bill held up the broad of his hand to say stop! And started laughing. Praman poured him another whiskey.

"In the most surveillanced era in the history of the world people keep asking me how do I know? I'm a DCI, I have A1 Clearance. That's how I know.

"Your letter, Praman, was spot on. By that time we were already investigating your case. In the letter you refer to the Network of Evil, an excellent expression. Well, we've got them all in custody. The Network of Evil. We've got them all under lock and Key."

Praman was puzzled and disbelieving. "Who have you got under lock and key?"

"You see, as you pointed out in your letter, it is intergenerational and goes back over sixty years. We had to stop somewhere, or to start somewhere. We will be sending our file to Pol City. Bronnie's first husband had a wife and two children before he came here. There may be victims still alive, or victims of the victims. Not all C.S.A. victims grow up to become C.S.A. perpetrators. There are all kinds of abuse - physical, emotional - but first things first. First, we have to tidy our own house and, believe me, it's messy. Many people may need counselling.

"So: we have Bronnie, an incestuous paedophile. If she didn't do it herself, she is certainly culpable. Furthermore, she covered it up for over sixty years and she encouraged her daughters, the victims, to join in the cover-up. All those lies and secrets," he was shaking his head in dismay, "have had monstrous consequences. What those two children went through is, well, I'm lost for words - *disgusting*? The ritualistic beatings: he stripped them, laid them face down on his bed and *flogged* them with his belt." He was silent. "I've had to watch all that stuff. I understand how it wasn't picked up by Human Operator. In those days it was normal to chastise children, and it still is.

"He raped them, sexually assaulted them in every known way - I don't need to go into the details - and beat them... for not *tidying up properly*. They were kids! He used to run his finger along the *top of the wardrobe* and, if he found dust, they got a hiding. This went on throughout their childhood and all of it was sexual. It stopped when they started having their periods at the age of thirteen, your ex-wife, Nasichisha, and her older sister, Jardena. Their mother didn't notice a thing?

"The Judges will find Bronnie guilty of Child Sexual Abuse and Sadism. She won't be able to talk her way out of that. Her dopy second husband stumbled into this and has no idea what's going on. He'll probably be offered counselling. Bronnie's two daughters, Nasichisha and Jardena, are both going to prison for *DEPS.*"

It was well after nightfall. Praman preferred the dark. He'd turned on table lamps (for guests) and the heating (for guests). The bottle of whiskey kept sentinel on the table. Cody was thinking that he had a light day tomorrow. Praman was thinking about gluttony and unpredictability.

"You called it P.A.S. in your letter," said Cody, glancing towards the books. "From an old book? Your brainwashed children ignored it."

"I was testing a hypothesis," said Praman in a low voice, as if to keep it secret.

"I know you were. Indeed, several."

"It comes from the Merkan Act after the old prof. who researched it. P.A.S. comes from pre-Cat times, believe it or not. It's actually called the *Denigration of the Individual* Act and the part that applies to you is Denigration of the Estranged Parent. Some people add an S for Syndrome, hence D.E.P.S., easy to remember. But nobody does. The Act was passed unhindered and, therefore, virtually unpublicised. It took several more years for the powers that be to form a Special Unit in Psychological Crimes.

"Most people can be stopped and the damage rectified. However," he gazed into the darkened room and looked across at the sad old hermit, "your case is the worst I've heard of so far."

"Nasichisha viciously set about destroying you in the eyes of your children when she gained possession of them post-divorce. She is so dysfunctional, the only way she could explain her amoral and destructive behaviour - reducing them to Welfare, refusing to get a job, the lowlife men in and out of their lives - was to prove that you were more dysfunctional than her. She rationalised her behaviour has *normal* in the circumstances.

"As they moved through their teenage days, you became increasingly irate. Not only were they teenagers, but their mother was casting her spells. They were increasingly ill-mannered, dismissive, sexist, racist, homophobic... That's when you started shouting the house down and effing and blinding!" Cody laughed. "Sorry, I know it's not funny, but really..." he started to chuckle again, "you must hold the World Record for warnings from Central Computer."

"Yes, I know," said Praman, "it was a mistake."

"But normal. As the years went by, the ironic thing is that *you* became more badly behaved than her and them! In the early years they started to make bizarre statements about you, which, over the years turned into positive insults that didn't make sense, which led to more shouting the house down! They were turning into mouthy idiots, although they're all multiple graduates, thanks to you. Your eldest son, Mosimanadue, seems to be a *knowing idiot*. He has no idea what's going on, although he received your, eh, *colourful* letter. Written bad language doesn't count, or you'd have an even bigger World Record! All that dumbing-down doesn't help. And the others: Halaigha, Lakota, and Psybunes, all dumbed-down fools, which made it easy for their mother. We're producing a society of highly educated, self-centred idiots! History is repeating itself."

There was a silence between them.

Praman spoke: "Too much positive reinforcement and too little accurate feedback."

"Probably," Bill said hesitantly, "Not my subject, but I'm sure you're right. What didn't help were your inevitable retaliations."

"Yes. It was spread over many years, but it was consistent. I should have noticed the pattern. It should have been punishment." Bill tried to concentrate. "But it *couldn't* have been because it kept happening. They did what children always do, although they weren't children. They turned it into classical conditioning: they were *eliciting* my behaviour, setting me up." He took a slug of his whiskey.

"They were having something *reinforced,* what their mother was drumming into them. Then she could say, "I told you what he was like: he's always been an angry man, jealous, resentment and impossible to live with.""

"The bottom line is that what's she's been doing is illegal," said Bill.

"Some of these other people are *Witnesses*. Jardena's two alcoholic children, Shachikaka and Makallee have been freed. Their moral development? Their disgusting mother has a lot to answer for.

"Your sister, Belbiana, and her husband, Tabatante, have also been freed. Belbiana's terribly... *sensitive* in her own right. As for Tabatante, it's all above his head. He thinks they're all obnoxious, including you, and I don't blame him!

"On the other hand," he drew a breath, "your other sister, Gelasia. Well, what a piece of work she is, what a joker, an uneducated, malicious," he searched for an acceptable word, "*witch.* Well, the joker is going to jail. She joined in thirty years ago. Why would she take your ex-wife's side? And she brought along her brainless husband, Purvanos. He should have known better. I daresay he will by the time he gets out.

"There are always victims: the grandchild you've never met? I suppose when Halaigha is in prison, her ridiculous, eh, *boy*friend, Damodural, will write a great poem... " He sighed.

"I know you understand all this and I'm here to confirm *it* and *you*, mete out justice, and draw a line under the whole appalling business. But it's only the beginning."

"There's a lot of healing needed," mused Praman.

We'll leave the two elderly men. I've accessed Spiraller No. 49. There are 100 pigeon-sized drones over the City at night, spiralling, circling.

49 is spiralling down to street-level where you can discern the dull sound of machines, mainly air conditioning systems. It's late and this part of the City is deserted except for Jeevalani the priest, striding purposefully (of course), under the influence (no doubt), broad hat, long black coat flowing behind him, and the ornate walking cane (all for show). He's probably worrying about his friend, Praman. What a terrible mess: that awful woman. But it takes two to tango. You never really know another person. If you're thinking that, Jeevalani, you're wrong.

And up we go! Ten thousand feet, twenty thousand, fifty thousand feet to a cloudless sky under a starry, starry night.

Dedicated to
Rita Pirotta:
the greatest friend
a person could have.

Lightning Source UK Ltd.
Milton Keynes UK
UKOW05f1106170117

292234UK00001B/56/P